MIRANDA

A ROWAN GANT INVESTIGATION

FINAL CHAPTER OF THE MIRANDA SAGA

An Occult/Paranormal Thriller

By

M. R. SELLARS

E.M.A. Mysteries

This book is a work of fiction. Names, characters, places, and incidents are either the product of the author's imagination, have been used fictitiously, or are used with permission. Any resemblance to actual events or locales or persons, living or dead, is entirely coincidental, unless otherwise noted.

MIRANDA: A Rowan Gant Investigation

An E.M.A. Mysteries Book
E.M.A. Mysteries is an imprint of WillowTree Press

PRINTING HISTORY
First Printing - Trade Paper Edition / July 2010

For information, contact WillowTree Press on the World Wide Web: http://www.willowtreepress.com

ISBN 13: 978-0-9794533-6-6

10 9 8 7 6 5 4 3 2

ACKNOWLEDGEMENTS

I would be sorely remiss if I didn't take a moment to thank at least a few of the individuals who were there to act as my sounding boards and as my moral support staff throughout the creation of this novel.

As the Rowan Gant series has been ongoing for more than a dozen years, the list of folks to whom I owe thanks has grown, with specific mentions for specific novels along the way. Given reprintings and revisions, if I were to include them all, the list would take up more pages than the novel itself. Therefore, in the interest of brevity—

The Usual Suspects—you all know who you are...

Other Persons of Interest—Virginia "Gina" Witt, MD, for being there to listen to an insane writer guy when he needs technical input on medicine, hospital procedures, and even ICU décor...

Scott "The Chunk Man" McCoy, for bringing me queso dip, corn chips, and wheat beer whenever I'm going down for the third time... And, for being a hell of a friend...

Martha Ackmann, for everything she taught me about journalism and writing, and for still being an inspiration to this day...

As well as countless others...

Of course, we cannot forget—black patent leather stiletto heels (preferably with my wife wearing them), cardboard, reusable shopping bags, pepper bacon, braunschweiger, grapefruit, capuchin monkeys, 18 year old scotch, Black Bush, garden gnomes, granola, electric pencil sharpeners, left-handed reversible skyhooks, hard salami, pigs in a blanket, clean sheets, bib overalls, breath mints, those little removable sticky things that point to where you are supposed to sign your tax return when it comes back from your accountant, magnifying glasses, and fiber tablets—*in that order...*

My personal playlist/soundtrack while writing this novel: *Dead Sound* (The Raveonettes), *These Are The Times* (Styx), *Kiss Me Hello* (Tommy Shaw), and as always, *Can't Stop The World* (Gavin Rossdale)...

And, as always, coffee...

For Joshua Landtroop.
1988 - 2010
You were a hell of a kid,
who became a hell of a young man.

You will be missed…

Mi•ran•da [mi-ran-duh] *–noun*: Invented by Shakespeare for the heroine of *The Tempest* (1611). It represents the feminine form of the Latin gerundive *mirandus* 'admirable', 'lovely', from *mirari* 'to wonder at', 'admire'; cf. Amanda.

—Oxford Concise Dictionary of First Names

Blanque, MIRANDA**:** A perverse and sadistic murderess of early and middle 1800's New Orleans, Louisiana, who is rumored to have derived autoerotic gratification from the intense suffering of her victims. Sister of Delphine LaLaurie, it has been theorized that the siblings were jointly responsible for the torture and subsequent deaths of numerous household slaves as reported in the *New Orleans Bee*, 1834. **[See also *Mistress Miranda; Devereaux, Annalise; LaLaurie, Delphine; paraphilia; sexual homicide; sadism; spirit possession, Voodoo*]**

—Excerpted from
Hell Hath No Fury: A Comprehensive Study of Women Who Kill
Luettecke, Seitz, & Witt – BCM Press
Revised Third Edition, March 2006

"Do you love me?"

Miranda, Prospero's Daughter
From William Shakespeare's, "*The Tempest*"
Act 3, Scene 1 - Circa 1611

"Now, let us see how much you love me."

Miranda Blanque
Prior to torturing a household slave
LaLaurie House Attic - New Orleans, Louisiana, April 1834

"*Relax, little man. I'm just showing you how much we love you...*"

Mistress Miranda /Annalise Devereaux
While torturing a subservient
The Whine Cellar BDSM Club – Bridge, Illinois, December 2005

Prologue

Excerpted from Rowan Gant's Personal Book of Shadows:

7/13 - 3:30 AM:

I can't sleep. I need to but I can't.

We have a really long day tomorrow. Almost 20 hours of sitting in airports and on airplanes, not to mention Ireland is 6 hours ahead of us, so that's going to screw me up too.

But, here I am wide-awake. I suppose I could blame it on excitement, but I know damn well that's not why. It's that time of the year. The anniversary of Ariel's murder is coming back around soon, and this is just par for the course. Hard to believe it's been less than a decade now. Not even a full ten years since her death turned my life into this unending nightmare. But, knowing that doesn't change a thing. It still seems like it all happened forever ago. Maybe it's because of this surreal existence of mine. Maybe it's because I wish it would just go away. I want to forget all of it. The horror, the pain, the images... But I can't. The nightmares never fade, and it doesn't matter if I'm asleep or awake. They're always there. I have a feeling they will be until I die. I guess that's what I get for being a Witch.

Of course, I'm not really a normal Witch now, am I? Hell, even other neo-Pagans think I'm more than a little out there. They go bang on drums and dance around a fire. Me, I have conversations with dead people. All things being equal, I'd much rather join them around the fire.

In retrospect I don't suppose I should have been shocked when the dead started talking to me. After all, I really brought it all upon myself when I purposely used WitchCraft to make a connection with their world in order to help solve Ariel's murder. Although, lately I've found myself wondering if my ethereal insight is truly borne of my practice of The Craft or if this would be happening to me even if I weren't a Witch. Maybe there's something wrong with me. Like that movie about the guy who turned into a supergenius because of a brain tumor. Maybe I've got one too. Who the hell knows? Maybe I'm just plain abnormal. Of course, I suppose it doesn't really matter. WitchCraft is where it all started, so it's what got me here in the first place. Whether I'm abnormal or not, the rest is really just a moot point I guess.

If only Ben hadn't noticed that I was wearing a pentacle around my neck. If only he hadn't asked for my help. If only, if only... It just never ends. I guess what it comes down to is that I should have stayed out of it. Just answered his questions and left it at that. If I'd been smart, that's what I would've done. Then I would never have opened the door that led me down this path. But I couldn't stay out of it. The victim was Ariel. She was my friend. In my mind I didn't have a choice.

Of course, like they say, hindsight is 20/20. There's nothing I can do about it now, other than drive myself crazy with all of the "if onlys" and second-guessing. The door between the world of the living and the realm of the dead is open for me now, whether I like it or not.

Live and learn, I guess... That's something else they say, whoever the hell "they" is.

I guess I'm just cursed. The dead are my personal bad pennies that keep turning up. I close my eyes and they're there. I open my eyes and they're there. Day, night, sleep, wake... It doesn't matter, they just won't go away. Ignoring them doesn't work either. I've tried. Gods how I've tried. And listening to them... Well, that just gets me into trouble. Everyone around me too. That's the worst part. I'm damned if I do, damned if I don't. Why Felicity puts up with it I don't know. Her life would be so much easier if she'd never even met me. But, if we'd never met I'd probably already be dead. Morbid, I know, but somehow she keeps me sane and alive. Somebody has to.

I'm just rambling now. I guess that's no surprise either. I really need to get some sleep.

Sunday, December 24
5:22 P.M.
Saint Louis, Missouri

"C'MERE AND TELL ME WHAT YA' THINK." BEN CALLED out over his shoulder then stood back and cocked his head to the side in order to inspect his handiwork.

Constance wandered in from the kitchen and stood next to him, hands resting on her hips. "What I think about what?"

At six-foot-six, Ben stood at least a head taller than her, so as she spoke, she glanced up at him then followed his obviously preoccupied gaze to the end of the living room.

"Whaddaya mean, about what?" he said as he gestured. "About that. So does it look better or not?"

She gazed quietly at the rank and file for several seconds, scanning back and forth with her eyes. Finally, she replied, "It looks like all you did was move the tall one."

"That's Big Ben."

"Big Ben? You're kidding, right?"

"Well, why not? He's as tall as I am, ain't he?"

"Taller, actually."

"So there ya' go."

"Okay..." She paused then scrunched her brow as incredulity crept into her voice. "But you named them?"

"Not all of 'em. Just some of 'em."

"I worry about you sometimes."

"Yeah, whatever. Look again. I did more'n just move Big Ben," he said, pointing at the mantle. "I swapped the two on the ends, and moved Sparky..."

"Sparky?"

"The fireman."

"Oh."

"So, anyway, then I rearranged all those small guys in the middle too. See?"

"Oh..." she said, a not quite hidden chuckle in her voice. "Well, I hate to say it, but other than the tall... I mean, *Big Ben*, it all looks the same to me."

"The same?" he blurted, disbelief underscoring the words. "I've been movin' 'em for half an hour. You're not very observant for a Feeb, are ya'?"

"Give me a break. There must be seventy of them for God's sake. Any more and we wouldn't even be able to see the Christmas tree."

His tone turned momentarily boastful as he pointed at the middle of the front row. “Seventy my ass. There’re a hundred and twenty-two countin’ the new guy there.”

“He have a name?”

“Not yet. Still thinkin’ about it.”

“I see. Well, suffice it to say you just made my case for me.”

“But the same?” he groused. “You’re kiddin’ me, right? It doesn’t look the same.”

She shrugged. “Sorry, but it does to me.”

“Dammit…” Ben muttered then huffed out a heavy sigh as he began to point. “Well, okay… So, what if I put Big Ben over there instead, and then put all the…”

Constance cut him off before he could continue. “Ben, relax, will you? They look just fine the way they are… And they looked fine when you started this… And they even looked fine when you set them up three week ago.”

“To you, maybe,” he grunted. “But they gotta be just right.”

“They’re fine,” she repeated a bit more forcefully, while continuing to stare at the display. After a moment she clucked her tongue and said, “You know, one of these days you’re going to have to explain to me exactly how you became so obsessed with nutcrackers.”

“I’m not obsessed.”

“One hundred twenty-two of them, Ben? And you buy at least one new one every year.”

“I collect ‘em. It’s a hobby.”

Constance shook her head. “Sure, okay. Whatever you say. Now quit playing with your dolls and come show me where you keep your paprika. Rowan and Felicity and your sister are going to be here soon, and I still have to change. I’d really like to have dinner ready on time.”

“Paprika… Ain’t that the red stuff ya’ use ta’ decorate deviled eggs?”

“It’s not for decorating,” she sighed. “It’s for seasoning. You do actually have some, don’t you? Please tell me you do.”

“Hell, I dunno,” he grunted as he followed her toward the kitchen. “I try not ta’ cook unless I absolutely have to.”

“Trust me, I’ve noticed. Well if you don’t have any, then you need to run to the store.”

“Why me?”

“Because I’m cooking, and like I said, I still have to change before our guests arrive. Not very observant for a cop, are you?”

He chuckled. “Funny. Real funny.”

A muted electronic tone sounded and then began to warble into a series of syncopated notes that steadily gained in volume. Ben pulled the chirruping cell phone from his belt and gave the screen a glance before quickly flashing it at Constance.

"Speakin' of our guests…" he announced and then exclaimed, "Oh, damn! I was s'posed to call Row about Firehair's present." He unfolded the phone then placed it against his ear and answered with, "Merry freakin' ho, ho, ho, Kemosabe…"

At first the only thing to greet him was a muffled thud.

He tried again. "Hello?"

This time the thud was replaced by a loud crash issuing from the small speaker. The noise was sharp enough that Ben jerked the phone away from his ear before bringing it back close enough to listen. A skittering hiss rolled out behind the crash and was punctuated by a hard clatter and thump.

"Rowan?" he barked. "Are you there?"

In answer, a woman's angry scream bled into his ear, only to be joined a split second later by his friend's voice calling out to him before it was suddenly choked off in a howl of pain.

Ben all but screamed into the phone, "…ROWAN? ROWAN?! GODDAMMIT! WHAT THE HELL'S HAPPENIN' OVER THERE?! JEEZUS H CHRIST… ROWAN!"

Eight Months Earlier

Saturday, April 22
9:32 A.M. – Flight 1695
On Final Approach To
Dallas Fort Worth International Airport

Chapter 1

"REVELATIONS?" MY WIFE, FELICITY, WHISPERED THE question.

"Chapter six, verse twelve," I replied. "And I beheld when he had opened the sixth seal, and, lo, there was a great earthquake... And the sun became black as sackcloth of hair, and the moon became as blood..."

"I suppose it's ironic, isn't it then?"

"That's one word for it," I replied. "Not the one I had in mind though."

"They're just stories, Rowan," she said. "You of all people know that. You can even quote them better than most Christians. The Bible is a book of allegorical prose. It's filled with misunderstood and misinterpreted metaphors and similes from a different age."

"I know," I sighed. "But everything has an element of truth to it somewhere... And sometimes...with everything I've seen... I just... Well, I just have to wonder if some prophecies are universal... If perhaps we're driving ourselves headlong into the darkened abyss of our own insanity. Why else would so many people do the horrible things they do?"

"Don't overanalyze," she offered. "Just try to forget about it. This is over. You've earned a rest."

I gave my head a slow shake. "Something tells me it isn't."

"Why?"

I let out a heavy sigh and pulled her closer as I struggled to find the words to express what I was feeling. "This wasn't right... I mean, the way it all happened. The killer escalated far too quickly. From a victim who disappeared several months ago, to a sudden spree."

"I'm sure the serial killer experts have an explanation for that."

"You're right, they probably do. But something still feels very wrong about it to me... And, that isn't the only thing. Ben made a valid point back at the rest area. I just handed him an address for the killer, and here we are. We all know that isn't how it happens. Everything usually comes to me in cryptic messages I have to decipher. That's how communication across the veil works. It's like a language barrier."

"Maybe you're just learning the language then," she replied.

"Maybe..." I said. "But that's not how it feels. It's almost as if someone was translating for me."

"Who?"

I sighed again. "That's the problem. I have no idea. I feel like I should, but I just don't..."

"Sir… Excuse me, sir…"

The voice drifted into my ears and floated around inside my skull like a distant whisper. It faintly registered, only in as much as I knew it was there, but nothing more. It seemed my misfiring neurons were still fixated on the endless loop of a perplexing memory that refused to be ignored.

"Maybe you're just learning the language then," she replied.

"Maybe..." I said. "But that's not how it feels. It's almost as if someone was translating for me."

"Who?"

I sighed again. "That's the problem. I have no idea. I feel like I should, but I just don't..."

"...I feel like I should, but I just don't..."

"...but I just don't..."

"...just don't..."

"Rowan…" A different voice now called me by name. This time however, I had the distinct feeling it belonged to someone familiar. Its tone was far more adamant, not to mention that it was also joined by a not-so-gentle nudge from something that felt curiously like an elbow.

I flinched at the sudden stab of discomfort, which only served to send a much sharper and far more enduring pain radiating up the back of my neck. It was at right about this moment I noticed I was leaning to my left with the side of my face pressed against something hard, effectively cocking my head at an uncomfortable angle. While this realization certainly explained the pain in my neck, it also seemed to have awakened a sore throb in my cheek.

My brain mulled all of this over for a fraction of a second then decided it had best pay attention to the voices now that pain was involved. Against my better judgment I sat up straighter and turned toward their sources.

"Huh?" I grunted as my eyes fluttered open.

The blurred countenance of a blue uniformed flight attendant shot me what appeared to be a quick smile and said, "Sir, I need for you to raise your seatback, please."

"What? Oh, umm, yeah… Sorry," I muttered the words through a haze of half sleep as I fumbled with the button on the side of the armrest and slowly leaned my creaking body forward.

I suspect the flight attendant didn't even hear my answer. By the time I looked up again, she was on the move and already several rows away as she continued toward the front of the MD-80's passenger cabin. At least that was my assumption—all I knew for certain was that a fuzzy blue shape was rapidly shrinking in the near distance, and it was no longer in my face.

I took in a deep breath and huffed out a heavy sigh. The fresh pains were starting to subside, but unfortunately, I was now becoming reacquainted with the fact that my skull was locked in a dire battle with a headache of questionable origin. I certainly could have done without the pounding inside my head, but I had been here countless times before. I knew simply by the way it felt that the pain had just about everything to do with the paranormal as opposed to earthly causes; and that was something painkillers couldn't usually make go away, no matter how much I abused them.

I reached up to rub my eyes and discovered my glasses were missing. I groped at my shirt pocket and found nothing, so I muttered a quick "dammit" under my breath and started feeling around in my lap for the fugitive spectacles.

"Here," Constance Mandalay said, nudging me once again as she held the bi-focals out to me. "I rescued them earlier before they ended up on the floor."

The petite FBI special agent was parked in the aisle seat next to me. She was my official escort for this emergency trip to FMC Carswell, the Federal Medical Center in Texas that housed female prison inmates in need of treatment, both mental and physical. The individual I was on my way to interview definitely fell into the mental category.

"Thanks," I mumbled, taking the glasses from her and sliding them onto my face. "Anyone ever tell you that you have sharp elbows?"

"It's been mentioned a time or two."

Why I needed an escort was still a mystery to me, but I wasn't about to complain. Fortunately for me, Constance was more than just a federal officer doing a job. She had been a good friend for several years as well, which made traveling with her far less stressful than it would have been with a stranger.

"Feeling better now?" she asked, augmenting the question with a quick smile.

"I'm not sure just yet," I replied, rolling my shoulders and turning my head slowly side to side. "But I think the crick in my neck is saying no."

"I'm not surprised. You really didn't move the whole time you were asleep."

"Yeah, but I wasn't out all that long was I?"

"Well over an hour," she replied. "Pushing two, actually. We're getting ready to land."

"We are? Already?"

"Did you think the flight attendant was just picking on you or something?"

"Honestly, it didn't even register. Guess I was still half asleep," I told her with a shake of my head, then winced and mumbled, "Almost two hours? Damn…"

"Almost. You were out cold before the landing gear was even all the way up; and we've been circling for a bit because of a delay on the ground."

"Man…" I sighed heavily once again. "Sorry about that. Guess I wasn't very good company."

"At least you didn't snore." She chuckled lightly then added, "Not too much, anyway."

"Great…" I mumbled. "Well, in my defense, I didn't really get any sleep last night."

She nodded. "I figured as much, which is exactly why I didn't wake you. Besides, it's okay. It gave me a chance to finish a trashy romance novel I've been reading."

"Well, at least you had…" I started then paused and scrunched my brow at her. "Wait… Did you just say you've been reading a romance novel?"

"No. I said I've been reading a *trashy* romance novel. There is a difference believe it or not."

"I hate to tell you this, but adding that particular adjective just makes the sentence even more unbelievable."

She shrugged. "We all have our guilty pleasures."

"Yeah..." I agreed. "I just figured yours would be *Guns and Ammo*, or something of that sort."

"That sounds like something Storm would say," she countered.

The Storm to whom she referred was Detective Benjamin Storm of the Saint Louis police department's homicide division. Ben and I had been friends for more years than I wanted to remember. He had even been best man when Felicity and I married.

Where he and Constance were concerned, however, the road to friendship had been paved with potholes and speed bumps. In fact, they clashed worse than plaids and stripes from the moment they met. To this day, the image of the petite federal agent going toe to toe with the six-foot-six Native American cop over a jurisdictional issue was not one I would ever forget—nor would most anyone else who had been there to witness it. Of course, with volatile chemistry like that to drive them, it was almost inevitable that they would end up in an on-again, off-again romance. Near as I could tell, as of last night they were still entrenched in an *on* phase of that seesawing dynamic.

"I guess after all this time he's rubbing off on me," I offered.

She shot me a quick grin then quipped, "I'm sorry to hear that. One of him is more than enough for society to deal with."

The moan of active hydraulic pumps rumbled through the cabin, followed by the clunk of the landing gear locking into place. I turned to gaze out the window as the landscape below steadily grew from a miniature diorama to a nearly life-sized sprawl of buildings and streets. Moments later the passenger jet thumped and shuddered as the pilot dropped it onto the end of a runway at DFW and began braking.

"Ladies and gentlemen, welcome to Dallas Fort Worth International Airport, where the local time is 9:42 a.m." A flight attendant's voice issued from the overhead speakers as soon as the airplane had slowed. She was barely audible over the warbling turbines as we taxied toward our arrival gate. "The current temperature is seventy-eight degrees under clear skies with a slight breeze from the southwest. You may now use cell phones, however all other portable electronic devices must remain off and stowed. On behalf of your Saint Louis based flight crew, I would like..."

"So, what's the plan?" I asked Constance, ignoring the rest of the attendant's corporate spiel.

"Doctor Jante said someone from Carswell would be meeting us at baggage claim," she replied.

"So they'll be taking us to the hotel, and we don't need to rent a car or anything?"

She shook her head. "We shouldn't need a rental. But considering the rush Jante put on this for the flight and everything else, my guess is we're heading straight to the facility, not the hotel."

"No rest for the Witch, eh?" I grunted.

"My guess would be no," she replied. "But if it's any consolation I'll make sure the bureau buys you a nice dinner this evening."

"I'll take you up on that if I'm not already asleep," I replied as I dug out my cell phone and thumbed it on. "I might need a rain check though, depending on how all this goes."

"We can do that," she said as she imitated my actions with her own cell. "Maybe you can grab another nap on the way. Carswell is about an hour from DFW."

"An hour, huh…" I grunted.

"A little over actually, according to Jante," Constance added. "She tried to get us on a regional flight into Meacham since it's closer, but DFW was the best she could do on short notice."

"So we get the dollar tour instead."

"Pretty much," she answered with a nod.

"Lovely," I sighed, watching my phone as the bars indicating signal strength appeared one after another. I shot a glance out the window then turned back and added, "Looks like we might be another minute or two getting to the gate. I'd better call Felicity and let her know we made it okay while I actually have the chance."

"Good idea." Constance nodded. "I need to call Ben too."

I hit the speed dial for my wife's number. Two rings later her mellifluous Celtic lilt poured into my ear.

"Row?"

"Yeah, honey, it's me," I told her. "Just wanted to let you know we're on the ground at DFW."

"Good. How was your flight?"

"Okay, I guess. I can't really say. According to Constance, I slept through most of it."

"Aye, that's a good thing then. You needed it. But you still sound tired."

"I am."

She paused for a moment then pressed with, "Your *headache* is worse…isn't it?" Her voice put audible quotes around the word headache to let me know exactly what she meant.

"It's not that bad," I told her.

"Don't lie."

My wife always seemed to know when I was holding things back from her, although she didn't usually point it out unless she was truly worried. She was also far more aware of what was really happening with me on a preternatural level than she tended to let on, but then, she too was a Witch. The simple fact of the matter was that I knew better than to try sheltering her from my ethereal curse with a mundane lie. However, protecting Felicity was a hard habit to break, especially after everything we had just been through, combined with the fact that it wasn't quite over yet. If it were that easy, I wouldn't even be making this trip.

Fortunately for me, she understood my motivation.

"Okay," I conceded. "You're right. It's bad enough, yeah... But I've had worse."

"Will you have a chance to rest? I mean...before you have to..." Her voice trailed off leaving even the barest details of the impending meeting unspoken.

I shook my head out of reflex and regretted the action immediately as it only served to enrage the ache inside my skull. Stifling a groan, I let out a sigh then answered, "Probably not. Someone from Carswell is supposed to pick us up, and based on what Constance was told by Doctor Jante, she thinks they might be taking us straight to the facility."

"They aren't even letting you check into your hotel first?"

"We aren't really sure. Just speculating at this point. But I guess we'll find out soon enough."

"They should at least let you get some rest," she said, concern making her voice rigid. "It's not like this is your actual job. You're doing the FBI a favor. You don't owe them."

"I know, honey, but in a way they're doing us a favor too. You know that. Besides, it really wouldn't matter," I soothed. "I'm here now. You know I'm not going to be able to rest until this is over. I'm amazed I actually fell asleep on the flight."

"Aye, I know...I know..."

"So, how are you doing?" I asked, changing the subject out of self-defense.

Felicity wasn't going to allow it. "I'm fine. I'm just worried about you."

"Well don't. I'm doing okay."

"We both know better than that, Rowan Linden Gant."

She always invoked a maternalesque use of my full name whenever she wanted to make it clear that she was serious—especially if being relatively soft-spoken, as she was right now. Other than simply agreeing with the statement, I didn't have an answer that wouldn't be just another lie meant to protect her from the horrors that had become my world, so I said nothing.

After a healthy pause she demanded, "Promise me you won't take any unnecessary chances then."

"I promise."

"You're lying again," she sighed.

"Yeah…but in my defense, you knew I would."

"Aye… I did…" She paused again before adding, "I have a bad feeling about this, Row…"

I told the truth this time. "Yeah… Me too, honey. Me too…"

"Very bad…" she whispered.

The airplane had finally stopped moving, tones had chimed, and seatbelts signs had gone dark. Passengers both ahead of and behind us were crowding the aisle to wrestle carry-ons from the overhead bins, compounding the already claustrophobic atmosphere of the passenger jet's cabin.

I hated for the call to end, but at the same time I knew if I stayed on the line with Felicity any longer, it was only going to make us both worry that much more. I had the distinct impression she was feeling the same way but simply couldn't bring herself to say goodbye.

Noticing that the travelers ahead were actually beginning to move toward the exit, I seized the opportunity for a mutual escape and told my wife, "Listen, sweetheart, we're at the gate. I'm afraid I need to go."

"Okay… Be careful."

"I will."

"You'll call me later then?"

"As soon as I'm settled in."

Her voice softened even more as she cooed her Gaelic pet name for me. "*Caorthann…*"

"Yes?"

"I'm loving you right now…"

"And I'm loving you right back."

I knew her parting comment was heartfelt, but it still couldn't mask the trepidation in her voice. I doubted mine was any better.

AS PLANNED, SOMEONE FROM CARSWELL WAS WAITING for us at our baggage carousel holding a small pasteboard rectangle, which boasted R GANT in hastily scribed block letters. I can't say it was welcome news, but having been forewarned I wasn't at all surprised to discover that Agent Mandalay's suspicion was dead on—a stop at our hotel was definitely *not* on the immediate itinerary.

CHAPTER 2

"WHILE INSIDE THE INTERVIEW ROOM YOU SHOULD remain seated until it is time for you to leave or unless there is an emergency. If for some reason you need to terminate the visit before the end of the allotted time simply inform the stationed officer. Do not engage in any physical contact with the prisoner. You are not permitted to give anything to the prisoner and you may not accept anything from her either. Do you understand?"

I nodded to the corrections officer while adding a vocal "yes" to back up my visible acknowledgement of the strict instructions. It hadn't been all that long ago that I learned audible responses were considered mandatory while inside prison walls. I didn't know for sure if this applied to visitors as well as prisoners, but I figured it was better to be safe than sorry. I couldn't afford for anything to screw this up, least of all something stupid like me not following a basic procedure.

The simple truth was that this meeting held far more importance for me than it did for the case investigators from the FBI's Behavioral Analysis Unit who had called me in. I'm certain they were well aware of that fact, but I doubted they knew exactly why. Only a small handful of individuals were privy to that answer, and even some of them didn't actually understand the explanation; they merely accepted it because they'd known me for so long.

"It's not like I have anything to give her anyway," I commented purely out of nervousness. "They had me put everything I own in a locker when they searched me out front."

"Then that should make this relatively easy. Raise your arms and hold them out to the side, sir," the officer instructed.

"I just told you they searched me out front," I said, somewhat confused.

"Yes, and I'm going to search you again, Mister Grant. It's procedure when dealing with this type of inmate visit."

"Gant."

"Excuse me?"

"My name is Gant. G-A-N-T. No R."

"Sorry. Raise your arms and hold them out to your sides, Mister *Gant*," he replied, stressing the pronunciation of my name this time.

Without further objection, I did as I was told, and he began to pat me down. This second search was no less thorough than the one to which I'd been subjected upon my arrival. In fact, it may have been even more comprehensive, which took some doing since I was literally walking in with nothing more than the clothes on my back and the shoes on my feet. Still, given the intense level of scrutiny, I couldn't have felt more naked even if it had been a full-out strip search.

"Turn toward the wall," he said and then continued to pat me down once I'd complied.

"I thought this place was less a prison and more of a medical facility," I ventured.

"It's a medical facility for federal inmates," he answered without missing a beat. "Patients here are convicts, plain and simple. That makes it a prison."

"Minimum security though, right?"

"Medium, with a few exceptions that lean toward maximum."

"Yeah, I think I'm starting to get that."

"Good," he replied in a matter-of-fact tone. "It's not something you want to lose sight of while you're inside, especially if you're a visitor. Okay, all done. You can relax and turn around now."

I let my arms drop to my sides and shuffled around in place as I added, "I'll keep that in mind. The prison thing, I mean."

"You'd better. This may be a medium-security installation for the most part, but we have our problem children, and you're here to see the worst of them all. Considering her history, your life could depend on staying alert and sticking to procedures."

"I guess that's why I had to spend almost thirty-minutes reading and signing release forms, huh?"

"That all? Thirty-minutes is nothing. Either way, like I said, this one's not your normal inmate. I'll be honest; we're not really set up for her type. If you ask me she belongs in a supermax, but when they're crazy, sometimes they send 'em here. Either way, she's bad enough that there's a whole special set of rules just for her," he explained. "She'll be staying in restraints for the duration of the visit, and as I mentioned before, an officer will be stationed in the interview room with you at all times, so I don't anticipate there'll be any problems. Still, I cannot stress to you enough, Mister Gant, just exactly how dangerous this prisoner is."

I glanced at his name badge and let out a half chuckle. "No offense intended, Officer Baker, I know why she's in here, but isn't that overkill? I mean, so far everyone has been making her out to sound like that serial killer from those movies who ate his victims with fava beans and Chianti."

"She's close enough in my book," he replied. Then he regarded me with a skewed stare before asking, "They didn't tell you, did they?"

"Tell me what?"

"A couple of months ago she went monkey-shit crazy during a one-on-one therapy session. Then, when the doc called for help she really lost it. Clawed the living shit out of an officer's face. Ended up taking five of us to restrain the bitch, and pepper spray didn't even faze her. Neither did the needle full of sedative they hit her with once she was in restraints.

"Worst part is that before we could pull her off she somehow managed to break the officer's jaw, gouge out one of his eyes, and bite off most of his right ear. But unlike our friend from the movies, she spit the ear back out." He stopped talking and stared at me for a moment then added, "And that, Mister Gant, is why she has her own special set of rules. Still think it's overkill?"

I can't say that Annalise having done this came as a great shock. Still, only just now hearing about it blindsided me quite a bit, and I felt like an ass for making the comparison. I paused briefly then answered him with noticeable hesitation in my voice, "No…they…didn't tell me about that."

"Yeah, well it's not exactly something we publicize," he told me. "If all that wasn't enough, when we finally pried her off him she was moaning like a twenty-dollar whore. Crazy bitch rolled around in her cell for the rest of the day and more than half the night acting like she was gettin' laid, and I mean hard, if you know what I'm saying."

"I do." I nodded and then offered. "Actually, I doubt she was acting though."

"What makes you say that?"

"She's a sexual sadist. She literally derives carnal pleasure from inflicting pain. What she did to the officer most likely brought her to a very real and very physical orgasm, which she then perpetuated by reliving the event in her mind. That's actually part of her signature where her kills are concerned. Beyond that…well…it starts to get a little weird."

"Like that isn't weird enough?" he asked then issued a thoughtful grunt before adding, "Like I said, crazy ass bitch."

"That's one way to put it," I agreed. "So…how is the officer doing? The one she attacked."

"Learning to live with a glass eye and spending a lot of time with a plastic surgeon and a shrink."

"I'm sorry to hear that."

"Yeah, me too," he grunted. "On the bright side they finally unwired his jaw and let him start back on solid food about a week ago."

I wasn't quite sure how to respond to that, so I continued with my apology. "I'm sorry about the movie reference too. I didn't mean…"

"Don't worry about it." He cut me off, underscoring the words with a shake of his head. "You aren't the first one to make it, and I doubt you'll be the last. What it comes down to is that I'm simply trying to warn you, Mister Gant. This woman isn't one of the run-of-the-mill head cases we get around here. She's psycho bitch insane." He wagged his finger in a spiraling loop next to his own head. "Insane inmates are unpredictable, and unpredictable inmates are the worst kind of dangerous."

I restrained myself from pointing out that Annalise Devereaux was even more dangerous than he imagined—but in a completely different fashion and for reasons he wouldn't begin to believe. Nobody on this planet knew that better than I.

Instead, I replied, "I appreciate the heads up," and left it at that.

"You're welcome," he said, his expression stoic. "Don't take it personal, but I'm just doing my job. I don't know you from Adam, so your problems are yours, not mine. But, you get hurt or killed while you're in there on my watch, then it *is* my problem. Doesn't matter what they had you sign, it's on me. And, I've still got seven more years before I can start collecting a pension, so I don't need a dead civilian on my hands fuckin' that up."

"I understand."

"Good."

In the wake of his comment he looked me over, one eyebrow cocked upward in a questioning arch. With a quick thrust of his chin toward me he said, "I have to admit I'm a bit curious about this whole square dance though. The way they fast-tracked you isn't exactly what we consider normal around here, if you get my meaning. Especially for an inmate like Devereaux."

I nodded. "I think I probably do."

"Rumor is you just flew here from Saint Louis a few hours ago."

"Well, rumor is correct. I did."

"Must have been an early flight."

"Too early."

He pursed his lips and nodded thoughtfully, as if chewing on that bit of information before swallowing it. A few seconds later he added, "Also seems like there's a whole lotta other red tape gettin' cut real quick like."

I shrugged and then built upon his metaphor. "I guess the FBI uses some pretty sharp scissors when they have to."

"Yeah, guess so," he grunted. "So mind if I ask what your story is? You a big shot criminal psychologist writing a book about freak jobs like Devereaux or something like that?"

"No," I replied, shaking my head. "I'm just a consultant."

"Consultant, huh? Well, you seem to know an awful lot about what makes this one tick."

"Yeah… Unfortunately she isn't exactly a stranger to me… But, I'm afraid 'consultant' is still pretty much the only real label for what I do."

"So what exactly do you consult about?"

I'd been under this spotlight before, and I knew better than to mention the occult. References to the paranormal generally caused people to look at you like you had lost your mind or simply dismiss you out of hand. I furrowed my brow and gave him a one-shouldered shrug. "Special circumstances. That's about the only way I can think of to describe it."

"Yeah…okay." He gave me a quizzical look. "So what you mean is you consult on crazy fucks."

"It gets a little more complicated than that."

"It always does… Well, all I can say is considering the strings that got pulled around here the *circumstances* must be pretty damn *special*."

I sighed then muttered as much to myself as to him, "You have no idea."

"I probably don't want to," Baker replied, then without any further questions he returned to an explanation of procedures. "Okay. So with her history and restrictions, this should actually be a non-contact visit, which means you're supposed to be talking to her through a pane of reinforced glass."

"I know. But for reasons I really can't get into, I need to be physically in the room with her."

“That’s some of the other red tape I was talking about,” he said with a quick nod. “Now, under these circumstances we’d normally bring her in first and secure her before letting you into the room, but again, we have a change in procedure. On high said to do it the other way around. Is that your understanding?”

“Yeah, that’s the plan.”

“Mind if I ask why?”

“Psychological advantage.”

“And if she goes monkey-shit before she’s locked down?”

“I’m pretty sure they had me sign something to cover that possibility.”

“Yeah, well like I said, it’d still end up being my ass in a sling, so let’s hope you’re right about this whole advantage thing.” He shook his head then turned and unlocked a heavy door. After swinging it outward on its hinges, he pointed through the opening and offered a new set of instructions. “Have a seat on this side of the table. I’ll let them know to bring her in.”

“Thanks,” I said with a nod as I moved past him.

“Thank me when you’re back on this side of the door in one piece,” he replied as he gave the door a push.

The barrier thumped closed behind me with the dull finality of a coffin lid slamming shut. I don’t know if it was a product of the eerie sound or simply because I had a very good idea what was coming next, but at that exact moment every hair on my body stood painfully at attention.

SOME NIGHTMARES ARE MEASURABLY WORSE THAN others. In my personal estimation, on a scale of one to ten, the terror sitting across the table from me at this very instant was at the minimum an eleven. Of course, I’ll admit I was biased. After all, she had tried to kill me on more than one occasion. But, she wasn’t the first, and I suspected she also wouldn’t be the last. The thing that truly colored my perception of her was the psychological scarring she had left on my wife. That was my personal line in the sand, and she had crossed it without apology.

The all too familiar thud of my otherworldly headache was continuing to pound out a painful rhythm at the base of my skull. However, the prickling gooseflesh that had accompanied me into the room was finally dying down, not that such turned out to be a true reprieve. One pain had simply faded away only to be replaced by another, that being my intestines twisting into a knot as bile churned deep in my gut. It seemed my body was just full of involuntary responses tied to my current struggle to maintain composure, and apparently it was determined to give them all a chance at an audition. Lucky me.

I tried to ignore the discomfort and focused my attention on the woman opposite me. Even up close and personal, as we were now, Annalise Devereaux's resemblance to my wife was a full three steps beyond uncanny. The fact that they shared the same father and their mothers had been identical twins made it a bit easier to imagine from a genetic standpoint, but even then the doppelganger effect was still at best a one in a billion occurrence. Extraordinary as it was, they were almost as indistinguishable in physical appearance as their biological mothers had been; and as we had found out through intensely trying circumstances, their DNA was very close to being just as eerily mirror-like.

Still, the carbon copy outward appearance was under the best of circumstances. The past few months spent as a guest of the federal corrections system had been less than kind to Annalise, effectively blurring those similarities in the worst way. Instead of a smooth, ivory complexion, she was tainted with a drawn, grey pallor. Her hair was cropped short, and though apparently clean, its once vibrant auburn was lackluster. Instead of bright, jade-green eyes like my wife's, hers were dull and lifeless. They were staring at me now from deep, darkly rimmed sockets.

While she was still the spitting image of Felicity, she appeared now as a frail and sickly version of her, which triggered an automatic surge of sympathy deep inside me that was hard to quell. I struggled with the new feeling for a moment, letting out a slow, quiet sigh while closing my eyes. When I reopened them nothing had changed—not that I'd expected such. Still, it was worth a try.

For all intents and purposes, Annalise Devereaux looked drained, both emotionally and physically. She was used up—for lack of a better expression. She appeared as if she'd had no rest at all for untold ages, and while appearances can sometimes be deceiving, this time it was dead on. I also had a better than sneaking suspicion that it was not just the incarceration that had done all of this to her. A good portion of it was due to the parasite she had invited to set up residence in her body.

Miranda.

Unholy wasn't a word I used often, but in this case it was the perfect descriptor for the brimstone-charred spirit that inhabited my wife's heretofore unknown half-sister. Miranda was the unfortunately immortal soul of a sadistic murderess from another century, brought back to life in the here and now by proxy—all because the woman sitting in front of me played with magick she didn't truly understand.

Of course, Annalise's already well-ingrained proclivities had served to fuel the spirit possession, turning her from a professional dominatrix who already walked a bit close to the edge of unbridled cruelty and into a perverted serial killer in her own right. Truth be told, if I believed in Hell then I would say the two of them were a match forged in its darkest bowels.

But, a trail of mutilated bodies wasn't the only horror their ethereal union had left in its wake. Felicity and I were the scarred and still bleeding proof of that fact. In the end, that was my primary reason for being here in this room now—to close a final gaping wound and put an end to Miranda, once and for all.

Whether or not that was actually possible remained to be seen.

I shifted in my seat then locked my fingers together and rested my hands on the table in front of me as Annalise continued to stare. Not a single word had been spoken by either of us since she was brought in and handcuffed to a circlet mounted on her side of the metal table. After another languid span of time had passed, I glanced at my empty wrist then remembered my watch was in a personal effects locker on the opposite side of several secure doors. I let out a much more audible sigh than before and then glanced around the room in search of a clock, but I found none. Just bare walls, save for a security camera mounted in an upper corner out of easy reach. Finally, I brought my gaze back to meet hers but remained silent.

I wasn't sure how much longer I could play this game. I knew her muteness was intentional, and in my mind it was a foregone conclusion she would win this staring contest hands down. She was just as stubborn as my wife, which was of no surprise. If genetics played any part whatsoever in such things, she had inherited the family trait honestly. Besides, she also had insanity in her corner, even if it was by proxy. However, even with those almost insurmountable odds stacked against me, I waited, all the while my brain wrestling with my tongue in order to keep it still.

What seemed to be another solid five minutes passed before my grey matter was finally down for the count and I gave in. I slowly shifted in my seat then cleared my throat and said, "You win, Annalise. I'm here, just like you wanted."

She remained silent and her expressionless stare never left my face.

I waited while several heartbeats thumped out a nervous cadence in my chest. I had questions I desperately wanted to ask, but I knew it was too soon. If I didn't allow her to open up at her own pace, I'd never learn what I needed to know. And if I showed my cards now, I was fairly certain I would lose any chance of ever finding the answers.

"You're the one who wanted to talk to me," I offered. "Remember?"

No change. Not even a flinch. If it weren't for the intensity of her stare, I would have started wondering if she was even conscious. Of course, I really had no idea exactly *who* was sitting across the table from me. The body ostensibly belonged to Annalise Devereaux, but for the most part she had relinquished it long ago. Who actually inhabited the flesh and blood shell at this particular moment was anyone's guess. I had my suspicions that the steadfast gaze was pure Miranda, but I really couldn't be sure just yet.

Time continued to drag, and the pain inside my skull kept gnawing away at what little patience I still had intact. After another half dozen minutes or so, I purposefully shifted my gaze to the corrections officer in the corner. I was a half second from opening my mouth to tell him I was ready to give up and leave when Annalise's voice broke the quietude.

I had expected that when she finally spoke, it was likely to be no more than a frail whisper, but what I heard now was far from it. Her comment was direct, and her voice was strong, calm, and even, as she said, "I really do not understand what it is she sees in you."

CHAPTER 3

THE CAUSTIC OBSERVATION CERTAINLY WASN'T EVERYTHING I had hoped for out of this meeting. However, depending on your perspective, hope and expectation can be two completely different things. To be honest, since I hadn't expected much at all, this was better than nothing. At the very least she was speaking instead of simply staring, and the subtext of her comment was purposely blatant.

I cleared my throat once again, shifted forward in my seat, and then nodded. "Actually, I've been asking myself that very question for several years now."

"I sincerely doubt it," she replied.

It didn't matter to me that she was being adversarial. In my mind, the fact that she responded at all was enough to push the dialogue forward. If she wanted to argue, I was willing to oblige.

"And why is that?"

"So you want to play psychologist, I see."

I shook my head. "No. As I recall, you're the one with the psych degree, not me. I'm just asking a question."

She launched an exasperated sigh into the air between us. "Fine, I will play along. I say I doubt it because you are pretending to assume the *she* I am referring to is your wife."

"I see," I answered with a slight nod.

My headache was still raging, not that I'd imagined it would magically subside just because she began to talk. However, the return of the prickling gooseflesh as my skin tightened in a physiological response to her comment had definitely not been on my list of expectations—especially since my stomach was still slowly working its way through the expanded edition of the *Handbook Of Knots*.

Apparently, this was going to be even harder on me than I thought. I took a moment to bolster my psychic defenses, but I feared I was already too late. Preternatural attacks were like flood waters—once they broke through there was precious little that could stop them, and I had no doubt that I was already bobbing in a dangerous current.

After a short pause I asked, "So, I take it you're talking about someone else then?"

"Of course. You know full well that I am."

She was correct, I did know, but I wasn't going to let on to that just yet. I wanted her to believe she was the one in control of the conversation. Unfortunately, what I wanted really didn't matter all that much because she actually did have the upper hand, whether I cared to admit it or not.

"Could've fooled me…" I said, purposely furrowing my brow. "Care to fill me in, or am I just supposed to make another assumption?"

She cocked her head and gave me a pitying glare. "You are nowhere near as clever as I expected you to be. What happened to the man who tracked me all the way to New Orleans?"

"Which one of you?" I asked. "As I recall I tracked you both."

"You tell me."

"I suppose it doesn't really matter, does it? After all, where one of you goes, so goes the other."

"For now," she said.

"Yeah… Okay…" I replied. "So anyway, to answer your question, I'm reasonably sure I'm sitting right here."

"I am not so certain that is true."

"Why do you say that?"

"Your pathetic attempt to make me believe you do not know of whom I speak."

"Maybe I'm just dense."

"I doubt it."

I shrugged. "Then maybe you set the bar too high."

"Do not try to make this about me."

"Isn't it though?" I asked. "About you, I mean? You're the one in control here."

"No, no, no…" she muttered, shaking her head. "That was clumsy. Ham handed. You are playing this game all wrong." She lifted her hands above the table as far as the chain on the cuffs would allow. "Besides, if I was the one in control, then you would be wearing these and crawling on the floor at my feet where you belong."

"Point taken," I said as I nodded. "But, even though you're the one who is physically restrained, by the same token you're in command of the situation. After all, you wanted me here and I showed up. No questions."

"Do you really think I do not know that you have been trying to arrange this meeting yourself? We both know you wanted it even more than I. And, we also both know you have questions."

"Okay, you got me. I have questions. But don't we all? At least I haven't asked them."

"Yet," she spat.

"True."

"But you want to."

I shrugged again. "Would you expect any less?"

"I thought we had established that you are already far less than I had expected?"

"Because I don't know who you're talking about?"

She shook her head, only slightly, but still enough to be perceptible. "You know exactly who I am talking about. What makes you dim is your belief that you can play stupid with me and that I will buy into it."

"Maybe I'm not playing."

"Do not continue to insult my intelligence. Do you really think you can fool me? I know everything you are thinking."

I steepled my index fingers then tapped them lightly against my pursed lips as I feigned introspection. After a moment I dropped them forward to point toward her. "So you're going to be the psychologist now?"

"Psychology is not necessary in order for me to recognize bad acting when I see it. I have already told you that you are not clever enough to play this game with me."

"Okay then. No games. Why did you ask for this meeting with me?"

"Why don't you tell me?"

"Who's playing games now?" I asked with a sigh. "Did you call me here just for your own entertainment?"

"What if I did?"

I took in a deep breath and then exhaled slowly. Leaning back in my chair, I cocked an eyebrow and gave her a half shrug. "If you did, then I think you're easily amused, and to borrow a phrase, we both know that isn't true. But what can I say? Go for it. Entertain yourself. And when you're done, we can talk about the real reason I'm here."

She arched an eyebrow, slowly glanced over her shoulder at the guard, then turned back to face me. "Have Officer Bardwell remove these handcuffs and leave us alone, and trust me, I will entertain *both* of us."

"I doubt we have the same ideas about what we find entertaining," I replied. "So if it's all the same to you, I think I'll pass."

"I thought as much." She sneered as she gave her head a haughty shake. "It does not matter. You do not have the time anyway."

I shrugged at the question. "Time? I've got all day."

She smiled and shook her head. "No. You do not."

"Sure I do."

"No," she replied, the corner of her mouth turning up in a wicked smirk. "You would love for me to believe that, but I know better."

"Okay," I conceded. "Then since I'm the dull-witted one here, why don't you fill me in?"

"Are you certain you really want to keep trying to play a game you are destined to lose?"

I clucked my tongue and paused before answering. "Truthfully, I haven't really been certain about much of anything where you've been concerned, except that you're an evil bitch."

She flashed a thin, condescending smile. "Finally… That is the first truly honest thing you have said to me since you arrived."

I answered with sarcasm. "Glad I could brighten your day."

"Would you like to continue the trend, or shall I do it for you?" she asked.

"This is your party," I replied. "Why should I have all the fun?"

"All right then," she returned. Shifting in her seat she allowed her expressionless gaze to dwell on my face for several heartbeats before speaking once again. "You do not have all day because you would not last that long and you know it. You are exhausted. You have barely slept and your nerves are on edge. Being this close to me is making you worry, and right now you want nothing more than to call your wife to make sure she is safe since you are not there to protect her. But most of all…you are afraid of her."

"I'm afraid of my wife?"

She furrowed her brow in admonishment. "I really am bored with you playing stupid. I have already pointed out that you are not any good at it."

I gave in. "Okay… By *her* I assume you mean Miranda."

"That is twice now with the honesty…. Very good… I am becoming somewhat heartened."

I splayed my hands out in a small shrug-like gesture as I rephrased her comment and repeated it back to her, "So you think I'm afraid of Miranda."

"I do not think you are afraid of her," she replied, shaking her head slowly. "I know you are."

I sighed then gave her a quick nod of assent. "Okay. I'll admit that I was once, but not for the reasons you imagine. And, I'm not anymore."

"How is it you think you know what I imagine?"

"Call it an educated guess."

She pursed her lips and rolled her eyes. "No, not the lying again. We were just starting to have a meaningful dialogue."

While I had been maintaining a passable front, on the inside I was going down for the third time. No matter how hard I had been trying to wall myself off from her malignant energies, she was finding a way in. The very core of my being was under assault, and the effects couldn't be contained much longer. I felt like a bomb, and she was holding the dead man switch that would set me off.

I shifted forward in my seat and growled, "Meaningful to whom? It sounded to me like all you did was state the obvious. Trust me, I've seen myself in the mirror today, and I know damn well I look exhausted, so you aren't telling me anything new. You want honesty, Annalise? Here it is. Everything you just said was a dime store observation anyone could make. Just like you said earlier, no psych degree necessary. So maybe it's you who isn't all that clever. Did you ever think of that?"

She leaned in, mimicking my posture. "Come now, be honest. You really do not believe that."

"No," I admitted, my voice even but still edgy. I huffed out a heavy breath and then sat back. "No, I don't. I just think you made a horrible error in judgment. Miranda is the one who isn't as clever as she thinks she is."

"Really? How do you know you are not talking to Miranda right now?"

"I don't." I shrugged. In point of fact, from her very first words I knew that's exactly whom I was talking to, but I lied anyway. "I suppose I could say I know who is *riding the horse* because of your initial comment to me." I kept close watch on her eyes as I spoke. I had purposely used the phraseology common in *Vodoun* to describe the act of a *Lwa*, or ancestral spirit, inhabiting a corporeal body. I knew it was a transparent attempt to provoke a reaction, but I tried it just the same. However, the reference didn't even garner a twitch, so I continued. "Or, maybe it's because you didn't even blink when I called you Annalise. I think we both know Miranda wouldn't really care for that. But if I gave you any of those reasons, I'd just be lying and you know it. The real truth is, I have no idea which one of you I am talking to at the moment."

She allowed herself an exaggerated sigh. "And it seemed like we were making such progress, but here you are lying to me again. Come now, telling me the truth did not hurt that much, did it?"

"Only a little," I replied. "So…before we go any further with this game of yours…"

She cut me off. "This is not *my* game. It is yours…"

"Fine," I grumbled. "Have it your way. So, if it's my game, then we play with my rules. Time to ante up. What are you wagering?"

"What about you?" she asked. "What are you putting on the table?"

"You first."

"Greedy, aren't you?" she replied. "Should you not be happy with what you have already won?"

"And what would that be?"

She smirked and cocked her head to the side. "You are alive, are you not?"

"I see. So then I guess that's what you meant with your comment about not understanding what she sees in me. Miranda has a soft spot for me so she let me live?"

She shook her head. "Of course not. You have Annalise to thank for your continued life."

I remained silent, eyes locked with hers as she waited for me to react to her purposely-clumsy move. I searched my grey matter for an appropriately biting response but found none. The harsh pain inside my skull had taken its toll and then some. In my mind I tried to blame it on the lack of sleep, but I had been down this road before. It was nothing new, and I had definitely gone longer than just a day without rest and still managed to function. The simple fact of the matter was that I had walked in here unprepared, and Miranda was draining me. In my haste to bring this all to a close I had underestimated her, just as I had done in New Orleans. She had bested me there twice. Now she was doing so here for the trifecta, and it seemed I was handing it to her without much of a fight.

The longer I sat there allowing this to happen, the more my psychic nerves throbbed, raw and bleeding. She knew this and was mercilessly grinding them under her heel while taking delight in every moment of my inadequately hidden agony. In the grand scheme of things, our verbal sparring had only just started, and here I was already face down on the mat. I couldn't help but wonder if I had made a fatal error by coming here at all.

I silently pondered the idea of trying to rally myself enough to at least finish this round. To somehow drag myself up and regain control… But all I could find was a resurgence of my earlier anger, which was now directed at myself more than anyone else. After a moment I simply gave in and allowed it to take over.

When I opened my mouth once again, my words were laced with venomous sarcasm. At this juncture, I knew the best I could hope for was a stalemate. Of course, given that I'd actually surrendered the game the minute she came into the room, hope and expectation were as always, two completely different things.

CHAPTER 4

I SHOOK MY HEAD SLOWLY AND SOMEHOW MANAGED TO snort out a short harrumph. "Referring to ourselves in the third person are we?"

"Are we?" she replied.

"Well now... If this isn't all creepy and spooky I don't know what is..." As I spoke the words I was simultaneously wavering my hands in the air between us to pantomime the mystical. I stared at her for a moment and then huffed out a second heavy breath while struggling to keep a tight reign on my anger. Weaving more of a sardonic tone into my voice I spat, "And embarrassing too. I mean, what a surprise. I've been talking to Miranda this whole time. Whoops. How awkward for me."

"Finally, the real truth comes out. You knew with whom you were conversing all along, little man," she stated without pause.

"I actually suspected it while you were busy playing stare down with me. Then once you opened your mouth it was fairly obvious. We've met before, or don't you recall?"

"Of course I remember." She leaned back in her seat as far as her restraints would allow and then purred, "We have actually met more times than you know."

"Believe me, I've got a pretty damn good idea," I countered. "You aren't exactly forgettable."

"Of course I am not."

"I hate to burst your bubble, but I didn't mean that in a good way."

"I am sorry to hear that. I enjoyed our times together very much."

"Well, I guess that makes one of us."

She feigned a melodramatic pout. "You really should not be like that. You see, if you are nice to me I just might keep you around when I take Felicity."

There it was, the figurative dead man switch. The trigger she had been squeezing in her fist, just waiting for the right moment to let go. From the moment she walked into the interview room she had been steering everything to this point, and now she relaxed her grip so she could watch me explode.

No more had the last syllable of my wife's name been pushed past her lips than I came up to my feet with a wildfire of rage consuming me from within. A sharp, metallic sound ricocheted from the walls as my chair toppled backwards and clattered across the tile floor. It was joined midstream by a loud smack echoing through the room when my left hand came down flat on the surface of the table. Propelling myself into a forward lunge, I thrust my right hand out, clipping her jaw in the process.

"You aren't coming anywhere near my wife, you fucking bitch!" I growled.

I allowed myself to fall across the table as I brought both hands to bear on her. In a flash I had my left tangled into her hair, wrenching her head back as my right gripped her throat. I heard no sound coming from her as I dug my thumb into her windpipe, but she kept her eyes locked with mine. There was no mistaking the contented look they now held. The smug air only served to enrage me further, and I resolved to bring about her end, here and now.

My blindly stupid act, however, was terminated before I could follow through.

I heard shouting filtering in through the sound of blood rushing in my ears. It was faint but unmistakable. I felt my fingers being pried off Miranda's thin neck, although there didn't seem to be much sense of urgency behind her rescue. I suspect that given what she had done to his colleague, the corrections officer wasn't overly concerned for her welfare. Eventually I heard a sharp gasp from Miranda as my grip was broken, but I saw no change in her expression. In fact, she didn't even blink.

Several seconds later my left arm was twisted behind my back, then I was pulled backwards and restrained, even though my rational self had instantly kicked in and I was no longer struggling.

"I'm afraid we're going to have to end this interview, Mister Grant." The voice belonged to Baker, the officer who had searched me prior to my entry into this room. He sounded almost apologetic.

I didn't realize he had joined us until now, but it only took a quick glance for me to see that both he and Officer Bardwell were holding me back.

"Not yet," Miranda said. "I'm not through with him."

"It's not your call, Devereaux," he shot back, adopting a far more gruff tone with her than he had with me.

"Look, I'm sorry…" I stuttered.

"Yeah, me too," he replied, softening again before grumbling. "But sometimes the job gets in the way." Directing himself at the other guard with a jerk of his head, he ordered, "Bardwell, take Devereaux to the infirmary. I'll take care of Mister Grant."

I didn't bother to correct him this time. I had far more serious matters to worry about than the massacre of my name. Of all the times I had found a way to screw up, if this one wasn't the crowning jewel of them all, at the very least it definitely ranked among the top three. I simply stood there with my mouth shut. I knew there was nothing I could say to fix this, and unfortunately I didn't believe in miracles.

A low warble sounded in the room, quickly increasing in volume. Officer Baker pulled a cell phone from his belt, glanced at the face of it, then muttered, "Hang on a sec there, Bardwell."

The other corrections officer had just unlocked one of Miranda's cuffs, so he clicked the restraint back into place and stepped back, keeping watch on the situation while he waited.

"This is Jeb," Officer Baker said into the cell phone as he placed it against the side of his head. "Yeah… Yeah… I thought you might have…"

I looked away from him and centered my gaze on Miranda once again. She stared back at me with a satisfied smile perched on her lips. Her earlier grayish pallor was now flushed, a fact less obvious than the smile but still a visual cue that she was stimulated. Blood trickled from one corner of her mouth where my hand had made contact when I first threw myself at her, and a bright red welt was already forming on her neck.

She arched her eyebrow and then asked, "Feel better now, little man?"

"Not really," I replied.

"I do."

"I'm not surprised. You got what you wanted."

"Not everything."

"…Are you sure about this?" Officer Baker's voice interrupted. He wasn't actually speaking to anyone in the room, but the obvious change in his tone diverted my attention all the same.

I glanced over at him and saw that he was looking up into the security camera while still talking into his cell. "All right. You're the boss."

He closed the phone and stuffed it back into the holder on his belt before addressing me. Shaking his head in disbelief, he said, "Like I said before, you must be one hell of an important sonofabitch, Grant."

He turned to Miranda and thrust his chin at her. "I'm only asking this once, Devereaux. Do you want to go to the infirmary?"

"No," she replied. "I do not."

"So, am I to understand that you are refusing medical treatment?"

"Yes."

"Officer Bardwell, did you hear the inmate?"

"Yes sir, she is refusing treatment."

Baker let go of my arm and took a few steps over to the toppled chair. He righted it, slid it behind me, then put a hand on my shoulder and somewhat forcefully guided me into the seat. As I sat down he said, "Psychological advantage, huh?"

"Apparently not," I replied sheepishly.

"Yeah, no kidding. Well, do us all a favor. Stay in the chair until the interview is over, and keep your hands to yourself, Mister Grant. Just like I told you the first time, okay?"

I nodded and answered, "Yes sir." Under the circumstances I still thought it best not to correct him about my name.

Once he had exited and Officer Bardwell resumed his station, I glared across the table at Miranda.

She smirked. "That was fun."

"You aren't getting Felicity," I told her. I kept my voice at an even timbre, but it was impossible to mask the hatred that drove it.

"And who is going to stop me? You?"

"Obviously I already have."

"Do you really think so?"

"You're here."

"No. Annalise is here. I am wherever I wish to be."

"No, you aren't. You're trapped here with her."

"Really?" She actually chuckled. "How do you know I am not trying Felicity on for size again right now?"

I steeled myself and clenched my fists at her question. What made it almost intolerable was her casual use of my wife's name. To an outside observer it wouldn't have meant a thing, but to me it inferred an unwanted intimacy between them.

As my fingernails bit deeply into my palms, I replied, "Because you're here talking to me."

"That means nothing, and you know it. Connections, little man."

"Not anymore. I broke your connection to her."

"Did you?"

"You know I did."

She laughed. “Is that the lie you have been telling yourself these past months?”

“It isn’t a lie, it’s a fact.”

“Be truthful, little man. You do not believe that.”

“How do you figure?”

“That is easy. You came here, did you not? If you truly believed you had broken *all* of the connections, you would never have shown up.”

She was a step ahead of me all the way. Maybe even two. However, I had already given up too much, so I wasn’t about to surrender anything else if I could help it.

“You’re the one who demanded to see me,” I spat. “Besides, if you know so much, you should be well aware that I came here to talk to Annalise. Not you.”

“Of course you did.”

“Then let me,” I said. “Or are you the one who’s afraid?”

She snorted out a laugh. “What is it you think I fear?”

“What Annalise might tell me.”

“Such a sad little man,” she told me, shaking her head. “Annalise has nothing to tell.”

“Then let me talk to her.”

“No.”

“I can make you go away.”

“And how do you propose to do that?”

“Thirsty at all, Miranda?” I threatened but remained still in my seat.

All it took was that simple phrase for her to know exactly what I meant. I had used salt water on more than one occasion to chase her out of Felicity’s body when she had managed to sneak her way in. That was before I had discovered the gateway that was allowing it to happen in the first place—one half of a paired necklace that had been charmed by magick well over a century ago, and more recently, re-empowered by blood.

My query didn’t sound like much of a threat, I know, but salt was the basest form of purification, and when it came to magick, sometimes the simplest path was the most effective. At this particular moment I was perfectly happy to test that theory by pouring some down Annalise’s throat.

She laughed again then shook her head. “Petty magic, little man. Is that your answer to everything?”

"It works," I growled.

"Perhaps not. Maybe I merely allowed you to believe that," she corrected.

Our eyes remained locked for a handful of heartbeats. Finally, I said, "You're lying."

"Am I?"

"Of course you are."

She laughed. "Go ahead and cling to your faulty beliefs. It only makes things easier for me. Although, I must admit, I was looking forward to a challenge from you. I should have known better."

Her words were audible but shrouded by the resurgence of blood rushing in my ears. In that instant the hammering in the back of my head spread forward to encompass my entire skull, and all I wanted to do was scream. Instead, I leaned back in my seat and closed my eyes as I rubbed my temples.

"Yeah… Whatever…" I mumbled.

"All right… Now I am done," Miranda said.

"Done what?" I asked in return while opening my eyes.

She ignored my question. Instead, she turned and called over her shoulder in a flat, matter-of-fact tone, "Officer Bardwell, we can go now."

"Hold on," I demanded, shifting forward and glaring at her. "We aren't finished here yet."

The corrections officer was already starting to disconnect her restraints from the table as I spoke.

"Yes, little man," she replied. "We are."

"Stand up," he ordered her.

She complied, waiting silently as he deftly reconnected the cuffs with the Martin chain looped around her waist. Taking hold of her upper arm, he guided her around the chair and away from me toward the door where they had entered earlier. I couldn't do anything but sit there quietly and watch them go. Hanging my head, I let out a long sigh. As if the agony trying to chisel its way out through the side of my skull wasn't enough, now I was stewing in self-recrimination over the fact that I had allowed her to win.

"Just a minute," Miranda said, her voice coming from a few steps away.

I looked up and saw the two of them standing next to the door. Miranda turned slightly and leveled yet another pitying stare upon me.

After a thick silence she stated coldly, "You want to know about the other half of the necklace."

My throat tightened as my heart jumped in my chest. Suddenly, her lead was no longer measured in steps. She had already lapped me and was still pulling out ahead. It really shouldn't have come as a surprise that she knew what I wanted. The dead always seemed to know things they shouldn't. I guess, under the circumstances, I was simply having trouble thinking of her as dead, and that was just another of my critical errors in all of this.

It was obvious that lying about the necklace wasn't going to work, so I replied, "Yes."

She regarded me coolly for a moment. "Come back tomorrow and maybe I will let you ask Annalise if she knows anything about it."

With that, she turned away from me. A few seconds later they were gone, and I was left alone with a blinding headache and an icy chill slowly working its way up my spine.

CHAPTER 5

"ARE YOU OKAY, ROWAN?" CONSTANCE ASKED. "YOU don't look well at all."

We were sitting in an office normally used by one of the staff psychologists. Actually, I was the one doing the sitting. Constance was pacing back and forth in front of me.

Following my less than productive visit with Miranda, Officer Baker had escorted me back to the administrative unit where the petite FBI agent was waiting. Although the thrum in my head had been blinding me to most everything else resembling lucid thought, I still somehow managed to make it a point to apologize to him again for my reckless outburst. Given the back-story he had relayed earlier, I wasn't terribly shocked by his contrite reply. The words themselves were innocuous but their hidden meaning clear—that being the fact that he would just as soon I had been successful in my attempt to choke the life from Annalise.

I rubbed my eyes, pushing my glasses up off the bridge of my nose with little regard for them. Finally I muttered, "The headache's finally started to dial back a bit, but honestly, I've been a hell of a lot better."

"Should we have one of the doctors take a look at you?"

"Wrong kind of headache. Wouldn't do any good," I breathed. "You've figured that pattern out by now."

"True enough," she sighed. "Even so, is there something I can get for you? Water? Coffee? Soft drink?"

"How about a bottle of Scotch?" I replied.

"I said soft drink. Scotch will have to wait until later."

"Yeah, I was afraid of that. Coffee would probably be good. Maybe some aspirin. It won't fix it, but it usually helps take the edge off at least…" I replied. "And a phone."

"Do you really need a phone?"

"Yeah, actually. I do."

From the sudden lack of audible footsteps, I could tell she stopped moving. A second later I felt something tapping against the back of my wrist and heard her say, "Here."

I lowered my hands from my face and looked up to see that she was offering me her cell.

"You can use mine," she said. "I know I can get you some coffee. I'll have to ask around about the aspirin."

"Two outta three…" I mumbled, leaving the rest of the cliché unspoken as I took the proffered device from her hand.

"I'll go see what I can do," she told me as I flipped the cell open. Stopping at the door, she turned and blurted, "What the hell were you thinking, Rowan?" Her tone was a jumble of admonishment and confusion, with neither one taking any real prominence over the other.

"Ben must be rubbing off on you too," I replied, skirting the query. "I'm pretty sure he's asked me the same thing at least a dozen times."

"Probably," she replied then deepened her voice and added, "But it's more likely he said, 'Jeezus H Christ, white man. What the fuck didja' think ya' were doin' in there?'"

"Yeah," I grunted, a slight chuckle in my voice. "That sounds more like it. Not a bad imitation, either. So I take it you were watching the show too?"

She nodded. "I was with Doctor Jante and Doctor Clayton."

"Who's Doctor Clayton?"

"Chief psychologist for the facility."

"Great. How many shrinks does it take to screw Rowan? Three. One to fuck him up and two to analyze." I sighed then asked, "Speaking of which, where are they? I would have thought Jante would be ready to read me the riot act."

"I asked them to let you have some time to decompress."

"I'm amazed she agreed," I mused. "Gives them some time to compare notes, I guess. They've probably got me diagnosed as a complete nutcase by now."

"Maybe, maybe not. But getting back to my original question," she pressed. "You don't usually go off the deep end like that. I'm serious, Rowan, what were you thinking?"

I closed my eyes and pinched the bridge of my nose between my thumb and forefinger as I tried to ground the pain. After a heartbeat or two I said, "I'm pretty sure we can safely say I wasn't."

She clucked her tongue. "Yeah… I think you're right…"

I grimaced then looked up at her. "I hate to even ask, but exactly how pissed off is Doctor Jante?"

"Believe it or not, I don't think she is. I doubt she's happy about it, but she really acted like what happened was no big surprise."

"What about the other guy?"

"Doctor Clayton? Pretty much the same. He seemed to follow her lead."

"Who was responsible for allowing the meeting to continue?"

"It was Doctor Clayton's call, but Jante pushed for it, and like I said, she seems to have quite a bit of influence over him."

I furrowed my brow and mumbled, "Curiouser and curiouser…"

"Okay, forget the *were*. What *are* you thinking?"

"That I'm being used for something and somebody didn't bother to clue me in."

"That crossed my mind as well," she replied with a shake of her head. "But what?"

"That's a good question."

She added, "Another good one would be why."

"No offense, but I've been asking myself that for quite awhile where the cops and feds are concerned. It's not like this would be the first time I'd been used and abused by someone with a badge."

Constance nodded, answering in a chagrined tone, "I know."

She wasn't paying me lip service. She really was well aware of the backstabbing Felicity and I had endured, not only from the Saint Louis police but the FBI as well. Over the years I had been used as bait for a serial killer without my knowledge, threatened, and even investigated. However, for me, none of that could begin to compare to how they'd tried to railroad my wife for crimes she didn't commit. And, all of this had been done by the very same authorities that had sought our help in the first place.

But, by the same token, I also had a tendency to be the beneficiary of nebulous bureaucratic intervention just when my hour seemed to be at its darkest. Who was playing the puppeteer was still a complete mystery to me, but to say I felt like I was firmly attached to the ends of their strings was an understatement. To say the least, my confidence in most law enforcement was growing thin. Were it not for Ben and Constance, it was doubtful I would trust anyone with a badge ever again.

After a moment I noticed an unsettled quiet had fallen in behind my friend's words, so I broke it with a heavy sigh. "I guess I need to go ahead and make these calls," I said.

She nodded again. "Sure. I'll see about that coffee and aspirin."

I was already stabbing out a number with my thumb when she exited the room. A pair of rings later a gruff, male voice came on the line.

"Only been a coupl'a hours. Missin' me that much, are ya'?" Ben almost cooed the words, an uncharacteristically tender note in his voice.

"Not really," I replied.

The immediate shift in his tone was almost jarring. "Row?"

"Yeah. I'm using Constance's phone, but I'll let her know you're fantasizing about her."

He ignored the jab. "You two all right? Everything okay down there?"

"Constance is fine," I told him. "Me…well, I'm about as okay as I can get under the circumstances."

"Yeah, sounds 'bout like you. So, you keepin' your hands off my girlfriend?"

"Depends. Are you keeping your hands off my wife?"

"Hell yeah, white man. I'm afraid of 'er."

"Me too."

He chuckled. "Well that answers that, doesn't it? So… I doubt ya' called ta' shoot the shit. Guess I oughta ask… What's really goin' on down there?"

"I sort of blew it with Miranda."

"How?"

"Believe me, you don't want to know."

"Jeezus, Row, I hate when you say crap like that…"

"Yeah, I know."

"Then tell me what the hell ya'…"

I cut him off before he could continue to press me on the subject. "I promise I'll fill you in on the whole story when I have time. But listen, right now I called about something way more important. You know that thing I gave you this morning when we were on the way to the airport?"

"That bottle with the jewelry in it?" he asked. "Yeah, what about it?"

"Where is it?"

"I dunno. Prob'ly sittin' in the console of my van where I left it."

"Dammit, Ben…"

This time he interrupted me instead. "Relax, will ya'? I'm just yankin' your chain. I got it right here in my pocket. You were pretty damn clear about not just leavin' it layin' around."

"You're sure it's there?"

I could hear him shuffling around a bit on the other end of the line, then he replied, "Well, now it's in my hand and I'm starin' right at it, so yeah, I'm sure."

"And you can see the necklace in there, not just the salt?"

"Salt. So that's what that is."

"Ben…"

"Yeah, yeah, Jeezus… Chill out white man, I can see the goddamn necklace floatin' around in the salt."

"Good."

"Where the hell'd ya' think it'd be?"

"I'm just checking, Ben. That's all."

"Uh-huh… So you really think a friggin' piece a jewelry is why Firehair got all *Twilight Zone* weird on us?" he mused, referring to Felicity by a favored nickname.

"Yes, I do," I replied. "And Miranda just all but confirmed it."

"How?"

"Something she said. She told me she knew I wanted to ask Annalise about the necklace."

"So?"

"So I hadn't even mentioned it."

"Yeah, okay," he replied. I could almost see him nodding. "So what you're really talkin' about is spooky, dead person, Witch shit."

"Something like that."

"Okay, so then ya' wanna tell me what's goin' on? You're soundin' a bit ramped up."

I let out a quiet but heavy sigh. "I'd like to say just me being paranoid, but we know how that usually turns out."

"Yeah," he grunted. "Usually you ain't paranoid, they really are out ta' get ya'. So, really, fill me in. What's the story?"

"I haven't really figured it all out yet, but I have a sneaking suspicion the FBI is keeping me in the dark about something," I said.

"Mushroom treatment, eh… No big surprise there," Ben grunted. "What's Constance think?"

"Same thing as me, unfortunately."

I could imagine him shaking his head as he breathed, "Fuckin' wunnerful… Goddamn Feebs."

"You date one."

"She's an exception."

"Yeah, I'd have to agree with you there."

My friend sighed heavily and then adopted a curious tone. "So, lemme ask ya' somethin'. Why are ya' puttin' yourself through all this shit? Why don't ya' just do some hocus-pocus on this Miranda bitch and be done with 'er?"

"I've tried. Believe me, I've tried."

"What's the deal? Your Witch-fu not good enough?"

"That's one way of saying it," I replied. "Hoodoo is some very intense stuff, Ben. It has no moral restrictions, and it's like the guerrilla warfare of magick."

"Yeah, so? I thought the stuff you do was pretty serious too."

"It is, but hoodoo is seriously down and dirty. It can…" I stopped mid-sentence and took a mental step back. Rather than giving him a detailed lesson in magick, what I really needed was a mundane analogy that would get the point across. "Look at it this way," I said after a short pause. "The particular magick I'm dealing with here is like two-part epoxy. You need both parts to make it work. Same basic principle applies. For me, or even an expert practitioner of *Vodoun* and hoodoo for that matter, in order to stop what Miranda has set in motion, both parts of the magickal working are necessary. That necklace you're holding onto for me is only half of it. Without the other, the situation is at best a stalemate."

"You ain't actin' like it's at its best," he observed.

"That's because it's not."

"Great," he grunted. "So what happens if ya' can't find the other half?"

"I'd rather not think about that."

"Yeah… I 'magine not."

I swallowed hard and slowly let out a breath. "Yeah… So, listen, I still really need to call Felicity and check in with her. Just do me a favor. Don't let that necklace out of your sight, okay? And don't go anywhere near Felicity with it."

"Yeah, okay," he agreed. "I kinda got that part already."

"Thanks, Ben."

"I'll put it on your tab. Hey…you do me a favor too. Have Constance call me when you're done screwin' around with 'er phone, okay?"

"Yeah, I will. Later." I stabbed the end button even as the last word was coming out of my mouth and then began dialing a new number.

A moment later my wife's near panicked voice issued from the earpiece. "Constance? What's wrong? Is Rowan okay?"

"It's me," I told her.

"Rowan? Sorry… The caller ID came up with Constance's cell number."

I explained. "My phone's still in a personal effects locker, so I'm using hers."

"Row… Is everything okay?" The concern that was initially apparent in her voice had dropped considerably, but a thread of tension was still palpable.

"Yeah…I'm okay…" I told her. "What about you?"

"I'm fine," she replied, her voice a bit hesitant. "Why?"

"You don't sound fine."

"I'm fine… Rowan, what's wrong?"

"Nothing… I just wanted to hear your voice, that's all."

"*Breugadair*."

I met the Gaelic insult head on. "I hate to tell you this honey, but you might want to look in a mirror. I can tell you're lying too."

"That would be *breugag*."

"You say potato…"

"One is masculine, the other feminine…"

"I'm sure it is, but I didn't call you for a lesson in Irish Gaelic, and I hate to tell you this, but you aren't any better at changing the subject than I am. Tell me what's wrong."

"You first."

"Good Gods, Felicity, I'm fine…"

"If you were really fine you wouldn't be calling then. Not yet," she chastised, then stated as much as asked, "You've been in to see her already, haven't you?"

"Unfortunately."

"Who was she?"

"Miranda. But that's pretty much who I expected."

"Aye… So…what happened?"

I stifled a snort. "Just what she wanted, I'm afraid. She pushed all the right buttons and set me off."

"Are you really okay then?"

"Yeah…" I half whispered. "Yeah… At the moment I think she bruised my ego mostly. But, she's not going down without a fight, and that has me worried."

"So…you didn't find out anything?"

"Other than the fact that Miranda is still in control, no, not really."

"Annalise?" she asked, a different sound of concern threading through her words.

"No…" I replied, shaking my head out of reflex. "Not even a glimmer. But Miranda is definitely dangling her out there in front of me like some kind of carrot."

"How do you mean?"

"When today's interview ended, she told me to come back tomorrow and she might let me speak to her."

"Do you think she really will?"

"I doubt it," I replied. "Why would she? Besides, other than the corporeal body itself, I honestly don't know if Annalise even exists anymore. If she does, she might not even be lucid at this point."

There was no reply, but I could hear Felicity breathing softly on the other end of the line. And based on some of our past conversations, I had a fairly good notion what she might be thinking.

Finally, I said, "Remember, honey, Annalise tried to kill you."

"Aye, that's true…but she's still blood."

"Blood you didn't even know existed until less than a year ago, and that discovery didn't come under the best of circumstances I might add."

"I know. But…" She allowed her voice to trail off before saying, "I suppose you're right then. I'm damned either way. One of them wants to consume me, the other wants to kill me."

"Not going to happen," I soothed. "Either one. I won't let it." I paused briefly and then said, "Okay…your turn."

"What do you mean?"

"I told you the truth, now you owe me the same. What's wrong?"

"I'd hoped you'd forgotten about that then," she replied.

"I know you did. But I didn't."

She tried to object. "It's nothing important."

"Then it shouldn't be a big deal for you to tell me, right?"

I heard her take a deep breath in resignation. After a suggestive pause she said, "I'm having…feelings…*urges*."

Her admission sent a fresh chill tap dancing along my spine. I knew all too well the kind of urges she meant, and the hollow feeling now expanding through the pit of my stomach told me I knew why.

"These aren't just your normal…you know…" I left the rest of the hopeful question hanging.

"You mean my normal desires to tie you up and play the dominatrix?" she answered, unabashed as always. "I thought so at first…but…no… That isn't exactly how they feel. These are…" She hesitated before finally saying, "These aren't just urges to play. They're…much darker."

The answer wasn't what I wanted to hear. I asked, "How dark?"

"Very," she replied, her voice leaning heavily on the word.

"How intense are they?"

"Enough. But, not so bad that I can't cope."

"You're sure?"

"Aye, Rowan, I'm sure. They're nothing I can't handle."

"You need to drink…"

She finished the sentence for me. "…salt water. I know, and I already am… And sage tea as well. You aren't the only Witch here, you know."

"Yeah, I know. Is it helping?"

"Aye. It seems to have taken the edge off then."

"But the feelings are still there…" I replied, offering the words as more of a statement than a question.

"I'll be okay, Row," she appealed. "Really, I will."

I wasn't convinced, and she didn't necessarily sound like she was either. But, right now there was a little too much distance between us for me to do anything other than worry.

"When did they start?" I pressed, a bit of hesitation creeping into my voice. I already knew what she was going to say, but I had to ask.

"About an hour ago," she replied. "Maybe a little more. Why?"

I closed my eyes and whispered, "While I was in the room with her… That's what I was afraid of."

The ache bouncing around inside my skull took on a new dimension, making the back of my throat tickle with a thin wave of nausea. Recent events stuttered through my brain like a cartoonist's flipbook until one exploded forth to fill my thoughts.

In my mind's eye I could clearly see Miranda's smug grin as she stared back at me. But even worse, I could also hear her mocking voice as she chuckled and said, *"Really? How do you know I am not trying Felicity on for size again right now?"*

CHAPTER 6

AS SOON AS MY MOUTH WAS ABLE TO SYNC UP WITH MY brain once again, I mumbled to Felicity, "Let me see about changing my flight. Just hang in there, and I'll be home as soon as I can, even if I have to buy a new ticket out of my own pocket."

"No," she replied, a sudden sternness in her voice.

"What do you mean, no?"

"Exactly that. No. You can't come home yet. You just told me you have to meet with Annalise tomorrow."

"Honey, I also told you I don't even know…"

She cut me off. "…if she even exists any longer, I know. And before you say it, I know Miranda might only be stringing you along with this."

"There's no might to it," I replied. "I know she is, and so do you. It's what she does. Besides, after the way things went today, the powers that be around here might not even allow another meeting to happen."

"Why?"

"Let's just say I doubt the FBI is very keen on their consultants losing their cool during an inmate interview."

"Oh, Rowan…" she sighed. "What did you do? You aren't in any trouble are you?"

"I'll tell you later, and I don't know for sure on the trouble just yet," I said. "But I don't think so, which seems a little weird in itself if you want to know the truth. I've had a bit of a hinky feeling about all this ever since the interview ended."

"Well, it is Miranda after all."

"Yeah, but not just that. It's something different. Something a little closer to home and definitely grounded in reality."

"What?"

"That's something else I don't know for sure," I admitted. "But I get the impression I haven't been told everything that's going on. Plus, with the way things have played out so far, it appears as though my presence here may be more important to the FBI than I originally thought it was."

"I told you I had a very bad feeling about this," she lamented.

“I know, honey. Me too. But it might all be moot. Like I said, after what happened today, I’d be surprised if they were actually willing to let me into a room with Miranda again.”

“I wish you would tell me. Not knowing is just going to make me worry more.”

I swallowed hard and said, “Let’s just say she’s going to have some bruises and I’m responsible.”

“Oh Gods, Rowan…” she breathed. “You assaulted her?”

“It’s okay,” I told her. “No permanent damage. It really sounds worse than it was.”

“You’d best be right. Should I call Jackie then?”

It didn’t surprise me that she brought up our attorney. Her name had crossed my mind too. “No. Not yet, anyway. If I get charged with something then yeah, for sure…”

“Okay then. If you’re certain.” After a pause, Felicity ventured, “Aye, but you still have to try to talk to Annalise if they will let you. That’s why you made this trip in the first place.”

“A trip that has turned out to be a huge mistake,” I told her. “Especially in light of what you just told me a minute ago. Your problems today started while I was in the room with Miranda. I’m willing to bet that she’s somehow using me as a conduit to get to you. That was something I didn’t even consider, which was stupid on my part. I should have thought of that.”

“Don’t allow her to use you then.”

“Easier said than done, obviously, or it wouldn’t have happened in the first place.”

“Maybe, maybe not,” she replied. “What if it’s you who should be drinking salt water?”

“I’ve tried that before, remember? Apparently I’m immune to its positive effects.”

“Try it again.”

“Felicity…” I said. “Even if that would work, it’s all a moot point. The door to Annalise has most likely been closed. On all fronts.”

“Only if you allow it to be.”

“You’re putting way too much faith in me, honey. Besides, we’re getting off track. The real issue here is you. I can’t stay here and leave you by yourself if she’s found a way to connect with you again. On top of that, if she’s using me as the conduit then the farther I am away from her the better.”

“But what if the closer you are to me the worse off I am?”

"Don't…" I stuttered, paused, and then said. "Dammit, Felicity."

"You know you have to take that into consideration too."

"You're being awfully damn logical, you know that?"

"One of us has to," she replied. "Besides, I told you, Rowan, I'll be fine."

"I wish I could make myself believe that."

"Aye, I wish you could too because it's the truth."

"I can't take the chance."

"You have to, Row… You know you do. I'll be fine. Really."

I sighed heavily, leaning forward and resting my elbows on the edge of the desk in front of me as I massaged my forehead with my free hand. "And what if you're wrong, Felicity? What if they'll let me talk to her again and she gets to you through me?"

She was quiet for a moment before answering softly. "What if she does? What do you think you could do if you were here?"

"Keep you safe."

"Could you?" she appealed.

"Yes."

"Aye, you would try… I know that… But at what cost?"

"That doesn't matter."

"It does to me." She fell silent for a moment then all but whispered the reason behind her objection, "I almost killed you once already."

"No, you didn't. That wasn't you. It was Miranda."

"Yes, but she was using *my* body," she replied, laying heavy emphasis on the my. Just from the sound of her voice, I could imagine the pained expression she was most likely wearing.

"Which is precisely why…" I began.

Once again she cut me off. "Which is precisely why you should stay there and find a way to stop her for good."

"You just aren't going to let me win this argument, are you?" I asked after a short pause.

"No." There was a brighter note in her voice this time. It was faint but there nonetheless. "When do I ever let you win?"

Even with my current mood, I had to smile at her rhetorical question. "You know if they won't let me see her, then there's not much I can do about it."

"You'll find a way. You always do."

I puffed out my cheeks and let go with a long exhale as I continued rubbing my forehead. "Promise me you'll call right away if the urges get stronger."

"I promise."

"I'm serious, Felicity."

"So am I."

I paused and shook my head in disbelief at what I had just agreed to do. After a moment I said, "You know I'll be checking back in with you later, right?"

The humor in her voice increased again as she murmured, "Aye, you'd damn well better then, Rowan Linden Gant… I don't take well to being stood up."

For the second time today, we ended our long-distance connection on a concerned note. We'd muddled through this waltz many times before, and as usual both of us wanted to lead. Most of the time we could make that work, but this go around the tempo was completely wrong and we were faltering through the steps. Unfortunately, as long as Miranda was playing the music, we had no choice but to dance.

"AFTER SOME DISCUSSION, WE'VE DECIDED WE WOULD like for you to go ahead and meet with Annalise again tomorrow, Mister Gant," Doctor Jante said to me. "Just as she suggested."

My momentary descent into violence went unmentioned. In fact, up until now, only the standard pleasantries and a cursory introduction between Doctor Clayton and myself had been exchanged, but not much else. Now, apparently break time was over.

I was in the middle of ripping the ends from two square paper packets of generic analgesic tablets when the verbal bomb was dropped on ground zero, which was, without a doubt, me. There was no ceremony whatsoever behind the statement, and I had to wonder if the heavy-handed delivery was calculated or truly as clumsy as it appeared on the surface.

Either way, the tone in her voice was unmistakable. She was telling me, not asking me.

I looked up at her for a moment then back down at my hands. Without a word I continued about my task of pouring the quartet of pills into my palm then wadding the empty packets and stuffing them into my pocket.

We were still in the same office where I'd been sequestered ever since returning from the ungodly mess that was posing as my interview with Miranda. Jante and the chief psychologist had followed Constance into the room when she returned with the coffee and painkillers, which was very shortly after I had finished my call with Felicity. Given their timing, I suspect they had been on the other side of the door listening for a cue to come in. Of course, they could have been watching me on a screen down the hall for all I knew. It seemed there were cameras everywhere you looked in this place. I hadn't noticed one in here just yet, but that didn't mean there wasn't a lens spying from above.

Still mute, I reached out and lifted a Styrofoam cup from the corner of the desk. I took a tentative sip of the coffee and found that it was far closer to lukewarm than hot. Since it had been given more than ample time to cool down, that suggested I was probably correct in my theory that they had been waiting outside the door for me to finish my call. I popped the handful of aspirin into my mouth, gave them a quick chew, and then washed the gritty results down with a healthy swig of the brew. Fortunately, the universal constant of bad cop coffee didn't seem to apply here. While it definitely wasn't the best I'd ever had, it also didn't bear the same taste profile as an industrial solvent—like the cup of sludge I was used to swilling whenever I visited the metropolitan homicide division at police headquarters back in Saint Louis. Under the circumstances, however, I think I might have preferred the sludge, so long as I could have it there instead of here.

Finally, after a second slug to wash the taste of the pills from my mouth, I set the cup aside and grunted, "Actually, I talked to Miranda. I haven't met with Annalise yet."

"A matter of semantics," Jante replied.

"Yeah, you just go right on believing that," I said with a nod. "It seems to have worked out well for you."

"I'll have a driver meet us out front," she offered, ignoring my sardonic gibe as she snatched up the handset from the telephone on the desk. "It's after noon so I'm sure you are hungry by now. We can discuss this over a late lunch and then take you to your hotel."

"Actually, I'd prefer you just change my airline reservation," I said.

"Excuse me?"

"Something that would get me home this afternoon or early evening would be perfect," I replied.

While I had promised Felicity I would take a shot at talking to Annalise, it was becoming more and more obvious to me that something else was going on here. I wasn't about to walk into it blindly. I'd already done enough of that for one day.

"Mister Grant…" Doctor Clayton began.

"Gant," I said, my voice terse as I cut him off. "G-A-N-T. What is it with you people around here? Do you have a surplus of R's or something?"

"My apologies," he replied.

I gave him a conciliatory wave of my hand as I shook my head. "No… No, I'm the one who should apologize. I realize it's no excuse, but if you knew what my head felt like right now…" I let out a heavy sigh.

"I understand," he said with a nod.

I raised my eyebrows. "Thanks, but no, you really don't… Believe me, I wish you did though."

"I see," he replied, however his expression said he didn't. "What I was going to say is that we are faced with a unique opportunity here."

"That's one word for it."

"So, Mister Gant," Doctor Jante interjected. "Are you saying you don't wish to meet with Annalise again?"

"Actually, I'm not saying anything of the sort. But, just so we're on the same page, I will say that I'm a bit confused by all this. Shouldn't I be the one trying to convince you to let this meeting take place?" I answered.

She nodded and stated the obvious reason. "Of course. Because of your unfortunate outburst."

"Well yeah, if that's what you want to call it," I said. "Where I come from it's referred to as assault." Even though I tried to keep it reined in, a hint of sarcasm crept out with the words anyway.

"You needn't worry about that."

"Why not? I mean think about it. I just attacked one of your inmates. Personal feelings aside and, as much as I hate to say it, she has rights, and I'm reasonably certain I violated them in spades."

"As far as we are concerned your actions were justified."

"Justified?" I threw my hands up into the air in front of me and added with a note of exasperation, "Hell, she hasn't even been tried and convicted yet. Not to mention that she was chained to the table when I went across it at her. My actions weren't justified and you know it. Shouldn't you be hauling me out of here and charging me with aggravated battery or something of that sort?"

"Rowan…" Constance warned in a quiet voice. "Don't push it."

"As I said," Jante told me. "You needn't worry. No criminal charges will be filed. The incident isn't even being reported."

I spat, "That doesn't make sense."

"You really should listen to S.A. Mandalay. We're doing you a favor."

"You're probably right, but I'm a little stubborn."

Jante crossed her arms and stared at me. "All right. Do you want to be arrested, Mister Gant?"

"No, I never said that's what I wanted." I shook my head to punctuate the response but didn't display any other reaction to the threat. "But I would like to know what's really going on."

"As I said, because of your history with the Saint Louis office of the bureau, we're doing you a favor," she replied. "However, if you'd rather not accept it, I can go ahead and have Special Agent Mandalay take you into custody."

"Now you're bluffing."

"Am I?"

"Yes," I told her, not wavering. "If arresting me was really an option, today's meeting never would have continued after my 'outburst' as you called it. Not to mention this whole favor thing would have never been put on the table."

"I have my reasons for allowing the interview to continue."

"Oh, I'm sure you do, and that's what has me wondering. But it also doesn't change the fact that you're bluffing right now."

"Why would I bluff you, Mister Gant?"

"Well, this is just a guess, but I'd say because there's something you want from me."

She cocked her head. "And how did you arrive at this conclusion?"

"No offense, Doctor Jante, but I've been played by people who are better at it than you." I shrugged. "Let's be honest. Other than arresting me, at the bare minimum, kicking my ass out of here is what would make the most sense in this situation. But instead, you're sweeping things under the rug and even wanting me to have another meeting with the Ice Queen. Your mistake here was assuming I still wanted that meeting too."

"You don't?"

"Right now, I'm not so sure," I said, giving my head a shake. "Miranda tore me apart in there, you know that. And that was just what you could see on the surface. There are things going on here that I don't expect you to understand."

Doctor Clayton spoke up again, a recognizable aura of academic curiosity in his voice. “I assume you are referring to your contention that the personality calling itself Miranda is actually a Voodoo spirit inhabiting Annalise Devereaux’s body?”

“They’re called *Lwa*,” I replied. “And yeah, that’s definitely part of it.”

“And you truly believe this?” he pressed.

“Yes, I do,” I huffed. “But go right ahead and feel free to think I’m a nutcase, Doc. Everyone else does, so join the club.”

He gestured with his hands as he shook his head. “Well, even you must admit that such a belief defies conventional logic.”

“Yeah, I do,” I grunted while giving him a nod. “Every friggin’ day of the week. So there you go. Welcome to my *unconventional* life.”

“Let’s get back to the issue at hand,” Doctor Jante interrupted. “Are you or are you not willing to meet with Annalise Devereaux tomorrow?”

“You tell me.”

“Mister Gant, I have no idea what game you are playing.”

“Same one as you,” I told her. “I just don’t have the benefit of knowing all of your rules, so I’m making them up as I go.”

“Excuse me?”

“Look, Doctor Jante, I’ll make you a deal. You come clean with me about what it is you want from me, and I’ll give it another go with Annalise.”

“I’m sure I have no idea what you are talking about.”

“Then let me help you understand. It’s obvious that you believe my involvement here outweighs my transgression, which is why you’re willing to put me back in a room with Annalise Devereaux, even though you can’t really be certain I won’t flip out again. This can only mean that there has to be something in it for you. Maybe not you personally, but for the FBI at least. The problem here is that I don’t know what that is. Can you understand my confusion now? Obviously something else is going on here, and even though it involves yours truly, I’m not in the loop and that makes me very nervous.”

“You’re imagining things.”

“If that’s the case then I must be delusional,” I replied. “All the more reason why you shouldn’t trust me in there with her.”

With a cloud of exasperation billowing around her words, Jante said, “Exactly what is it you think I can tell you, Mister Gant?”

“I’m guessing plenty, but it wouldn’t hurt my feelings if you’d start with explaining why you're so willing to overlook what happened. And while you're at it, maybe you could tell me exactly who the Behavioral Analysis Unit is studying here—Annalise Devereaux or Rowan Gant?"

CHAPTER 7

JANTE'S OUTWARD DEMEANOR HARDENED. SHE REGARDED me coolly, as if sizing up an adversary before throwing a punch. Taking the approach of putting us at odds with one another probably wasn't my smartest move ever; but I'd already blown the bell curve for the day in that particular department, so in the grand scheme of things it really didn't matter all that much. At any rate, my reply to her query had definitely struck a nerve, so I was either going to get my answers or find out I was wrong about her bluffing. Either way, I figured I would be ahead of the game in one sense or another.

"S.A. Mandalay," she finally said, verbally addressing Constance but never taking her eyes off of me. "Would you mind escorting Doctor Clayton out of the room for a few minutes."

Like earlier, even though she had phrased the words as a question, she wasn't asking. She was giving an order. I realized she was officially the one in charge, but her demanding verbal mannerism was starting to wear on me.

Unable to hold my tongue, I asked, "Why break up the party, Doc?" This time I made no attempt to hide my sarcasm.

"This is strictly FBI business."

"Fine. Send Doctor Clayton out for a coffee break." I gestured toward the now uncomfortable looking chief psychologist then glanced in his direction and added, "No offense intended, Doc." Leveling my gaze back on Jante I said, "But Constance is FBI and I'd really prefer she stick around."

"That isn't possible."

"And why is that?"

She shook her head. "In this case I'm afraid that what you are wanting to discuss is above her pay grade."

"Above her pay grade?" I chuckled. "And Ben tells me I watch too many movies. Hell, I'm starting to feel like I'm in one… Here's the thing, we both know if it's above her pay grade then it's way the hell above mine. I want her to stay."

"I'm trying to work with you, Mister Gant, but you're being unreasonable."

"It's one of my more endearing qualities. Just ask my wife."

"You really aren't in a position to negotiate."

"I don't know about that... You're the one who called me, remember?"

"Only because Devereaux was so insistent upon speaking with you."

"I don't buy that," I said. "She could have had her lawyer contact me if that's all it was. There's more to it than that."

"Perhaps I was merely doing you another favor. I'm well aware that you had already exhausted every contact you have trying to arrange a meeting with Devereaux prior to my calling you. In fact, just over a month ago you told me yourself that you needed this meeting with her."

"Yeah, I did. But with today's blind eye added to the mix, that would make two awfully big favors for someone you don't really know all that well." I shrugged. "So what's in it for you?"

"Research, Mister Gant. Data."

"Then I guess we both stand to lose something if we can't make nice on the playground."

"I can still have you arrested and brought up on charges," she threatened.

"I have no doubt that you can," I agreed. "Hell, I'm the one who suggested it. But I'm pretty sure I already called your bluff on that one, didn't I?"

"The thought of being arrested doesn't concern you at all, does it?"

"Oh, it concerns me," I said with a nod. "It concerns me quite a bit. But I happen to have a pit bull of an attorney, not to mention two corrections officers and an FBI agent who know exactly what went down in that interview room after my screwup. I'm sure a few procedures and rules were ignored today, and I'm betting that would have some bearing on how things play out for everyone concerned. So, even if I go down, I'll take you with me."

"So you're resorting to blackmail?"

"Just taking a page from your playbook, Doc."

"All of this posturing is accomplishing nothing," she admonished.

I agreed. "You're right. But since it's mutual, let me see if I can break the cycle." Turning to Constance I held out my wrists and asked, "You want me like this, or should I put my hands on top of my head, or behind my back, or something like that?"

"Stop it, Rowan..." Constance scolded me under her breath.

"They've already patted me down a couple of times today," I

continued. "But if you have to do it again just watch where you grab, if you know what I mean. I'm sure Felicity will understand as long as you're careful."

Constance growled at me again, much more audibly this time. "Dammit, Rowan… This isn't a joke…"

"You should listen to her, Mister Gant," Doctor Jante snapped. "You don't seem to be taking this situation very seriously."

I turned back to her and adopted a deliberate tone. "And that's where you're dead wrong. To my knowledge I'm the only damn person in this room with anything really at stake here, so I'm far more serious about this than you even imagine. But, the simple fact is I've already been manipulated as much as I'm going to allow, by both you and Miranda. So either have Constance arrest me, or tell me what's really going on. Your choice."

She pursed her lips and cocked one eyebrow slightly upward as she studied my face. The silence in the room became so thick that I could easily hear the second hand on the analog desk clock dutifully announcing the precisely measured expiration of time.

Eventually, Doctor Jante forced out a quiet harrumph and then addressed Doctor Clayton. "William, would you give us a few minutes please?"

Though still terse, her tone was noticeably more cordial toward her peer.

"Certainly, Ellie," he muttered. "I'll be in my office when you're finished." As he turned toward the door he glanced at Constance and me. "Mister Gant, Special Agent Mandalay."

Jante watched him go then addressed me again. "Before we begin I would like to suggest one more time that you reconsider your wish to have S.A. Mandalay present."

I snapped back at her. "I thought we'd…"

She cut me off quickly, holding up her hand in a stalling gesture. "I am merely making a suggestion, Mister Gant. But you need to be aware that I am doing so for your sake."

"What's that supposed to mean?" I asked.

"It simply means that what I am willing to say will be tempered by who is in this room."

"Sounds to me like someone is covering her ass," I spat.

She dismissed my comment with a shrug and then made one of her own. "If you really want an answer to your questions…"

With the sentence still hanging in the air, purposely unfinished, I stared back, searching her face for any indication that would tell me if I could push her any further. I saw none.

"It's up to you, Rowan," Constance told me. "I can wait outside."

"Yeah…" I murmured, nodding my head and then raising my voice to a more audible level. "Yeah, I give up. Maybe you'd better."

"You're sure?"

"Yeah. I'll be fine."

Constance reached out, lightly squeezed my shoulder and said, "Okay. I'll be right outside in the hallway."

Once her fellow agent had exited and the door was shut behind her, Doctor Jante carefully perched herself on the corner of the desk. Looking down, she smoothed her skirt in a deliberate motion, picked off an imaginary piece of lint, and then focused her attention back onto me.

"She's obviously very fond of you."

"My wife and I are very fond of her as well," I replied, a hard edge in my voice. "She's a good friend to both of us. But you already knew that."

"I didn't mean to imply anything else."

"It makes sense now though," I mused aloud. "I mean, why you so easily agreed to her escorting me on this trip instead of some other random agent. I actually couldn't figure out why I even needed an escort up until just now. You knew I'd request Constance, and you think having her here gives you leverage against me if you need it."

"That sounds rather like paranoia."

"Is that an official diagnosis or a friendly observation?"

She smirked. "For someone who appeared to be in a state of severe psychological distress during that interview, you seem to be holding your own now, Mister Gant."

"Trust me, the distress was real."

"But you're fine now?"

"I still have a headache from hell," I replied. "But yeah, I got a second wind."

"Apparently."

"Listen Doc, the crazy bitch in the prison khakis already put me in a seriously foul mood, as I'm sure you've noticed. And our little skirmish hasn't exactly helped either, although no offense here, but dealing with you is a friggin' cakewalk compared to her. But, you said it yourself; all this posturing is getting us nowhere. So, can we just stop circling each other like a couple of rabid dogs and get down to it? Otherwise we're going to be here forever."

She sighed heavily. "All right then. First, I need you to understand that what I am going to say to you is completely confidential."

"I pretty much figured that part out when you started clearing the room," I replied.

"Should you repeat any of what I tell you, rest assured, I will deny this conversation ever took place."

"Who's paranoid now?" I asked.

"Not paranoid, Mister Gant. Careful."

"Like I said, someone's covering her ass. Fine. I get it. Confidential. Top secret. Eyes only. This tape will self destruct. Just between you and me… Can we get on with it?"

"Good," she acknowledged. "In answer to your earlier question, the focus of this case study has always been Annalise Devereaux. However, as of late, you have been under observation as well."

"Okay. I think I pretty much had that one pegged. Although, the rhetoric sounds generically clinical," I said.

"It is meant to."

"I assume 'as of late' means this has been going on a little bit longer than just today?"

She nodded as she uttered, "More or less." Neither her tone, nor her noncommittal words inspired confidence in the ambiguous answer.

"Okay, so the admission was a nice overture to start, but how about telling me something that I haven't already figured out? Like maybe why I'm being observed? Am I under some kind of super secret criminal investigation or something?"

"No, nothing like that. Not since prior to our meeting in Saint Louis."

"But before the meeting I was?"

"Yes, of course," she replied, a slightly confused expression on her face as she shook her head. "Given the circumstances of Devereaux's crimes and your wife's apparent connection to them, both of you were the subjects of an investigation. But you already knew that."

I shook my head and quietly snorted. "Yes, I did. But, something told me that whole meeting with you was a ration of bullshit from the word go."

"Not entirely. You'd both been cleared prior to that meeting."

I repeated her words. "Not entirely… Which implies you weren't completely truthful about its purpose then, which means I'm right about it being bullshit. So am I to assume that's when the observing started?"

She remained silent, and her expression neither confirmed nor denied my question.

I pressed, "Okay, so if I'm not under some sort of criminal investigation, why don't you tell me what all this observing is about?"

"It's for the purpose of evaluation."

"Of what?"

"Potential, for lack of a better explanation."

"Okay, I'll bite. Potential what?"

She shifted slightly and began to explain. "As I'm sure you are aware, a good portion of your exploits are a matter of record."

"By exploits I guess you mean my helping with murder investigations?"

"Exactly. And since there are some very detailed reports, as well as some obviously sanitized accountings, you have become a bit of a curiosity. In any event, the depths of your talents have not escaped the notice of the bureau, and in particular the BAU."

"So what you're saying is that the FBI is treating me like a lab rat because I'm a Witch?"

She gave me a shallow nod and said, "Actually, Mister Gant, in a very real sense, yes."

CHAPTER 8

WHILE MY TALENTS, AS SHE PUT IT, HAD NOT ESCAPED the attention of the FBI, at this particular moment in time, they were most certainly escaping mine—at least as far as anything precognitive was concerned. I had to admit, I was fully expecting her to laugh in answer to my last question, and therefore, this turn in the conversation wasn't one I had foreseen. Not entirely sure what to say next, I sat mutely staring back at the psychologist.

"Allow me to elaborate," she said.

I nodded. "Please do."

"You, Mister Gant, have an amazing capacity for connecting dots no one else can see in order to find a killer. That is something of a rare talent."

"Not really." I explained. "Dead people talk to me, Doctor Jante. That's it. I know you think that's crazy and that it sounds like a Hollywood cliché, but it's the truth. And it's also definitely not what I'd call a talent. In fact, I personally view it as a curse."

"Whatever explanation you wish to believe is up to you. Still, it has captured the attention of the bureau."

"Yeah… Well to be honest I don't see what the big deal is here. I thought the whole criminal profiling thing was what the Behavioral Analysis Unit was all about?"

"It is."

"Okay. So don't you have all sorts of highly trained people, like you for instance, running around connecting the imaginary dots?"

"Yes, we do," she agreed. "But not as many as you think."

"How many could you possibly need?"

"More than you would imagine."

"Why don't either of those answers surprise me," I sighed. "Well, what does any of this have to do with me?"

"Very few people have a natural talent for creating a profile from a crime scene. It can be learned, yes, but only the truly exceptional have an innate ability such as yours. Fewer still have your particular affinity for seeing beyond the visible scope of the scene and making the necessary leap wherever the science fails to provide a bridge."

"I believe they call that intuition," I replied.

"Yes, Mister Gant, I am well aware of what it is called. My point being that it is something with which you appear to be blessed in abundance."

"Well, like I just told you, what I do isn't intuition, or science either for that matter. I can't take the credit for what the spirits of homicide victims insist on screaming into my ears."

She gave me a dismissive roll of her eyes. "As I said, however you wish to explain it to yourself is your business. We are primarily interested in the results."

"I've never held anything back," I said. "So what's the problem?"

"Your territory."

"My territory?"

"Yes, Mister Gant. It is a bit limited, geographically."

I cast a sidelong glance at her as the words sank in. Finally I said, "Wait a minute… Let me get this straight. What all this really comes down to is that I'm being evaluated by the FBI for a friggin' job?"

Jante simply stared back at me without offering a reply.

I sighed. "This is nuts."

"Why do you say that?"

"Because for one thing I already have a job."

"Your software consulting firm."

"Yes."

"Business hasn't been all that brisk lately, has it?"

"Business has been fine."

"Yet your income has dropped off."

"And you know this how?" I asked.

"That's confidential."

"Yeah. Figures. Well, I have plenty of consulting work to keep me busy, thank you."

"But somehow you're still free to spend an excessive amount of time helping the Major Case Squad in Saint Louis with their investigations? That can't be good for business."

I shrugged. "I wouldn't say excessive."

"I would," she replied. "Especially for someone with plenty of consulting work to keep him busy."

"I guess it all depends on your definition of the word 'excessive,'" I told her. "Besides, I only get involved when I don't really have any choice."

"You always have a choice, Mister Gant."

"Yeah, well try telling that to a pissed off spirit of a murder victim.

When they find someone on this side of the veil who can actually hear them, they tend to latch on and not take no for an answer."

"I will have to take your word for that."

"I've got scars to prove it," I spat.

"So I've read," she replied.

"Is that it?" I asked.

"What do you mean?"

"I mean is that it? This whole FBI headhunter, recruit the Witch thing… That's what was so top secret that everyone had to leave the room?"

"There are circumstances that dictate extreme discretion where this is concerned."

"Yeah, whatever," I said, unconvinced. "So, here's a question. Why do you have me talking to Annalise? You already have your case against her. Wouldn't it be a better test of my *potential*," I made quotes in the air with my fingers to offset the word, "to see what I can do with an unknown?"

She nodded. "Yes, but the mutual fixation between Devereaux and you is one of the things that has us curious."

"About what?"

"Why the fixation, of course."

"If I'm remembering my freshman psych class properly, it's not all that unusual for sociopaths to fixate on objects, or people they objectify, especially if they are afflicted with a paraphilia like she is," I said. "But I'm not telling you anything new, am I?"

"Of course. That, however, doesn't explain your fixation with her, unless, of course, you are a sociopath as well."

"Maybe I am."

"I think we both know better than that, Mister Gant."

"Well, I would think it's pretty obvious, especially to a psychologist. She tried to kill my wife and me both."

"A logical consideration," she agreed. "But, no. Not in this case. There's something more. When we first met in Saint Louis, you told me you needed to make Miranda go away."

I huffed out an exasperated breath and massaged my forehead for a moment. The headache had settled somewhat but was still more than enough to make me wish I'd stayed home. Finally I said, "Yes. I did. So are we switching gears? Is that what this is about now?"

She nodded. "Partly. It is obvious that your belief in the Miranda personality being some sort of malevolent spirit is what has compelled you thus far. And, moreover, why you are here now."

"I've never kept that a secret, but by the same token I've never expected anyone to understand it. If you did you'd know Miranda is exactly what I say she is. Besides, that doesn't answer my question. What I personally believe doesn't explain why you are so intent on me going back in there and talking to her. What more do you think you're going to learn?"

"Actually, Mister Gant, that's what we were hoping you were going to tell us."

"Well then, we're both screwed," I replied. "Because in case you missed it, right now Miranda is the one with all the answers, not me. And, she's in no big hurry to hand them over."

"...SO, THERE YOU HAVE IT. APPARENTLY I'M IN THE process of being recruited by the FBI," I said while dipping the end of a wedge-shaped French fry into a puddle of catsup on the edge of my plate. "What I really don't get is why all the cloak and dagger about it."

"Good question," Constance replied while attacking her much healthier lunch selection with a fork.

"And why was Jante so worried about anyone else knowing?"

"Actually, that's easier to answer. It's probably a by-product of the overall secrecy. Like you said to her back at the office, she's covering her ass. And, she's doing so because she and whoever else is involved in this are violating bureau protocols left and right. She might even be covering for someone higher up the food chain. It's hard to say. In any case, she probably didn't want anyone who would realize this is all out of bounds to be a witness to what she was saying."

"It's that big a deal, huh?"

She shrugged. "It really depends. The fact that she mentioned your business being slow tells me you're being looked at pretty hard. That information may well have come from the prior criminal investigation when Felicity was confused with Annalise, but it shouldn't be applied here. Technically, it still equates to an unauthorized background check."

"Which isn't good, I take it?"

"No, it's not. It isn't the end of the world, but it would most likely be enough to get her censured. Although, I really doubt much more would come of it than that, unless it could be proven that your constitutional rights had been willfully and intentionally violated and that you had suffered harm because of it. Other than that, it could definitely open the FBI up to a lawsuit."

"Well, I don't know about that. I do feel pretty manipulated though."

"I can understand that," she agreed. "And speaking of being used, just so you know, I came pretty close to violating your rights myself, and you would have had bruises to prove it."

"Yeah, for a couple of minutes there you didn't seem very pleased with me. Sorry about that."

"I understood where you were coming from, but just do us both a favor—don't put me in that position again, or I *will* hurt you," she said, then flashed a wry grin.

I nodded. "I promise."

We were parked across from one another in a booth at the restaurant connected to our hotel. It was late enough that the lunch rush was over but still far too early for dinner, so we had the place almost completely to ourselves. We'd been dropped off here less than an hour ago after officially declining the earlier lunch invitation we'd received. I don't know if the food would have been any more upscale, but in my opinion the company would have been almost intolerable. Given all that had transpired, by the time my conversation with Doctor Jante ended, I'd had more than enough of her for one day; and I was fairly certain the feeling was mutual. Sharing a meal with her really wasn't an appealing option as far as I was concerned.

However, since Constance and I were both running on coffee and the quickly waning benefits of an overpriced airport breakfast back in Saint Louis, sustenance was definitely in order. Therefore, we checked in, dropped our luggage in our rooms, and headed straight back down here.

I had begun telling her what transpired behind closed doors back at Carswell as soon as we sat down, pausing only long enough for us to place our orders. I hadn't actually told Doctor Jante I would keep her secret; therefore I wasn't particularly worried about violating a confidence to which I'd never agreed. I came here for answers, not more questions, so I wasn't about to play her game.

I mulled over Constance's earlier comment while chewing the mouthful of potato, then swallowed and asked, "So the FBI isn't allowed to recruit?"

"Sure we are," she said. "We do it all the time, but not like this."

"Well, apparently you do."

She rolled her eyes at me. "You know what I mean."

"Yeah," I agreed. "I do."

Stabbing at her salad, she commented, "I know I'm changing the subject, but I have to say you sure seem to be in a lot better mood now."

"Actually, yeah, I am," I said while turning my plate in a slow semi-circle as I looked for a suitable angle at which to attack the oversized cheeseburger that was competing for space with the equally massive pile of fries. "Not euphoric by any stretch of the imagination, but way better than I was. Don't know why. I suppose just getting out of there helped."

"I've had days like that," Constance agreed.

After a quiet pause I confessed, "I'm actually feeling a little guilty about it."

"Why?"

"It's not like this is done," I said. "Miranda is still looming over us. I still need to make a decision about tomorrow. And, Felicity…"

"Didn't she say she was fine though?"

"Yeah. Yeah she did…" I admitted. I had called her again while we were being driven to the hotel, and she had assured me everything was back to normal. In fact, she had sounded as relieved as I now seemed to be feeling.

"Then let yourself relax for a change, Rowan," Constance said. "You live under that dark cloud way too much. It's not good for you."

"You're probably right," I agreed. "I just hope this isn't some sort of calm before the storm type of thing."

"There you go again. The eternal pessimist."

"Sorry. It's become a bit of a habit."

"I've noticed."

"Not without good reason," I reminded her. "Look at my track record."

"I know." She looked up from her meal and watched for several seconds as I visibly struggled to figure out how I was going to get my lunch from the plate to my mouth without ending up wearing some of it. Finally, she shook her head and commented, "I still can't believe you ordered that thing."

"Yeah, I'm beginning to feel the same way," I replied with a chuckle. "But I'm really hungry and it looked good in the picture on the menu."

"So your mood is obviously better. What about your headache?"

"Down to a dull roar. Actually, it's even better than it was earlier this morning on the plane," I answered while smashing down the top of the burger with my hand in an attempt to make it flat enough to fit my mouth. "So, still there, but much better than it was a couple of hours ago."

"Well that's a good thing, right?"

"Yeah, about as good as it gets for me. I've gotten used to living with the pain I guess. Unfortunately, the lull is just another one of those red flags that makes me wonder when the piano is going to fall on my head."

"I thought we were trying optimism this time?"

"It's kind of a foreign concept for me, but yeah, you're right."

She shrugged. "Who knows? Maybe food will help."

"Maybe. If I can ever manage to actually eat it."

She glanced at the monstrosity on my plate and raised an eyebrow. "I'm really thinking a knife and fork are in order for that thing."

"It's a cheeseburger, Constance. I'm pretty sure they would revoke my membership to the man club if I did that."

She shook her head. "You really have been hanging out with Ben too much."

I decided that I was simply going to have to dive in and take my chances. Still, as a precaution I tucked my napkin into my shirt collar to form a makeshift bib, then finally managed to get my hands around the sandwich and haul it up from the plate.

Constance chuckled as she joked, "Should I flag down the waiter and ask for extra napkins?"

"Now you sound like Felicity," I said.

"Well, she did tell me to look after you."

"Did she teach you any Gaelic?" I asked. "Then I'd feel right at home."

"Maybe I should call her and ask for a lesson or two."

"I'm sure she'd be happy to oblige."

I returned my attention to the mammoth burger. All of my smashing at least allowed me to take a bite but not without a significant amount of struggle involved in actually getting my mouth around it. Of course, a side effect of the manhandling also produced a bit of a mess, just as I'd expected, most of which I was able to contain over the plate. However, some of it still ended up accenting my shirtsleeve, not to mention my face.

I laid the burger back onto the plate and began cleaning the catsup and such from my chin. Constance grinned at me, shaking her head before once again stabbing at her bowl full of healthful greens. I continued chewing while stifling my own urge to laugh.

The cheeseburger actually did taste as good as it had looked on the menu. Unfortunately, my enjoyment of it ended with that first bite because when I swallowed I felt a quick stab of pain along the side of my neck. What made it even worse was the fact that the stinging sensation was too familiar for words.

A swath of panic instantly rushed over me as I winced and reached upward, feeling around with my fingers. The burning sensation gave way to a tingling discomfort. When I pulled my hand away and looked, it was wet and smeared bright red. The light fixture over our table instantly bloomed, casting everything in a stark contrast of washed out colors and hard shadows.

Constance's voice echoed in my ears. "You missed some, Rowan."

I tried to look at her as a gelid chill penetrated my skin, leaching directly into my bones.

"How did you manage to get catsup on your…" Her voice rattled in my head again but stopped with a sudden yelp, leaving the question to dangle, unasked.

The room began to spin, and I pushed my hands against the edge of the table in an attempt to stop myself from sliding downward, but to no avail. I had already begun pitching sideways as darkness slipped in to replace the garish light.

I could feel pressure against my neck as I heard Constance, shouting the command, "Call 9-1-1. NOW!" Her voice was no longer jovial. It was authoritative and controlled but still couldn't hide the twist of fear that corkscrewed through its tone.

As consciousness slipped away, I was certain I could hear Miranda laughing.

CHAPTER 9

"HAVE YOU TRAVELED OUT OF THE COUNTRY RECENTLY?" the paramedic asked as he took my pulse.

"No," I replied. The word was muffled by the oxygen mask covering my nose and mouth, so I shook my head for good measure.

"Have you been in contact with anyone who has recently traveled abroad, or have you…"

"No," I replied again, cutting him off. This time I pulled the oxygen mask down away from my face. "And before you…"

"Sir, you need to leave that on." He interrupted me and tried to move the mask back over my nose and mouth, but I pushed his hand away.

I continued with my objection. "Look, I know where you're going with this, and I understand, believe me. But, you're wasting your time. I haven't contracted any virus, and I'm not contagious."

"Sir, you don't have any visible wounds, and…"

"…And I just bled all over the place, yeah, I know. Listen, just give me a minute here…"

Leaning to the side and looking past him, I moved on to a more pressing issue as I directed myself to Constance, "Do me a favor… Call Felicity and check on her…" I could hear the thread of near panic starting to unwind through my own voice, so I was certain she could too. "Make sure she's still okay."

"I'm sure she is," she said, shooting me a puzzled look.

"Just call her and check for me, please?" I appealed. "Miranda has something to do with this, I'm certain of it."

She nodded as she pulled her cell phone from her belt. "Okay. But don't worry, I'm certain she's fine."

I nodded. "I know, but I just need to be sure."

"You realize she's going to want to know why it's me calling instead of you, right? What do you want me to tell her?"

"The truth I guess. She'll know if you're lying to her."

"Great," she mumbled as she stabbed in the number. Then she tucked the phone up to her ear while wandering a few feet to the side so as to be removed from the commotion surrounding me.

I couldn't hear what she was saying because her voice was

drowned out by the paramedic once again insisting that I keep the oxygen mask in place. However, I watched her until she turned back to face me. Once she waved and gave me a vigorous nod, I relaxed as much as I could and allowed the poking and prodding to continue.

We were still in the hotel restaurant, with me sitting in a chair at the center of the mess. The scant few patrons who had earlier been enjoying a late lunch were long gone. That was understandable, of course. After all, the sight of a man bleeding profusely all over a table tended to have a dampening affect where appetites were concerned. Since the dining area was temporarily closed by the management, the only gawkers present were the wait staff, and they were at least keeping their distance.

"Follow my finger," the paramedic instructed, holding his gloved digit in front of my face.

I'd been down this road so many times I suspected I could conduct the examination for him. It seemed as though every time I became involved in an investigation, I ended up in the back of an ambulance or sitting in an emergency room, whether I needed treatment or not. Still, I complied with the instruction then continued to sit quietly while he took my vitals for the second time.

"BP one-forty over ninety," he called out to his partner.

"See," I mumbled through the oxygen mask. "I'm fine."

"That's actually a little to the high side of normal, sir," he replied.

"Especially for a guy who just bled all over the place, right?"

"There's an explanation for…"

"I know there is," I interrupted, voice still muffled but taking on a harder edge. "It's because I'm starting to get really annoyed with all this."

"Just calm down, Mister Gant."

"Yeah," I muttered. "Right."

A few moments later I heard Constance say, "Rowan. Look up here at me."

I brought my face upward, and the deceptively bright strobe of the small flash on her cell phone flickered in my eyes. At the same time, the electronically produced noise of a clicking camera shutter sounded in my ears.

I pulled the mask down again over the further objections of the paramedic and asked, "What's that for?"

"It's a compromise," she said, eyes focused on her cell phone screen instead of me as she rapidly thumbed the keypad. "I'm messaging it to your wife as proof that you're okay, so she doesn't buy herself a ticket on the next flight she can find."

"But she sounded okay, right?"

"Other than worried sick about you, yes. She says she's fine."

I glanced down at my blood-covered shirt and briefly tried to imagine what the photo she had just snapped must look like. The image I conjured wasn't pretty. "You really think that picture is going to calm her down?"

"Believe me, I mentioned that to her myself, but she insisted."

"Yeah," I grunted. "Sounds like her. But I guess she's seen me looking worse than this."

Constance nodded. "She said something to that effect when I gave her a description. You're still going to need to call her though. She wanted to talk to you right this minute, but I convinced her to let them finish checking you over first"

"Yeah, I know I will. Thanks."

"Sir, I really need you to put the oxygen mask back on," the paramedic insisted yet again.

"No," I said, giving my head a shake as I pulled the mask up over my head before he could stop me, and then handed it to him.

He took it but continued trying to convince me it was necessary. "You need to leave this on while we transport you to the hospital."

"I'm not going to any hospital," I replied.

"Sir, you've obviously lost a significant amount of blood for some unknown reason," he pressed. "I would really suggest that you allow us to take you to the hospital."

"You should probably listen to him, Rowan," Constance told me.

"This isn't anything new," I told her. "Trust me, I'll be fine."

"This has happened to you before?" the paramedic asked.

"A few times, yeah."

"Then you should definitely let us take you to the hospital. They can run some tests to determine what caused this," he pressed.

"I can tell you exactly what caused it," I replied. "The spirit of a hundred and fifty-year-old sociopath."

He furrowed his brow and glanced toward the police officer who had responded to the call with them then looked back to me, "I'm not sure I understand. Are you saying that you were attacked?"

"Not like you think I mean…" I grumbled.

"How then?"

"It's a long story with too many chapters for me to get into at the moment."

"But when you said spirit, did you mean like a ghost or something?" he asked.

"She's definitely an 'or something,' that's for sure."

"Mister Gant, I need to ask if you are under the care of a psychiatrist, or…"

I looked up at my friend then sighed heavily and spoke over the paramedic, "Constance? A little help here."

She shook her head as she extracted her credentials from her pocket and gave the case a practiced flip so that she could display them to both him and the police officer. "Special Agent Mandalay," she said. "Don't worry about it, I'll vouch for him. Mister Gant is one of our consultants. He isn't insane that we're aware of. Just a little…" She paused thoughtfully then added, "Quirky would probably be the best way to describe it."

I shot her an annoyed look. She returned fire with a glare that said in no uncertain terms "shut up and let me handle this." Since I had asked her to intervene on my behalf, I figured it best to comply. Besides, she could have easily told them something quite a bit worse and still been completely truthful.

The paramedic objected, "Unexplained hemorrhaging isn't 'quirky,' ma'am, it's possibly a life threatening issue."

"Believe me," she replied. "He knows."

He turned back to me. "Mister Gant, you really need to go to the hospital."

"I appreciate your concern, but my vitals are pretty much normal, right?"

"Yes, but that…"

I interrupted again. "And I have the right to refuse medical treatment, am I correct?"

"Yes, sir, you do."

"Okay then. That's what I'm doing."

"Sir, if you still insist on refusing treatment then I would strongly advise that you call your personal physician as soon as possible," he told me. "You might have a serious underlying condition."

"Trust me, I'm not the one with th…" I started but noticed Constance glaring at me once again before I could finish. Changing my tone midstream, I nodded and lied. "Yeah. Okay. I'll make sure I do that."

ONCE THE PARAMEDICS HAD GONE, CONSTANCE AND I headed back up to our rooms. The restaurant staff gave us a wide berth, which was fine as far as I was concerned. At this point, the light of my earlier brightened mood had officially been extinguished, so I definitely wasn't up to the intrusion, no matter how well meaning it might be.

Constance finally broke the silence as the elevator gave a slight jerk and started upward to the seventh floor. "Are you sure you're okay?"

I turned toward her and nodded. "Physically, yeah. Mentally, that's a whole different story I'm afraid."

She leaned back against the side wall and crossed her arms. "So, is this whole incident about what I think it is?"

I backed up and imitated her posture by resting against the opposite wall. "Guess that depends on what you're thinking. I experienced spontaneous hemorrhaging just like this in connection with the case I worked last month."

"Ben told me about it, and yeah…that's exactly what I'm thinking," she said. "The guy the media was calling Count Dracula."

I gave her another nod. "Then yes, I'd say we're probably on the same page."

The elevator stopped with a quiet thump, and then the brushed metal doors parted down the center, revealing the opposite wall of the corridor. Fortunately, no one was waiting on the other side, so for the moment at least, my somewhat gory appearance was a non-issue. If I could make it to my room without running into anyone else, all would be fine. I motioned Constance ahead of me and then followed her out and to the left.

"But isn't that investigation closed?" she asked as we walked down the hallway. "As I recall the suspect is dead, correct?"

"Suspect, yes," I replied. "But maybe he wasn't the actual killer. Or maybe there was more than one… I don't know… All I can say is something felt very wrong about the way that case ended."

"Wrong how?"

"Wrong unfinished. Like it was some kind of a set up."

"Set up how?"

"It was too convenient. Especially from my end with the visions and such. The answers came too easily."

"Okay, then set up by whom?"

"That's the burning question. I'm beginning to think maybe Miranda."

"How could she do that?"

"Another good question, and one I need to find an answer to before it goes any further."

"Did you tell Ben about this?"

"Of course I did. And to his credit, he was perfectly willing to follow up on it too… But no more victims surfaced, so in the short term it appeared that the killings had stopped… Plus, I didn't have any more episodes… And then there was all the hard evidence at the scene itself…" I allowed my voice to trail off for a moment before continuing. "We pursued it for a couple of weeks, but I couldn't give him anything solid to go on. All I could say was that something still didn't feel right."

"And now this happens."

"Yeah. Now this. Which also feels very wrong to me."

"Because of the timing?"

"Yeah… Pretty much."

"I haven't seen all of the details on the original case," she said with a shrug. "So I only know what Ben told me, but wasn't it all actually connected to the vampire subculture?"

"That's how it appeared on the surface," I said. "Sanguinarian vampirism. People who have actually convinced themselves that they are vampires and really do drink blood. Everything from Renfield's syndrome to kids looking for attention. It's pretty strange, even by my standards. But in the end, everything stopped at the dead suspect. No solid connections to the local vampire community that we could find."

She pursed her lips and nodded. "Maybe you were dealing with a transient."

"I guess it's possible, but that wasn't how it felt to me."

"Well, we know what it usually means when you have one of your feelings…"

"Unfortunately."

"Okay, for sake of argument, say we assume the suspect had a partner who has now resurfaced. If you apply the Holmes criteria for defining serial killers, the timing itself could speak to an emotional cooling-off period between murders. It's been what, a little over five weeks? That could easily fit depending on the original cycle of activity and the triggering stressor."

I nodded. “True. But the original case had a period of acceleration. A spree that occurred in the days leading up to a full moon. We’re a few days past that this month. So, why now? Why today of all days?”

“Maybe the killer isn’t actually on a lunar cycle. There could be a different stressor,” she said. “This might just be a coincidence. They do happen, you know.”

“Yes, I do. And maybe that’s the case this time, but something in my gut says no.”

“Well, like I said, we know what your gut feelings usually mean.”

We stopped at our rooms, which were positioned directly across the hall from one another. I dug around in my pocket for my keycard. Constance already had hers in hand.

“But what about the loss of the partner?” I asked.

“What do you mean?”

“Wouldn’t that affect the pattern somehow?”

“That would all depend on the emotional investment. There’s almost always a primary partner with paired killers. The one who calls the shots and most often literally controls the actions of the other. There may or may not have been a bond between them.”

“So a dominant and a submissive.”

She nodded. “More or less.”

“Miranda is definitely dominant,” I offered.

“She would certainly fit the profile, but she’s currently incarcerated.”

“No. Annalise is, not Miranda.”

“Okay, that’s more your area of expertise than mine.”

I cocked an eyebrow. “Speaking of expertise, with all that information floating around in your head, why aren’t you working with the BAU yourself?”

She shrugged. “Having that sort of information and having the talent to put it into practice are two different things.”

“Yeah. So I’ve been told.”

She smiled. “Besides, right now I like it right where I am.”

“Yeah. I get that.”

“Okay…” she said, paused, and then nudged the conversation back to its original track. “So what about this whole gut feeling of yours? Obviously that’s leading you back to Miranda as well.”

I gave her a quick nod along with a shrug. “Yeah, it is. I’m not sure exactly what she has to do with all this, but she’s involved somehow. I’m convinced of that much.”

She shook her head and sighed, “Dammit, Rowan. Why do you always have to be right?”

I could tell she meant the words to be rhetorical, but I still answered with a “Huh?”

“What you said earlier,” she explained. “The calm before the storm. It didn’t last very long, did it?”

“No, it didn’t.” I shook my head. “But then, it never does.”

“Yeah…” She allowed her voice to trail off for a moment. “Well, I’d better call Ben,” she finally said, turning and unlocking the door to her room. “If you’re correct, and they don’t already have a body on their hands, he needs to know they’ve probably got one coming.”

“Yeah, good idea.”

She made a half turn back toward me, holding the door ajar with her palm. “Okay, so since you didn’t get to finish your lunch, do you want to clean up then try grabbing something to eat somewhere else in a little bit?”

I shook my head. “I think I’ll wait until dinner this evening. What about you? I kind of interrupted your lunch too.”

“I’m fine, actually. Besides, I have some protein bars in my bag. Do you want one to hold you over?”

“No, but thanks anyway. What I really need to do is call Jante and let her know I’ll talk to Miranda again.”

“Are you sure you want to go ahead with that, especially after what just happened?”

“Actually that’s all the more reason why I need to do it.”

“But if you’re right and she has something to do with what just happened to you, wouldn’t that be a little too dangerous?”

“Obviously it’s dangerous no matter what I do, Constance,” I replied. “But this time I plan to play by my rules, not hers.”

“And what are those?”

“I don’t know. I haven’t made them up yet.”

Constance shook her head and rolled her eyes. “Well, call Felicity before you do anything else,” she instructed. “I promised her you would, and I don’t want her angry with me because you didn’t follow instructions.”

“Yeah,” I said. “Been there. It’s not pleasant.”

“Well then start dialing,” she replied as she pushed her door farther open and stepped across the threshold. “Because you’re already giving me more than my share of unpleasantness all by yourself. I don’t need any from her.”

"That's what friends are for, right?" I quipped.

"Sure, why not?" she replied, a note of good-natured sarcasm briefly echoing in her words before she turned serious for a moment. "So you're certain you're okay, right?"

"Yeah. Tired, but I'll be fine. Why?"

"Double checking. You just bled all over a restaurant, you know."

I acquiesced. "True."

"If you need anything, just call me or bang on the door, okay?"

"I'll be fine, Constance. Don't worry so much."

"Okay, get some rest. But just so you know, I plan to check in on you."

I half chuckled, "You're almost as bad as Felicity."

"That's what friends are for, right?"

"Touché."

As she started swinging the door shut she added, "Now, speaking of your wife, go call her. And just so you know, I have her permission to use force with you if necessary."

The door was closed before I could answer, so I shook my head and turned toward my own. Back down the hallway, I heard the elevator chime then start opening, so I quickly swiped the keycard and pushed into my room. Once inside I parked myself on the corner of the bed and made the call to Felicity.

The conversation with her went much as I expected. A full gamut of emotions and a few torrents of Gaelic, some of which were as yet unfamiliar to me. I had the distinct impression from the tone by which they were delivered it would be better to keep it that way.

By the time we eventually said our goodbyes, she had calmed down. Still, she made it a point to remind me that she kept an overnight bag packed for emergencies and that she would find a way to get here if necessary. Since she wasn't one to bluff, I took her threat to heart and promised to play it safe.

Unfortunately, as I never seemed to be the one in control of my own destiny, I wasn't entirely sure what good that promise was going to do either of us.

CHAPTER 10

THE AFTERMATH OF THE PSEUDO-HEMORRHAGE WAS still clinging to me, so I needed to get myself cleaned up, especially if I planned to venture out into public for dinner at some point. I also still needed to call Doctor Jante, but given the events of the day, I found myself procrastinating. Even though I felt I had no choice but to meet with Miranda again, the idea of putting myself in that position was already taking its toll. I wasn't kidding when I told Constance that I'd yet to make up a new set of rules, and so far that fact hadn't changed.

My headache was already starting to ramp up again, although this time it was coming at me from both sides of the veil. As a preemptive move, I rummaged through my suitcase and pulled out a bottle of aspirin. After pouring a pile of them into my palm out of habit, I scooped the majority back into the container, leaving only two behind. I'd overdosed myself too many times in the past, and I didn't need a repeat performance right now. I tore the sanitary wrap from a small glass and filled it with water from the tap. Tossing the pills into my mouth, I washed them down then set the glass aside and flipped the switch for the light over the vanity.

The reflection staring back at me from the large mirror was a train wreck. My eyes were half-lidded with a desperate need for sleep, which only served to deepen the semi-circular shadows of exhaustion already evident beneath them. While the paramedics had cleaned away some of the blood in a futile attempt to find a wound that was all but gone before they ever arrived, my clothing wasn't the only part of me still sporting the darkening residue. I had smears on the side of my face and down my neck as well as a good amount in my hair.

I placed my palms against the vanity for support then closed my eyes and allowed my head to hang as I muttered, "Why me?" It wasn't the first time I'd asked the universe that question, and judging from the notable lack of response, it probably wouldn't be the last.

After a few moments of quiet self-pity, I huffed out a breath then pushed back from the vanity and stripped off my shirt. For a moment I considered soaking it in the sink but then decided it just wasn't worth the effort, so I tossed it into the waste can. The garment was clearly beyond redemption, and I was beginning to feel like maybe I was too.

After drenching a washcloth in a stream of hot water, I began washing the dried blood off my face. By the second pass it was apparent that I definitely had my work cut out where cleaning up was concerned. At least this time there wasn't a wound that needed tending, which was more than I could say for some of my other adventures.

I sighed at my reflection as I began to feel sorry for myself once again, then muttered aloud, "Don't even go there, Gant…"

I knew I couldn't keep putting off the inevitable, so as I started rinsing the washcloth with one hand, I plucked my cell phone from my belt with the other, flipped it open with my thumb then scrolled through the stored contacts and dialed a number. I was just starting a fourth round with the wet rag when Doctor Jante's voice issued from the speaker and into my ear, so I stopped scrubbing and shut off the water.

"Mister Gant," she said, her tone noticeably cool. "Given our earlier discussion, I wasn't expecting to hear from you quite this soon, if at all."

"Believe me, I didn't expect to be calling."

"I'm sure."

I was operating under the assumption that she was still just as interested in having me meet with Annalise again as I now needed to be. But, by the same token I was also well aware that I was preparing to start across a bridge I'd all but set ablaze earlier in the day. Therefore, I swallowed my pride and endeavored to douse any remnants of the fire.

"Look, I need to apologize," I told her. "I know we didn't exactly part on the best of terms this afternoon, and I'm truly sorry for my role in that."

"Accepted. Now, are you merely calling to apologize, or should I assume this also means you've changed your mind?"

"About the meeting, actually, yes. I would like for you to go ahead and arrange that, if it's still on the table."

"And if it isn't?"

"Then I guess I have to figure out how to talk you into it again, which admittedly won't be easy for me. So, I'm hoping I don't have to."

She paused for a moment and then said, "Do you mind if I ask why this sudden change of heart?"

"I'm working on a theory."

"I see. Is this theory something we should know, Mister Gant?"

"I'm not really sure just yet," I replied. "Can you tell me if Annalise is monitored at all?"

"Yes she is. Why do you ask?"

I glanced at my watch and did a quick mental calculation. "Because if it's possible, I'd like to find out who she was roughly an hour and a half ago. Annalise or Miranda."

"Why is that important?"

"Let's just say it has something to do with that uncanny intuition thing you're so interested in."

"Mister Gant..."

"Listen, Doctor Jante, I'm honestly not trying to start another argument with you. Believe me, I've had more than enough drama for one day. But, this is very important and not all that easy for me to explain."

She sighed. "Well, I'm not currently at the facility. Let me make a call and see what I can do about arranging the meeting. Where are you now?"

"My hotel room. I'll be here for a while, but I'll have my cell with me if I leave."

"Give me a few minutes to see what can be arranged, and I will call you back."

"Thanks," I told her. "And don't forget to find out about who she was."

"I'll try," she agreed. "But that's something that may be hard to determine depending upon the circumstances."

"I understand," I said, nodding as I spoke, simply from force of habit. "But if it's at all possible, it's very important that I find out."

"Can I assume you'll give me a more coherent explanation about all of this in the not too distant future?"

"Yes, as soon as I can give you one, I will. I promise."

"Fine then. I'll call you back as soon as I know something."

"Thanks."

I closed the phone and laid it aside before returning to the cleanup task at hand. Less than five minutes later the device was warbling out an electronic peal. This time the conversation was exceptionally brief, and while I still didn't end up with an answer to my question, I did have a scheduled meeting with Miranda at 10 the next morning. Now, I desperately needed to start worrying about exactly what I was going to do once I was back in the same room with her.

I absently clipped the phone onto my belt and then started back in on the task of trying to make myself presentable. Unfortunately, the face staring back at me from the mirror really wasn't looking much better than it had when I started. Giving in to the futility, I tossed the now pinkish washcloth aside and headed for the shower.

As I stood under the steaming jets of water, I forced myself to relax in hopes that would help me formulate a strategy. Of course, I was also well aware that even my best-laid plans were virtually guaranteed to go astray. I had too many years of anecdotal evidence to support that fact. Even so, I gave it a try. And, as always I kept coming back around to one fundamental issue: Above all else, I had to keep Felicity safe.

The real question was how.

"YOU AIN'T BLEEDIN' ALL OVER MY GIRLFRIEND AGAIN, are ya'?" Ben asked. The question sounded half serious and came in place of a simple hello when he answered my call.

Without missing a beat I replied, "If I was, I probably wouldn't be the one calling you, now would I?"

"Yeah, well stranger shit has happened where you're concerned."

"Yeah, I guess it has," I agreed. "Well, don't worry. I haven't done any bleeding since lunch."

"Good," he grunted. "You had Constance a bit worried."

"Really? She seemed to handle it like a pro."

"That's 'cause she's a copper," he replied. "She *is* a pro. We deal with shit then worry about it later. It's part of the job. So listen, if you're callin' about a body, we still don't have one yet. Not that I've heard, anyway. But if ya' got any ideas where we should look, I'm more'n happy ta' listen."

"No, not yet."

"Okay…" he said with a questioning note in his voice, then allowed a short pause to hang in the air before pressing, "Okay… So, are ya' callin' about that necklace again? 'Cause it's still right here in my pocket."

"That's good to know," I replied. "But, no, I actually wanted to talk to you about something else."

"Okay, spit it out, white man. You called me, remember? I ain't in the mood ta' play twenty questions."

"Sorry…" I sighed. "I guess I'm still a bit preoccupied by all this."

"Yeah, no shit. I've interviewed suspects with more to say."

"So, anyway, I was wondering… Do you have anyone you trust who owes you a favor?"

"Yeah," he quipped. "You. And by my count it's more like several favors."

"I'm serious, Ben."

"So am I," he huffed in retort. "But since you're the one askin', my guess is ya' mean somebody besides you, huh?"

"Given that I'm in Texas right now, yes."

"Well, I dunno. What exactly are ya' needin'?"

"Someone to keep an eye on Felicity tomorrow morning."

"What for? You don't think she's screwin' around or somethin' do ya'?"

"No," I scoffed. "Nothing like that. Worse actually. I have another meeting with Miranda at ten."

"Okay. So what's that got to do with Firehair? I mean, besides… Well, you know what I mean."

"When I talked to her earlier today she said she was having some *issues…*" I leaned heavily on the word and paused for effect. "The thing is, it seems they coincided with the timing of my meeting with Miranda."

"So when you say 'issues' you mean that kinky *Twilight Zone* stuff like before when…" He allowed the sentence to remain unfinished.

"Yeah," I replied. "The homicidal dominatrix urges like when Miranda was possessing her. She kept herself under control this go around, but I really don't want to take the chance that she might not be able to do the same if it happens again."

"Man, you'd think I'd be used to this shit by now, but workin' with you two is just off-the-charts weird sometimes."

"Believe me, I feel the same way more often than you realize."

"Yeah… So tell me somethin'… I know ya' said ya' need both parts of this thing to make it go away, but I thought you at least had part of the Voodoo crap covered with this jewelry in a jar thing. I mean, Miranda down there, Firehair up here, salty necklace in my pocket all adds up to no psycho redhead. Right?"

"Obviously I was wrong about that."

He huffed and then muttered a sarcastic, "Well shit. Hold on a sec while I write that one down on the friggin' calendar."

I snapped at him, "This isn't a joke, Ben."

"I know, I know…" he said.

I pushed back my momentary annoyance and tried to offer an explanation. "Yes, the necklace is definitely the primary conduit. But Miranda knows I've figured that out. She's searching for another way in, and unfortunately I think maybe I'm it."

"How?"

"I'm connected to both of them."

"So, unconnect."

"I wish I could, but with that magick in place and Annalise acting as a host, I can't."

"Lucky you," he grunted. "So's that why ya' tried to choke the fuck out of 'er today?"

I let out a long sigh. "Constance told you about that too, huh?"

"Yeah," he chided. "She filled me in on the whole deal since you wouldn't."

I ignored the baiting remark and answered the original question. "Well, I didn't actually find out about what was happening to Felicity until after that whole mess was well over, so it wasn't the direct cause. But yeah, during the interview she made a few comments that set me off and I lost control."

"Wunnerful… And they're actually lettin' you back in a room with 'er?"

Obviously, Constance hadn't told him everything. "That's a long story in itself."

"With you it usually is," he grunted. "Guess I'll hafta wait for Constance to tell me about that too?"

Once again I ignored the bait and redirected. "Anyway, back to my original question?"

"Yeah… Okay… I get it… So you're just wantin' someone ta' hang out with the little woman in case she goes all la-la land freaky, right?"

"Pretty much. But it needs to be someone who understands what's going on and can actually do something about it, if you know what I mean. You've seen how quick it can happen and where it leads."

"Oh yeah, been there…" he mumbled then huffed out a heavy sigh. "So what we really need is somebody with handcuffs and eyes in the back of their head."

"That pretty much describes it, yes."

"Well, with Constance outta town I don't have any plans. I could go over and hang out."

I objected immediately. "No. You can't. You have the necklace."

"Yeah, so? You pack it around all the time when you two are together."

"I'm a Witch, you aren't."

"Great…" he moaned. "You mean ta' tell me the hocus-pocus shit on this thing is that bad, and you pawned it off on me?"

"It's focused on Felicity, Ben, not you. You're fine."

"You sure?"

"Yes."

"Well, okay… But if the damn thing makes me go all fruitloopy, I'm kickin' your ass."

"Don't worry, if it does, it will probably make killing me your first priority all by itself."

He almost yelped, "Hey, I thought ya' just said it wouldn't…"

"Relax, Ben. Just leave it in the salt, keep it away from Felicity, and you'll be fine," I reassured him and then pressed further on my query. "So, anyone else in mind?"

He let out a quiet harrumph. Upon hearing it I could easily imagine that he was smoothing back his hair then allowing his hand to slide down to his neck and begin absently massaging. It was a physical mannerism he'd had at least as long as I'd known him, and it was a sure sign he was concentrating. The gesture was so much a part of his makeup that I didn't have to physically see him to know he was doing it.

Finally, he said, "Yeah…maybe. Lemme call Charlee. She's been around for some of the woo-woo shit, so she's kinda up ta' speed with that part. Plus she knows Firehair already, so that'd prob'ly help."

The name more than rang a bell. Detective Charlene McLaughlin had been assigned to several investigations where I was involved, and Ben was correct—she had certainly seen some things that tended to defy logical explanation. Of course, that sort of thing wasn't all that unusual whenever I came into the picture.

Just as important though, she had pulled a few shifts watching over Felicity and me a few years ago when a spree killer named Eldon Porter had set his sights on us. Therefore, as Ben had mentioned, she wasn't a stranger, which would make things easier for all concerned.

"Good suggestion. I'd definitely trust Charlee," I told him. "Thanks, Chief, I appreciate you making the call."

"Yeah," he grunted. "I'll just keep addin' to your tab, Kemosabe."

"Right… So, do me a favor and call me back when you find out if she's up for it. Then I can give Felicity a heads up so she expects her."

"Firehair doesn't know about this?"

"Not yet."

"Jeezus, Row. Do ya' actually believe she's gonna go for it?"

"I'm not going to give her any choice."

He snorted. "Yeah, right. Good luck with that."

"I don't think it's going to be an issue, Ben," I told him. "I'm pretty sure she's as concerned about this as I am."

"I hope you're right. About it not bein' a problem I mean."

"I guess we'll see."

"Okay, well, lemme call Charlee and see what I can work out. Ten tomorrow you said?"

"Yeah, but I'll probably be at the facility a bit earlier than that. She might want to figure for around nine."

"Okay. Talk to ya' in a bit."

"Later."

I closed the phone and then glanced at the LCD display before clipping it back on my belt. It read 6:13 PM. Later than I thought it was, but earlier than it felt like it should be. Everything was starting to catch up to me with a vengeance—the lack of sleep, the tension, the uncertainty about tomorrow, and even the pervasive headache.

I sat waiting for the return call but grew oddly uncomfortable with each passing minute. Eventually, I hauled myself up out of the straight-backed desk chair and padded slowly around the room in an aimless circle. As tired as I was, I just couldn't seem to sit idle.

I pulled my cell from my belt and looked at the display. Less than ten minutes had passed, yet it seemed more like an hour. I had to admit, impatience was definitely one of my faults, but I wasn't usually this bad. I sighed and then continued staring at the numbers on my phone. After what seemed an eternity the display incremented.

Then, as if on cue, the reason for my restlessness became painfully obvious.

I felt a familiar friction born of unearthly influence begin to rub me raw just beneath the skin. I purposely shuddered in an attempt to shake it off, but as usual it clung to me even tighter. Seconds later I felt simultaneously chilled to the core and flushed with fever.

I'd been here too many times before, unfortunately. It seemed that whenever the dead wanted to talk, this was how they made sure they had my undivided attention. But, this was also just the beginning; it would only get worse—*much worse*.

"Dammit…" I muttered to myself. "Not right now…"

I knew whoever it was wouldn't be dissuaded. They never were, and that meant I didn't have much time before I would find myself standing in the void between the living and the dead, having a one-sided conversation that was no less than a psychotic excuse for a puzzle with missing pieces. Something else I knew in spades was that I was going to become very vulnerable on more than one level. Historically, it hadn't always been a good idea for me to go through this sort of thing alone, and it was a sure bet that this time was no exception. Since Constance was just across the hallway, I turned and started toward the door. However, it seemed I had even less time than I had originally thought. Before I managed to take my first step, the lights in the room began to bloom in a harsh display of prismatic colors. My vision tunneled, and in that instant the door became a far-away and wholly unattainable goal.

As the carpeted floor rushed toward my face, my world became an empty void, darker than dark, and colder than cold. The last thing I heard was an electronic warble of the *William Tell Overture* as the cell phone, still clasped in my now paralyzed hand, started to ring.

CHAPTER 11

I'M WALKING.

At least, I think I am.

I cannot see.

I cannot hear.

I can only feel.

I'm walking.

To where, I do not know.

Darkness surrounds me. But, it isn't mere indigo like the dark of a moonless night.

Or even the darkness of sleep.

It is blacker still.

Disturbing.

Maddening.

It is the total absence of everything.

It is the black of nothingness, and not only does it surround me, it is in me…

It is me.

Cold…

Void…

Nothing…

I'm walking.

"Rowan…" A distantly familiar voice calls to me.

I stop.

Hollowness consumes me from within and without.

I am nothing.

"Rowan. I'm right here," the voice calls again.

I turn in the blackness, spinning slowly in place, eyes searching though I cannot see.

I blink.

Though all else remains void, a petite, strawberry blonde woman appears, standing before me.

I ask, "Ariel? Is that you?" My voice echoes and folds in upon itself to become a jumble of disjointed syllables that make no sense. They solidify and shatter into sparkling shards around me.

The broken words shimmer like semi-precious stones. I watch as they disappear, taking with them my question.

I turn my face back to the woman. I have not seen her move; yet she now has my hand in hers. She shakes her head, a forlorn expression painted across her face as a tear wells in the corner of her eye. "It's been too long, Rowan. You never come to see me anymore."

I try to talk, but the faded jewels of my words took not only my question but my voice as well.

I feel dampness on my cheek.

I feel dampness on my arm.

It is beginning to rain.

I turn my face upward and the rain turns to blood.

I am alone now.

The cold downpour of blood soaks me.

Envelops me.

Its iciness burns me.

I try to scream as the pain bores inward.

I watch in horror as my body begins to disintegrate.

Skin peels away in rigid, frozen strips...

Followed by muscle, frost burned and crumbling...

And finally bone, gelid, brittle and shattering...

I am no more...

A hollow, pounding noise thumped inside my head. A moment later it repeated and was followed by the distant, muffled sound of a voice buzzing in my ears. "Rowan, it's Constance. Open the door."

There was a short pause then another round of the hollow thumping. This time the voice that came in its wake sounded far more concerned. "Rowan! It's Constance. Can you hear me?!"

Hearing her was the easy part. Responding was something else entirely. I could feel that my entire body was shaking against the unearthly cold. The burn beneath my skin was eating its way inward, and I wanted to scream. Unfortunately, my jaw was clenched so tightly I couldn't even manage a whimper.

"Rowan!" the muffled voice called to me again. "Answer me!"

Something brushed my hand and pain exploded through my soul. I could feel myself trying to withdraw from the touch.

Another muffled voice joined the first. I couldn't understand what it said, but it sounded almost as frantic. An electronic rendition of the *William Tell Overture* began chirping in my ears once again.

After that I heard nothing because the darkness was coming to take me back.

I'm running.

The rain has stopped, and this time I am not alone.

A cold fire is chasing me.

I can feel it blistering my back with its gelid fingers.

I open my mouth to scream but can project only silence in a deafening wave.

The fire catches me.

Consumes me.

I am no more...

"Rowan." The distantly familiar voice lances my ears again.

Ariel is still holding my hand.

I look at her and she cocks her head to the side. "Stay with me, Rowan. I will protect you. Come... She's waiting. She's been waiting for you for a very long time."

I try to talk again. "Who is waiting for me, Ariel?"

The words rattle inside my skull, but when I open my mouth to speak them, only silence spews forth from my lips. I can literally see it spreading out from me—a dense cloud of nothing, creating an acoustic void in its wake.

Ariel gently presses two fingers against my lips and shakes her head.

"Come with me," she says. "She's waiting."

We're walking...

Constance Mandalay's voice ricocheted around inside my ear canal before finally connecting with my brain and allowing it to eavesdrop. She sounded as if she was nearby. Sharp and clear, as opposed to the earlier muddied tone.

"Someone from the hotel is calling nine-one-one," she said, her voice businesslike but edged with concern. "No... He's on the floor, shaking like he's having some type of seizure. Yes, I guess it could be one of his trances."

I could still feel myself vibrating from the intensity of the cold. Every inch of my skin prickled like countless needles were being repeatedly plunged into it, and my head felt as if it was going to split open and spill its contents at any moment.

I heard her say, "No, he's not bleeding this time… Yes, I've tried that… No… Dammit, Ben, I can't just sit here and watch. Yes, I know that's what he says, but… I know… I think maybe I should call Felicity."

I wanted to scream "no," but the returning darkness wouldn't let me.

"She's been waiting for you," Ariel says, pointing off into the void.

I follow the line of her arm and see that a large wooden door has appeared. It looks heavy and old. Intricate carvings cover its surface, but when I try to focus on any of the detail it becomes blurry and nondescript.

I'm certain the door wasn't there a second ago...

Or was it an hour ago?

Or maybe it was a day ago...

I have no idea how long I've been here. It seems like forever. And it seems like I've only just arrived.

"Go," Ariel says. "She's waiting."

"Who?" I ask.

The word flips and tumbles as it falls from my mouth, and then it liquefies and drips slowly into the darkness to disappear. Seen, but not heard.

Ariel repeats in earnest, "She's been waiting for you, Rowan. She's been waiting for so very long now... She needs you. Go to her."

I look at the door and then back to Ariel. However, only the dark void remains where she once stood. Her voice echoes in my ears, coming from no direction, and all directions. "She's waiting..."

I cautiously step forward and rest my hand on what appears to be an ornate handle. I push the door inward, allowing it to swing open on groaning hinges.

The creaking of metal against metal is all that I hear.

Beyond the threshold I see nothing but blackness.

"She's waiting for you," Ariel's voice says.

I turn to find that she is standing behind me.

"Go to her..." she says, nodding as if to urge me along. "She's waiting."

Ariel reaches forward and presses her palms against my chest. The touch seems light, but I am unable to resist the incredible force it carries.

My balance is gone.

I topple backward.

I'm falling...

Falling...

Impact.

"Get me some salt," Constance said. "Now."

An unfamiliar voice questioned, "Salt?"

"Yes, salt," she barked. "Get it, now dammit!"

Whoever belonged to the other voice didn't press the subject. I could hear feet against carpet receding in a quick scamper.

"Felicity?" Constance said. "Are you still there? No... He's not shaking anymore. He just jerked suddenly, and now he's not moving at all... Yes, he's still breathing... Do what? Are you sure? Okay..."

The darkness is replaced by grey.

I'm standing in the center of a small room.

The walls are close.

Too close...

Claustrophobia claws at me.

I close my eyes, but when I open them again nothing has changed.

The discordant unharmony of silence is suddenly replaced by quiet sobbing.

I turn toward the sound.

An ivory skinned woman is huddled in the corner.

She is nude, which makes the fact that she is emaciated even more obvious and pronounced.

Her body is bruised and covered with weeping abrasions.

I cannot even imagine the abuses she has suffered.

A long cascade of hair falls around her, matted and filthy. Here and there, a wisp of its original fiery red can be seen.

I kneel in front of her.

She continues to sob.

I reach out and gently touch her.

Slowly, she brings her face up and stares at me with vacant eyes.

She looks familiar.

Too familiar...

The recognition frightens me.

"Felicity?" I ask, not wanting to hear the answer.

Terror burns through my stomach, and I can no longer breathe.

The darkness is gone.

This time it is the light that comes for me.

The first thing I felt was a sharp sting against my cheek.

The second thing I felt was my body spasming as it drew in a quick breath.

The third thing I felt was bile rushing up my throat.

I heard a woman's yelp filter into my ears, followed by a quickly muttered, "Dammit." The latter belonged to the same voice.

A moment later I was pushing myself up from the floor, groaning as my head resumed its earlier intimate relationship with a near blinding migraine.

"I think he's coming out of it now, Felicity," Constance said, a mix of relief and disgust in her voice. "He just threw up on my shoes."

CHAPTER 12

"AT LEAST IT WAS A DIFFERENT SET OF PARAMEDICS THIS time," Constance said as she pushed open the door and walked into my room. On her way through, she reached up and flipped the security latch out of the way so that the door would now be able to fully close. Advancing farther inward she continued the verbal observation, "I really don't think the pair from this afternoon would have bought my story that this was just a false alarm."

"Yeah, I think you're right," I agreed. "Thanks for taking care of that. I really wasn't up to another argument."

"No problem." She stepped over to the side of the bed where I was perched and thrust a plastic bottle of sports drink into my hands. "Here. Felicity told me to make sure you drank at least one of these right away."

"Yeah, she said she gave you care and feeding instructions for the wayward Witch," I replied, absently giving the cap a twist to break the seal. "Thanks."

I had spoken briefly with my wife once I was back to something resembling lucid. As I expected she was no happier about the current situation than she had been about the earlier one, but she took it somewhat easy on me anyway. It really wasn't as if this was anything new. The big difference was that she was too many miles away to do much more than worry. Of course, she claimed she tried to make good on her earlier threat but was unable to find a seat on a flight out until the next afternoon. Had it been earlier in the day, I wouldn't have put it past her to make the eleven-hour drive; although, knowing Felicity and her lead foot, she probably would have done it in nine.

Constance frowned and gave me an obvious once over before announcing, "I still really wish you would have let the paramedics check you out anyway. Just to be sure you're okay."

"I'm fine."

"Yeah, Rowan, you're the poster boy for fine," she snorted, making no attempt to hide her sarcasm. "In the past twelve hours you've dealt with a constant headache, hemorrhaged all over a restaurant, and experienced some kind of unidentified seizure that had you curled up in a ball on the floor. You just can't get any better than this."

"It's not like you haven't been down this road with me before, Constance."

"True, but I don't think I'll ever really get used to it," she countered. "Do you know the night manager asked me three different times if they needed to worry that a housekeeper might find you dead in the morning when she comes in here to clean the room?"

"What'd you tell…"

"Him," she finished for me. "I told the truth. I said that right now I don't know. I mean, let's be honest. If Ben hadn't called me when you didn't answer your phone, you'd probably still be laying there."

"Maybe," I said. "Maybe not. Hard to say."

"It's the maybe part that bothers me, Rowan," she spat. "It bothers all of us."

"I understand," I replied. "It takes its toll on me too, Constance. And, just in case you forgot, it's not like I have any control over it. I wish like hell I did."

Her voice took on a more soothing tone. "I know. It's just… I don't know…"

"Freakish?"

She nodded vigorously. "I guess that's as good a word as any. Even Ben thinks so, and he's more used to it than I am."

"Well, I can't say that I disagree with either of you…but if it makes you feel any better, you don't need to worry… They won't…find me dead that is. Not yet, anyway."

"I hate to tell you this, but the events of the day aren't really inspiring much confidence in that statement." She sighed heavily then stepped over to the nightstand and parked an extra bottle of the sports drink before simply standing there and watching me. After a long moment she motioned and said, "Go on. Drink it."

I eyed the bottle then glanced up at her, "It's blue, Constance."

"Sorry, but that was the only flavor they had in the machine. And blue usually means it's raspberry."

"Raspberries are *not* electric blue."

"I don't care, just drink it," she ordered.

"I'd really rather have Scotch," I complained in a half-hearted voice.

"Felicity told me you'd probably say that," she replied. "Besides, they don't sell Scotch in vending machines. Now will you just drink the damn thing before I have to pin you and pour it down your throat?"

I wasn't going to force the subject any further. I'd seen her take down bigger guys than me without breaking a sweat, and she was obviously intent on carrying out my wife's instructions. The truth is, I didn't know why I'd even argued in the first place, except that maybe it helped keep my brain occupied so I didn't have to think about what I'd recently witnessed with my mind's eye. Giving in, I took a long gulp of the cold liquid and then loosely screwed the cap back onto the plastic mouth.

"Good enough?" I asked.

"It's a start," she grumbled.

Momentarily satisfied, she wandered away from me, stepped over the freshly scrubbed spot on the carpet, and then parked herself in the desk chair. Once she was settled she unscrewed the cap on the bottle of water she was still carrying.

"Actually, I happen to have…" I started.

She immediately finished the sentence for me. "…some Scotch miniatures in your luggage. Felicity told me that too."

"I see. Should I even look or did she also tell you to hide them from me?" I asked.

She took a drink then shook her head and pointed at the plastic bottle in my hand. "No. She just told me to make sure you drank all of one of those before I let you have any alcohol."

"Well at least there's that," I said. I removed the cap and took another swallow then added, "Even if she is mothering me by proxy."

"She's just worried about you. Like I said, we all are."

"I know." After a short pause I nodded toward her now unshod feet and added, "By the way, sorry about your shoes."

"Don't worry, I'm putting them on your tab."

I raised an eyebrow. "What? I already owe Ben. I have a tab with you now too?"

"I'm not Ben, so whatever you owe him doesn't help me a bit," she replied then nodded and gave me a half smile. "And to answer your question, you started a tab with me this afternoon. That was a brand new blazer you bled on."

"Oh," I grunted. "Well, for the record that wasn't actually my blood."

"Not my point," she replied.

"So I guess my credit card will be tagging along the next time you and Felicity go shopping."

"We'll work it out," she replied. "No hurry."

"Yeah…"

An uncomfortable quiet flowed in behind the conversation, which was actually no big surprise. There had been a palpable tension running between us for the past half hour, and it had nothing at all to do with me ruining her wardrobe or even my arguing with her over the drink.

Although we'd worked together on numerous occasions, and she'd seen me go through similar events, usually it was Ben sitting where she was now. And, more often than not, even he would be playing second chair to Felicity. Sometimes there were just things that only another Witch could understand.

For all intents and purposes, Constance was navigating somewhat unfamiliar territory. It was one thing to witness my bouts with the supernatural; it was something else entirely to be charged with reaching into one and pulling me back from the brink. I think she was still adjusting to playing the part of my handler.

Of course, it also didn't help that I wasn't being all that forthcoming. What's worse is that I was reticent on purpose. The instant replay of what I'd seen in the vision was still looping inside my head—just as it had been ever since I'd regained consciousness. Unfortunately, instead of becoming desensitized to the images, I was experiencing much the opposite. Since it already wasn't getting any easier for me to watch, talking about it was several slots down from the top of my to-do list.

I took another long pull on the bottle of blue liquid. Then noticing that not much was left, I went ahead and finished it with a final pair of gulps before capping the empty bottle and tossing it aside. Sighing, I allowed my head to hang while I endeavored to massage away the painful movie that was being featured on the main screen inside my skull.

Apparently Constance finally grew tired of waiting because without provocation, she asked, "Do you want to talk about it?"

"About what?"

"What you saw when you were face down on the floor having that seizure. That's what."

"Nothing to talk about," I grunted. "Like I told you earlier. It wasn't really much of a vision. Just a lot of disjointed, meaningless imagery… Sometimes it just happens like that."

"Uh-hmm, so you said," she mumbled. After a short pause she pushed harder. "What disjointed imagery did you see that you're so afraid to tell Felicity?"

"What are you talking about?" I asked in return. "I just told you I didn't see anything important."

"You saw *something*, Rowan," she pressed. "Or felt something. I don't really know how it works. But whatever it was, it scared you, and for some reason you're afraid to tell your wife about it."

"You're imagining things."

"Okay, but that makes two of us."

"What do you mean?"

"I mean Felicity knows you're holding something back, and she's not happy about it," she chided. "Just in case that makes any difference to you."

"She tell you that?"

"Yes. As a matter of fact, she did."

I slowly blew out a breath through puffed cheeks while continuing to work my fingers against my scalp. My pause was long, and when I finally replied, my words were unconvincing, even to me. "Well, you're both wrong. There's nothing to tell. So if you don't mind, I'd prefer we just drop it."

"Fine," she replied. "But do yourself a favor, Row. Don't ever turn to a life of crime. You've got to be one of the worst liars I've ever met."

"I'll keep that in mind."

A short lull intervened then Constance said, "It's a little after eight. Do you want to see about grabbing some dinner?"

I gave up on the fruitless massage and looked over at her. "Actually, I need to call Ben. He was working on something…"

"It's already taken care of," she said, cutting me off. "Detective McLaughlin is already on her way to your house."

"But she wasn't…"

She didn't let me finish. "After what happened tonight, Ben thought it might be a good idea to cover all the bases."

"Yeah… He's probably right. Then I guess I need to…"

"That's taken care of too. Felicity is on board with it and is expecting her."

"Well…" I mumbled. "I guess I should say thanks."

"You're welcome. So…dinner?"

"Honestly, I'm not all that hungry," I replied. "I know it's still early, but since I didn't really get any sleep last night, I think maybe I'd just like to turn in."

"That sounds like a good plan," she agreed. "It's been a long day for both of us."

Standing up, she walked over to the closet, slid the door open, and then pulled the extra pillow and blanket down from the shelf. I watched in silence as she headed back over to one of the more comfortable chairs in the corner of the room. After unfolding the blanket and spreading it out, she extracted her Sig Sauer and laid it on the table next to the chair. The firearm was followed a moment later by her handcuffs, credentials and room key.

"What are you doing?" I asked.

She looked over at me. "Getting ready to turn in."

"Something wrong with your room?"

"No." She shook her head. "It's just fine."

"I take it you've decided that you're spending the night in here with me." My words were more a statement than a question.

"Obviously."

"Why?"

"Can you promise me you aren't going to have another episode of some sort during the night?"

"Yes. I promise."

She parked herself in the chair and settled in. "Like I said, Rowan. You're just about the worst liar on the planet."

"I'll be fine," I objected.

She pulled the blanket over herself and said, "Goodnight, Rowan."

Sunday, April 23
9:17 A.M.
FMC Carswell / Carswell NAS JRB
Fort Worth, Texas

CHAPTER 13

"I SPOKE TO THE ASSIGNED OFFICER PERSONALLY," Doctor Jante told me then shook her head to underscore the statement that followed. "Unfortunately, she said that Devereaux was sleeping during the period of time in question."

As was the case the day before, Constance and I had been hastily escorted onto the grounds of the Naval Air Station where FMC Carswell was located. I had felt a bit self-conscious as we were brought forward and checked through ahead of the other visitors who were obligated to wait en masse. However, the feeling was quickly overshadowed by everything else that was weighing on me.

I finished shoving my belongings into a personal effects locker once again, and then as I rechecked my pockets I asked, "So the guard is certain she was asleep?"

"As certain as she can be under the circumstances," she replied. "So I'm afraid there's really no way to answer your original query."

"Actually, I think you just did. If she was sleeping then she was Annalise…or what's left of her, anyway."

"I'm not sure I follow your logic. Would you care to enlighten me?"

"By your definition of what's going on with her, I can see where you might not," I explained. "But, if you're willing to accept the fact that you aren't dealing with a fractured personality here and that you're actually up against a parasitic spirit that's using Annalise's body, then it should make perfect sense."

"How so?"

"Simple deduction. Miranda doesn't need sleep. Annalise does."

"Actually, Mister Gant, a similar argument could still be made in the case of dissociative identity disorder. The manifestation of a given personality can easily trigger the release of stress hormones, which can in turn inhibit the ability to sleep. And to be honest, whenever the Annalise personality is in control, she always displays far more agitation, which would effectively counter your theory. Therefore, what you are saying doesn't prove your claim that this is a spirit possession at all, nor does it accurately indicate which personality was truly in control at the time."

I held up my hands in mock surrender. "No problem, Doc. I'm not here to argue the point. Feel free to rationalize it any way you want, that's fine by me. But whether you agree or not, as far as I'm concerned if she was sleeping, then Annalise Devereaux was the one in the cell, not Miranda."

"Aren't you making a rather large assumption?"

"I prefer to call it a necessary leap when science fails," I said, parroting back to her the words she'd used earlier to describe why the FBI was taking such a vested interest in me of late. I purposely refrained from making a point of that fact since Constance was standing nearby; I didn't want to cause her any undue trouble by possibly bringing to light that I'd told her everything I was supposed to have kept secret. Fortunately, it was apparent from the doctor's expression that no explanation was necessary and that the verbal jab had landed directly where it was aimed.

Jante raised an eyebrow and gave me a stern look. "An interesting choice of words. Still, even if you are correct, what does this prove? Why is it so important?"

"It tells me that Miranda wasn't here. And if I'm right, that means she was using someone else's body to commit another murder."

"A murder? Where?"

"My best guess, Saint Louis."

"Best guess?" She cocked her head to the side. "So this is just part of your theory then? You don't actually know that a murder has been committed, correct?"

"I can't point you to a body if that's what you mean, but my gut feeling is that she's killed again."

Constance piped up, "I already contacted Detective Storm with the Saint Louis city homicide division, and he alerted the Major Case Squad. They don't have anything yet, but I've worked with Rowan before. If he says…"

Doctor Jante held up a hand to stop her. "I'm familiar with Mister Gant's track record." She sighed then pursed her lips and studied the floor for a moment before looking back up to my face.

"Hypothetically, if I were to believe this whole story of yours, what makes you think *Miranda* murdered someone in Saint Louis?"

"In her own way, she told me she did."

She furrowed her brow. "Are you basing that on something she said during yesterday's interview?"

"Actually, no. She chose a somewhat more perverse route to get my attention."

"What is that?"

"Believe it or not, she caused me to bleed all over my lunch."

"Mister Gant, now you're making even less sense than before."

"I know that's how it seems, but you're just going to have to take my word for it," I said. "Intuition, remember?"

"Yes, I do. But I also remember that you promised me a coherent explanation, and I've yet to hear one."

"That's true, I did. But, I'm afraid this is about as coherent as talking to dead people gets. Honestly, it all comes down to a matter of connecting some unrelated dots."

She cast another skewed glare at me and sighed once more. "Again, assuming I accept your story as even remotely possible, whose body did she use? Obviously not your wife's, as you seem to fear will happen, or I suspect you wouldn't be this calm."

"No," I replied while shaking my head vigorously. "She didn't use Felicity, although I can guarantee you that's her end game with all of this."

"So you've said. Who then?" Jante pressed.

"Only Annalise and Miranda know that answer."

"And you think you can convince one of them to tell you?"

"No, actually, I don't."

"Then what exactly is your intention here?"

"I'm just looking for some more dots to connect, Doctor Jante. Related, unrelated, I don't care. I just want to stop her."

"She's behind bars, Mister Gant."

"No, she isn't. You took a body off the streets, that's all," I replied. "That's not going to stop Miranda, and she's on a mission to prove that."

She regarded me in silence. I waited several heartbeats then let out a heavy sigh and rubbed my forehead for a moment. I was about to speak when a sharp trill sounded nearby. I glanced over to see Constance pulling her cell phone out and thumbing it on. As she stepped away from us, I heard her say, "This is Mandalay."

I turned back to Doctor Jante and found that she was still frowning at me. Rather than continue the stare down and wait to see which one of us was going to flinch first, I simply gave in and said, "Look, I was under the impression you were all for me going back in there with her."

"I was," she replied.

"By 'was,' do you mean you aren't any longer?"

"What I mean is that since our discussion yesterday, there have been some concerns raised about your effectiveness in this situation."

"By you or by someone farther up the food chain?" I asked.

"The concerns came from higher up."

"Yeah, I'm not surprised." I shook my head. No longer caring about secrets, I spat, "So since this lab rat isn't behaving the way you want him to, you're ending the experiment."

She glared at me. "That option is being seriously considered."

"Then why the hell am I even standing here arguing with you?" I barked, raising my voice slightly. "Why did you bother to set this meeting up in the first place if you weren't going to let it happen?"

I was now attracting the attention of staff as well as a group of other visitors that had entered the lobby area. Jante shot me a hard look then grabbed me by the arm and pulled me aside.

In a hushed voice she demanded, "Calm down, please. Your lack of self-control is the primary concern."

"It didn't seem to be an issue yesterday."

"Actually, it was for some."

"Well, if you think this is a lack of self-control, then you haven't seen anything yet," I growled. "Now, why don't you answer my question?"

"Mister Gant, you're here because even with the concerns, you still have your advocates."

"Lucky me," I returned, tone still edgy. "Listen, I think I made it crystal clear yesterday that I wasn't all that excited about being the subject of an experiment to begin with, but now I've had enough of this bullshit. So, if you need to take a vote or something, then get on the horn and do it; because, if all we're going to do is stand here and argue, I'm done."

"Excuse me," Constance said, interjecting herself into the close quarters conversation. "Sorry to interrupt, but I think you both need to hear this. That call was Detective Storm in Saint Louis. They found a body that fits with what Rowan predicted."

"And that would be?" Doctor Jante replied.

"Mid to late twenties with what appears to be a bite mark on her neck," I announced. "And she will have been exsanguinated."

"Yes," Constance confirmed. "Except it's he, not she. The victim is male."

"Male?" I questioned, furrowing my brow.

"Yes," she replied. "I know the gender is a deviation, but listen to me—there are a couple of other things you need to know. Unlike the women killed last month, his body also shows signs of extreme physical tortures which are consistent with the type found on many of Miranda's victims."

"She's sending a message," I said.

Constance added, "And it's addressed to you, Rowan. There was something protruding from his mouth. An Emerald Photographic Services business card."

As if the signs of torture weren't obvious enough, my wife's business card drove the point home.

"Dammit," I muttered. "Felicity?"

"Ben already checked. Detective McLaughlin is with her and everything is fine."

"Good," I said then brought a spate of calm sarcasm to bear on Jante. "Well, Doc, is that enough confirmation for you?"

"Fine," she said, voice flat. "I'll have you escorted over."

"Great," I returned, my tone just as businesslike. I looked over at Constance and asked, "While I'm in there, would you mind doing me a couple of favors?"

"Of course. What do you need?"

"First, call Ben back and ask if he can get Charlee to stay with Felicity until I get home."

"You mean overnight?"

"Actually, no, that's the second favor. See if you can either change our tickets to something that will get us out of here as soon as possible, or buy new ones if you have to. I'll pay whatever it costs."

"I can do that," she replied.

"Thanks," I told her then turned back to Doctor Jante. "Where can I get some bottled water and some salt around here?"

She wrinkled her brow and asked, "Why?"

"It's an *intuition* thing," I replied.

"There's a vending machine on the way over," she offered, shaking her head. "I'll have to see what I can do about the salt."

"I appreciate it. Oh, and I'm going to need something else from you too."

"And that would be?"

"A waiver of the visitation restrictions because I'm taking the water in there with me."

CHAPTER 14

A SMUG GRIN TWEAKED MIRANDA'S DRAWN FACE AS SHE was led into the interview room. Following the same procedure as the day before, I was waiting for her in my seat at the table. Her escort disconnected her handcuffs from the Martin chain around her waist and then guided her into the chair opposite me.

"So…you decided to come back," Miranda said, cocking her head to see me around the corrections officer who was reconnecting her handcuffs to the ring on the table.

A purplish bruise wrapped almost halfway around her thin neck. The garish colors were mottled and faded toward the edges, but a solid, dark area of discoloration was evident where my thumb had pressed into her windpipe. It didn't take any imagination at all to see my own handprint in the outline of the contusion.

"You knew I would," I said.

"Of course. You missed me."

I shrugged. "No. Not really."

"Face it, little man. You are obsessed with me."

"I'll give you that," I nodded. "But it's definitely a different kind of obsession than what you would like to believe."

"What do you think?" she asked, executing a disjointed change of subject. She pointed her chin upward and turned her head slightly so as to call attention to the large bruise. "I wore it just for you."

"I see."

"Tell me, little man," she continued. "Do you abuse your wife too, or is it just me who gets to be the lucky one?"

I let out a carefully measured sigh but chose to hold my tongue.

Without missing a beat, she returned to the original subject. "Getting back to Felicity, how does she feel about this lurid preoccupation of yours? Is she jealous of me?"

"Actually, she's okay with it," I replied.

"Of course she is," Miranda replied. "Because she knows you will bring us together again."

"That's not going to happen." I reached out and lifted the bottle of salt water from the table and unscrewed the cap. I'd downed a full one before ever walking into the room, and something told me I'd likely drain this one before I walked out.

"Salt water?" Miranda asked, nodding toward the bottle in my hand.

"Yes. Want some?"

"I thought we talked about this. That will not work on me."

"Doesn't really matter," I replied. "It isn't for you. It's for me." I took a long swallow and then carefully replaced the cap, never breaking eye contact with her.

She didn't even blink, but I could tell by her silence that this was a move she hadn't expected. I knew she was trying to get inside me, just as she had done yesterday. I could feel it. My head was throbbing, and there was even a slight tingle pricking my skin. But none of it was anywhere near the intensity of the day before.

My defenses were up and holding. The pain was manageable so far. It seemed the infusion of salt was working for the moment, but I had the distinct feeling that it was nothing more than a stopgap. Given enough time, Miranda would find a way around it.

"Don't you want her to be happy?" she pressed, moving on.

I dipped my head in a shallow nod. "You know I do."

"Well then, why are you trying so hard to keep us apart?"

"Obviously I'm doing more than just trying."

"Which means you do not really love her. If you did, then you would not stand between us."

"Why is that, Miranda?"

"Because I can give her so much more than you. I can make her happy in ways that you cannot fathom."

I knew this was only a precursor. Her intent was to bait me into a repeat of my outburst. If I lost control, salt water or not, she would be able to take the reins, and just like before, there would be no turning back. However, I wasn't going to allow that to happen this time. I steeled myself and simply replied, "So I've heard."

"I am sure that you have." She smiled. "In great detail I suspect."

"No, not as much as you would imagine."

"So I am her secret then. That is even better."

"Not a secret, really," I replied. "She just has a lot more class than you."

She ignored the insult and continued her attempt at provocation. "Tell me, little man, does it not make you jealous that I can pleasure her in ways that you cannot?"

"Can you? It seems to me that you actually just use her as a vehicle to pleasure yourself."

"A pleasure from which she benefits."

"I think that might be a matter of perspective."

"Really? Are you familiar with the remora?" she asked.

I nodded. "It's a fish as I recall."

"Very good. Yes, it is," she replied. "You see, the remora attaches itself to sharks, whales, and other large sea creatures. In exchange for the ride, it grooms its host, keeping it free of bacteria and harmful parasites. The arrangement is called mutualism. Both of them reap benefits from the symbiotic relationship."

"And so you're telling me that you and my wife have that same type of relationship I take it?"

"Of course."

"And you fancy yourself the remora, and not the shark."

"See?" she replied, saccharine sweet sarcasm glazing her words. "You do understand."

"Actually, I don't, because what I see is something completely the opposite. Like the lamprey eel, you attach yourself to a host then proceed to suck the life out of her before moving to the next and so on. Therefore, you benefit at the host's expense. That arrangement is called parasitism."

"Interesting. I did not know you had a background in marine biology," she quipped.

"I had to dissect a lamprey when I was in high school," I replied. "It left a distasteful impression on me then, just like you have now."

"Yet here you are."

"Yes. Here I am," I agreed. "So… How about you? That analogy with the remora seems like a fairly obscure piece of knowledge for a self-involved head case whose waterlogged corpse was found floating face down in the Mississippi back in eighteen fifty-one."

I unscrewed the cap on the bottle and took another drink of the salt-laced water while she glared at me in silence. Apparently it was my turn to strike a nerve.

"I've wondered about that for a while now," I continued as I set the bottle aside. "The newspaper article I found mentioned that you were seen jumping into the river. Why would you do something like that? Or, were you maybe pushed?"

She continued to stare.

"I have a theory. Want to hear it? It has to do with your sister, Delphine…"

She cut me off, announcing in a cold tone, "You never answered my question."

"Answer mine and I'll see what I can do."

"No."

"That doesn't seem terribly symbiotic of you."

She allowed the gibe to go unanswered and instead, verbally forced the subject back onto the original track. "Felicity and I are meant for one another. You need to come to terms with that, little man."

I nodded. "That's what you keep saying."

She gave me a sidelong glance then raised an eyebrow. "You are handling this much better than you did yesterday."

"Thank you," I replied. "However, you seem to be a little more on edge today. Ironic, don't you think?"

She ignored the observation and pressed forward. "I am afraid that your visit is in vain. I have decided not to let you speak to Annalise."

I harrumphed. "I hate to break it to you, but I knew that yesterday."

"But you came anyway."

"Well, to be honest I wasn't going to, but then I got your message."

She feigned an innocent smile. "What message?"

"I think you know the message I mean," I said, keeping my tone even and calm. "After all, you found it necessary to interrupt my lunch in order to deliver it."

"Maybe you should eat faster."

"I tried that once. It's bad for my digestion."

"Really. Perhaps you have an ulcer. You should probably have that checked."

"Good advice. I'll do that."

She stared at me across the table, her expression blank. Rather than return the favor, I focused my gaze over her shoulder at a random point on the wall. After a long wait, I forced myself to yawn then stared back at her without saying a word.

"I still have no idea what message you are talking about," she finally said.

"Really?"

"Why would I?"

"Because it came from you."

"You really do need some rest, little man."

"You'll get no argument from me there. How about you? You're looking a bit rough around the edges yourself."

"I'm fine."

"Don't they let you look in the mirror around here? That body you're wearing is in sad shape, lady. Annalise isn't looking too well at all, and you know it."

"That is because she is weak."

"I guess that nap yesterday afternoon just wasn't enough for her, was it?"

She simply stared back at me again, expressionless.

"I know what you're doing, Miranda," I told her. "They've found the body. But then, you already know that, don't you?"

There was a flicker in her eye as she smiled, but other than that she remained silent.

I nodded. "Still no comment, I see. So, tell me…" I gestured at her. "Is this your grand plan for my wife? Ride her until nothing is left like you've done to Annalise. Then move on to the next horse? And then the next?"

She finally ended her purposeful reticence. "Felicity is different."

"I can't argue with you there. But even she wouldn't be able to take the abuse you dish out forever. You would eventually burn her out too."

"We will see."

"No." I shook my head. "No, we won't."

"I can make them stop, you know," she said, stressing the sentence heavily.

The abruptness of the comment, as much as the words and tone, told me she was switching topics in an attempt to regain control.

"Make who stop?" I asked.

"Them," she repeated. "The dead. I can make them leave you alone."

"I doubt it."

"Why, I made you understand them, did I not?"

In the wake of her question, a flash of memory played through my grey matter. To say it was familiar would have been the ultimate in understatements.

"Maybe…" I said. "But that's not how it feels. It's almost as if someone was translating for me."

"Who?"

I sighed again. "That's the problem. I have no idea. I feel like I should, but I just don't..."

A line formed between a pair of the unrelated dots then continued on to another. Unfortunately, the picture that was starting to be revealed was far from pretty.

I nodded. "I guess I should have known it was you."

"If I had wanted you to know it was me, you would have."

I paused then picked up the bottle of water and drained it. Miranda watched me in silence.

Several heartbeats thudded inside my chest before I finally asked, "So, now you're offering me a bribe?"

The corner of her mouth curled upward in a vile sneer. "I said that I could, little man. I never said that I would."

"That's right. You didn't, did you..."

I looked over to the corrections officer in the corner and calmly said, "Okay. I'm done."

He came forward and set about disconnecting the handcuffs from the table. I remained seated, watching the process unfold.

"You are not finished," Miranda said. Her tone was flat.

"Yes, I am," I replied.

"You still want to speak with Annalise," she countered. There was no desperation or even urgency in her calm voice. It was simply a statement of fact.

"Yes. You're right, I do. But you won't let me, and I'm tired of playing your game."

"You need me. You will be back."

"No, Miranda, I don't. And, I won't." I shook my head to punctuate the words. "Not this time."

"Stand up," the guard told her.

She complied but never took her eyes off of me. As the officer proceeded to connect the handcuffs to the belly chain around her waist, Miranda twisted her mouth into a wicked smile.

"Are you certain you want to do it this way?" she asked.

"You aren't leaving me any choice, are you?"

"I suppose that is your perception," she replied. "We will be seeing each other again soon, little man." The comment was brimming over with innuendo, which she underscored with, "You know I will be coming for her."

I nodded. "What I know is that you'll try."

"And I will succeed."

"And why are you so sure of that?"

"Because, you no longer amuse me, and like you, I have tired of this game."

"Meaning?"

"I will be coming to kill you first. Then, you cannot stop me."

"I see. Well, that's definitely what it's going to take to get to her." I shrugged. "Just out of curiosity, I don't suppose you'd like to tell me who you're going to be when you come to do this?"

"That would spoil the surprise, now would it not?"

"I suppose that is your perception," I repeated her words back. "But, I thought you were tired of this game?"

"This is a new game."

"So…how will I be able to play if I don't know it's you?"

"You will know," she said. "But if it will help, I will wear something… or *someone*… special."

Sunday, April 23
11:58 P.M.
Lambert Saint Louis International Airport
Baggage Carousel 3
Saint Louis, Missouri

CHAPTER 15

I COULD FEEL NOTHING.

Well, nothing in a preternatural sense, anyway. On a physical level it was a different story, even though travel weariness had managed to numb me a bit in that arena too. While I certainly realized that exhaustion took a major toll, in the past it had never seemed to make any difference where the ethereal was concerned. If anything, it served to heighten my sensitivity to it by lowering my defenses. So, no matter what, I always felt something.

Always.

It was just an accepted part of my existence. Evil would seek me out, and I would always know it was there. Why? Because without fail, I would be able to *feel it*... But, right now, even while holding it in the palm of my hand, I could feel nothing.

I twisted the small bottle in my fingers, spinning it slowly while I watched the white crystals cascade across one another like sand trickling into the bottom of an hourglass. With each turn, as the necklace inside tumbled, a shiny flash of its metal surface would peek through and then almost instantly disappear once again beneath the grains of salt.

Ben had been waiting for us on the opposite side of the security gate at Concourse C, and the very first thing he had done was shove the bottle containing the cursed jewelry into my hand—before he even uttered a single word of greeting in fact. I could tell by the look on his face that he was three steps beyond mere relief just to be rid of it. Apparently, my reassurances that he was safe from its effects hadn't been enough to allay his fears.

My concentration was broken by an alarm sounding nearby, so I looked up from the distraction in my hands. The attention light over the baggage chute winked several times, and the delivery belt began to move. Seconds later an unseen motor began humming, and the metal slats of the time worn carousel itself jerked hesitantly. Once they shuddered and began sliding around the elongated oval, their unsynchronized rattling was punctuated by tinny scrapes as they proceeded to accordion in and out of one another around the semicircular ends. A full sixty seconds passed before the first suitcase finally appeared at the top of the conveyor; then, with a clunk, followed by a swoosh of nylon against metal, it toppled from the edge and slid onto the rotating carousel, ending with a dull thud against the lip at the bottom. A moment later it was followed by another and then another.

However, thus far none of the luggage riding the horseless merry-go-round belonged to me.

I glanced over to the status board and saw that our flight number was still listed, which ostensibly meant our carousel hadn't been switched while we weren't paying attention. Then I looked at my watch and saw that it was almost midnight. Whether by mere suggestion, from the exhaustion, or a combination of both, I yawned.

We'd been on the ground now for better than thirty minutes, and the information on the lighted board had already been announcing the arrival of our luggage on this particular carousel for the last fifteen of them. The delay was par for the course in my experience, even at this late hour with the airport approaching deserted, save for overnight staff and the small clutch of passengers milling around this particular baggage claim. Still, typical or not, I couldn't say I was overly excited about the wait—not that I could do anything to change it, of course.

I sighed and rubbed the back of my neck with my free hand. Wherever I wasn't numb, I ached from the tension of the day. Still, I was feeling much better than I had been earlier. At least now I was back in Saint Louis and no longer sitting 700 plus miles away at DFW with a standby ticket in my hand, a crowd of confirmed passengers ahead of me, and an attack of anxiety so intense that it had me either calling or text messaging Felicity every half hour. Now, even as tired as I was, the drudgery of waiting for my luggage seemed almost normal in a sense, which was something I knew I should find comforting. But, right now normal was anything but. In fact, it was more along the lines of disconcerting.

"That one yours, Row?" Ben asked, thumping my arm hard with the back of his hand in order to get my attention.

I shot a glance toward where he was pointing and saw a dark green suitcase rumbling my direction on the slanted metal plates.

I shook my head. "It's close, but mine's just a little smaller than that and should have a laminated tag on the top handle."

"Yeah, I thought so," Ben grunted. "Just wanted ta' be sure."

"All good. Thanks."

"Well, there's mine," Constance said as a roll-around skidded down and then toppled onto its side and began moving our way. Her voice was a quiet drone as she slowly started forward to retrieve it.

"Relax, hon. I got it," Ben said as he stepped past her and quickly reached in with a long arm to scoop it up. Setting the luggage to the side and extending the pull handle up, he slipped his free arm gently around the petite federal agent's shoulders while we continued to wait. She leaned into him and let out a long, weary sigh.

My friend looked like he was probably just as tired as Constance and I both were. His angular Native American features were expressionless and sagging beneath his salt and pepper hair, a fact that served to accentuate some of the age lines that had started forming on his face over the last decade. Always one for a good cliché, he liked to say it wasn't the years, it was the mileage. He'd go on to add that those lines were just his personal road map to prove he'd been there and that any scars were simply souvenirs from his stops along the way.

Truth is, we had both racked up more than our share of miles and souvenirs, and our journey just seemed to get longer every day. Still, my friend remained on top of his game through it all, and even at this moment his dark eyes kept vigilant watch over our surroundings. Mine, on the other hand, ignored the outside world and drifted back to my hand to once again focus on the bottled jewelry.

Since the twin of this necklace had been an integral part of some very intense blood magick on Miranda's behalf, in my own way I suppose I was attempting to keep an equally vigilant watch out for a different kind of threat. Not only had the two pieces of jewelry connected her to my wife, the missing mate was now being used to provide her with an interim host that was allowing her to roam beyond the walls of Carswell. Her thinly veiled parting comment earlier today had confirmed that and had been just that much more evidence to support my belief that it was the key to ending this nightmare once and for all.

My only question at this point was why she had not yet employed the free host to directly contact Felicity. In my mind, it seemed that would be the logical end run, as it would definitely be a way to get around me with much less effort. In retrospect, luring me to Texas should have provided the perfect opportunity to simply have the new horse walk up to our front door and ring the bell then pounce on my wife the moment she answered. The fact that this hadn't occurred was a relief, of course, but at the same time it was troubling. What's more, there was also the fact that until now I hadn't foreseen another host besides Annalise as a possibility at all. That in itself just added another entire shot of anxiety to my already overflowing cup of worry.

I kept trying to tell myself that the lack of direct contact meant that something else was stopping her. What it was, I had no idea, but if it was in fact true, and I could figure it out, maybe I could use it to my advantage. Unfortunately, I also knew that what it might really mean is that she had something else planned that I couldn't even begin to imagine. After all, when you are dealing with an insane person, it is almost impossible to predict the next move she will make. And when you are dealing with an insane person who is also the very definition of evil, all bets are off. Yet, here I stood with my chips on the table, waiting for the wheel to spin and the ball to drop. Feeling helpless wasn't doing my disquiet any favors.

It also made me wonder if I was just as insane as she.

"Here, Row," Ben said to me as he gave my arm a bump once again. I heard the metal on plastic hiss of a suitcase pull handle being telescoped, followed by the click of it locking into place. Out of reflex, I looked toward the sound. It appeared that my friend had retrieved my bag while I was being held captive by my inner thoughts. Leaning it toward me, he added, "C'mon. You ready to get outta here?"

"Yeah," I grunted in agreement, my attention anything but focused.

"You okay, white man?" he asked.

"What?"

"Are you oh-kay?" he repeated, exaggerating the enunciation on each of the three words. "You're actin' a little more la-la land than normal, even for you."

"Oh…that…" I nodded, then took hold of the handle on my suitcase and followed along as he and Constance arced out and around the few passengers still waiting. "Actually it's not that at all, believe it or not. I guess I've just got a lot on my mind. That and I'm worn out."

"Yeah, I can relate." He glanced over at me as we walked toward the exit. "That bitch really got to ya' down there, didn't she?"

"Yeah, I guess so…" I replied. "I just wish I knew what she's planning."

"Besides goin' after Firehair, ya' mean?"

"Yeah, but really more of the how she plans to do it, I guess."

"Uh-huh, yeah, well you'n me both," he replied.

"I guess I should have seen this whole thing coming. Especially given my reservations about the resolution of that last case."

"You ain't Superman, Row."

I grumbled. "Yeah, well sometimes I feel like I have to be."

He nodded. "Yeah, I know. Been there." He was quiet for a second then asked, "Do ya' think you're gonna be able ta' end this?"

"Superman or not, I have to. I don't have any choice."

We continued for a moment in relative silence, save for the vibrating drone of the suitcase wheels clacking against the non-skid surface of the floor. As we approached the automatic doors at the bottom of the sloping ramp they slid open, and we exited into the terminal level of the parking garage. Compared to the dimness of the baggage claim area, the exterior lights around the entrance cast harsh, yellowish illumination down from above. I blinked several times as my eyes adjusted to the sudden glare.

"To the left, next level up," Ben said, pointing as he guided us toward the stairwell.

The night itself was mild, with the temperature hovering somewhere in the low sixties. Cool, but not cold. A slight breeze wafted through, stirring the funk of old exhaust fumes and dirty concrete that forever permeated the structure.

As we approached the stairs, Ben asked, "So you ain't gonna do the *Twilight Zone* thing anytime soon, right?"

"You mean right now?"

"Yeah. Like right here or somethin'."

"Honestly, I don't think I could if I wanted to, why?"

"Just checkin'," he replied. "When you get like this I start worryin' 'cause it usually means you're about ta' fall down an' flop around on the floor or some shit. I don't need your sorry ass rollin' backwards down the stairs right now."

"It's not always that bad," I objected.

He gave me a one-eyed stare. "Aren't you the guy who just bled all over the place and shit?"

"Yeah, yeah, I get your point. But that doesn't always happen."

"No, maybe not, but whatever does happen is always weird and kinda freaky."

"So you're saying I embarrass you?"

"Hell no," he snorted. "You embarrass yourself. I'm just along for the ride." Constance was already halfway up the stairwell, so Ben gestured and said, "After you, white man. Just in case and all, ya'know."

I huffed out a tired snort, hefted my suitcase by the grip, and then started upward. "You know, Constance didn't give me this much grief. Maybe I should just work with her instead of you."

"Leave me out of it," she called down at us from the landing. "Right now the only partner I want to work with is my pillow."

"I won't argue with you there," I said. "I just want to get home myself."

"So listen, Row," Ben started. "On this whole…"

Before he could finish the sentence, a syncopated warble began issuing from his belt, growing louder with each beat. He grumbled and said, "Hold that thought."

I had just stepped onto the landing next to Constance when my friend topped the stairs with his cell phone in hand. He held it up and waved the chirping device at us as he announced, "Speakin' of home, I think McLaughlin must be gettin' antsy…"

Flipping it open, he answered with, "Yeah, Charlee, we're on our way. I just picked 'em up." As he spoke my friend dipped his head in the direction of his van, and we started walking toward it while he listened to the caller. "Do what? Awww, Jeezus. You'n Firehair are okay, right?"

Adrenalin instantly dumped into my bloodstream at the mention of Felicity, especially considering the apparent nature of his question to Detective McLauglin.

"What's going on, Ben?" I asked, concern tightening my throat and causing my voice to rise slightly in pitch.

He shook his head to stave me off while he concentrated on the call. "But you're both okay, right? Good…"

His vehicle hadn't been parked very far away, so we arrived at it quickly. He let go of Constance's suitcase and hurriedly dug around in his pocket for his keys, which he immediately handed to her. She proceeded to unlock the van, but my attention never wavered from him.

"You call it in ta' Major Case? Yeah… Well don't let the locals fuck with anything. Just have 'em secure the scene until MCS gets there…" He continued. "Yeah… Good… Okay, so what about the vic? Are ya' sure? Yeah, sounds just like the last one… What? Jeezus… Okay… Yeah, well hang tight. We'll be there in twenty." Ben folded the phone and slipped it back onto his belt. A look of distress now hardened his features, and his hand shot up to smooth back his hair.

His silence was punctuated by a sharp click as Constance pushed down the pull handle on her luggage. We both stood watching him and waiting. However, I didn't hold out for very long.

"Are you going to tell me what's going on?" I demanded. "What happened?"

His side of the conversation had been enough for me to figure out that Miranda apparently hadn't waited to kill again and that somehow Felicity was involved. Obviously, that latter fact had put me immediately on edge, especially considering all the possible implications. However, it was my friend's sudden switch in demeanor that disturbed me most. Something about it said there was more going on than just the discovery of a body.

He sighed. "Listen, Row, Felicity's okay. She's just fine and Charlee's with 'er. So don't worry about that."

"What the…" I started. "Okay…but, what's going on? Why is she even involved? She… She didn't…"

He shook his head and then gestured at me with one hand. "What? No… No, she was with Charlee. She didn't go all kinky *Twilight Zone* or anything, so that's all good…"

"Then what's going on?"

He sighed. "Apparently your front yard just became the killer's latest dump site."

I muttered, "Damn that bitch…" I sighed heavily as I closed my eyes then reached up with both hands and began massaging my scalp. Oddly enough, I think the gesture was more out of habit than anything else because there was no pain.

I still felt nothing.

In fact, I realized in that moment that not only did I feel nothing, but also for the first time in a very long while, the din inside my skull had fallen quiet. No screams, no murmurs, not even a whisper.

The voices of the dead were gone, and it seemed I was very much alone.

CHAPTER 16

BEN HAD AFFIXED HIS MAGNETIC-BASED EMERGENCY light to the roof of his van, and it was sending out oscillating waves of bright red as he whipped the vehicle through quiet intersections, completely ignoring speed limits and traffic signals in the process. Riding with him was always an adventure to begin with, and when an emergency was involved, it was akin to being aboard a runaway train. Fortunately, there wasn't much traffic to get in his way at this hour.

In my usual attempt at self-preservation, I cinched my seatbelt even tighter and tried to keep my eyes focused forward through the windshield. However, even with that, I could feel the bottom drop out of my stomach when we arced along the ramp from I-70 to I-170 Southbound. For a moment or two, I found myself wishing I had one of the airsickness bags from my recent flight handy.

I couldn't see the speedometer from where I was sitting, but my best guess was that we had to have been traveling at better than eighty miles per hour because by the time all was said and done, it had only taken us five minutes to reach I-64. Shortly after that, we were turning down my street, and although we were still a few blocks away, in the distance we could already see the flickering lights of the squad cars in front of my house. Their stark flashes of red and white strobed like an ugly blemish on the night, and once again the pit of my stomach was gone.

Blowing through the stop signs as the blocks ticked past, it took less than a minute for us to reach our destination. My friend had barely started braking the van when I unbuckled my seatbelt and grabbed the handle on the sliding side door.

"Dammit, Row!" he shouted. "Hold on a sec! Ya' can't get..."

I didn't hear the rest of his comment because I had already levered the door backward on its raspy tracks and then launched myself through the opening. The vehicle was literally still rolling when my feet hit the pavement. Although I stumbled, I somehow managed to keep my footing and started jogging toward my house. I probably would have stepped it up and broken into a dead run had it not been for the uniformed officer who met me at the end of the driveway.

"Whoa!" he barked, one hand out toward me and the other resting on his sidearm. "Hold up! Where do you think you're going?"

I stumbled to a halt and spat, "Where does it look like?"

"Lockup if you keep being a smartass," he replied without missing a beat. "Now how about answering my question?"

My next response was more in line with what he was after but still flat and succinct. I pointed past him and said, "In the house. I live here."

"Okay. Are you Mister O'Brien?"

"Gant, actually," I replied. "Felicity O'Brien is my wife. Is she still in there?"

He nodded. "Calm down. The detectives are taking her statement. I'm going to need to see some ID, sir."

I sighed and reached for my wallet. Before I could fully extract it from my pocket, however, Ben drew up alongside me, his badge hanging around his neck on a thick cord.

"Detective Storm, Major Case Squad," he told the officer while flashing his official ID. Then he wagged his thumb at me. "It's okay. Go ahead an' sign 'im in, he really does live here. And besides, he's actually a consultant for the MCS."

By now I had my driver's license in my hand and was holding it out to the cop. He went ahead and gave it a cursory glance then nodded.

"Okay, you can put that away now, Mister Gant," he told me, then made a half turn and called to another officer who was positioned at the opposite corner of the yard where the crux of the activity was going on. "Yo, Foreman. I need that log over here for a sec… Hey… Foreman…" He glanced quickly back to us as he started trekking toward the man with the sign-in sheet. "Hang on…"

Once he was out of earshot, my friend grumbled at me, "See, Row? I tried ta' tell ya' ta' fuckin' wait."

I didn't respond. I was too busy being mesmerized by the gruesome carnival that had taken up residence in my front yard. A sagging ribbon of bright yellow crime-scene tape cordoned off my property line, extending out past the sidewalk and even beyond the curb itself. Spotlights from a pair of squad cars were aimed at the area, and a stark pool of light filled the lawn. Swimming in it was a woman wearing a windbreaker emblazoned with the words CRIME SCENE UNIT, a clipboard and numbered tent-shaped markers in hands. The true centerpiece of the entire spectacle, however, was the nude body sprawled on the grass.

As much as I hated to admit it, over the years I had become increasingly jaded about crime scenes. Once you'd stood in the middle of enough of them, the experience tended to take on a clinical edge. It was always surreal in its own way but dispassionate nonetheless. Each scene was different, and each was the same. Every one of them had a story to tell—and often times even more than one if you listened closely enough. You just had to figure out which voices were telling you the truth.

But, this one was different.

Here, my repetition-cultivated indifference was overpowered by the pain of violation. Variations of this scene had played out on this very ground far too many times.

When Eldon Porter had come here to kill me…

When Felicity was kidnapped…

When Miranda had left her first calling card…

Just to name a few.

And now, it was happening yet again. While it was almost certain that our home held some sort of morbid record for the most instances as an active crime scene, it was one of those dubious honors I definitely could have done without. As callous as I had become about such things, I could simply never get used to having the horror land directly on my doorstep.

Ben, apparently misunderstanding my daze, offered in a consoling voice, "She's okay, Row. I already told ya' that. Relax."

I remained mute and continued to watch splashes of red and white from the active light bars atop the municipal police cruisers as they flickered across the fronts of my neighbors' houses—and in some instances, my neighbors' faces. Even at well past midnight, some of them were intent on gawking. No big surprise really because I'd seen it before. I would have liked to think there was an element of compassion in the stares, but unfortunately, I knew better. I'd learned way too much about human nature to believe that was true. Besides, empathy definitely didn't fit with the rumors that had been circulating about us around our neighborhood for the past few years.

Ben gave my arm a nudge. "Hey, white man. Did'ja hear what I said? She's fine. Felicity's okay. Stop worryin'."

I finally nodded. "Yeah…I know, Ben. I know. But…I'm not entirely sure that I am."

"What? You gettin' ready ta' zone out on us?" he asked.

"I really don't think so," I replied.

"Okay. So what's wrong?"

"I'm not exactly sure... I mean...it's strange... There's nothing there, Ben. I'm not feeling anything..."

"Ya' mean like physically, or like the la-la land shit?"

"The la-la land," I echoed as I shook my head. "I'm not connecting. It's weird."

"It's prob'ly just 'cause you're wore out, Row."

"Maybe... But that's never made..." Before I could finish the thought, I was interrupted by the uniformed officer returning with the crime scene log.

"Here," he said as he came walking back toward us and offered Ben a clipboard. "You know the drill."

My friend quickly scribbled his information on the page and then handed it to me. "So...you were sayin'?"

"Being exhausted has never affected me like this before." I mimicked my friend's actions and then returned the log to the officer. "Usually it's the opposite."

Ben shrugged. "Yeah, well you're good for a lotta firsts, ya'know. Maybe this is just somethin' new."

"Maybe," I returned. "But whatever it is, something just isn't right."

"Man..." he mumbled as he shook his head. "I hate when you say shit like that. It usually means somethin' bad's about ta' happen, and we're gonna be in the middle of it."

"It's already happening, don't you think?"

"Yeah, but I mean somethin' worse. You're pretty fuckin' good for that darkest before it goes completely black crap too, ya'know." Ben pulled the crime scene tape upward and jerked his head toward the house. "Well c'mon..."

I started to duck under but stopped halfway through and asked, "Where's Constance?"

"She was makin' some calls," he answered, glancing back toward his van then back to me. "Yeah...she's still sittin' there. Looks like she ain't done just yet. She'll prob'ly be along in a bit." As he finished the sentence, he motioned for me to keep moving.

I nodded then continued beneath the tape and started up the driveway with my friend close behind. I was still several yards from the near end of the flagstone walk when the front door of the house opened and a man I recognized to be one of the aforementioned detectives stepped out onto the porch. My wife followed behind him almost immediately.

With the exception of a few stray curls, her fiery auburn hair was pulled back into a ponytail, revealing her pale ivory face. Her expression was hard, and I could see her lips moving as she spoke to the cop, but at this distance I couldn't actually hear what she was saying. The moment I saw her I broke into a jog and yelled out, "Felicity!"

Several people on the scene turned and glanced toward me when I made the abrupt call, but my wife was the only one who mattered. The second she made eye contact she came bounding down the front stairs. Increasing my jog to a brisk run, I met her at the bottom.

"*Damnaigh go saigh...*" She growled the words softly in my ear as she fell into me and looped her arms around my neck. "*Damnaigh a, damnaigh a...*"

Not only was she slipping into Irish Gaelic, her normal background Celtic lilt had thickened noticeably. That was a sure sign she was either tired, angry, or both. Judging from the hour and harshness of the words themselves, my money was on the latter of the three.

"I know," I soothed, slipping my arms about her waist and pulling her close. "I know... I said the same thing when I heard... Are you okay?"

"No," she said, her heavy brogue wrapping itself around a voice sharply edged with sarcasm. "I'm not okay. And I won't be okay until that *ban-àibhistear* is gone forever."

"I understand..."

"I wish you'd just killed her then."

Given our present company, I was glad that our conversation was taking place in close quarters and hushed tones, although I had no doubt we could still be heard.

I replied, "You don't mean that."

"Aye, but I do."

"That wouldn't stop Miranda, honey. You know that."

"Aye..." she sighed heavily. "But this has to end, Rowan... It has to..." Her words were a staunch demand as opposed to a weeping lament.

"It will. It will..."

"Aye, but how?"

I sighed. Right now I was just trying to say the right thing, whether it was true or not. Unfortunately, I simply didn't have a solid answer for her. "We'll figure something out..."

"We'd better soon or I'll just go kill her myself. I swear I will..."

I felt a tap on my shoulder then heard Ben's questioning voice, "Hey… Row?"

"Yeah, Ben?" I replied, turning slightly though still holding tight to my wife.

"I…" he started hesitantly, giving us a careful once over. It was obvious he wasn't sure quite what either of our emotional states might be at the moment, so he was treading lightly. "Look…I hate ta' interrupt ya'… And, listen…Felicity…if ya' still need some time or somethin' I can back off… But…"

Hearing his comment, she immediately loosened her grip and pushed back from me enough so that she could look him in the eye. Shaking her head, she admonished, "Aye, Ben, get your fekking head out of your arse. You know I'm not some whining sap, then. I'm just pissed off."

He huffed out a breath and nodded. "Yeah…s'pose I forgot who I was dealin' with there for a minute… Guess I shoulda figured that out from the accent, huh?"

As usual, my wife retorted, "I don't have an accent. You do."

"Oh yeah, I can see you're just fine," he replied with a slightly relieved tone and then jerked his head toward the illuminated yard. "So, anyway, Row, ya' wanna have a look at this before they haul the body off ta' the morgue?"

I looked over my shoulder then reluctantly let go of Felicity and turned fully toward the horror. The crime scene investigator was still walking her grid-like search pattern around the involved section of the lawn. Thus far, not a single one of the numbered markers had left her hands, which wasn't a big surprise. From all appearances, the dump had been quick, and since the ground was fairly dry, the chances of any collateral evidence such as shoeprints would be slim. Still, it was always a possibility, so they had to go through all the motions just in case.

Allowing my gaze to drift to the center of the tableau, I could see that a death investigator from the county medical examiner's office had recently joined the fray. I didn't think he could have been on-site very long because I hadn't noticed him when we signed in. Of course, at this point there was little for him to do here, save for transport the body, which is something he appeared to be preparing to do. He had a rubberized body bag already spread out nearby, and at the moment, he was engaged in the process of paper-bagging the victim's hands so as to protect any possible evidence.

I continued to watch in silence as the two of them worked independently of one another. Usually by this point on a scene, I would be all but blinded by a preternatural migraine, as the dead would be attempting to use my brain as a stage for an esoteric play. A disjointed horror drama, fraught with hidden messages I would then be forced to decipher. This was my unofficial job—to be a lightning rod and personal translator for tortured spirits with a story to tell. It was what I was used to doing.

But at this particular moment, I wasn't being a very good employee.

All I could sense was a mind-numbing silence filling my skull. The constant din of voices was still squelched for the first time in many years, and in that quiet, it occurred to me that this really was what it was like to be "normal." Then, as I stood there wondering why this was happening, a recent conversation rolled through my tired grey matter.

"Them," she repeated. "The dead. I can make them leave you alone."

At that moment I realized exactly who had control of the ethereal volume knob. Unfortunately, it definitely wasn't me.

Ben gave me a verbal nudge. "Row?"

"I'm sorry," I replied, my voice flat.

"Seriously, Kemosabe…ya' sure you're not goin' *Twilight Zone*?"

I shook my head. "I can't."

"Whaddaya' mean, ya' can't?"

"I mean I can't. Not anymore."

"Are you okay?"

I sighed. "I guess that depends on what you mean by okay."

"Dammit, Row… Don't be difficult. You know what I mean."

"I'm sorry… I'm not trying to be… But…they're gone… I don't think I can help you with this, Ben."

"You still ain't makin' sense. Whaddaya mean gone? They who?"

"The visions… The voices… All of it…"

He shook his head. "No *Twilight Zone*?"

"No," I replied.

"Are you sure?"

"Yes…I'm sure. I can't help you with this, Ben… To be honest, right now I'm not even sure I can help myself…"

CHAPTER 17

STEAM SPEWED FROM THE GAP AROUND THE SMALL filter basket on the half-sized coffeemaker, alternating between light wisps and briefly pressurized jets, as the machine slurped the last of the water from its reservoir with a loud gurgle. Still caught up in a misty haze somewhere between sleep and wakefulness, I watched it with quiet anticipation while standing at the counter and holding an empty ceramic mug cradled in my hand.

The machine heaved a final moist sigh, sending out a cloud of dissipating vapor as it sputtered and then wheezed itself into silence. I gave a languid glance to the side at the small microwave positioned immediately next to it. If the clock on its face was correct, it was pushing 7 a.m. That meant I was already more than an hour off my normal morning schedule. But then, I didn't really have any place to be but here, so I don't suppose it mattered all that much.

"Mmmmm…" my wife murmured sleepily as she padded up and slipped her arms around me from behind then squeezed, pressing herself against my back. Letting out a long sigh, she mumbled, "You're being awfully noisy this morning, you know."

"Sorry…" I told her. "I didn't want to wake you, but I desperately needed coffee, and this thing apparently wasn't built for stealth."

"It's okay, me too," she said. "Is it ready then?"

"Yeah," I grunted. "Finally. You'd think since it only holds two or three cups it'd work a little faster."

I filled the mug I was already holding and then set it to the side in front of the microwave as I said, "There you go."

Knowing she would want to doctor the brew as usual, I pushed a cellophane-wrapped packet of sugar and creamer over next to it. Then I grabbed a fresh cup from the small tray and tossed its packet of the same on top of the first. After inspecting the inside of the empty mug out of habit and finding it clean, I poured some coffee for myself.

Felicity let go of me then stepped over to her cup. She immediately began tearing open the thin plastic wrapper on the drink condiments, biting the sealed edge to get it started then ripping it lengthwise with her nails.

"I should have just had you bring it to me in bed then," she announced with a slight chuckle.

I cocked an eyebrow as I looked at her and said, "That's just one of your regular 'dominant Irish Princess' moods talking, I hope?"

"Aye. It is."

"Good. That I can do."

"Don't worry," she said with a pained softness to her voice. "I'm not her. I'm me…"

"I'm sorry hon. I didn't mean… I just guess I'm a little gun-shy after…"

"I know," she said as my voice trailed off. Her tone was still hushed but now carried with it a note of sympathy. "It's okay. I understand. I probably shouldn't be bringing that sort of thing up right now anyway."

"Don't worry about it. As long as it's you, I'm all good with it."

I gave her shoulder a squeeze then turned and leaned back against the counter and watched as she emptied both powdered creamers and then all four packets of sugar into her cup. Once she finished mixing the concoction she quickly drew the plastic stirrer between her lips and then tossed it onto the counter.

"So, how did you sleep?" she asked before taking a sip of her coffee.

"Okay, I guess," I replied with a shrug. "Not great by any stretch. But then I wasn't expecting to come home just to end up staying in another hotel, so my whole system is a little off I think."

"Aye, I can imagine." She shook her head as she continued, "But Ben was pretty insistent that we not stay at the house, and when you agreed… Well, I just wasn't up to arguing."

"I think that's a first for you, isn't it?" I quipped.

"Very funny," she admonished, but her good humor was betrayed by a slight grin.

I smiled. "Just making an observation. After all, you have to admit that you're pretty stubborn."

"True."

"And, you were wound pretty tight last night too."

"At first, but I think I finally just crashed once you were here."

I nodded. "Yeah. Been down that road."

"Well, in my defense I did make him take the dogs home with him, so they wouldn't be left alone," she countered.

"Yes, you did do that," I agreed. "I wonder how that's working out?"

"I'm sure they're fine."

"I'm not actually worried about them. I'm wondering about him."

"He'll live," she chuckled and then paused before lowering her voice to a more soothing timbre. "I know this wasn't a very good homecoming, Rowan…"

I sighed. "It's not like it's anything all that new, sweetheart…"

"Well, I know it's not exactly a silver lining, but you have to admit, this really is a nice suite we're in."

"Yeah…it is…" I looked around and then added with more than a hint of sarcasm, "It has a really nice price tag too, which is coming out of our pockets."

"It's not like we can't afford it then."

"I know, but that's not the point."

"Aye, I realize that, but at least we're here together."

"True." I smiled then leaned over and kissed her on the forehead before settling back against the counter once again. "So, what about you? How did you sleep in this *nice suite*?"

"Honestly, not all that well."

I took a swig of my java then nodded. "Yeah, I thought that might be the case. I couldn't help but notice you were tossing and turning most of the night."

After a thick pause she almost whispered, "I just couldn't stop thinking about it."

"Yeah…not surprised…" I let out a sigh and then sipped my coffee for a moment. I wasn't sure how to get around talking about what had happened, but I really didn't want to go there. Finally, I offered a generic reply, "Don't worry. Hopefully this will all be over soon."

"Not soon enough," she mumbled.

"I know…but soon."

She gave me a questioning look. "How will you be able to…"

I had a fairly good notion I knew what she was about to ask, so I headed her off. "I wonder how long Ben is going to want us to stay away from the house?"

Felicity cocked her head and stared at me, obviously nonplussed by my overt and unapologetic shift of subject. I could tell by her expression that she was trying to decide how to proceed with the conversation. I just hoped she didn't try to push it back onto her original track.

Finally, she said, "Well…if it's going to be for very long I'll be needing to go by the house for a few more things then. I didn't pack much last night…or should I say, this morning."

"Same here," I agreed.

"And we'll need to get someone to look after the cats," she added. "A day or two is fine, but no longer than that."

"Yeah, true. We could probably get RJ to do that."

"Aye, maybe."

I shrugged and said, "Well, if we end up having to extend our stay, I guess we could just pretend it's a vacation."

"We could," Felicity said, nodding. "And since you mention it…"

Even as she started to speak I remembered our conversation just prior to my leaving for Carswell. With everything that had happened in the past forty-eight hours, it had completely slipped my mind. Until now, that is.

"Yeah… Yeah… I know," I replied, shaking my head. "Vacation… I promised we'd get away and go to Ireland, didn't I?"

"You did…" she said. "And I'm holding you to it…"

It was my own fault. I had managed to shove us directly into this topic with my offhand remark, and unfortunately, it required a response that wasn't as far removed from the current situation as I would have liked. Having no choice, however, I started to appeal. "Felicity, honey, we will, I promise…but I'm not sure it would be a good idea for…"

"Hold on then," she interrupted, shaking her head. "Let me finish. I'll be needing some time to clear my schedule, so it's not like we can leave just yet anyway. But…I did go ahead and reserve our airline tickets for mid July."

I sighed and nodded. "Okay… Good. That'll work. I've got to line up some time off myself. That should give me plenty of time."

"Aye. I thought as much," she said with a nod.

"How long am I taking off?"

"Four weeks."

"Yeah…I think I can probably arrange that. I'll just have to farm some stuff out."

"Me too," she said. "Oh, and I also talked to Austin. He insists we stay with him for at least part of the trip."

"I'm good with that. But, are you really sure you want me hanging out in pubs with your brother?" I gibed.

She shook her head and snorted. "Like it matters. I can drink the both of you under the table and you know it."

"You have a point."

"Of course I do."

"Okay," I said, feeling relieved that we'd managed to veer off the morbid path I'd inadvertently started us down. "So I guess if we're staying here for a bit, we can just call this a pre-vacation warm-up."

Felicity leaned to one side in order to look around and past me. "Aye, well there's a refrigerator behind you. If we're going to pretend, then I'm thinking some *Guinness* is in order. And maybe a bottle of *Black Bush*, and a few other things as well."

"We can do that," I said then drained my cup and turned toward the coffeemaker. "Need some more?" I asked as I took the small carafe in hand and glanced back at her over my shoulder.

"Is there any more sugar?"

I twisted my head back around and looked on the tray where the glasses and mugs were arranged but came up empty.

Looking back at her, I shook my head. "Afraid not."

"We'll have to fix that too," she announced as she held her cup toward me. "Just a little then."

I slowly added some of the hot java to her mug and then emptied the remaining contents of the carafe into my own. Once I'd placed the vessel back onto the base and switched it off, we continued to stand in the kitchenette-like alcove. An awkward quiet welled up between us to fill the room. The vacation talk had apparently played itself out, and that didn't bode well for keeping the subject off last night's events.

I wasn't absolutely certain what my wife was thinking about, but I had a good idea. And I was crystal clear on what was occupying my own brain. Unfortunately, it was a sure bet we were both back on the same page, which is exactly where I didn't want to be. The problem was, I couldn't think of anything else to say that wouldn't just be another obviously heavy-handed attempt at a verbal diversion.

Felicity cleared her throat then took a sip of her coffee, all the while keeping her jade green eyes fixed firmly on my face over the rim of the cup. A few seconds stretched into several and then eventually folded themselves into a minute plus. Finally, she spoke.

"How's your head?" she asked.

Apparently, my assumption was correct, and we were going back to square one. She was just going to take a different approach.

I looked at her and shrugged. "Fine."

"No headache?"

"Nope."

"And nothing else either?"

I kept my mouth shut and simply shook my head.

She regarded me quietly for a moment, waiting for me to expand on the answer. When I didn't, she pressed forward. "So first you changed the subject, now you're playing mute," she began. "Would you mind telling me what we are going to do with this gorilla in the corner? Do we just keep ignoring it then?"

"I take it you mean the voices…" I grumbled. "Or, lack thereof, I guess."

She huffed out an exasperated breath. "Aye, Rowan, for a start. Although we both know there's more you're not saying."

I exhaled heavily myself and then turned up my mug and drained what was left of my now lukewarm coffee. After setting the empty cup aside, I shrugged and said, "I don't think we've really ignored it. We just haven't fed it, so to speak."

"*Cac capaill*," she spat. "Be honest, Row… You're avoiding it like the damn plague and you know it."

I shrugged. "Okay, maybe a little."

"A little?" she yelped.

"All right… Fine… More than a little," I admitted as I pushed off from the counter and walked out into the bedroom area. I knew I couldn't escape, but I didn't want to fight with her, and that's probably where this was heading.

She was right behind me. "And you call me stubborn," she snapped. "What's going on? Why are you avoiding this?"

"Because I don't want to talk about it."

"Well, I think maybe it's time you did."

"What for?"

"Because, obviously it's bothering you."

I turned around and looked at her. "Well hell yes, it's bothering me. Is it not supposed to?"

She stared back and chewed her lower lip for a moment then shrugged and said, "And?"

"And what?" I asked.

She bobbed her head and pressed, "What else then?"

"And it bothers me. What more do you want me to say?"

"Tell me what you're hiding."

"Nothing."

"I know better."

"Well, it's not something for you to worry about," I told her.

"*Cac capaill.* No. I'm not letting you do this. I want you to tell me," she demanded.

"Not happening."

"All right then, if you won't tell me what you're hiding, then tell me why not hearing the voices bothers you so much."

"Because I'm sick of being screwed with by Miranda."

"What else?"

"What do you mean, what else?"

"I mean that's not all. What else?"

"Come on, Felicity," I barked. "I'm pretty sure you already know the answer to that."

"Aye, I do. But you need to say it."

I shook my head at her. "What the hell for?

"So that you can face it."

"Good Gods, honey… Have you been taking psychiatrist lessons from Helen or something?"

"Would you rather talk to her about this? I'm sure she would fit you in today."

"I'm not in a hurry to talk to anyone about it," I snapped and then announced, "Now if you'll excuse me, I'm going to go take a shower."

I made a move to step past her in my bid to seek temporary refuge in the bathroom. However, my wife wasn't going to allow that to happen. She mirrored my movement and placed her hand against my chest to stop me.

"You aren't walking away from me, Rowan," she said.

"I'm not talking about this anymore," I replied, my voice tense.

I began to move again, but she still wouldn't give up. However, instead of simply continuing the argument, she let out a low shriek then launched herself forward and pushed me. Caught completely off-guard, I tried in vain to retreat as her palms struck hard against my chest, but there was no place for me to go. The bed was immediately behind me, and between my clumsy footing and the force she applied, I stumbled. I attempted to sidestep in order to regain my balance, but Felicity angled in and hooked her leg behind mine while continuing to drive forward. I collapsed backward onto the bed, with her on top of me.

In a flash, my fiery, redheaded wife had scrambled upward and was sitting on my stomach with her knees pressing down across my arms right at the elbow. Her hands were gripping tight around my wrists and she was pitched forward, holding me down with everything her petite frame had to give.

Her face was just inches from mine when she snarled, "Damn your eyes, Rowan Linden Gant! Damn your eyes!"

"Dammit, Felicity!" I barked as I struggled. "What the hell?!"

"You're not doing this. You're going to talk to me," she hissed, clamping her thighs tight on my ribcage to keep me from wriggling free.

"Are you enjoying yourself?" I snipped.

She blasted back with a quick retort. "That's not what this is about. Talk to me, *damnú ort*!"

I knew I could probably escape her hold, but it would involve someone getting hurt, and that someone wasn't me. I was also well aware that this was still my wife on top of me, not Miranda using her body, and the last thing I wanted was to injure her. Given the leverage she had, I eventually just gave in and conceded the battle. Felicity, however, didn't release her hold on me, even after I relaxed.

I sighed and simply lay there looking up into her imploring eyes. Finally, I said, "I don't want to talk about this because I'm afraid. There. I said it."

"Aye..." she whispered. "I know. And that's why you have to talk about it. Tell me why."

She definitely wasn't going to give up, but then, I knew better than to believe she would. I'd told her the truth because lying to her would get me nowhere. But, I also hadn't told her all of it, and she obviously knew that. How much of it I could continue to keep a secret remained to be seen.

The hollowness of fear started pooling in my chest as my emotions took over.

"She's blinded me, honey... I can't feel anything..."

"I know..."

"Felicity... If I can't..." I stammered and then stopped as my throat tightened, causing me to choke on the words. Gathering myself, I started again. "If I can't feel her coming then I might not be able to stop her. And if I can't... If I can't stop her then I could lose you."

"You won't," she murmured. "I promise."

"You can't..."

"Sshhhh..." she hushed. "You won't."

I wanted nothing more than to believe her words, but what I had kept secret wouldn't let me. I finally felt her vise-like grip on my ribcage begin to relax as she laid forward and slowly pressed herself against me. Apparently, I'd satisfied enough of her demand for the moment.

Once again I'd told only part of the truth, keeping hidden from her that which was already too painful for me. The image of her wasting away in that cold vision was something I felt I simply could not allow her to know.

When she released my arms I slid them around her and held tight. I'm certain we would have stayed in that position for the rest of the day had the room phone not begun to ring less than five minutes later.

"Do we have to answer it then?" Felicity asked.

"No," I said, hugging her close.

The peal of the phone stopped after the fourth ring. Half a minute later, my cell phone began to rattle and warble out the *William Tell Overture* as it vibrated across the surface of the desk on the other side of the room.

My wife issued a resigned sigh. "It must be Ben…"

"Yeah," I agreed. "That's his ring tone."

"You'd best answer it then."

"I know…" I sighed. "I know."

We disentangled ourselves, and I slowly sat up on the edge of the bed. My cell had already sent the call to voicemail and fallen into silence. Before I could stand up, however, the room phone began to ring once again. I shifted left then reached across Felicity's legs and snatched the handset from the cradle.

"Hello," I said.

"Ever hear of answerin' your phone?" Ben replied to the greeting.

"Sorry, I was busy."

"You two ain't…well gettin'…ya'know…"

"No, Ben, we aren't," I said.

Under different circumstances, I would have replied with something suitably risqué in order to razz him about his characteristic attack of modesty wherever sex was concerned. But, right now I didn't feel all that amused.

"Well, are ya' dressed?" he asked.

"Not yet, why?"

"'Cause ya' got about an hour, and then I'm gonna be in the lobby waitin' for ya'," he replied. "Both of ya'."

"Why?"

"We got a bad guy ta' find."

"Ben, I already told you I'm not…"

I didn't get a chance to finish my objection because he spoke right over the top of me, "Meet me in the lobby. See ya' in sixty."

At the end of the sentence, there was a dull click followed by a hollow silence. I realized he had simply hung up in order to cut me off.

I sighed heavily then settled the handset back into the cradle. Then I gently patted my wife on the back of her calf.

“What’s the story?” Felicity asked.

“We need to get cleaned up,” I told her. “I’m afraid the gorilla’s keeper will be here in just a bit.”

CHAPTER 18

FELICITY AND I WERE BACKED INTO A CORNER ON THE crowed elevator. Apparently, everyone staying in the hotel had a meeting at the same time this morning, or so it seemed. We pressed ourselves farther into the wall as the car stopped at each successive floor on the way down. We gained more passengers on the first three stops, but after that, it was simply an exercise in waiting since the elevator was full.

Eventually, we reached the lobby, and the crush of suits in front of us began to filter outward. By the time they'd cleared and we were able to exit, the doors were already sliding shut. Felicity made it through unscathed, but since it was an older model elevator, I ended up purposely shouldering the mechanical safety edge and sent the sliding panels into a hasty retreat so that I could follow.

"He's over there," my wife announced, pointing across the expanse of marble tile and expensive looking area rugs.

Ben was lounged in one of the sitting area chairs near the center of the lobby, his attention focused on a folded newspaper in his hands. We walked toward him then skirted around the sofa just opposite where he was seated.

As we drew closer I announced, "I'd say good morning, but it hasn't really started out that way."

Our friend looked up from the newsprint then tossed it on the large coffee table and stood. "What the hell kept ya'? I've been waitin' down here for fifteen minutes, and some jackass took the comic section, so I got stuck readin' about how bad my 401k is tankin'."

I glanced at my watch and shook my head. "You said an hour, Ben. It's only been about forty-five minutes. Maybe fifty. Besides, you're not one to talk. I tried calling you back four times after you hung up on me, and you didn't even bother to answer."

"Yeah, well I was kinda busy," he snorted, repeating back to me the excuse I'd given him earlier. He then addressed himself to Felicity with one of his typical baiting remarks. "So what's the deal, Firehair? You runnin' a bit long with all the girly stuff this mornin'?"

Not being any more in the mood for his joviality than me, she muttered, "*Póg mo thóin*, Ben."

"Okay," he shot back with a nod and a grin. "Bare it an' share it, Irish."

My wife instantly raised an eyebrow and regarded him with a quiet stare, a slightly surprised mask plastered across her delicate ivory features.

"Yeah," he said, a self-assured cockiness in his voice. "Didn't think I knew what that meant, did'ja? See there? I'm catchin' on."

"Aye, are you really then?" she puffed, annoyance clearly evident in her voice. "*Go bpléasca scata Fomhórach ólta do bhall fearga.*"

She cocked her head and smirked as she stared at him. The grin faded from Ben's face while he stared back at her silently for a few seconds, apparently waiting for her to clarify. When she remained mute he finally turned his questioning gaze in my direction.

"Don't look at me," I replied while giving my head a shake. "I've never heard that one, so I couldn't begin to translate. Besides, you started it."

"Yeah, whatever," he grunted, shaking his head. "Just tryin' ta' lighten the mood a bit, ya'know."

"Sorry, but it's not working," I told him. "Not today, anyway."

"Yeah, no shit, I kinda noticed. So, anyway, you two ready ta' roll?"

"Hold on just a second; ready for what?" I said, gesturing for him to wait. "I already explained that I'm no good to you on this one. The visions are gone." I pointed my index finger and double-tapped myself in the middle of my forehead with it for effect. "There's nothing but dead air, Ben. Nada."

"So's that make ya' an airhead?"

"Dammit, I'm serious," I growled.

"Jeezus, lighten up, Row. I know ya' get kinda hard ta' deal with whenever you're workin' a case, but damn…"

"I'm sorry, Ben, but I'm just not in the mood to joke around. And, I'm not working this case."

"Yeah…okay, whatever."

"I'm serious."

"Then why didn't ya' just stay in your room?" he asked.

"Because you wouldn't answer your goddamned phone. Otherwise I would have told you exactly what I'm telling you now."

He shrugged. "Okay, well since you're already here, might as well give it a go anyway…"

"What? Are you not listening? Exactly what is it you want from me?" I asked.

"The usual. Your help on the case."

"Okay, I'm asking you again... Did you not hear what I just said? The visions disappeared last night, and that hasn't miraculously changed in the past eight hours." I raised my volume a notch and stressed the enunciation of the last four words, " I... Can't... Help... You."

He nodded. "I ain't deaf, Row. I ain't a moron either. I just talk like one to throw people off. Listen, I get what you're sayin'. But you want this bitch stopped, right?"

"Of course," I returned, a fresh wisp of incredulity woven through my voice. "What the hell kind of question is that?"

"It's the kinda question I ask ta' get your attention whenever you're rampin' up ta' be an asshole," he replied with a slightly harsher edge. "Zactly like you're doin' right now for instance. Now, if you wanna play Mister Serious, okay, I can do that, so listen up. Whether the *Twilight Zone* thing is workin' for ya' right now or not doesn't matter. I don't give a shit about that." He wagged his finger back and forth between Felicity and me. "Simple fact is the two of ya' know more about Miranda and how she does whatever the hell it is she does than anyone else around. Plain and simple. And, right now, the MCS needs that input from you. End of story. Got me?"

"Okay, fine. But I'm telling you up front, I really don't think I'm up to this, Ben."

He huffed out an annoyed sigh then shook his head and stared at me for a moment. Finally, he splayed out his hands in mock surrender and asked, "What the hell's goin' on with you, Row?"

"Do you really have to ask?" I snapped.

"Yeah," he replied. "'Cause I just don't get it. You sure as hell ain't actin' like the Rowan Gant I used ta' know."

"Well, think about what I've been through, then ask yourself what's wrong with me."

"Yeah, look, you think I don't know what you've had ta' deal with? I realize you're a victim here, trust me, nobody's disputin' that fact. But I also know that ain't somethin' new where you're concerned. And I gotta be honest, I've never seen ya' play the 'pity me' part. Up till now, that is."

"Maybe I've just finally had enough."

He nodded. "Okay, I'll buy that. I've heard ya' say it before, but fine, maybe you're for real this time, so I'll go along with ya'. We all get burned out, and I'm not surprised if you really are. Hell, I've been worried about ya' more'n once. You know that.

"But, guess what? This ain't over, and you ain't off the clock yet. At least not until this one's done. You can't walk away from it, and you know that as well as I do."

"Dammit, Ben."

"Go ahead and damn me all ya' want if it makes ya' happy. But we need ya' on this. Felicity needs ya' on this. Hell, you need you on this."

"Okay, fine," I conceded. "But I'm still not sure how much good I can do."

"Like I said, you know how Miranda works. Besides, you're the only one who's broken, ain't ya?" He turned his gaze toward Felicity and said, "I mean, I know you ain't quite as tuned in as Row, you still got the whole woo-woo thing happenin', right Firehair?"

"No way!" I spat before she could answer him. I hadn't exactly been keeping my voice down during this conversation, but now it rose in volume by several notches. "Dammit, Ben, no friggin' way. I said I'd help you, but you aren't dragging Felicity into this, do you understand me?! I won't allow it!"

"I beg your pardon?" my wife interjected. Her comment was clearly aimed at me, but I was focused on Ben and all but ignored it.

"Excuse me," a new and unfamiliar voice sharply insinuated itself into our conversation.

I looked toward it and found a middle-aged woman in a neatly pressed business suit glaring at us. Based on where she was standing, she had likely approached from the side that was partially obscured by a row of large potted plants. Her gold nametag identified her as the front desk manager.

"We bein' too loud?" Ben grunted.

She nodded. "You could say that. Are all of you guests here at the hotel?"

"They are," Ben said, waving his finger at us. Then he withdrew his badge case and flipped it open to display his credentials. "I'm just their ride."

She glanced at Felicity and me with an air of quickly rising suspicion as she noticeably took a step back from us. Returning her gaze to Ben she asked, "Is there a problem, officer…"

"Storm. Detective Storm," he answered, sliding the case back into his pocket. "No. No problem, really. Just a discussion that got a bit outta hand is all. Sorry 'bout that."

"I see," she replied with a nod then carefully choosing her words said, "Well, if I could ask that you either tone it down a bit or take the discussion elsewhere, I'm sure our other guests would appreciate it."

He nodded. "Yeah. We can do that. Sorry again."

As she walked away, my friend turned back to me with a frown then clamped a large hand on my shoulder and leaned in while pulling me a bit closer. In a low tone he said, "See what I mean about you rampin' up to asshole intensity? Now, number one, calm your ass down before the hotel kicks you outta here. Number two, I hate ta' tell ya' this, Row, but I ain't draggin' Felicity anywhere. In case you've forgotten, whether ya' like it or not, she's already in this shit just as deep as you. Maybe even deeper."

"Aye, he's right, Rowan," Felicity said. "I am."

"That's different," I objected, although much less boisterously than before.

"Only in your eyes, because as usual, you're trying to protect me," she replied. "Besides, I'm the one she's after. And there's something else you may have forgotten… What I do is ultimately my decision, not yours."

"Dammit, Felicity," I grumbled.

"You know I'm right," she said, softening her voice to a soothing tone. Still, the stern intent was there, and I knew I'd best give in.

I was only two hours into my day, and already it wasn't favoring me in the least. I huffed out a heavy sigh and told her, "Yes, you are. But that doesn't mean I have to like it."

"Aye, that's true. No more than I like it when you do the same to me then."

On that point, I couldn't even begin to argue. Over the years I'd seesawed between embracing my curse and trying to ignore it completely. The attempts to deny it never lasted long, and when all was said and done, I would put myself right into the middle of the strife, no matter what anyone else said. Unfortunately, it didn't always end well, and Felicity was the one charged with picking up the pieces and putting me back together. I fully realized that task exacted its own kind of toll; still, that didn't mean I wanted her to trade places with me.

But, now that I'd finally come to terms with accepting my unwanted abilities as an ever-present part of my life, they had been unceremoniously taken away. Since I had no real inkling of exactly how Miranda had done this to me, I was at a loss as to how to circumvent or change it, which left me standing on unfamiliar ground.

Never in my wildest dreams did I imagine that I would find myself silently begging the universe to re-open a door I'd been trying to shut for what seemed like a huge slice of forever. And in keeping with the status quo, today was no different than all of those before it because my pleas were apparently still falling upon deaf ears.

The decision was being made for me, against my will and without opportunity for appeal. If we were going to stop Miranda, then I needed to let Felicity take the lead, and that wasn't going to be an easy task for me. Especially given what I'd been forced to see.

"So…" Ben said. "We good here?"

"No," I mumbled. "No, we aren't."

"Rowan…" Felicity appealed.

I sighed, "Yeah, honey, I know… I don't guess I have any choice, do I?"

"Aye, you're right. You don't."

"Fine…but we go at it with our eyes open. No taking unnecessary risks."

She shook her head and gave me a mocking chuckle. "In other words, don't be like you then?"

"Yeah…" I agreed. "Don't be like me."

We fell quiet for a moment then Ben glanced back and forth between us and interjected. "Okay, are we all good *now*?"

I nodded. "Yeah. Let's give it a try, I guess."

I heard myself saying the words, but in my heart and soul I wasn't comfortable with them at all. Before the last syllable faded, I was already regretting the decision.

"That's more like it," my friend said.

"All right then, so where do we start?" Felicity asked.

"Breakfast," he replied. "That's actually the reason I got down here early."

"Okay, and after that?" she pressed.

"After that we head ta' the county medical examiner's office and make nuisances or ourselves."

Felicity shook her head and commented, "And you want to eat breakfast first?"

"Yeah. I'm hungry," Ben replied then jerked his thumb toward an archway leading off from the lobby. "Wanna go ahead an' grab somethin' in the restaurant since we're already here?"

I glanced down the short corridor then turned back to him and shook my head. "I didn't exactly have a good dining experience at the last hotel restaurant where I ate. How about we try somewhere else."

"Your call." He shrugged then ushered us ahead of him toward the door. "We could hit a pancake house or somethin' on the way, long as it's quick."

"Are we in a hurry now?" I asked.

"A little. Ya' kinda hafta get there at the right time, if ya' know what I mean," he replied.

I sighed. "We don't actually have an appointment, do we?"

"Relax. I got it covered. We just need ta' make a coupl'a quick stops before we get there and it'll all be good."

"Oh, by the way, I meant to ask," Felicity said. "How are the dogs doing?"

"Okay, I guess." Ben gave her a sarcastic grunt. "The big one seems fine, but I don't think the other one likes me."

"Quigley? What's wrong?" she pressed.

"Little bastard stole my towel and tore it ta' shreds while I was in the shower this mornin'."

CHAPTER 19

"WHEN WE GO INSIDE, JUST HANG LOOSE AND LET ME handle it," Ben told us as we climbed out of his van in front of the squat brown building on Helen Avenue. He elbowed his door shut then came around the front of the vehicle and waited for us, adding, "There's kind of a process I gotta go through ta' get things rollin'."

Timing what it was, breakfast itself had ended up being rushed, tasteless, fast food eaten while on the way to our next stop. Of course, given that an autopsy suite containing a dead body was our intended destination, we probably didn't need to have too much sitting on our stomachs right now anyway. Although, I'm not sure our greasy selection was going to be much better in the long run.

As he'd mentioned earlier, upon drawing closer to the county medical examiner's office, we made a pair of side trips into some nearby drive-thrus. Between them, Ben shelled out more than twice as much as he'd spent on his earlier meal.

I levered the sliding side door of the Chevy closed and then followed Felicity up onto the sidewalk where Ben was waiting. I gestured at the items in my friend's hands and said, "By process, I take it you mean bribe, right?"

"Not a real good word ta' use around coppers, white man," he grunted while shaking his head.

Since Ben was taking the lead, I held open the entry door while he and Felicity filed through and then followed behind them into the lobby area. Once inside I sidled up next to my wife and glanced around, but we both remained mute just as we'd been instructed to do.

Behind the low counter in front of us was seated a woman who looked to be in her late forties to early fifties. She was dressed in scrubs and wore her dark brown hair in a short but stylish bob. As the door was closing behind us, she looked up, her expression blank; then without uttering a word she returned to her work.

"Krystal not in today?" Ben asked.

"She's running late," the woman said without looking up.

"Ahh," my friend muttered then announced, "Well…don't guess it matters really. This is actually for you anyway." He placed the large cup he was carrying onto the surface of the counter in front of her. It was wrapped in a heat resistant sleeve that bore a logo made up of an anthropomorphized coffee bean depicted leaning against a trio of interlocking J's. Beneath it were the words, Jenna's Java Joint. The actual contents of the vessel made up more than half the money he'd spent a few minutes earlier. He waited the better part of a minute for a response, but when none was forthcoming he added, "Dull-duh-somethin'-somethin' coffee."

The woman on the other side still didn't look up. She simply kept pushing an ink pen across a form she had in front of her on the lower portion of the desk. As she continued to write, she replied, "Dulce de Leche Latte, Detective Storm. Dulce de Leche."

"Yeah, that," Ben grunted.

"I know you know how to say it."

"Yeah, but it's more fun this way."

"For you it seems," she acknowledged and then asked, "Large I presume?"

"Biggest one they'd sell me, yeah."

"Whole milk, of course?"

"Uh-huh. And an extra shot of the duh-letchee stuff."

"*Day Lay-chay*."

"I thought that's what I just said."

She sighed and shook her head but still didn't break her gaze from the task before her. A moment later she held out her free hand, fingers and thumb crooked in a semicircle as if she was already grasping the cup. Ben took the cue, picked up the drink and pushed it into her waiting grip. She carefully withdrew the appendage, took a tentative sip of the latte and then let out a small sigh as she curled her hand in and cradled the cup against her shoulder. She still didn't look up at us. Instead, she shifted down to the next line on the form and continued writing. As she scribbled, she held her head tilted slightly and peered at her work through rectangular reading glasses that were perched low on the bridge of her nose. Her lips moved slightly, though no words were uttered, as she appeared to mouth the sentences she was putting onto the page.

I looked at Ben and gave him a quick nudge. When he turned to me, I shot him a questioning raise of my eyebrow. He simply furrowed his own brow and shook his head then turned back to her and continued to patiently wait. After a good three to four minutes had expired, the woman took another sip of the drink then laid her pen aside and looked up at him.

"Do you know what would go just perfectly with this?" she asked.

Ben lifted his arm and placed a small, white paper bag on the counter where the coffee cup had been. The side visible to me bore several translucent, greasy blotches where the contents came into contact with it.

"If I had ta' guess, I'd say a fresh apple fritter, right outta the fryer, from Airway Donuts down the street," Ben replied. "But like I said. I'm just guessin'. Oh, and ya' might wanna be careful. I think it's still kinda hot."

The woman shook her head and smiled. "I know I've asked this before, but please explain something to me, Detective Storm. How is it that you, a city cop with whom I've only had dealings a handful of times, knows exactly what it takes to brighten my morning, when your counterparts here in the county who have to work with me on an almost daily basis don't have the vaguest notion?"

"'Cause I'm a hell of lot better detective than them," he replied with a grin.

"I see," she said, rolling her eyes. "If I recall correctly, that's what you told me the last time. And the time before that."

"Yeah, prob'ly," he added with a shrug. "Lookin' for a different answer, are ya'?"

"Is there one?"

"Between you and me, yeah. Just so happens I was pretty tight with Carl Deckert."

"Ahh, finally the truth comes out," she said with a nod at the mention of the former county homicide detective. "I guess I should have known. Although, he always brought me a cherry-cheese Danish with my latte."

"Yeah, I know. But I overheard ya' talkin' one day when you were all excited about gettin' one of the apple fritters they'd just pulled."

"And you remembered that?" She chuckled. "So you really are a good detective."

"That's the rumor, but don't spread it around. It'll blow my cover."

"Carl Deckert was a good man," she offered sadly. "I hated when he retired, and I was very sorry to hear he had passed."

"Yeah, me too. He was a hell of a copper," Ben agreed with a solemn nod.

"Too bad the other county detectives didn't learn from him the way you did," she added.

"Yeah, well if it's any consolation, Doc Sanders down in the city isn't exactly my biggest fan. I think she's immune to my charms if ya' know what I mean."

"Hard to believe," she replied. "Of course, Christine isn't easy to charm. But then, neither am I." She took another sip of the latte.

"Nahh," Ben said. "You're plenty easy. You just ain't cheap."

"I'll remember you said that," she quipped and then focused on me. "All right then, don't be rude, Detective. Introduce your friends."

"Doctor Audrey Kingston, Chief Medical Examiner for Saint Louis County," Ben said while gesturing back and forth between her and us. "Rowan Gant and Felicity O'Brien... Rowan an' Felicity, Doc Kingston."

I nodded and said, "Nice to meet you."

Felicity did the same.

Ben had already focused his attention back on the doctor and offered, "Row is a..."

"You're the Witch," she said, interrupting him as she directed herself at me. "I've heard quite a bit about you."

"Yeah, I get that a lot," I said with a pained smile.

She nodded. "I'm sure you do. The newspapers and television seem to take great delight in your exploits." She shifted her nod toward Felicity. "Both of you."

"Yes, they do at that... But, they also have a tendency to blow things out of proportion," I offered. "So, don't believe everything you hear."

I felt odd making the comment. The very idea of stories about me being exaggerated was really a matter of perspective. The media definitely leaned toward sensationalizing everything where I was involved, but that was something I'd learned to live with. The fact that they'd almost tried and convicted Felicity on the airwaves and in newsprint was a different story. However, that was only one side of the coin. There were many things that actually did happen and, moreover, were vastly more shocking than even the media had managed to distort thus far. Fortunately, those particular events had remained out of the public eye for the time being, and if we were lucky, they always would.

Doctor Kingston nodded at me and parroted the complete maxim, "I believe that's actually *anything* you hear... As well as, anything you read, and only half of what you see."

"Exactly."

She smiled and looked back to Ben. "So…since you arrived bearing gifts, I assume this isn't a social call. What is it you need from me, Detective Storm?"

"Should be easy," my friend answered. "Your people brought in a body early this mornin', and we kinda need ta' have a look at it."

She shot Felicity and me a sympathetic frown. "I'm sorry. Is this an identification? Are you the next of kin?"

"No, actually," I replied, shaking my head.

"Homicide investigation," Ben explained, waving toward us. "They're consulting on it for the MCS."

"Ahh, then it must be something unusual."

"You could say that," he agreed.

"Well, if the body just came in early this morning, then we won't have even started the post, so I don't have any results for you."

"Yeah, I know," he replied. "That's not really what we're here for."

"I see. So then exactly what is it you would be here for?" she asked.

He shrugged and gave her a half nod, "That part's a little complicated, Doc."

"I thought you said this should be easy?"

"It mostly is."

She peered over the top rim of her glasses at Felicity and then me. "So is something I've heard but I'm not supposed to believe what makes this so complicated, Mister Gant?"

I nodded. "That about covers it."

She shot Ben a slightly bothered look then rolled her chair a few feet to the right and absently remarked, "Well, if the body came in early this morning, then the paperwork should be right over here on…" Her voice trailed off for a moment, then she lifted a clipboard from the top of the neatly arranged stack. She pushed her glasses farther up on the bridge of her nose then read aloud, "Doe, John… Caucasian, approximate age early twenties… Found nude in a front yard in Briarwood…"

"That'd be the one," Ben told her.

She scanned the rest of the page in silence then lifted it and looked over the one beneath. Finally she said, "It looks as though the death investigator is finished and any external evidence has been collected…" She paused, frowned, and then said, "That's interesting…"

"What's that?" Ben asked.

"Possible cause of death acute hypovolemia, but no blood found at the scene."

"Yeah…" Ben grunted. "It was a dump. We got another stiff just like 'im in the cooler downtown too."

"Really? Same apparent C.O.D. and circumstances?"

"Yeah."

She nodded, muttered, "Interesting," and then went back to scanning the pages. We stood there in silence while she continued to read. Eventually she arched an eyebrow and said, "Hmmm."

Ben pressed, "And *hmmm* means?"

"Another layer to your complication, Detective," she replied. After a brief pause, she looked up at me. "Among the evidence recovered was one of your business cards, Mister Gant. Apparently it was lodged in the victim's mouth."

Given that the first victim had been tagged with Felicity's business card, I can't say that this bit of news surprised me all that much. However, the fact that it was my card and not hers was definitely somewhat unexpected.

"Great," I mumbled.

"And," she continued, glancing briefly back at the page. "According to this, it seems that 'welcome home little man' was written on the back of it. Does that mean something to you?"

"Unfortunately, yes. I'm afraid it does."

Doctor Kingston lowered the clipboard then pushed her glasses back down to the end of her nose and stared at all of us expectantly. "And you say you have another body downtown, Detective?"

"Yeah Doc, it's a serial."

"And the business card?"

Felicity piped up, "That time it was mine, actually."

"Like I said, Doc," Ben told her. "Complicated."

"I'm not entirely certain that's a strong enough word, Detective," she replied.

"Yeah…" he agreed. "You got a better one?"

"Not one that I wish to use in mixed company."

Ben nodded. "Uh-huh. That was my first choice, actually."

"From you, I'm not surprised."

"Sorry I'm late, Doctor Kingston," a new voice joined the conversation as a harried young woman juggling her purse and a lunch tote shot past us. "Traffic on one-seventy was horrible this morning."

"That's okay, Krystal," the doctor replied. "But now that you're here, I have some things to take care of in the back."

"Okay," she replied as she tucked her belongings beneath the counter. Glancing at us, she smiled and said, "Good morning."

"It's been quiet so far," Kingston told the receptionist as she vacated her chair. "But do me a favor and hold my calls for the next hour or so, okay?" She shot us a quick glance and added, "I have a feeling I'm going to be busy for a while."

"No problem."

Still clutching the latte, the doctor re-addressed herself to Ben as she snatched the pastry-filled bag from the countertop. Giving her head an animated nod toward the doorway where the receptionist had gone through to slip around behind the counter, she said, "Why don't the three of you come back here and try to un-complicate this situation for me." Holding up the bag while she turned, she added, "And fair warning. I'm eating this while I listen, and I don't share my apple fritter with anybody."

WE WERE GATHERED IN DOCTOR KINGSTON'S OFFICE with the door closed. She was seated behind her desk and, as promised, working very hard at making a portion of the huge pastry Ben had supplied to her disappear. Felicity and I were on the opposite side of the workspace, parked next to one another in a pair of moderately comfortable but still patently institutional-style chairs. Ben, on the other hand, was standing off to one side, in a not-quite-relaxed posture, with his back firmly against the wall so that he could see the entire room, including the door.

My friend had taken up his usual sentry-like position once the rest of us had settled in. He did this most everywhere, but I especially noticed it whenever he was at a morgue. I'd once asked him about the peculiar habit, and he had simply grinned and said, "Don'tcha ever watch zombie movies, white man?"

I knew the answer was intended as a joke; or at least, I assumed it was. Still, I suppose I couldn't really blame him if it wasn't. After all, his unofficial partner was a Witch who talks to the dead—or used to, anyway. In his mind, I doubt zombies were much of a stretch.

"All right, Detective Storm, let's hear it," Kingston said, focusing her attention squarely on him as she swiveled her chair his direction then leaned back with a piece of apple fritter between her fingers.

"Like I said," Ben replied, executing a one-shouldered shrug in the process. "We just need ta' have a look at the body."

She nodded. "Okay. Why?"

"Part of the ongoing investigation."

"Detective, I think we can all agree that's fairly obvious. After all, it's what we do," she replied. "And before we waste any more time, you've already told me that it's complicated, so let's not go there again. How about something new and different that I don't already know?"

Her demeanor was serious but didn't seem particularly adversarial. At least things were starting off better than I'd seen them go during some of our visits with her city counterpart.

"Come on, Doc..." Ben groaned. "I'm just tryin' ta' do my job."

"That makes two of us."

"So let's make it easy," he said. "Give us ten minutes. Fifteen tops, and we're outta your hair."

"Look, Detective, the latte and fritter got you this far, but you're going to have to work for the rest," she explained. "Besides, I'm not saying no. I just want you to bring me up to speed before I allow the three of you to traipse around an autopsy suite. I don't care if it's only for sixty-seconds. My turf, my rules."

"We just want ta' check a coupl'a things against the stiff we have downtown," Ben replied. "That's all."

"Before we've even started the post?" she asked.

"Yeah," he grunted. "See. It's not a big deal."

"If it's not a big deal then it can wait for the preliminary autopsy report, correct?"

Ben muttered, "Aww, Jeez... Doc..."

"You're going to have to try a little harder, Detective."

"Well, technically the fact that I'm workin' a case here should be enough, don'tcha think? It may be your turf, but I'm the one with the shield."

"Oh, I have one too," she replied. "Want to see it?"

Ben shook his head. "Yeah, I know. But mine says COP, not DOC."

"That doesn't really matter."

"This investigation is being run by the MCS."

"I understand that, but since you showed up unannounced, it makes me wonder exactly what's going on."

"Friggin' wunnerful…"

"Well, how about this," she offered. "What do you normally say to Doctor Sanders at the city M.E.'s office in order to get through the door with her?"

"Honestly?" my friend huffed. "I try not ta' say anything 'cause that just starts an argument. We usually sneak in when she's at lunch and then end up gettin' caught anyway."

"Easier to apologize than to ask permission," she observed.

"With her, pretty much."

Doctor Kingston dipped her head and chuckled. "Well, at least you're honest about that."

"Yeah, well I figure she's already told ya' about it at some point, so lyin' ain't gonna help me any."

"You really are a very good detective," she joked.

"Okay, come on, Doc… Are we just wastin' our time here or what? I can get my lieutenant on the phone if that's what you're needin' for us ta' make this happen."

She tore off a small piece of the fritter then popped it into her mouth and chewed thoughtfully. Once she swallowed, she nodded as if agreeing with herself then looked up at him and said, "Okay, so tell me this…when do we get to the part where you tell me about the WitchCraft?"

Ben snorted and splayed out his hands in surrender then looked over at me. "All right, Row. I'm done. You're on."

Problem is, "on" was the last place I wanted to be.

CHAPTER 20

USUALLY, WHENEVER I WOULD FIND MYSELF SITTING IN A morgue, I'd be in a much worse state than I was right now. The pain trying to claw its way out through the side of my skull would be so intense that I'd be wishing for a family-sized bottle of aspirin. And, the voices inside my head would be so loud that I'd want to wash every last one of those pills down with enough alcohol to send myself into a coma.

What's worse, all of that torment would be happening before I had even come face to face with the corpse of the victim I was trying to help. It was all just part of the territory.

But today that simply wasn't the case. For all intents and purposes, outwardly I was just fine. Of course, that determination really was dependent upon your particular point of view. I was certainly stressed, but for a change, the cause behind it was definitely grounded in the here and now, as opposed to the preternatural ether.

The simple fact was that, after all the years of inescapable chatter, the silence filling my head at this very moment was, to say the least, unnerving. Hearing the tortured souls of the dead had become my norm, so their glaring absence was an alien concept as far as I was concerned—especially here, in a place where they normally gathered as if they were attending a morbid party being thrown in their honor.

In a very real way, the unbreakable quiet had taken with it not only their voices but my own identity as well. I was no longer "The Witch" who helped the police. I was just some guy going through the motions and trying to pretend nothing had changed, when in fact, almost the exact opposite was true; nothing was the same. This minor personal epiphany made me realize that when Miranda had said she could make the voices stop, she had not been making an offer for the purpose of bribing or even baiting me; she had been issuing a clear and explicit threat.

And now, obviously, she was making good on it.

However, as bad as this oddly foreign experience seemed to be, it was actually the least of my tortures at the moment. The worst actually had an unseen manifestation, which took the form of a sinking hollowness in the pit of my stomach. But, unlike its ethereal cousins that normally plagued me under circumstances such as these, this one was of my own making. My rampant fear regarding the horrific vision Ariel had guided me through was now fueling my reservations about allowing Felicity to go forward with standing in for me as a conduit. If the added fuel wasn't bad enough, explaining the process to Doctor Kingston was fanning the flames even more. And, quite simply, every last bit of it was starting to make me feel physically ill.

"So let me see if I understand, Mister Gant," the county M.E. said, summing up the explanation I'd just tried to give her. "What you're telling me is that you somehow psychically connect with the immortal soul of the deceased and then proceed to conduct a pseudo-forensic interview about the crime. Correct?"

"Close, but not exactly." I scrunched my face and gave my head a tentative sideways dip. My anxiety was competing with everything else for my undivided attention, not to mention that I was already struggling to explain a nebulous concept to someone who was likely a skeptic. So, getting my point across definitely wasn't coming easy for me this morning. I shrugged and told her, "Something of that sort would be ideal, of course, but I'm afraid it just doesn't happen that way."

"Then how does it happen?"

"Well, you were right about the connection part. But once that's done, I really just turn into an observer. What I see generally doesn't make much sense, but I watch anyway and try to remember whatever I can. Usually that's fairly easy. It's the forgetting that I have problems with. But anyway, I also listen… And then afterwards, when it's over, it all comes down to me trying to shove a bunch of really bizarre puzzle pieces together.

"If it works the way it's supposed to, I pick up enough clues to actually make them fit and form at least a partial picture. And, if I'm lucky, that picture fills in some blanks for the police, which in turn helps solve the crime."

"You make it sound fairly simple."

"Believe me, it isn't. I wish it was."

"So you still get these clues from the spirit of the deceased though, right?"

"Sometimes yes. Other times…well…it's pretty hard to explain, but the victim definitely plays a role in it, yes."

"So you're saying it's a 'had to be there' kind of thing," Doctor Kingston said, boiling down the ambiguity of my answer to a simple phrase. However, her tone didn't sound at all mocking, which was a bit of a surprise given some of my previous experiences, in particular with persons of the scientific ilk.

I nodded. "Yeah, pretty much."

"I see," she replied, leaning back in her chair. A crease formed across her forehead, and it was obvious that she was carefully digesting everything I'd told her thus far. Finally she said, "So what if it doesn't work like it's supposed to?"

"Best case scenario, I just don't get anything," I told her.

"That implies there is also a worst case scenario," she prompted.

I shrugged. "There always is with just about everything, isn't there?"

"Can you give me an example?" Doctor Kingston asked.

Under the circumstances, I really didn't want to start down that path. I was having enough trouble going along with this as it was. Dredging up the things that could go wrong certainly wouldn't help.

I tried to circumvent the question while still reassuring her and at the same time myself. "It's nothing that you would need to be concerned about."

"But what about you?" she pressed.

I lied, not that I expected it to go unnoticed, but I gave it a shot anyway. "Not really."

As expected, she looked at me with something akin to suspicion. "Are you absolutely certain about that?"

"I take it we're coming back around to something you've heard?" I asked.

She acknowledged with a dip of her head. "Yes, I've been privy to a few stories."

I shrugged. She obviously wasn't going to let up, so I had no choice but to address her concern, like it or not. "Then maybe it would be easier for me to answer you if you share what you've heard," I said. "Then I can tell you if it's legitimate or unfounded."

"All right then," she said. "I've been told by an extremely reliable source that while doing this sort of thing you have experienced maladies ranging from violent seizures to an apparent cardiac arrest. Spontaneous hemorrhaging and the sudden appearance of stigmata-like wounds were also mentioned."

I let out a heavy sigh in the wake of the comment. As the memories conjured by it began to overtake my brain, I muttered, "Well, unfortunately, I'm afraid I can't deny any of that."

"So then you can see my concern?" she pressed.

The question didn't register. My attention had already taken a hard right turn and was now well off course, speeding headlong through a darkened tunnel of foreboding. I knew she had said something to me, but since the words didn't connect, I simply grunted what I thought might be an appropriate response. "Yeah…"

"All of those things sound fairly serious to me. So for my own peace of mind, what I really need to know is if they are something that could possibly happen today if I were to allow you to go through with this?"

The question echoed past me as I stared through her at the wall. Again, the words were nothing more than noise rattling in my ears, with no meaning or reason.

The painful memories that were now assaulting me had already been in the back of my mind; they always were. However, I purposely kept them locked away. That tactic seemed to work for the most part, until someone would come along and manage to let them out, that is. Just like was happening right now.

With them now on the loose and running unchecked through the front of my brain, my anxiety received an unwanted boost that felt like it all but stopped my heart. I couldn't keep myself from extrapolating the experiences and applying them to the current situation. Unfortunately, in each of these mental simulations, I was not the subject, Felicity was.

The hole in the pit of my stomach was growing. I could feel it expanding through my gut as the bile churned and gnawed around the edges.

I felt a thump against the back of my leg but ignored it. A moment later it came again, a bit harder. Through my self-imposed fog, I finally realized it was the toe of Felicity's tennis shoe. She hadn't assaulted me with a full-fledged kick, but the force of the second thud told me it wasn't merely an accident either; it was definitely on purpose and meant to get my attention. I slowly glanced over at her and saw that she was staring at me with more than a little concern in her eyes.

"Rowan?" she said. "Are you okay then?"

Doctor Kingston was speaking almost simultaneously. "Mister Gant, is something wrong?"

"I'm… I'm sorry," I stuttered in apology, turning back to her. "Sorry… Just… Ummm… What was the question again?"

She gave me a cautious stare and then paraphrased her earlier query, “Should I be concerned that you might experience some sort of life-threatening reaction if I let you go through with this?”

“Well…” I began with a heavy sigh. “I really don’t think it’s anything to worry about in this case…” I forced myself to say the words, even though I didn’t believe a single one of them myself.

“Are you certain?” she pressed. “No offense intended, but you don’t sound particularly convinced.”

I reached up and rubbed my forehead. The onslaught of images set loose by my unrestrained imagination was still ravaging my brain. And now, the endless loop of the vision depicting my battered and emaciated wife was playing over the top of them in vivid, contrasty hues. The acute distress they caused was consuming me in violent waves, and I could no longer maintain the calm charade.

“Mister Gant?”

“I’m sorry,” I told her, shaking my head. “I just… I just…”

“Is something wrong?” she asked.

“What?” I asked. I understood her words, but anything resembling a coherent response escaped me. I looked over at my wife then over to Ben. They were both staring at me with worried expressions.

“You okay, Kemosabe?” my friend asked. “Somethin’ change all of a sudden? You goin’ *Twilight Zone*?”

Panic set in.

I felt the room starting to close in around me, and my chest tightened as a low hum began pulsing against my eardrums. I glanced quickly between all their faces once again then said, “I’m…I’m sorry. I think…I…I just need to get some air.”

I pushed up from the chair and turned. Then I stumbled around the piece of furniture as I aimed myself at the door. I heard the hollow drone of both Ben and Felicity calling out my name behind me, but I was already putting distance between them and me at an increasingly rapid pace. Less than a half minute later, I was standing in the middle of the parking lot with my eyes closed and the heels of my palms pressed against them while I tried to recapture my breath.

CHAPTER 21

IT WASN'T VERY LONG BEFORE I HEARD A PAIR OF VOICES engaged in a hesitant conversation. They were coming from a point that sounded to be several feet behind me, and both of them were just barely audible over the traffic on the nearby highway. However, they were still clear enough for me to recognize as Ben and Felicity.

I knew, of course, that my sudden rush out of the building couldn't be ignored. So at the very least I'd fully expected my wife to follow after me. The fact that Ben joined her was no big surprise at all. He'd been down this road with me several times himself.

I had only just begun to find my breath, and my heart was still hammering against my ribcage as it threw its frenzied tantrum. The horror projecting inside my skull remained clear and inescapable; it didn't matter whether my eyes were closed or open. I was honestly beginning to wonder if this was all just another part of Miranda's plan to remove me as a threat. To torture me into submission by leaning on the weakness I had so blatantly displayed to her over and over again. It was just like something she would do, and she would enjoy every minute of it.

I sensed someone standing next to me and heard a quick series of shuffling noises, but I didn't open my eyes. I had a good feeling I knew who it was without even looking, and when the light breeze shifted allowing me to catch a hint of familiar perfume, my suspicion was instantly confirmed.

I wasn't actually ready to talk to anyone just yet, even my wife, but I suspected that soon I wasn't going to have much choice in the matter. I suppose I could have simply turned and started walking away, but I realized that I wasn't going to be able to put off the inevitable forever. And running down the road like a madman with a petite redhead in hot pursuit wasn't going to solve anything for either of us.

Still, right now, I needed to think. Unfortunately, what I needed to think about wasn't what kept replaying through my mind.

"I'm sorry, honey…" I finally muttered. "Pretty dramatic exit, huh?"

"Aye, I'd give it a weak five," Felicity answered softly, with an audible shrug in her voice. "Honestly, you were fairly subdued in the drama department."

"I'm glad you're able to joke about it," I said. "Because I'm not."

"I'm sorry…" she said. "Are you okay then?"

"Not really," I admitted.

I could hear her measured breathing as she waited for me to embellish upon the comment. After a long pause she reached out and placed her hand softly against my arm and simply held it there. When I still remained quiet, she elected to probe for a more complete answer. "Headache? Voices?"

"No…" I said. "Gods, if only that's what it was. Then maybe this wouldn't be happening."

"What is it then?"

I paused for a moment and then simply said, "This."

"This?" she asked.

I lowered my hands and opened my eyes. The blurred image of my wife was no more than a foot away, staring back at me with what appeared to be concern and curiosity twisting her face. She gently rubbed her palm against my arm then brought up her other hand and offered me my eyeglasses.

"You dropped these," she told me. "How they didn't end up scratched I'll never know."

"Thanks," I muttered, taking them from her and slipping them onto my face.

Her pale countenance came sharply into focus, wide eyes fixed firmly upon mine. The previously fuzzy expression of inquisitive disquiet creasing her face was now crisp and clear.

She waited a moment and then verbally pushed me once again, "You said 'this.' What did you mean?"

"This," I repeated, shaking my head and gesturing back toward the building. "This place. This situation. You. All of it."

"What about it then?"

I shook my head. "I can't let you do it, Felicity. I just can't."

While she still held concern in her eyes, the curiosity in her face seemed to morph into something resembling slight annoyance. "Aye, Rowan, we just had this conversation. I told you that you cannot make this decision for me. And, we've already discussed…"

"I know," I said, cutting her off. "I know. But, trust me, I have a valid reason."

"All right then, tell me. I'm listening."

"It's not that simple," I objected.

She sighed heavily. "I'm not someone off the street who's

unaware, Rowan. You aren't alone in this. I understand… I believe… Talk to me."

"I know that, honey. But this is…" I let my voice fade as the necessary words hid from me.

"*Caorthann*," she urged. "I'm not blind. I know this has something to do with what you've been keeping from me… The thing you saw in that last vision that you won't say. The thing that's eating away at you."

"Yeah…" I whispered. "It does."

"And that's what I was really after you to tell me this morning," she added.

"I know you were."

"Obviously whatever it is you saw has something to do with me… And whatever that is, it terrifies you."

"It does," I agreed.

"Tell me then."

"Felicity…"

"No…" she interrupted. "No excuses. You told me this morning you were afraid that Miranda would take me away from you. Well, you need to know that I'm afraid too because right now she's taking you away from me…"

I sighed and looked past her for a moment. There was more than mere sentiment in her words. She had a valid point. Miranda was dividing in order to conquer, and I was letting her. I drew in a deep breath then brought my gaze back to meet my wife's and unburdened myself, just as she wanted. "Ariel showed up in that vision."

"You mean Ariel Tanner?" she asked.

I nodded.

"But you haven't connected to her across the veil in years," Felicity continued. "I assumed her spirit had moved on."

"I know, me too," I agreed. "But apparently that isn't the case."

"What did she say then?" Felicity pressed.

"It's not so much what she said," I told her. "It's something that she showed me."

"Something about me, I assume?"

"Yes," I almost whispered. "She showed me you…or, what little is left after Miranda pushes you out of your own body."

"Aye, and that's what has you so troubled?"

"Shouldn't it?" I asked.

"Rowan…" Felicity shook her head as she breathed my name. "You know the future is not set."

"But I also know that the things Ariel showed to me before actually did come to pass."

"Not true," she contended. "They happened, yes, but not exactly as you'd seen. You changed them. Because of the one possible future Ariel showed you, you were able to change the outcome. You saved a little girl's life if you remember."

"I know," I said. "And now I'm trying to save yours."

"By stopping me from doing this," she observed softly.

"Yes."

She stared off to the side for a moment then shook her head and looked back into my eyes. "Aye, but what if you aren't saving me?"

"What do you mean?"

"What if this is exactly what Miranda wants? For you to give in to your fears and keep me from finding a way to stop her."

"I considered that. But what if it's the other way around? What if she's just luring you in? She's the one who's blocking me, Felicity. You know that."

"Aye, I do," she said with a nod. "But we can't know for sure which path to take if all we do is stand here worrying over the outcome."

"Inaction is a path unto itself," I objected.

"A stagnant path with no future," she replied. "I can be just as pseudo-philosophical as you."

"I'm still not excited about the other options."

"But we have to at least choose one."

"I thought I had."

"I said *we*," she replied. "We have to choose it together. If we're wrong, we can always turn back."

"Can you?"

"We have to try."

"That's my point," I objected. "When it comes to this, there is no we. There's just you. I'm as good as blind, Felicity."

She shook her head. "Aye, but I'm not."

"And that's what makes you vulnerable."

"Which is why I need you with me. Blind or not, you can still keep me grounded."

"Need I remind you that the one time you did this, your reaction to channeling a victim was far worse than anything that's ever happened to me?"

She shook her head and quietly snorted. "Rowan…you only say

that because you were on the outside looking in for a change. I've watched far worse happen to you…and cried over it more times than you know."

"Honey…"

"Shhh…" she hushed me as she briefly touched her fingers against my lips. "We have to do this. You know it. She already knows how to find us. We can't hide forever."

"So this is where you draw the line in the sand?"

"Aye."

I sighed. "But, if you're wrong, and you can't turn back?"

"I keep going forward."

"And, if it's a trap?"

She looked away for a second then back into my eyes. "Then you will find a way to come rescue me."

She was correct. If it came to that, I would, no matter what the personal cost. Unfortunately, I couldn't help but hear Ariel's voice in my head saying, *"She's been waiting for you, Rowan. She's been waiting for so very long now…"*

"SORRY ABOUT ALL THAT," I APOLOGIZED.

Ben shook his head. "I'm kinda used to it by now, Row."

"Yeah, I guess you would be, wouldn't you?"

"You feelin' better?" he asked.

"Not really," I told him. "But I've got it under control."

We were still outside, although Felicity and I had moved out of the center of the parking lot and joined our friend up on the sidewalk near his van. The fissure at the bottom of my stomach had been continuing to grow and like an aggressive cancer was even now spreading to the rest of my body. Emptiness welled in my chest, sending its painful hollowness radiating outward. Intellectually, I knew my wife was correct in her belief that we needed to meet the threat head on. Emotionally, however, I was a half step away from being a basket case. At the moment, I just happened to be hiding it fairly well, or so I thought.

Ben gave me a once over and grunted sarcastically, "You've got it under control? Yeah. Right."

"Seriously."

"No offense, white man, but I think I need a second opinion," he said and then turned his attention to Felicity. "Whaddaya think, Firehair, he gonna be okay?"

"He'll be fine then."

"You sure about that?"

"Aye."

"Okay, if you say so." He shook his head and sighed before admitting, "I just dunno, man. Now I'm actually feelin' kinda guilty about pushin' you two into this."

"Don't worry about it," I replied then glanced at Felicity. "You had help."

"Yeah, so?" he grunted. "That somehow s'posed ta' make me feel okay about it?"

"It doesn't really matter, Ben. You know that eventually I would have ended up in the middle of it anyway, no matter how much I objected."

He nodded. "Yeah, prob'ly."

A thick pause fell between the three of us. I could tell Ben was thinking about something, so I was expecting him to start massaging his own neck at any moment.

"So…" I spoke after several heartbeats. "How bad did I screw things up with Doctor Kingston?"

Ben grunted out a relieved half chuckle. "Believe it or not, ya' didn't. Apparently she's heard enough stories about ya' through the grapevine ta' think this is just normal for you."

"Terrific," I said with a thin grimace. "Not exactly the reputation I was trying to foster."

"Yeah, well, I guess it could be worse."

"I suppose you're right about that."

Ben fell quiet again then looked at the ground and reached up to smooth back his hair, just as I'd expected. Allowing his hand to slide downward it came to rest on the back of his neck, and he began working his fingers against it in a slow massage.

"What is it, Ben?" I asked.

"That obvious?"

"It always is."

"Yeah, great… So listen, I got a call from Constance while you two were over there talkin'."

"Something wrong?"

"Depends on how ya' look at it, I guess," he replied, allowing his hand to drop back to his side. “Apparently she got a call from someone at the prison down in Texas this mornin’. Seems Miranda had a message for ya’.”

“Gods, Ben, not another victim already…” I sighed.

“Not yet,” he told me. “This one was a question, and it’s strictly verbal.”

“Well at least there’s that.” I drew in a deep breath and gave him a nod. “Go ahead. What’s she want?”

“She wanted ta’ know if you were ‘enjoyin’ your quiet time.’”

“Not as much as I thought I would.”

“Yeah…I figured that’d be the answer… So you ready ta’ go back in? The doc’s waitin’…”

CHAPTER 22

AS AUTOPSY SUITES GO, THIS ONE DIDN'T SEEM ALL THAT different from any other I'd been in over the years. A quick glance around showed me that it was laid out a bit differently, but then that was to be expected. They all were. In the end, it was still a cold room with a tiled floor, tiled walls, and an overabundance of stainless steel making up the decor. The centerpiece of it all was, of course, the pedestal table with a built-in sink at the end.

"Will this suffice?" Doctor Kingston asked, sweeping her arm around the room.

"I don't see why not," I said with a shrug. "All we really need is privacy. And hopefully this won't take long."

It struck me as odd how open and receptive Doctor Kingston seemed regarding this entire exercise. I certainly didn't get the impression that she was ready to embrace it as science, but one could tell simply by her tone and actions that her curiosity was more than just a little piqued by it all. Even after my momentary lapse, her inquisitiveness showed little sign of tapering off. If anything, it was becoming more intense.

"Privacy isn't a problem," she replied. "Now, before I bring in the body, just so I understand, how is it you're going to go about doing this?"

"Nothing radical. It usually involves close proximity to the deceased—and maybe limited physical contact, though not always." I shrugged. "After that it pretty much either happens or it doesn't."

"That's it?" she replied. "You don't need to burn any incense or light candles or draw pentagrams on the floor or anything like that?"

"Is that one of those stories you heard?"

"No, actually."

I cast her a skewed glance for a moment then pressed, "Okay…then I have to ask. Cable psuedo-documentary or a bad horror movie?"

She cracked a lopsided smile. "A little of both, I guess. And a lot of reading."

"Well, there won't be any of that nonsense, so you don't have to worry there," I replied. "At most we might walk in a circle initially while invoking protection, and we usually have salt on hand…" As I allowed my voice to fade, I glanced over at Felicity. "But in all honesty, that's not really for me to say. I guess that's actually your call this time, hon. This one is really your show, not mine."

"Aye, I suppose it is then," my wife replied.

Doctor Kingston shot me a confused look. "I was always under the impression you were the one who did this, Mister Gant."

"Usually, I am," I replied. "However, there are some extenuating circumstances in this case."

"Anything I should know?"

"Not really," I told her, shaking my head. "But, don't worry. Felicity is a Witch too."

"That's fine," she said.

Felicity chimed in. "Like Rowan was saying, there's no need for theatrics. I have some salt for protection. Other than maybe sprinkling a bit of it on your floor, we shouldn't be leaving a mess."

"Okay then," the doctor said. "Sounds reasonable. Just one last question…" Her voice was tempered with something that oddly enough sounded like a note of excitement. "Would it affect you adversely if I turned on the recorders in here?"

Since I couldn't be absolutely certain what it was I had detected in her tone, plus given the earlier questions about risk, I cocked my head and gave her a questioning stare. "C.Y.A., Doctor Kingston?"

"No, actually," she replied. "Personal research."

"Research?" Felicity asked.

"Yes. Just something for my own edification."

I raised an eyebrow. "So apparently you don't think we're insane like most everyone else does."

She shook her head and chuckled, "Well, you might be for all I know. But you certainly have a reputation among law enforcement."

"Yes, unfortunately," I replied.

"I suppose that came out wrong. I'm actually talking about the good reputation," she explained. "Besides, I have an admission to make. I've always had a bit of a fascination with the occult."

"Which would explain the reading you mentioned earlier," I said.

"Exactly," she agreed. "To be honest, I'm actually a little disappointed that there isn't any more to all of this than what you've told me."

"I'm afraid it's rather unremarkable, for the most part," Felicity told her. "But I'll be happy to make use of a broom if it would enhance the experience for you."

"Seriously?" the doctor asked.

"Aye, it's not necessary, but I can do it. Brooms make for excellent protection spells, and a little extra warding won't hurt a thing."

Kingston nodded with a bit of a grin. "I'll get one for you."

THERE ARE PLENTY OF OLD SAYINGS AND METAPHORS meant to illustrate just how quickly some things can change, and every single one of them came crashing down upon my wife. In a matter of a few short minutes, I had seen her earlier confidence dissipate as if it was being leeched directly out of her by the cold of the room. I was still allowing her to take the lead on this, but I had to admit, I was beginning to worry even more than I had at the outset.

"So whaddaya gonna want me ta' do?" Ben asked.

The three of us were standing in the autopsy suite awaiting Doctor Kingston's return. The M.E. had already ducked back in earlier with the broom and was now supposed to be retrieving the body that would set this all into motion. I gave my friend a quick shrug in response to his query.

"I guess whatever it is you normally do, but you should probably ask Felicity," I said. Then I looked over at my wife and called her name a bit louder, "Felicity?"

She continued staring blankly off into space, so to finally get her attention, I had to reach out and rest my hand on her shoulder as I called again, "Felicity, honey?"

She glanced toward me, her eyes shining with a glassy vacancy. Blinking, she stuttered, "Ummm… Oh, sorry… What?"

"Ben needs to know what you want him to do," I explained.

"Oh…" She creased her brow then looked at him and asked, "Did you already put the broom in the corner?"

"Yeah," he replied, a bit of confusion in his voice. "A coupl'a minutes ago."

"With the bristles up?"

"Yeah," he said again, pointing toward the upended implement several feet away. "Right over there where ya' told me, and exactly like ya' said. Ya' just stood right here and watched me do it."

"Oh…" she mumbled. "Right."

"So is there anything else ya' want me ta' do?" he pressed.

He kept his eyes locked on her as she appeared to concentrate hard on the question, but both of them remained mute. After a quiet moment he asked, "Are you okay, Firehair?"

She looked at him blankly, and then as his words appeared to register, she nodded.

"You sure? You ain't already goin' all *Twilight Zone* on us are ya'?"

"Aye..." She nodded again. "I mean, no... I... Yes, I'm fine... I'm not... I don't... I'm not sure what you can..." she stammered through unfinished sentences as she glanced around. Finally, she shook her head and said, "Well...I guess if you just want to stay out of the way, that would probably be best then."

"Yeah, that part's kinda a given," he grunted. "I'm just offerin' ta' help if ya' need somethin' else is all."

"I know," she replied, shaking her head. "I'm sorry. This is a little..."

He nodded slowly as her voice trailed off. When she had fallen mute once again, he said, "Yeah, I'm kinda startin' ta' get that... Don't worry about it. S'all good, as long as you're okay."

"What? Oh...I'll be fine," she returned.

I hoped she was correct, but her rapidly deteriorating state wasn't filling me with confidence. Inside my head, every objection imaginable was screaming at me, presenting themselves with explicit detail and backup arguments tailored to overcome any opposition. However, I left every last one of them unspoken. Felicity was obviously edgy enough as it was, and I couldn't afford to add fragility to that mix. Me casting any further aspersion upon this undertaking wouldn't help her at all if we intended to continue. In fact, it might well be dangerous if I piled my misgivings on top of the latent doubts that were now peaking through her slack expression.

My friend turned a questioning glance in my direction and then jerked his head to the side indicating that I should follow him as he began to wander away from Felicity. I looked at my wife, who was once again staring off into space, then stepped over to where he was waiting.

"The little woman seems pretty out of it there, white man," he whispered. "I'm sorta used to it outta you. Her, not so much."

"Yeah, I know," I replied in a hushed tone.

"She was fine a little bit ago, so what's goin' on?"

"She's just starting to get nervous, Ben," I told him, as much to reassure myself as anyone. "This isn't her normal role. And, she has a lot to worry about on the periphery as well."

"Yeah..." he breathed, nodding. "The psychobitch."

"Exactly."

"So...she gonna be able ta' do it?"

"Maybe. She definitely wants to try."

"How 'bout you?" he pressed quietly, thrusting his chin toward me. "You seem to have calmed down quite a bit."

I shook my head. "Only on the outside."

"Not feelin' any better about this?"

"Not really," I replied and then glanced back at Felicity for a moment. She hadn't moved and seemed almost catatonic. I turned back to my friend and added, "Maybe a little worse, actually."

Ben reached up and smoothed back his hair. "So, I hate ta' ask, but what if somethin' with this goes south? You gonna be able ta' hold it together?"

"I don't have any choice, Ben. I'm all she's got on this side."

"Yeah, Row. That's pretty much 'zactly why I'm askin'. Can you handle it, or should we just stop right now?"

"Aren't you doing a bit of an..."

Across the room from us a pair of doors swung inward and interrupted me mid-sentence. We both turned toward the sound and saw the end of a gurney appear as it nosed its way through the opening. The elongated cart was swiftly followed by the rest of its length and brought up on the opposite end by Doctor Kingston who was providing both the propulsion and steering. She finished pushing it toward Felicity then brought it to a halt and locked the wheels in place. Although we certainly weren't finished, Ben and I broke from our whispered conversation and joined them.

Resting atop the stainless steel surface of the gurney was a rubberized body bag. Given its current bulk and shape, it was definitely engaged in doing exactly what it was designed to do. I kept my eyes on my wife as I slipped around the end and came up next to her. I could see that she had moved, but not much. She was now staring at the bag in front of her, unblinking, with a faint look of dread now twisting itself into her features.

"Sorry I was gone so long," the doctor announced. "I wanted to make sure everyone knew this suite was off limits for the time being. So...are we ready?"

I remained quiet, watching and waiting to see if Felicity was going to respond. She was still squarely focused on the black zippered sheath, seemingly transfixed in a moment only she could see.

After several seconds passed, I gave her arm a gentle nudge and called softly, "Felicity?"

"Aye..." she muttered, her voice even thinner and more distracted than before. "I'm okay."

I didn't believe her. The arrival of this newest member to the party was obviously pushing her apprehension beyond the next level. Of course, I had already been hovering up against the red line for hours, so I knew exactly how she felt. Unfortunately, that knowledge wasn't comforting to me in the least.

No matter how hard Felicity had tried to reassure me otherwise, we both knew that channeling the dead wasn't exactly her long suit. Other than her body being hijacked by Miranda, she had only done this once before, and it had been strictly involuntary.

She was as skilled a magickal practitioner as I'd ever met. In fact, I would even readily admit that she was more advanced than me in that arena. But, this wasn't magick. It was something completely different. Still, in reality, we had no way of knowing whether or not this would even work. Under the present circumstances, I found myself hoping that it wouldn't.

The tone of Ben's next exchange with my wife told me that his second thoughts about this were starting to bother him even more.

"You think you're gonna be able ta' do this, Felicity?" he asked.

She gave her head a slight shake. "I don't know."

"Fair enough. You still good with tryin'?"

"Aye," she replied, her voice soft and distant. "I think so."

He waited a moment, still watching her carefully. Eventually he told her, "You can back out, if you don't want ta' go through with it. It's not a problem. I'll understand."

"No..." she mumbled. "We need to do this."

My friend looked over at me, more concern in his eyes than I'd seen for quite some time. "Row...I'm leavin' it up ta' you. Wanna pull the plug?"

The litany of objections presented themselves once again, ricocheting around the inside of my skull as they looked for an exit. However, I simply gave my head a barely perceptible shake and said, "No. She's probably right. We should try."

"Is everything okay?" Doctor Kingston asked.

"Just makin' sure everyone's still on the same page, Doc," Ben replied. "It's a Witch thing."

Had the situation been different, I likely would have guffawed at Ben's use of that phrase.

"All right then," she began, addressing me directly. "Mister Gant, earlier you said you may need physical contact with the deceased?"

"It helps," I replied and dipped my head toward my wife. "But it will only be Felicity, not me."

"Then you'll need to put these on, Miz O'Brien," the doctor replied, holding a pair of surgical gloves out to her.

Felicity was staring again, so I gave her a nudge. She looked at me then turned and focused in on the gloves and took them from Doctor Kingston. I continued to watch as she began trying to stretch one over her hand. There was an unmistakable hesitation in all of her actions, and her steadily growing uneasiness was becoming more than simply palpable. I had been here countless times myself, so I knew all too well that it was starting to exact a painful toll. As I watched my wife struggle with the glove, I began to wonder if I should take the out Ben had offered and just go ahead and stop this before it even started.

But, I forced myself not to give in, took a deep breath, and fought to hold my tongue. Instead of objecting, I reached out and took the surgical glove from Felicity and told her, "Here. Let me help."

She looked at me in silence, chewing at her lower lip, and then slowly held out her hand. I stretched the rubber sheath and carefully slipped it onto her right appendage. She started to offer the other hand, and I shook my head.

"No. Just your right," I told her. "I'll be hanging on to your left."

She gave me a slow nod.

I held her gaze for a moment then reached up and brushed the hair back out of her eyes. In a quiet voice I asked, "Are you sure you're ready?"

She nodded again, this time attempting a verbal response as well but only managing a barely audible whisper. She stopped, cleared her throat and then repeated, "Yes."

"Okay…then let's give this a try."

I reached into my pocket and withdrew the small handful of salt packets I had earlier retrieved from her purse. I counted them out while glancing at the space around us and running through a quick mental calculation at the same time. Then I counted through them again, peeled off four, stuffed two of them back into my pocket and held the other two out to Ben.

"Whaddaya want me ta' do?" he whispered.

"Remember how I chased Miranda out before?" I returned, my own voice low.

"Yeah," he said then opened his mouth and pantomimed eating the salt as he nodded toward Felicity.

"Exactly…" I replied. "So…hang on to them…just in case."

It would have been easier to go ahead and use everything I had in my hand, but I wanted something to fall back on if necessary, and this was what I had. I was carrying the backup. Ben was going to be my failsafe. I hoped I would need neither.

Tearing the remainder of the packets open, I poured the crystals into the palm of my hand and then began walking in a tight circle, barely a few feet out from our small clutch around the gurney. As I slowly shuffled along the perimeter, I sprinkled pinches of the salt in my wake.

Halfway through the circumference, I heard Ben's voice somewhere behind me as he whispered to Doctor Kingston, "Relax, it doesn't usually get weird for another coupl'a minutes yet."

I continued along my arc without acknowledging that I'd heard him. At the moment I had someone far more important on whom my attention needed to be focused.

Once I'd completed the orbit, I took the crumpled handful of empty salt packets and shoved them into my other pocket. I closed my eyes then took a deep breath in through my nose and held it for several heartbeats before allowing the warmed air to vent in a slow stream out via my mouth. Even though Miranda had taken away my connection to the dead and my ability to feel, she couldn't keep me from executing the simplest of exercises where WitchCraft was concerned—grounding and centering.

I repeated the pattern of breathing several more times as I visualized a solid connection between the Earth and myself. I imagined a conduit forming between the floor and my body, and in my mind it took the form of a spire of light. It acted as a channel through which energy could pass in both directions. This would be my anchor in the here and now, and I would be Felicity's sole tether between the worlds of life and death.

After a handful of minutes, I finally felt myself beginning to relax. The emptiness that had begun earlier in the pit of my stomach and then spread throughout my body was still making a home in my chest. However, it no longer consumed me. I knew I hadn't arrived at a perfect calm, but it was the best I was going to be able to manage, so it would have to do. I took one last cleansing breath then stepped over and resumed my earlier station next to my wife.

I reached down and slipped my hand into hers, pressing our palms together and intertwining our fingers in a tight weave. I felt her squeeze out of reflex, and she slowly swiveled her head and looked into my face.

"Like you said," I told her softly. "Don't be like me. No chances... No risks... And, don't you dare let go."

"You either," she whispered.

"We ready?" Ben asked.

"Aye," Felicity responded, giving him a shallow nod.

He looked at her, then at me. The reluctance was clear in his eyes. Finally, he held up the two salt packets and stared at them briefly before returning his gaze to mine. He wagged the square packets at me as if to say, "I've got your back."

I simply nodded.

Ben sighed then looked at the M.E. and said, "Go on. Open it up, Doc."

Doctor Kingston stepped around the end of the gurney then reached out a gloved hand and tugged on the zipper. In a smooth motion she pulled the closure, creating an ever-widening gap down the center of the shroud. Once she reached the midpoint, she stopped.

Moving back to the head of the gurney, she carefully folded back the sides of the rubberized fabric and revealed the body that had been sprawled in our front yard less than ten hours ago. After the medical examiner had moved out of the way, Felicity slowly reached out, her gloved hand hovering a few inches above the pale flesh of the corpse.

And then, through our clasped hands, I felt her entire body go completely stiff.

CHAPTER 23

USING THE TINES OF HER SALAD FORK, FELICITY SLOWLY batted a small hunk of tomato back and forth on her plate. After a few seconds of the cat-like behavior, she pushed the deep red triangle close to the edge using the back of the utensil. Lazily piercing the bite-sized chunk, she then maneuvered it around the layers of thinly sliced red onion, other slabs of extraordinarily crimson-hued tomato, and dollops of fresh mozzarella cheese that were all swimming in a translucent green pool of olive oil. So far, other than a few initial bites, she had barely touched her lunch other than to engage in the absent-minded activity currently at hand.

The restaurant was unusually quiet, but then it was early yet. The sharp-edged, raspy beat of the Raveonettes *Dead Sound* floated through the room as the last verse of the song filtered from the overhead speakers nearby. It was underscored by the muffled sound of a distant emergency siren somewhere outside. The mélange of noises seemed to echo the tone of our day thus far.

"I'm sorry," my wife finally muttered, her voice riding on the back of a dejected sigh.

It was now coming up on two hours since we'd left the county medical examiner's office, and I'd lost track of the number of times she'd apologized during that span. I'd actually stopped counting somewhere around the tenth, and that was better than forty-five minutes ago. I figured Ben had given up on keeping a tally as well, but since he had disappeared to the restroom, he wasn't around to hear this latest verbal atonement. So even if I was wrong, it was really a moot point.

I slipped my hand over beneath the table and placed it on my wife's denim-covered thigh. Giving her leg a gentle rub, I tried to soothe her mood with the same words I'd already spoken several times. "I'm sorry too, honey. But all you could do was try."

"Don't lie, Rowan," she replied. Her voice was quiet but didn't lack for seriousness. "You aren't sorry. You're happy it didn't work."

"I wouldn't say happy," I told her. "But, yeah, sure, I'll admit I'm more than a little relieved."

In all honesty, I was completely sincere in my words of

consolation. I hated to see her beating herself up about something over which she had no control. I'd been there more than once myself and knew it was an exercise in futility. And, I also knew that given the unproductive outcome of our visit, we were still flying blind. Without a doubt, that was the real issue here. But no matter what I said, my wife hadn't yet been willing to let go of her self-recriminations.

"That's the problem. I am too," she said. Her tone was harsh, and she was obviously flogging herself with the words.

"You don't think you should be?"

"No." She shook her head but kept her eyes aimed toward the dark red chunk of tomato she was still pushing around her plate. "Maybe that's why I failed…because I was too afraid."

I sighed. "Honey, first off, you didn't fail. It just wasn't happening, that's all. Secondly, I've got news for you. If fear is what keeps an ethereal connection with the dead from happening, then I'd never channel a single spirit because I'm usually pretty terrified."

"*Cac capaill*," she muttered.

"It's the truth, whether you want to believe it or not," I told her. "Besides, even if you had made a connection, we still might not be any better off. You know as well as I do that you don't always get what you're after."

She objected. "But there might have been something."

"Or not, just like I said. You just don't know. Miranda is pretty good at covering her tracks when she wants to be."

"*Fekking saigh…*" my wife grumbled.

"You'll get no argument from me there," I agreed. "Listen, I know how you feel, but you're just going to have to get over it. We'll have to find another way of doing this."

"I'm still sorry."

"I know. You've already said that." I watched her for a moment as she continued to play with the food on her plate. Then I pushed the salt and pepper shakers toward her. "Would you like some salt for that?"

She shot me an odd glance as she lifted her fork and stabbed it hard into one of the tomato slabs. "No. Salt is bad for you."

I hoped her mood wouldn't continue. Felicity was usually far too stubborn to stay in a funk for very long, especially if she saw a way out. However, where the subject of Miranda was concerned, it could sometimes be a different story.

Ben's voice came from the side as he breezed past me. "Jeezus…is she apologizin' again?" I looked up and saw him sliding back into the booth on the opposite side as he continued, "I was only gone five friggin' minutes. How many this time?"

Apparently he was still keeping track after all.

"Just twice," I told him.

"Twice? Lemme see." He grunted and then rolled his eyes up in an animated fashion while he scribbled in the air with his index finger. A second or two later, he dropped his gaze down and focused on her as he reached for his burger. "Yeah, those two make it an even twenty-five, Firehair. That's the daily limit on apologizin'. Now ya' hafta stop. It's a law."

"I haven't apologized twenty-five times," she snapped.

"Yeah, actually, ya' have."

"He could be right, honey," I offered. "I lost track at ten."

"*Fealltóir*."

"No, I'm not a traitor," I replied. "I'm just telling it like it is."

She turned her attention back to Ben and countered, "Well, twenty-five isn't an even number."

"Doesn't matter, you know exactly what I mean," he replied then bit off a chunk of his sandwich and began to chew.

"Well, I'm terribly sorry if I'm annoying you," she snipped.

He swallowed and then shot back. "That's twenty-six, Irish."

"That's the second time you've called me that today."

"Yeah, so?"

"You've never called me that before."

"Yeah, well I didn't know you were still a foreigner before."

"I'm sorry?"

"Twenty-seven."

She huffed out an annoyed breath. "I think you know exactly what I meant."

Ben raised his eyebrows and shook his head at her. "Last Friday when we were all at that restaurant with the weird name."

"Flipdoodles?"

"Yeah, that one."

"What about it?"

"We were talkin' and ya' said ya' had dual citizenship, right?"

"Aye."

"There ya' go. Makes ya' a foreigner in my book."

Felicity stabbed her lunch hard and muttered, "*Go ifreann leat*."

"Yeah, go ahead and get it all outta your system. You ain't any good to me if your just gonna sit there an' pout."

"What's it matter? I'm obviously not any good to you anyway."

"Not like this, that's for damn sure."

"Well, at least I didn't just stand around wringing my hands like a big sissy."

"Do what?" Ben shot back.

"You heard me then."

He gave her a hard stare for a moment, then the corner of his mouth turned up in a half grin. "For a second there I thought you were serious."

"Are you certain I'm not?"

"I'm never sure of anything with you."

"Good. That's the way it should be."

My friend sighed and grunted, "Well, I wouldn't let it go to your head if I was you."

"Are you two aware that you sound like an old married couple?" I asked.

"Blame your wife," Ben replied as he returned his attention to the hamburger he still had pinched in his hand. "She started it."

"I think you're probably both equally at fault," I said.

"Actually, no, it's him," my wife quipped. "I think it's probably all the sexual tension."

"The what?" Ben yipped.

"Sexual tension. You've been dying to sleep with me ever since we met."

"Awww, Jeezus…" Ben groaned, dropping his sandwich onto his plate. He was obviously caught off guard by her gibe. "Dammit, Firehair, you know that ain't so."

"What? I'm not good enough for you?"

"I didn't say… I mean… You… Dammit… Now you're just goin' too far. Why the hell do ya' say crap like that?"

"Because I find you very entertaining when you're embarrassed," my wife replied. "That's why."

"Rowan?" he appealed, glancing over at me.

"Why are you crying to him?" Felicity snipped.

"Backup," he retorted.

"I've told you before, Ben," I said with a shrug. "She knows the mere mention of sex is a hot button with you."

"Well, ya' know I'm not wantin' ta'…ya'know… I mean… Jeezus, she's your wife for Chrissakes."

"Believe me, Ben, I'm not worried. And, it doesn't bother me if you find her attractive."

"Don't you start too."

I shook my head. "I'm not. You know, I don't get why you're always so surprised when she pushes this button to get a reaction out of you. It's not like she hasn't done it before."

"Yeah, that's true. But she ain't usually this ill behaved in public," Ben replied, stressing the last word.

"So sorry I can't say the same for you," Felicity remarked.

"Jeezus H Christ…" he sighed. "Are you done yet, Felicity?"

"I suppose so…" She paused then added the caveat, "For now."

He shook his head and let out a protracted "Fuck me…"

"Aye, you wish."

"Well, at least you seem to be coming out of your funk," I announced. "But I also have to say that you two are starting to annoy me a bit."

"You're just grouchy because you're hungry," Felicity replied.

I drew in a deep breath then puffed my cheeks out as I exhaled in exasperation. "Trust me, when you two really get going you can be annoying whether I'm hungry or not," I said. "But, yeah, you might have a point. I actually am starting to get annoyed that my food isn't here yet."

"Yeah, you been waitin' awhile," Ben commented as he scooped up his burger once again. "Wonder if they had ta' go kill another cow or somethin'."

"Pig. I ordered a BLT."

"Cow, pig, whatever," he grunted before biting into his sandwich once again. "Bet you're re-thinkin' your order now, ain't ya'?"

"I'm definitely beginning to wonder," I said.

"Speakin' of food," Ben said. "You ain't eatin' much, Firehair. Ya' maybe want some salt for that?"

"I wish the two of you would stop trying to give me salt," she snipped. "It's bad for you."

The nostalgic chords of an electric guitar twanged overhead as a woman's voice followed behind them in a haunting harmonization, repeating two simple words, "dead sound." I looked upward at the speakers out of reflex then back down and glanced between Ben and Felicity.

"Didn't they already play this?" I asked.

"Maybe she's stuck," Ben offered.

"She?"

"Whatever."

"Well, I think maybe that siren is too," I complained, nodding toward the window.

"Here you are, Rowan," a voice drifted into my ears as a plate slid onto the table in front of me.

I looked up and found Ariel Tanner staring back at me with a sad frown torturing her face. She shook her head and sighed, "I'm so sorry about the wait."

After that, pain was all I knew.

And after that, there was nothing at all.

CHAPTER 24

I FELT HEAVY.

That was the only way I could describe it. It was like my muscles had turned to lead and I was slowly sinking into oblivion.

My head was thick.

It was dense, as if it had been emptied of its contents and then stuffed beyond its capacity with cotton, if for no other reason than to soak up any random thoughts even before I was allowed to have them. I reached for memories anyway but found none. Only the tightly packed nothing remained inside my skull, a solid void from which there was no escape.

I wondered if this was what it was like to be dead. Then I tried to remember what it was I had been wondering. Then I gave up and stopped wondering altogether.

One side of my face was hot and the other was cold. My neck was stiff and my shoulders felt tired. At least, that is what my body seemed to be telling me. How it was getting this message across in a coherent fashion I had no idea. The connection between the stuffing in my head and the rest of me didn't appear to be on very good terms at the moment.

I noticed an uncomfortable dullness was now burrowing beneath my skin. It was as if I was numb, but not numb. I was teetering somewhere in between. Physical sensations were still there, but they made no sense. They were a long time coming, and when they arrived, they were almost impossible to identify.

It occurred to me that it was dark, so I tried to open my eyes. My eyelids fought that decision with everything they had, but I was determined. The struggle seemed to last forever, and by the time it was over I had forgotten why I even started, so I gave up.

Then, my left eyelid opened without any prompting from me, and a bright light exploded in front of it. I wanted to blink, but I couldn't. Just as suddenly as it had opened, it closed. But even as the residual starbursts began to fade, my right eye snapped open in much the same way, only to have the sun go supernova into it as well.

Finally, the darkness returned. I decided not to try opening my eyes again. Apparently, there was nothing I wanted to see.

“Can you tell me your name?” a voice filtered into my ears.

I ignored it.

Sometime later—how long I had no idea at all—I thought maybe I felt something pushing against my shoulder. The voice came again, “Sir, can you tell me your name?”

Apparently, ignoring the voice was not an option. I worked my jaw and tried to force my thick tongue to move. My throat felt raw, and it burned as I slowly pushed air out of my mouth in an attempt to form words.

“Rowmim Gahn…” I heard myself say. It didn’t make sense to me, but it seemed to mean something to the voice.

“Good. Can you tell me what day this is, Mister Gant?”

I took in a slow breath and then allowed my mouth to say whatever it wanted. “Money.”

“Good,” the voice replied.

I was starting to drift again, so the fact that the voice was pleased didn’t really matter to me.

I felt pressure against my palm, and the voice droned on some more, but I had no idea what it said. It was just so much background noise.

The heaviness pressed down on me again, and then it was gone. I was floating. And then I wasn’t. I was simply there. Now, I could feel myself breathing, or at least that’s what I thought. But that thought was fleeting as my cottony brain absorbed it and left me with nothing to think.

I knew I didn’t like this. How I knew, I couldn’t be sure. I had no thoughts. At least, I didn’t think I had any thoughts. But if I didn’t have them, then how was I thinking? It confused me. But being confused required thought, and that just sent me into a deepening spiral. I stopped trying to think.

At least the voice was gone.

I realized I was breathing and chose to concentrate on that instead.

Breathe in…

Breathe out…

Breathe in…

Breathe…

Now I was feeling heavy again. The troublesome dullness rolled through me like a sudden crashing wave and then ebbed slowly on a receding tide. In its wake it left only pain.

I tensed in a reflexive answer to this new sensation. There was something both familiar and alien about it. As my muscles involuntarily tightened, my hands clenched, and I felt that something was clasped in my right palm.

A rampant thought escaped the cotton and dripped into being.

Felicity?

I was holding her hand, wasn't I?

We were… somewhere…

I couldn't remember where…

I squeezed and waited for her to squeeze back. The acknowledgement coursed along sluggish nerves, reaching dead ends before turning around and re-tracing the way back out. Eventually, the weakened signal reached what now passed for my brain, but the information it gave was completely unfamiliar.

I squeezed tightly once again, hoping for a different message. My hope was rewarded, but not in the way I had wanted.

A soft buzz drifted into my ears.

A click followed.

My hand relaxed of its own accord.

The pain was no longer.

The uncomfortable dullness gave way to a pleasant lack of any sensation whatsoever.

The darkness grew darker.

Then everything became nothing.

Monday, April 24
7:17 P.M.
University Hospital Northeast
ICU
Saint Louis, Missouri

CHAPTER 25

"ROW?" A GRUFF BUT UNMISTAKABLY FAMILIAR VOICE echoed in my ears. "Rowan… Come on, Row, wake up."

I wasn't at all clear on what had transpired. Anything involving memories seemed to be staying just out of reach, although for some reason I knew who was speaking to me.

I tried to concentrate.

Something had to be in there somewhere. I vaguely remembered my head being stuffed with cotton. However, that's not how it was feeling right now. At the moment it felt as if someone had replaced the cotton with dark, viscous mud. I couldn't say that I liked this sensation any better than the previous; however, there did at least seem to be a little more feedback from the rest of my body making it through. Not that all of said feedback was particularly pleasant, mind you.

I could tell that I was lying on my back, or at least that's how it felt. For all I knew, my equilibrium was shot and I was hanging upside down. But, if I could believe the pressure against my spine, I was definitely laying on it. Of course, I wasn't sure that it really mattered. Rather than wrack my lethargic brain over trying to figure it out, I just decided to rely on first impressions and leave it at that.

As my body continued to file updated status reports—none of which were good—it came to my attention that my neck and shoulders were throbbing with a dull ache. The pain itself wasn't exactly excruciating, but it made me uncomfortable enough that I desperately wanted to move in order to relieve some of the pressure. I gave in to the desire and tried to shift into a more comfortable position. Unfortunately, the moment I began to tense the necessary muscles to affect the motion, a sharp pain arced through my upper abdomen and then into my chest. In response, I drew in a quick breath, which only served to send a second lance of pain to skewer along behind the first. I held the breath and then let it out slowly as I tried to force myself to relax.

"C'mon, Kemosabe. Wake up…" the voice said again.

After what seemed like an eternity, I carefully opened one eye and saw a face hovering a few feet in front of mine while staring down at me. The image was fuzzy, so I couldn't fully make out his expression, but I definitely recognized the countenance as belonging to Ben.

I groaned, "Am I dead?"

My throat was still sore, and now it was dry too, so the three words hurt like hell on the way out of my mouth.

"Yeah, you're dead, and I'm a fuckin' angel," he replied.

A woman's voice instantly admonished, "Detective! He's still dealing with the effects of the anesthesia. You shouldn't make jokes like that."

"Trust me," Ben said, glancing off in the direction of her voice. "Anesthesia or no, I'm the last S.O.B. he'd ask for confirmation if 'e really thought 'e was dead. He'd just know…" He looked back at me and added, "Right, white man?"

"Fuck you," I muttered. That pair of words hurt too, but they were worth it.

His face disappeared from my view, and I heard him announce, "Yeah, he's gonna be just fine."

I closed my eye and tried to remember, but the mud still caked my brain. I knew there was something just below its surface. Something important. If only I could seize onto what it was.

I felt fingers pressing against the side of my wrist, and the woman's voice came again, this time apparently directed at me. "Mister Gant, do you remember that you're in the hospital?"

"Do now…" I moaned. "Why?"

"You just had surgery, but you're doing fine. Are you in any pain?"

"Yeah," I croaked.

A moment later I felt a coolness encroach upon me as a blanket was pulled back. Something snaked against me with a tickle. I felt my arm being lifted slightly, and then it was lowered once again. The blanket slipped back over me, and the coolness was replaced by warmth. I felt pressure against my palm, and then a hand closed my fingers around a small cylinder.

"This is your morphine pump," the woman told me. "You must have dropped it. Just press the button if the pain gets to be too much."

I remembered, at some point I had squeezed my hand and then passed out. I don't know when it happened, but it seemed recent. Now I guess I knew why. On the heels of the memory, another more vivid recollection pushed through the mire of my confused brain.

"Felicity…" I groaned.

As disjointed thoughts of my wife flashed through my head, I felt my heart begin to race. A wave of panic rushed over me. I opened my eyes and began trying to push myself upward.

Razor sharp agony ripped through me, just below my ribcage. I yelped and felt the pain ramp up for a second round.

"Try not to move just yet, Mister Gant," the woman ordered.

"Listen to her, Row…" Ben told me, concern threading through his words.

I ignored both of them, and the pain as well. Even as it twisted deep inside me, ripping the breath from my lungs, I struggled to pull myself upright.

The nurse pressed gently against my shoulder and I fell back, gritting my teeth. "Just press the button, Mister Gant. It will help."

"Fel…" I tried to say my wife's name again, but the pain caused it to catch in my throat, unfinished.

Ben came back into view as he reached across me. I felt a large hand slip around mine and then squeeze, pushing down against my thumb. I heard a soft buzz then a click, and numbness began to spread through my body

"Detective," the woman admonished. "You can't do that."

Ben replied, flat sarcasm in his voice, "Yeah, well it was an accident. Whoops."

"Felicity… Feliss…city…" I whispered.

"Don't worry, white man…" Ben's voice said, but there was something about his tone that just didn't sound right.

Darkness slipped over me once again.

Tuesday, April 25
2:03 A.M.
University Hospital Northeast
ICU
Saint Louis, Missouri

CHAPTER 26

I WAS SWIMMING UP FROM AN EMPTY BLACK VOID. WITH a painstaking slowness, the black became less black, until finally it spread into a deep dark grey. Noises, some recognizable some not, began to filter in through the murk, and though I couldn't see, at least I could hear.

"Somethin' wrong? He okay?" Ben Storm's drowsy voice drifted into my head with a languid echo. Although he sounded as if he'd just awakened, there was an air of alertness about the words; not to mention they were darkly tinted with concern.

Assuming my ears were working the way they should, I guessed he was several feet away. From that same direction I could now hear movement, and it was starting to come closer.

Immediately nearby, a calmer female voice replied to him in a half-whisper. "Just making the regular rounds, Detective. Checking vitals and such."

"How's 'e doin'?" my friend asked, his tone a bit less intense. His voice was louder, so I assumed he was much closer to me now.

I was still swimming up through the greyness, groping for the light with each passing second.

"He's stable," she told him.

I heard my friend sigh heavily then shuffle in place.

I could feel something tightening around my arm as the low hum of an air pump filled my ears. It felt as if my heart was beating in my hand as the constriction slowly started to subside between brief, evenly spaced hisses. Finally, the quiet whoosh of escaping air flowed past me, and the squeeze encircling my bicep was gone.

My friend grunted. "Still a uniform out there, right?"

"There's an officer just outside the door, yes."

"Okay, good…" he huffed.

There was a short pause, then I heard the woman say, "You can't use that cell phone in here, Detective."

"Why not?"

"It interferes with the monitors."

"Yeah, okay…" my friend breathed. "Any way we can get a phone tempororarily hooked up in here then? 'Cause we're gonna need one."

"That shouldn't be a problem," she replied. "But it won't be until morning. You can use the phone out at the desk if you'd like."

"Yeah. That'll work for right now." There was another pause then he said, "Ya' got any coffee around here?"

"At the desk," she told him. "Help yourself."

"Thanks. I'll be right back…"

I could hear him turning to leave just as I broke through the surface of consciousness.

"Me too…" I groaned softly.

I heard him stop and turn back toward me.

"Row?" he said.

"Black," I told him for an answer, my voice a little stronger. "And maybe some sugar."

"Mister Gant?" the nurse asked. "How are you feeling?"

I allowed my eyes to flutter open. I was propped up slightly, but not necessarily comfortably. It was dark except for the subdued glow of vitals telemetry on the screen next to me and a small wedge of soft light streaming in from the partially open door. I could just make out their faces as they stood on either side of the bed looking back at me.

"I hurt like hell," I replied.

"You have the morphine…" she started.

"Don't touch it," I said, curling my hand in to guard the button, and then winced at the sharp pain my sudden action evoked.

"Mister Gant…"

"Talk," I managed to say as I caught my breath. "I need to talk…to Ben…"

"Yeah, Row?"

"Felicity?"

"Don't worry. We're keepin' 'er safe," he replied. "Constance is with 'er."

Like the foggy memory from before, something simply wasn't right about his answer. I didn't get the feeling he was outright lying to me, but something about the choice of words told me he was engaged in the sin of omission.

"Where is she?" I pressed.

"She's here at the hospital."

"Where?"

He huffed out a breath as he reached up to work his fingers against his neck. Shaking his head slightly, he replied, "In a different room, Row."

"Is she okay?" I demanded with as much intensity as my current state would allow.

He remained silent and continued massaging the bundle of muscles right where his neck met his shoulder.

"Answer me, Ben…"

"Physically, she hasn't got a scratch on 'er," he said.

Anger was starting to brew inside me, and it helped me ignore the pain as I lifted my head from the pillow and glared at him. "You're not answering my question."

He grimaced then blurted out, "She's in some kinda coma or somethin', Row."

I let my head fall back against the pillow as a cold terror flooded into my chest, pushing away the anger. I felt a burn down the back of my throat as it tightened. My eyes began to water and I blinked hard.

After a moment I asked, "What the hell happened?"

"You don't remember?" he answered.

I sighed and shook my head. "We were at the diner having lunch. She was upset about not being able to connect with…"

"Whoa…" Ben interrupted me. "Diner? What diner?"

"I don't remember the name," I snapped back at him. "We went there after she wasn't able to connect with the victim at the morgue. You should know this. You were there…"

"Row…" my friend began, shaking his head. "We never went to a diner."

"What do you mean?"

"You really don't remember what happened?"

"Dammit, Ben…"

The pain in my abdomen was now arcing from the left to the right and then back again. It bored deep and felt like my insides were on fire.

"I'm sorry, Row… Sorry…" He apologized. "Maybe you should just rest now."

"That would be best," the nurse interjected.

"What happened?" I demanded again.

Ben took in a deep breath and blew it out slowly. Shooting the nurse a glance, he said, "Wanna give us a minute?"

"Detective Storm… Mister Gant needs to…"

"Please," I appealed, cutting her off. "Just give us a couple of minutes, okay?"

She looked to the monitors and stared at them for a moment. My eyes were adjusted to the ambient light in the room, so I could see that she pursed her lips as she frowned and watched my vitals spike on the display. It was apparent that she was weighing the options. After a few heartbeats she turned to Ben.

"How do you take your coffee?" she asked.

"Black, why?"

"I'm going to go get you some," she replied. "I'm not going to be gone very long, and when I come back you need to be finished with the talking."

"Yeah, okay," Ben said with a nod. "Just don't hurry."

"I'm serious," she replied as she started out.

"Yeah, I got it," he called after her. "Me too."

Once she had vacated the small room, Ben turned back to face me. "Whaddaya remember from the morgue, Row?"

"I don't know…" I muttered. "We got there, met with Doctor Kingston. I had a minor meltdown…"

"Yeah, anything else?" he asked.

"She brought in the body and Felicity tried to make a connection."

"That it?"

I sighed and concentrated on the event, searching for the next part of the story, but came up blank. Finally, I said, "Yeah, I guess."

My friend gave me a slight nod and said, "Well, you're all good up to there, but you're missin' a big ass piece." He paused and took in a deep breath before continuing. "It all started out just like ya' said. Usual Witch stuff like you've done before. You'n Firehair were standin' there doin' the *Twilight Zone* thing. Doc Kingston and I were watchin'. It was quiet, nothin' goin' on. Hell, I was startin' ta' think maybe it wasn't workin'."

"You mean it did?" I asked.

"Well, somethin' sure as fuck happened," he said. "One minute everything was calm, the next minute Felicity was screamin' bloody murder. Any of that ring a bell?"

"No…" I replied.

"Yeah… Prob'ly a good thing, I guess," he grunted.

"Why?"

"'Cause it went downhill from there… Fast… When she started screamin', she went berserk. You had hold of 'er, tryin' ta' calm 'er down…" He stopped and puffed out a long breath. The pained look on his face was a good indicator that he was reliving the story even as he told it. After a short pause, he started speaking once again, outlining the events in short, fragmented sentences. "Looked like you had it under control… She was startin' ta' settle. It got all quiet again… You were across the room…" He paused again, staring off for a second. "Dammit… If you just hadn't been all the way across the fuckin' room…"

"What happened?" I pressed.

He sighed again. "You let go of 'er and pulled out one of those salt packets…and that was it. Like it was some kinda trigger or somethin'…" He shook his head. "Next thing I knew she had an autopsy knife off'a one of the trays in 'er hand…one of the big ones… Jeezus… You were all the way across the room… And the stiff was between us… I just couldn't get to you in time, Row… She managed ta' stab ya' twice before I could tackle 'er."

A flash of memory rolled through my grey matter.

"You will know. But if it will help, I will wear something… or someone… special."

I swallowed hard. "That wasn't Felicity, Ben. She didn't do this. Miranda did. Somehow she managed to get in…"

"I know that…" he said. "I know… I could tell just by the look on 'er face that it wasn't Firehair… And don't worry. I already talked ta' Doc Kingston about it. She's freaked, but I don't think she'll be a problem. I got 'er ta' erase the tape that was runnin', so Felicity ain't gonna get charged with anything. Not if I can help it."

"Thanks..."

"Don't worry about it."

"Where's the necklace?" I asked.

"Right here," he said, pulling the small bottle out of his pocket and holding it up where I could see it. "Ya' made me take it right before ya' passed out."

I sighed. "Okay…good."

"Ya' want it back?"

"No. Not yet. Hang on to it for me, okay?" I could tell he wasn't excited by the prospect.

"Yeah… Okay," He nodded and then glanced warily at the vial before shoving it back into his pocket. With a sigh he added, "Feel like I'm carryin' the goddamn nuclear football."

Silence fell between us as the sound of his voice trailed off. I closed my eyes and lay there, trying to find even an inkling of remembrance that connected with what I'd just been told. But there was nothing there. My mind had apparently shifted into self-preservation mode and was blocking out the trauma.

Finally I asked, "What about Felicity? How did she end up in a coma?"

"I dunno," he said. "It just happened outta the blue. I pulled her off ya' and managed ta' get 'er cuffed before she could stab ya' any more. She kept screamin' and kickin'… The doc was with you… Jeezus… There was blood everywhere, and you were just layin' there… But ya' kept tryin' ta' tell me somethin'."

"You needed to give her salt."

He nodded. "Yeah. Ya' still had it in your hand, and ya' kept tryin' ta' hold it out to me. So I pulled out one of the ones you gave me, held Firehair down and poured it into 'er mouth. She kept fightin' right at first, but it didn't take long, and all of a sudden she just went limp. A few minutes after that it was like she was unconscious or somethin'."

"She's not unconscious, Ben," I said with a soft lament. "She's gone."

"Whaddaya mean gone?"

"Miranda pushed her out," I said. "And then you pushed Miranda out. Now she's holding my wife hostage."

"How?"

"That's what I have to find out," I said, starting to lever myself up. "I need to see her."

"Whoa, Kemosabe, I get what you're sayin', but you ain't in any condition ta' do anything right now."

"I don't care," I growled between clenched teeth as a fresh wave of pain ripped through me.

He put a large hand on my shoulder and carefully pushed me back. It didn't take much because I didn't have enough strength to fight.

"Row," he said. "You were in surgery for almost six friggin' hours. Hell, I thought ya' were gonna bleed ta' death before we even got ya' here."

The door pushed open and the nurse walked back in. "Okay, time's up," she said, placing a Styrofoam cup onto the rolling tray at the end of the bed as she passed it by. "There's your coffee, Detective."

She continued up to the head of the bed and fiddled with my IV for a moment. "I just spoke with the doctor and he ordered something for you as well, Mister Gant," she announced and then withdrew a hypodermic from her pocket, uncapped it, and slid it into a port on the tubing.

I didn't give what she had said much thought. Instead, I continued pressing my friend. "Ben, I need to see her."

"You will, Row," he told me. "But right now ya' need ta' rest."

"The detective is right," the nurse echoed as she recapped the needle on the now empty syringe. "Just relax. This should take effect in just a minute or two."

"Was that a sedative?" I asked.

"Uhm-hmmm."

"No…" I objected. "I have to see Felicity."

"That will have to wait," she said.

"You bitch!" I spat with everything I could muster.

"I'll pretend you didn't say that, Mister Gant," she replied. "Now like I said, just relax. I'll be back in to check on you in a bit."

It wasn't long before the darkness came to take me again.

CHAPTER 27

"SOME PEOPLE JUST DON'T WANT TO STAY DEAD, ROWAN."

The voice coming from behind me was familiar and under the circumstances not entirely unexpected, so I didn't turn around. Instead, I kept my gaze focused straight ahead on the remnants of the inscription in the weatherworn stone before me. There was actually very little of it still visible, but that didn't matter. The particular mystery surrounding the missing letters had already been solved, and though only a few fragments of the letters remained, I knew exactly what it was supposed to say—Miranda Blanque 1808 - 1851.

I was standing near the back of Saint Louis Cemetery Number One, not far from the French Quarter in New Orleans. Shafts of pale light were stenciling my surroundings in not-so-random patterns, all courtesy of the jagged template of tombs and monuments that formed the immediate skyline. Grey shadows filled the areas in-between, laying a darkened patina across aged masonry, narrow pathways, and me. The air was still, and other than the voice and the sound of my own breathing, there was nothing in my ears but silence.

I had been here before, but that time I had been chasing Miranda. Now in a very real sense, she was chasing me. I suppose it made a poetic statement of sorts that her tomb would once again be the center point of it all.

"Does anyone really want to be dead?" I finally asked aloud, responding to the comment.

"There are a few."

I turned around to face Ariel Tanner's ghost. "Like maybe you for instance?"

"What makes you say that?"

"You're still dead," I told her. "You died almost ten years ago."

"That's true."

"And?" I asked.

"And what?"

"And shouldn't you have moved on by now? Been reborn into a new life? Or is Summerland and the whole reincarnation thing just a pipe dream after all?"

"Don't over think it, Rowan," she replied. "You'll find the answer when the time is right for you."

"Pretty typical non-committal answer, don't you think?"

"You just need to..."

"You aren't going to tell me I just need to believe, are you?" I asked, cutting her off before she could finish. "Because I'm running a little short on faith these days."

"Actually, I was going to say wait. But would it help revive your faith if I said believe?"

I ignored the question and held her gaze for a long while before finally speaking again. "I'm not really used to this, you know."

"Used to what?" she asked.

"Well, for one thing, up until very recently you've been non-existent. I haven't even seen you for several years. I just assumed that when I solved your murder you had moved on."

"To Summerland?"

"Or life. Knowing you, I figured you were probably a precocious kid somewhere, making life hard on some parents."

"No over thinking," she replied.

"Yeah. I suppose I should have known you would say that," I replied with a shrug. "But, I guess what really has me perplexed at the moment is that I'm actually carrying on a conversation with you. In the past you would just point me at things and say something completely off the wall. Then I would have to give myself a migraine figuring out what you were trying to tell me."

"The more things change, the more they stay the same."

"So, you're saying that this conversation has a hidden meaning?"

"I love autumn, don't you?"

"Well, at least that part is," I muttered, punctuating the comment with a low snort. "Staying the same, I mean."

"Which part is that?"

"The cryptic answers, within non-answers, within hidden answers that make my head hurt."

"Did you expect it to be any different?"

I shook my head. "No. I don't suppose so. To be honest, I didn't expect much at all."

"I love autumn," she repeated.

"Since I'm having this unique opportunity to actually talk, mind if I ask how this is even happening?" As I spoke I twisted back toward

the tomb and gestured. "I was fairly certain Miranda had somehow revoked my visiting privileges to your side of the fence."

"Did she?"

"Help me out here, Ariel," I said, turning back to her. "Am I answering that question for you, or for myself?"

"For whom do you usually answer them?"

I gave her a nod. "So...class is once again in session, I see."

"You learn quickly."

"Seems I used to say that about you."

She smiled. "I had a good teacher."

"And now you want to return the favor?"

"Have you ever imagined how you will die?" she asked.

"Unfortunately, yes. Way too many times."

She stared back at me without saying another word. I held her eyes with mine, waiting for the next non sequitur to fall from her lips.

A moderate breeze began to blow, seemingly from nowhere. I looked at my surroundings and watched as it kicked its way through the cemetery. Fallen leaves tumbled over one another, caught up on the rising current of cool air, making a dry sound in the midst of the quiet. Slowly, the wind tapered off and silence cascaded around us once again.

I glanced back at Ariel. "You aren't even really here, are you?"

"Perhaps I should ask you the same thing," she replied.

I snorted and shook my head. "We both know I'm not."

"Do you?"

"I know I'm in a hospital bed and pretty well drugged up. I also know that a seriously nasty spirit has managed to shut the door between the worlds for me. So, I have to assume that either I conjured you from recent memories and this is just a really screwed up dream, or I just went ahead and died," I announced, holding out my arms and twisting in place. "I don't feel dead, at least I don't think I do. So, my guess? All of this is drug induced. Just a bad trip is all."

"Are you sure?"

I settled my focus back on her and said, "Yes."

Ariel shrugged. "If that's what you want to believe."

"Can you give me a reason why I shouldn't?"

Instead of answering verbally, she simply reached out, placed her palm against my chest and gave me a gentle push. I stumbled back and then went into freefall.

As darkness folded in around me, I heard her say, "Some people just don't want to stay dead, Rowan."

I heard a woman scream.
Her scream was my scream.

I felt pain as she struck the hard surface of the water.
Her pain was my pain.

I felt panic as the swift current pulled her under.
Her panic was my panic.

I felt death as the silty river flowed into her lungs.
Her death was my death.

CHAPTER 28

"WHAT TIME IS IT?" I ASKED.

"'Bout thirty seconds past the last time ya' asked me," Ben replied. He didn't look up from the folded magazine in his hands. He just kept intently scanning the column of text then said, "Hey, did'ju know Isaac Newton was obsessed with the occult? Bet he woulda just loved hangin' out with you."

"Seriously, Ben."

"Yeah, seriously."

"I mean seriously I was talking about the time."

"Uh-huh," he grunted. "So was I."

"Ben…"

"Really, Row." He glanced at his watch and then returned his attention to the magazine. "Now it's been a whole minute. Why don't we see if ya' can make it five before ya' ask again, okay?"

"Dammit…" I mumbled. "What's taking so long?"

"Nothin'. You just think it is 'cause you're an impatient patient." He chuckled to himself at the pun.

"Not really funny," I said.

"'Scuse me for tryin' ta' cheer you up a bit."

I ignored him and bemoaned my original train of thought once again, "It's definitely taking too long."

"Will ya' just try ta' relax, white man."

I pressed my head back into the pillow and puffed out my cheeks as I exhaled a long sigh. Directly in front of me, the curtain was open on the floor to ceiling windows that formed the wall, but there really wasn't anything unique to see beyond the panes. I already knew the routine on the other side of the glass by heart because I had been watching the activity for the better part of the day. It was like an endless, boring television show marathon where all of the episodes were exactly the same. Doctors and nurses would come and go, and then they would come and go again, and again, and so on. Obviously, I couldn't change the channel, but the anti-drama was interrupted here and there by random commercial breaks whenever I drifted off to sleep, as the occasional self-administered bolus of morphine would tend to push me over the precipice into fitful slumber.

I actually wasn't all that excited about being drugged into a brain sucking stupor, so I would wait until I simply couldn't take the pain any longer before finally mashing my thumb down on the button of the pump's control pendant. Of course, whenever such a moment would come around, my body would wonder why I had waited so long. My mind, on the other hand, would curse me for being weak and giving in—right up until the moment when the opiate would make me forget why I even cared, which didn't take very long at all.

Soon after that, darkness would seep in, and harsh nightmares were never far behind. Unfortunately, all of them seemed to feature a perplexing visit from Ariel Tanner and would end with me drowning. I still had no sense that anything had changed on an ethereal level. No voices, and no feelings from the other side. No indication that the door between the worlds had been reopened for me. Therefore, I was relatively certain the nightmares were simply that, nightmares. No hidden meanings, just my subconscious unloading on me at the behest of the drugs. Because of that, I was very quickly developing an intense hatred for the apparent side effects of morphine.

"What time is…" I began.

"Jeezus, Row," Ben cut me off in a huff as he snapped the magazine against his knee. "It's been less than a minute. You're worse than a damn kid. I think maybe the drugs are screwin' with your concept of time."

"Maybe…but…I just need to see her, Ben…" I replied.

"I know ya' do. I'm the one who argued your case with the fuckin' doctor, remember?"

"Yeah…yeah, I know… I'm sorry… How did you manage to get him to agree anyway?"

"Less anyone knows, the better," he grunted. "Trust me."

"That bad, huh?"

"Let's just say I happen ta' know his teenager can't afford any more tickets, and we'll leave it at that."

"Yeah…thought it might be something like that… Okay… Well, thanks."

"Don't sweat it. But I'm tellin' ya' man, you really just need ta' relax. She'll be here soon enough."

"Soon enough has already come and gone," I replied.

"Jeezus…" he mumbled and gave his head a shake.

I waited for what seemed like several minutes but in reality was probably once again only a handful of seconds. I lolled my head to the side, so I could see my friend and asked, “How was she when you saw her earlier?”

He sighed heavily, and the resigned look on his face told me he was finally giving up on finishing the article he’d been trying to read. He laid the magazine aside then shifted in his seat and shook his head at me. “Pretty much like I said, Row. She just stares off inta’ space. Kinda like she’s…” he stopped mid-sentence and then craned his neck to the side as he appeared to spot something out the window wall. With a quick nod he said, “Looks like ya’ can see for yourself. Here they come.”

I turned my head and out of reflex tried to push myself upward on my elbows, not that I had enough strength to get very far. It had only been a little over twenty-four hours since I’d been rushed into surgery, so my body was still rebelling against sudden movements. The pain in my gut immediately erupted from a smoldering ache to a violent conflagration of agony. I stifled a groan as I lay back then fumbled for the bed controls and used them to slowly raise myself farther into a sitting position.

Through the windows and to the side of the nurses’ station, I could see a uniformed police officer. Next to him was a wheelchair. Due to its position at the desk, I couldn’t actually see the occupant, but I knew who it was. On the opposite side of the chair, Ben’s sister, Helen Storm, was nodding and chatting with a nurse.

As my heart began to beat a little faster, the fresh twinge in my abdomen started settling toward a dull but very prominent ache. I could tell by the way it lingered I would be reaching for the morphine button in the not too distant future, no matter how much I hated the inevitable nightmare that would be sure to follow.

By the time I had adjusted myself into something resembling an upright position, the door was already open and Helen was maneuvering the wheelchair into the room. She bore the same angular Native American features as her younger brother, and looking at them side by side there was no denying their familial ties, even though she stood quite a number of inches shorter than he. While her face still retained a youthful look, her long hair had gone almost completely grey just in the years that I had known her.

Once she was through the opening, she finessed the chair around Ben, who was already looking for a place to stand where he would be out of the way. Almost immediately behind her was the nurse who had been assigned to me for the shift.

"How are you feeling, Mister Gant?" she asked while Helen pushed the wheelchair close to the side of the bed and parked it.

"I'm fine," I told her in an absent tone. My attention was focused on the occupant of the rolling seat.

"The doctor says you have about ten minutes with your visitors," she explained. "Okay?"

"Yeah…" I muttered, still not tearing my eyes from Felicity.

"I'll come back when it's time," the nurse reminded us as she exited, carefully closing the door behind her.

My wife was arranged in the wheelchair with what had been obvious care, but even so, she was now slumped to one side like a crumpled rag doll. She was dressed in a hospital gown with a soft restraint loosely encircling her mid-section, apparently to hold her upright in the seat. A blanket was tucked in around the lower half of her body, covering her from the waist down, and her hands rested atop it in her lap, palms turned slightly upward and fingers curled in a relaxed posture. Her head was canted to the right, and Helen or someone had positioned a small pillow beneath it and against her shoulder for support.

I continued to stare at Felicity without saying a word. She was pale even beyond her usual ivory complexion but from what I could tell had not yet slipped into an obvious unhealthy pallor. Still, her face was slack, lips parted slightly, and her half-lidded eyes stared vacantly into space, just as Ben had described. Now and again she would slowly blink, and if one watched closely, there would be the barest hint of movement in her neck, and she would appear to swallow.

"How are you doing, Rowan?" Helen asked.

"I've been better…" I whispered.

"That is certainly understandable," she replied, genuine sympathy in her voice.

I tried to reach for Felicity, but the side rail of the hospital bed proved to be an insurmountable barrier in my present condition. Without any prompting other than my obvious distress, Helen immediately stepped forward and lowered the rail. When I reached again, she lifted my wife's hand and slipped it carefully into mine.

"Thank you," I said softly.

Felicity's fingers were cold and felt lifeless, but I held tight and squeezed as much as my own lethargic muscles would allow. I watched as she stared, looking through me at nothing.

"How is she?" I finally asked, still not taking my eyes from her expressionless face.

"Physically, she seems to be in good shape, especially considering the circumstances," Helen told me. "She is presenting in a state of catatonic stupor, the most prominent symptoms being mutism and immobility, quite obviously. However, she does appear to maintain a strong degree of reflexive and occasionally volitional motor control. For instance, she responds to being fed orally. If her condition persists for any length of time, as long as she can be fed, there will not be a need for a feeding tube. That is a very good thing.

"She has also been observed suddenly changing position of her own accord, but the movements are neither frantic nor labored, which is a good sign. Still, she displays little or no response to other external stimuli."

"Hey," I murmured in my wife's direction while slowly stroking my thumb against the back of her hand.

I already knew that right now the body in front of me was for all intents and purposes nothing more than an empty shell. In my mind, that much was a given. The consciousness, the memories, and everything else that made Felicity who she was, had been forced into a dark void, and they were being held captive there by Miranda. Still, that didn't stop me from seeing the woman I loved right there in front of me.

Helen cleared her throat and said, "There is something else I need to tell you, Rowan. Due to the violent outburst that culminated in Felicity's attack on you, her tentative diagnosis made by the doctor on staff was catatonic schizophrenia."

"But that was before you arrived, right?" I asked.

"Yes."

I turned my face toward her and tried to shake my head. "Well, you of all people know that isn't what this is," I objected.

Helen was more than just Ben's older sister, and more than a psychiatrist as well. She had known my wife and me for years and was intimately aware of the preternatural events that were my bane. She had even seen Felicity through her original possession by Miranda, so I trusted her with the truth, as bizarre as it was.

She nodded. "I know what Benjamin told me. And, I know what I have seen. I also know that I have never known you to be wrong, Rowan. However, what I know and believe is not at issue here."

"What is then?"

"The beliefs of others. I am here because you requested me to be," she replied. "However, there is opposition. Because of your own current status as a patient in intensive care, Felicity's parents are taking legal steps to assume guardianship over her and wish to begin the hospital's recommended course of treatment with anti-psychotics."

"Jeezus," Ben spat. "That was quick. When the hell did this happen?"

"They arrived upstairs at the mental health center with the paperwork and their attorney just as we were preparing to come down here."

I closed my eyes and sighed. I should have expected something like this. Felicity's father was definitely not in any danger of starting a Rowan Gant fan club, and this wasn't the first time he'd tried to intervene in our marriage.

I concentrated for a moment and then opened my eyes. "Would those drugs have any negative effects on her?"

"In all likelihood, no," Helen explained. "However, given the unique situation, I cannot say how they might affect your ability to reunite her consciousness with her corporeal form."

The words weren't exactly something you expected to hear from someone who made her living via the scientific method. But then, Helen was different, and she definitely understood what was at stake.

I glanced toward Ben, grimacing as the news brought a new stress to bear—one that only served to negatively enhance my already growing pain. "Do me a favor and call Jackie," I said, instructing him to contact our attorney. "She should be listed in my cell. Tell her what's hap…"

He was already digging through my personal effects for my phone as he cut me off, "I'll take care of it, Kemosabe. Don't worry. We'll get this straightened out." He extracted the device then gave me a nod. "Can't turn it on in here 'cause of the monitors. I'll take it out ta' the lounge in a minute. It's all good."

Helen added, "Rowan, I am not sure if it matters to you, but I should note that your mother-in-law was largely responsible for keeping their attorney from attempting to stop today's visit with you from happening at all."

"I'm not surprised. Maggie has her faults, but she's not a hothead like Shamus," I said, steeling myself against a wave of abdominal pain as the last word tumbled from my mouth.

"She also asked about you and seemed genuinely concerned for your well-being," she added.

The door to the room opened and the nurse followed it in. As she skirted quickly around Ben, she asked, "How are you feeling, Mister Gant?"

"I'm fine," I told her, tensing in order to hide a grimace that was threatening to erupt across my face. "My ten minutes aren't up yet."

"We had an alarm on your monitors," she replied, checking the stats on display next to the bed as she pressed two fingers against my wrist.

As if on cue, an electronic buzzer chirped, so she reached out and pressed a button with her free hand while continuing to check my pulse. Felicity's hand suddenly twitched against mine, and I rolled my head quickly to the side. Her motion was barely noticeable, but I was certain of what I had felt.

However, my wife was still staring into space, and her position in the chair hadn't changed.

"Felicity?" I whispered.

I waited several heartbeats, watching her intently, but there was no response. I squeezed her hand, still to no avail. Her small, almost unnoticeable spasm had probably been nothing more than a random signal firing along otherwise empty nerves.

I closed my eyes and swallowed hard as a burst of pain ripped through my abdomen on a mission to remind me just how vulnerable I was at the moment. The only thing keeping me from reaching for the button on the morphine pump was Felicity. However, given that she wasn't really here, I was beginning to wonder how much more I could take. The universe, or whoever happened to be piloting it at the moment, apparently wondered the same thing as well.

In that moment, it decided that not quite enough turmoil had rained down upon my particular piece of real estate. A quick knock came against the still open door of my room, and a uniformed police officer leaned in through the opening. "Detective Storm?"

"Yeah?" my friend grunted, glancing toward him.

"Sorry to bother you, but Lieutenant Sheets from the Major Case Squad is out in the lounge," he said. "He wants to talk to you right away."

"Sheets? L. T. is here?" Ben made a demonstrative gesture at the floor with his index finger as he spoke. "Did 'e say why?"

"He said it's urgent. Something about another victim in the bloodsucker case."

"Aww Jeezus, fuck me…" Ben spat and immediately turned to leave. As he stepped past Helen, he handed her my cell phone and began to say something.

"I will take care of it," she told him before he could even get the first word off the end of his tongue.

"Thanks," he told her.

I called out, "Ben…"

He stopped, "What?"

"You're coming back to fill me in, right?"

"Jeezus fuckin' Christ… You're layin' there in… Fuck!" He replied then shook his head and started out the door. "Forget about it, Row," he barked back over his shoulder. "This is my job, not yours. Not anymore. You're fired."

Adding to the ever-increasing tumult, the nurse announced, "Mister Gant, it's time for your visitors to go."

"No," I objected.

"Yes," she replied.

"She is correct, Rowan. I think it would be for the best," Helen told me, shifting around to unlock the brake on the wheelchair.

"Wait!" I yelped.

Continuing to hold tight to Felicity's hand, I gritted my teeth and twisted my body so that I could roll closer to her.

"Mister Gant, what are you doing?!" the nurse protested, taking hold of my shoulder as I almost rolled myself out of the bed.

Leaning off the side and bringing my face as close to my wife's as possible, I struggled out a whisper between labored breaths, "You hang on, Felicity… You hear me? Hang on… I'm coming to get you soon… I promise…"

Chapter 29

PANIC SPREADS THROUGH MY CHEST.

Dark water rushes up toward me…

Or am I rushing down toward it?

The muddy surface roils with tight eddies that appear then disappear.

The pain rips into me as I strike.

The water is hard like brick.

I am being pulled under.

The current has me now.

I need to breathe.

I gasp.

The silty water makes me gag as it rushes down my throat…

And then into my lungs…

I feel heavy now…

I'm sinking…

Darkness is coming…

I felt myself tense and then suddenly gasp. My eyes were still closed, but the narcotic haze that was ruling my existence off and on as of late finally seemed to be clearing once again. Images still played inside my boggy skull, and I knew immediately that I had dreamt of New Orleans cemeteries and drowning once again. I had expected it, but as usual that didn't keep me from being startled awake by the inevitable ending. I still wasn't quite sure why my subconscious had picked this particular nightmare to dwell upon. I assumed it had something to do with how Miranda had originally died back in 1851, but if there was some deeper meaning behind it, my rational brain wasn't getting the message. One thing I did know for a fact, however, was that the repetitious aberration was starting to get very old, and I was ready for it to go away.

As the haze continued to dissipate, I found my voice and mumbled, "You in here, Ben?"

Prior to the onset of the nightmare, I had been laying here adrift in a comfortable drowse, existing somewhere between wake and sleep. I had been able to hear everything around me with an unfettered clarity—magazine pages as they turned, footsteps that sounded lightly against the floor, and even the soft rush of air as the door opened and closed. But, none of it had truly made any sense in the fuzzy darkness that surrounded my world. It was all just an underlying soundtrack to which I'd grudgingly become accustomed. Apparently, so accustomed that it had lulled me back into a deepening sleep, where a darkened dream lay in wait.

Flowing into the quiet lull behind my voice, a new jumble of noises tapped out a rhythm against my eardrums. The medley began with the light rustle of fabric against fabric and the dull slap of a magazine carefully dropped against a flat surface, both happening in the near distance. Those sounds were soon followed by footsteps coming toward me and then quiet breathing close by.

Although my olfactory sense had been assaulted by the antiseptic smells of the hospital, which were less than pleasant in and of themselves, the smell of muddy water currently lingered in my nose—an illusion carried with me into wakefulness after each episode. Fortunately however, it appeared that a much more pleasant scent was now pushing it out as I picked up the barest hint of sweet vanilla.

"It's Constance, Row," Agent Mandalay told me. "You're on my watch now."

"Constance…" I began slowly. "If you're here…"

Apparently she anticipated my question and rushed to reassure me. "Don't worry," she said. "Agent Parker is with Felicity. As of this afternoon, the bureau officially took over from the local law enforcement. Until this is all done, you're both under federal protection, twenty-four-seven."

I finally allowed my eyes to flutter open and then rolled my head in the direction of her voice. Her face wasn't crystal clear, but I'd become used to being without my glasses, so at least it wasn't a complete blur. I could see that she was standing there looking at me with her head cocked to the side, and I was able to pick out the mix of concern and relief fighting for control over her features.

I sighed. "I suppose I have you to thank for that?"

She shook her head. "It came from much higher up, actually."

"I see… I thought the Federal Marshall Service handled protection details," I said.

"It depends on the situation," she said with a nod. "Obviously, you're a special case."

"Go figure," I mumbled then drew in a deep breath and said, "Guess it didn't matter how much I acted like an ass. I'm still being viewed as a possible asset, huh?"

"That's the rumor… But I'm sure there's more to it than that," she replied.

"So, how is she?" I asked.

"Felicity? I'm afraid she's pretty much the same," she replied, a detectable note of apology in her voice.

"What about her parents?"

"Helen spoke to your attorney, and she's on top of it. She said she'd come by and meet with you about it tomorrow."

"Good."

"So what about you?" Constance asked. "Are you doing okay?"

I swallowed then quietly breathed, "I guess that depends on your definition of okay."

"Same old Rowan," she replied. "I think you're allergic to straight answers."

"Not really. I just think out loud a lot."

"I've noticed. So…can I get you anything? Are you thirsty?"

"Yeah… Actually I think I am."

"Right now all they'll let you have are ice chips. The nurse brought a fresh container in just a few minutes ago. Would you like some?"

"That works," I muttered. "Just put 'em in a glass and pour some Scotch over them."

"Mm-hmm, I don't think so. Besides, why would you want Scotch when you already have something even better tapped right into a vein?"

"What? This?" I said, slightly lifting the hand that still grasped the pendant from the morphine pump and then letting it fall back onto the blankets. "Not really a big fan of the side effects."

"What side effects?"

"The nightmares."

"Hmm," she replied. "I didn't have any of those, myself. It just made the pain go away and I slept a lot."

My brain was still a bit sluggish, so it took a moment for me to connect the dots where her remark was concerned. However, within a second or two, I remembered that it wasn't all that long ago that Constance had been in a position very similar to this. Instead of a knife, her wound had been produced by a bullet making it through a gap in her protective vest, but the method behind the injury really didn't matter. Hers had still been courtesy of Miranda, just like mine.

"Guess it's just me then," I sighed.

"You should probably tell the nurse about it though. They might need to put you on something else for the pain."

"Maybe," I agreed.

Constance waited a moment then nodded toward the tray at the foot of the bed. "So...do you still want some of those ice chips?"

"Sure..." I replied.

She smiled and stepped away as I sent my fingers in search of the bed controls. Finding them mostly by touch, I eventually managed to start the top half into an upward tilt.

"How long was I asleep?" I asked once I'd struggled through the pain of adjusting myself into something resembling a reclined sitting position.

Constance handed me a half full cup of the crushed ice and shook her head. "I'm not entirely sure. You had already been out for a while when I took over, and that was..." She gave her watch a quick glance and said, "A little over four hours ago now. So probably five hours at least."

"Hope you brought another one of your romance novels to pass the time," I quipped.

She let out a light chuckle. "Some law enforcement bulletins and a copy of *Guns and Ammo*, actually."

"Seriously? But..."

She cut me off. "I never said that I *didn't* read it."

"True. You didn't." I paused and tried to focus on more recent memories. Unfortunately, they were still a bit of a blur. "So...I guess I should check... It's still Tuesday, right?" I asked, then tilted the cup to my lips and shook a few small chunks of the ice into my mouth. As they began to melt, I allowed the cool water to run down the back of my dry throat. The sensation made me realize just how thirsty I really was, so I tipped the cup to my mouth again.

"Yes," she said with a nod. "Still Tuesday. Although it's early evening. Coming up on seven."

I laid my head back and sighed as I did the mental calculation. Once I had swallowed the rest of the water, I turned my face to her. She had stepped the short distance back across the room and parked herself in the chair again. "Any word from Ben? When he left earlier there was something going on with another victim."

Constance nodded as she answered. "Yes, actually. I talked to him an hour or so ago, and they were finally starting the interview."

"Interview?" I asked, scrunching my brow. "What do you mean? I'm not sure I follow."

"I'm sorry," she replied. "I thought you already knew. The victim is still alive. He somehow managed to escape before the killer had a chance to bleed him out."

"Are you serious?" I asked.

"Yes," she replied. "He was picked up not far from here as a matter of fact. He was wandering down the middle of a street in Saint Flora, naked, and apparently in a complete daze. It appeared he had been tortured for a while, and he's in pretty rough shape but stable now, as far as I've heard. They brought him here to the emergency room." She extended her index finger and pointed at the ceiling. "He's in a bed two floors up at the moment, being interviewed by Ben and his lieutenant."

"Amazing…" I almost whispered as I stared off. Something still wasn't registering for me, but I couldn't yet put my finger on it.

Constance nodded. "You aren't the first person to use that word."

"I've had some pretty crazy nightmares lately," I said. "You aren't about to morph into a giant rabbit and tell me that's what this is, are you?"

"Your nightmares have been about giant rabbits?"

I gave my head a small shake. "No. Just making up an example."

"Well, you aren't dreaming this time," she assured me. "I can pinch you if you'd like."

"Thanks, I'll pass."

"Good call. I pinch pretty hard."

I rolled my head back up and slowly shook some more of the chipped ice into my mouth. I chewed it and once again allowed the melt to run down my throat.

The mind fog was lifting even more, but at the same time, I was already feeling twinges of pain in my gut—the trade off for clarity I suppose. Fortunately though, they were still dull and remote. With luck I'd have plenty of time before they became unbearable enough for me to be willing to endure the nightmare for the umpteenth time.

I started to lift the cup to my lips again but stopped and held it hanging in mid-air as my opiate intoxicated synapses continued to sober up. A series of misfires between neurons finally captured and then generated a shaky connection. As it continued to flicker and arc, a question floated through my brain. Rolling my head to the side once again, I lent a voice to the query.

"So, Constance…"

"Yes?"

"If they just now started the interview, how did they know earlier that he was a victim of the same killer?" I asked.

She frowned and shook her head. "It's not that important, Rowan. Just trust me. There was some very compelling evidence."

"Go ahead and pinch me," I said.

"What?"

"Go ahead and tell me what you're hiding," I replied. "That should be as good as any pinch."

"I can if you really want to know," she said. "But I don't see how it will help, and you aren't going to wake up from this. It's not that kind of nightmare."

"Yeah, I kind of got that already," I told her. "How'd they know, Constance?"

She sighed and shook her head again. "They knew because your name had been carved into his chest…and his back, and his arms, and even his forehead… Honestly, from what I understand, it's just about anywhere on his body there's room enough for it to fit."

Chapter 30

"OH," I REPLIED.

The word was patently anticlimactic in and of itself, but there really wasn't much one could say in response to an explanation such as Constance had just given—especially in this line of work and having seen some of the horrors I had witnessed over the years. Once upon a time, such a revelation would have been shocking to me. Absolutely horrifying on levels I couldn't even imagine, in fact. But, that was then. Now, such a violent reaction was a part of my distant past, and atrocities like these were just a matter of course in my painful world.

However, this isn't to say I was completely cold-blooded.

I was beyond disgusted by the news—that much was absolutely certain. It made me sick just to think about it. Still, surprise just didn't fit into the equation at all.

The simple fact of the matter was that carving my name into a victim was exactly the sort of thing Miranda would do, especially if she was working some type of hoodoo against me. She'd gone that route several times before, so there was no reason to believe she wouldn't do so again. The only question in my mind was exactly what kind of magick it was?

If I had to guess, I would say she was probably trying to kill me. On the surface, that's definitely how it looked. And, after all, we knew for certain that particular errand was at the top of her agenda, so it made perfect sense. Basic sympathetic magick—name the victim for me and then kill him as me. It was almost as simplistic as my use of salt to ward against her. In fact, it made me wonder if I had revealed too much during that meeting in Texas. Maybe she was taking a page from my own playbook and using my belief in the KISS principle against me. Given my currently weakened state, who knows, it might even have worked.

If those were in fact the circumstances, I guess it was a good thing for both of us that the victim had escaped when he did. I silently admonished myself for having such a self-serving thought, but pretty or not, it was the truth.

I rolled my head up and stared at the ceiling for a minute or two. I didn't find any comfort there, not that I was really expecting to.

As if the twinges in my gut weren't enough to deal with, my neck was now starting to ache and the pain was threatening to advance into my skull. As a countermeasure, I slowly worked my shoulders up and down then tried to move myself into a more comfortable position. I'd only been in this bed for a little over a day now, but it was already taking its own toll on my body. Unfortunately, I had a vague recollection of a doctor telling me that I wasn't likely to be leaving here for several more days yet.

I let out a groan as I settled back against my pillow. Unfortunately, my new physical arrangement didn't seem to be any better than its predecessor.

"Are you okay?" Constance asked.

"Yeah," I grumbled. "My neck is bothering me a bit. I guess I'm not used to laying around like this."

"Do you need another pillow or something like that?"

"Nahh…I don't think so. But thanks anyway."

"No problem."

I waited for a moment then added, "And I mean thanks for everything, Constance. You're a hell of a friend, and I want you to know I appreciate everything you've done. I know you've put up with a lot these past few days."

"That's what friends do," she replied.

"I know, but I just wanted to say it. Ya'know what I mean?"

She chuckled. "Don't get maudlin on me, Rowan. I'm not sure I'd know what to do."

I allowed myself a grin. "So I guess this wouldn't be the time to tell you that you're like family to Felicity and me and that we put you in our wills?"

"I'd say most definitely not. Unless there's a huge amount of money involved."

I snorted. "Don't worry. I think it's just the drugs talking anyway."

"Probably," she agreed. The melody of another chuckle fell in behind the comment before she added, "But seriously, thanks. And just so you know, the feeling is mutual."

"You're welcome," I said. "And thanks."

Quiet flowed into the room once again, so I tilted my head forward to watch the activity on the other side of the window wall. As expected, it was much the same as earlier, but at least it was something to look at.

The small amount of ice that remained in my cup had melted for the most part, so I took a sip then gave the Styrofoam vessel a tilt and completely drained it. After swallowing I let out a thin sigh and continued to stare through the glass.

"Do you want some more?" Constance asked.

I looked over at her. "Don't worry about it… You just sat down."

She pulled herself up from the seat and then shrugged. "Now I just stood up. Would you like some more?"

"I guess since you put it that way, yeah," I said. "Thanks."

"It's not a problem, Rowan."

She stepped over and took the cup from me then set about refilling it from the container on the tray at the end of the bed. I started working my shoulders in small circles as best I could in an attempt to loosen some of the kinks in my neck. The ache seemed to have blossomed now and was creeping upward into the base of my skull. As I slowly twisted my head side to side, I felt a tingle working its way up my spine. In that same moment, I noticed a mild burning sensation on my arms. I tilted my head forward as I raised the appendages and immediately saw small patches of gooseflesh erupting here and there across my skin. The tingle along my spine settled into my neck, and I felt myself shiver involuntarily.

Constance had apparently just turned back around to hand me the cup when the tremor began.

"Are you sure you're okay, Rowan?" she asked, arching an eyebrow upward as she watched me shake.

"I guess so," I said. "I think maybe I'm just feeling a chill."

She nodded. "Okay. That makes sense. They keep it pretty cold in hospitals. I had chills too when I was laid up. Let me see about getting you an extra blanket."

"Thanks," I told her.

I was still tensing my body against the sudden cold, and my abdomen was starting to announce its displeasure with me because of it. Constance abandoned the cup to the tray and stepped out the door of the room. The moment it opened, I could hear the scratchy buzz of a radio, probably coming from the nurse's station. I couldn't tell exactly what they were listening to, but it sounded like it might be some kind of round-table talk show. Whoever the guests were, however, they didn't seem to care if they talked over the top of one another. Fortunately, it was out there and I was in here, so it wasn't as annoying as it could have been.

A minute or so later, Constance was back at the bedside, and a nurse carrying a blanket came through the door shortly afterward. The strain on my muscles was now squeezing the nerves in my neck, so the ache was crawling across my scalp and leeching into my skull. Of course, in comparison to my old norm where headaches were concerned, this one was an amateur with no skill.

"How are you feeling this evening, Mister Gant?" the nurse asked as she began to unfold the pre-warmed cloth on top of me.

"Okay, I guess," I said, teeth chattering a bit. "A little cold, obviously."

She nodded as she continued tucking the blanket around me. "That's not unusual." She shot me a smile and then leaned a bit closer and adopted a faux confidential tone. "I'm always cold around here too. I even keep a sweater here all year 'round."

When finished, she turned and gave the vitals monitors a once over then directed herself to me once again. "Okay, well my name is Anastasia. I didn't get to introduce myself earlier because you were still asleep, but I'll be taking care of you tonight. Is there anything you need right now?"

I shook my head as I consciously tried to soak in the warmth of the blanket. "No, I don't think so."

She gave the morphine pump a quick check. "It looks like you're okay there. How is your pain this evening?"

"Not bad," I answered. "Although, I am starting to get a bit of a headache."

"How bad is it?"

"Not bad I don't guess. I don't really know."

"Well, how would you rate the pain on a scale of one to ten?"

"Maybe a high seven," I replied.

She raised an eyebrow. "A high seven? I thought you said it wasn't that bad?"

"I know…I know… But I'm sort of used to them being more like a twenty-five with occasional attacks of fifty or better."

She chuckled, but I didn't bother to point out to her that I wasn't joking. I really didn't feel up to inventing an explanation at the moment, and the real one certainly wouldn't do. Especially if my in-laws were trying to have me declared incompetent so that they could take over the decisions about Felicity's treatment. The last thing I needed to do was provide them with a witness who would testify that I qualified as delusional.

"I think we can probably get you something for that," Anastasia told me. "Let me check with the doctor just to be sure, and I'll be right back. Okay?"

"Yeah. Thanks."

Once the nurse had exited, Constance cocked her head and watched me carefully. After a short pause she said, "That came on pretty quickly, didn't it?"

"Yeah," I agreed, pushing out a heavy sigh.

The high seven had now progressed into a solid eight and seemed to be on the climb. It was still nothing by my usual standards, but it was definitely enough to let me know it was there. I looked past Constance and noticed the door had been left ajar, which explained why I could still hear the drone of the radio talk show wafting in from the nurses station. It seemed a bit louder now, and it was starting to annoy me.

"I wish they would…" I began.

Before I could finish the thought, a light rap of knuckles sounded against the door, and it slowly swung inward. Ben followed it and came cautiously through the opening.

"Hey, Kemosabe," he said.

"Yo, Tonto," I replied, teeth chattering slightly.

He strode over and gave Constance a light squeeze on her shoulder, but that was as far as he took the semi-public display of affection.

"We're takin' a break upstairs," he said. "So just thought I'd come down and check on ya'." He looked me up and down then said, "No offense, Row, but you ain't lookin' so good."

I was certain he had a valid point. The solid eight had very quickly advanced to a twelve with little ceremony or warning, and it was still on the move. I grimaced but brushed off his comment and went straight for a question of my own. "How's the interview going?"

He shook his head. "Right now, it ain't."

"I thought the victim was stable and alert?" Constance said.

"Yeah, he's stable, I guess," he replied. "And he's awake, but I'm not so sure about alert. They got 'im pretty drugged up, not that I can fault 'em for that. He's pretty tore up. But that ain't the real problem."

"Then what is?" Constance asked.

Ben hadn't closed the door, so it was now hanging wide open. It wouldn't have mattered except that someone had again turned up the volume on the radio out at the nurse's station, and the frenetic talk show was now blaring through the opening. However, I still couldn't make out what was being said because it seemed the host and all of the guests were stuck in a free-for-all with no regard for any type of order.

Ben shook his head in disgust and then proceeded to explain, "Fuckin' bitch did somethin' to his eyes, which is prob'ly why he was wanderin' in the middle of a street when they found 'im. Doc says he might regain part of his vision, but right now they're all bandaged up." He shrugged and then added, "And, of course, on toppa that she cut off all 'is damn fingers."

"What's that…" I started then shook my head and changed course mid-sentence while nodding at the door. "Ben, could you please shut that?"

He gave me an odd glance then stepped over and pushed the door closed as he said, "Yeah, sure."

The blare of the talk show didn't stop. If anything, it became a little louder still.

"Is something wrong, Rowan?" Constance asked.

"That damn radio," I said. "I wish they'd turn it down."

"What radio?" she asked.

"You can't hear that?" I replied, giving my head a shake.

Ben backed her up. "There ain't a radio playin', white man, trust me. This is the quietest floor in the whole damn place."

The twelve had now become an eighteen, and a sharp stab of pain lanced from the base of my skull and directly into my frontal lobes. I winced and closed my eyes as my whole body tensed, which in turn set off the pain in my abdomen once again. Even under the warmth of the multiple blankets I became ice cold, and I felt the intense prickling of every hair on my body standing to rapt attention.

"Jeezus, Row, you definitely ain't lookin' good now," Ben observed. "I think we need ta' call the nurse."

"Why the fingers?" I asked, pushing the question out through clenched teeth.

I didn't quite understand why I so desperately felt the need to know the answer, but it was more than a mere curiosity. It had literally taken on an unearthly urgency. For some reason, in my mind, it seemed as if my very life depended upon hearing it.

"'Cause she's a goddamn sadistic bitch, I guess," Ben answered from the hip with a healthy shot of sarcasm chasing the words. "Who the fuck knows? Hang on, I'm gettin'…"

"No," I pressed, cutting him off while squinting my eyes together as the eighteen ramped up to a twenty-two. I literally growled the demand, “I mean why do the fingers matter now?”

Constance’s urgent voice barked, “I just hit the call button.”

A high-pitched peal suddenly began issuing from the vitals monitor as an alarm started to sound. For some reason, even though only a portion of the telemetry was actually connected to me, the tone was swiftly followed by another, and then another, until it cascaded into an unscored symphony of electronic noise. Through my watering eyes, I could see frantic movement on the other side of the glass.

The door to the room flew open and bodies dressed in scrubs piled in through the opening, barking orders as they shoved Constance and Ben out of the way.

“Dammit Ben,” I groaned.

“Jeezus Row…” he huffed as he backpedaled out of the way.

“Why? Why the fingers?” I demanded once more, forcing the words out with everything I could muster.

“The guy’s a deaf-mute,” my friend called to me as he was being pushed out the door. His confusion about my curiosity was evident in his voice as he added, “He can’t communicate with us, and we can’t communicate with him.”

Twenty-two jumped straight to fifty, light bloomed in a harsh explosion of contrast, and the radio blared as thousands of dead, screaming voices poured directly into my skull.

When simple magick works, it works well. When simple magick fails, it fails big. However, this sudden collapse of SpellCraft wasn’t just a catastrophic failure; it was flat out epic, and I was at the center of it all.

CHAPTER 31

"YOU HAD SOME OF US WORRIED FOR A LITTLE WHILE, Rowan," Constance said.

"Yeah, I kind of got that impression," I replied.

Ben snorted and then quipped, "Not me. It was all them. I knew you were fine."

"Liar," I sighed.

"Yeah, okay. So maybe I was worried just a little."

"Uh-huh. Just a little. Sure." I answered him with a sarcastic grunt and then said, "Thanks though. I appreciate the concern."

"Yeah," he replied. "It's all good."

I let out another labored sigh then closed my eyes and attempted to will myself to relax. I hadn't been having much luck with that exercise so far, and I wasn't expecting to now, but that didn't keep me from trying.

The somewhat overestimated crisis itself had ended almost as quickly as it began, probably even quicker, in fact. Even so, it was nearly an hour before Ben and Constance were allowed back into the room with me; and that only happened once it had been decided that my shivering had somehow caused abnormal readings to feed back through the monitors, thereby falsely setting off the alarms. Since various and repeated checks of my vitals showed they were as normal as they could possibly be given my current physical condition, that was the only explanation that seemed to fit the minds of the medical professionals tending to me.

Of course, I knew better. There was definitely something else going on. While I certainly wasn't an expert, I doubted that it was my shaking or that there were system anomalies causing the alarms. My money was on the fact that a door between the worlds of the living and dead was once again propped wide open. I even had the familiar pounding headache and background drone in my ears to prove it, both of which were ailments I had never imagined I would be glad to have back.

Until now, that is.

Still, I just let the doctors and nurses believe their faulty conclusion. It would be better for everyone concerned if I left it that way.

"Are you still feeling okay, Rowan?" Constance asked.

"Okay as can be expected, I guess."

"Do you want to try sleeping now? I can make Storm shut up if you want me to."

"Hey!" Ben exclaimed. "I'm not the one yammerin', you are."

"Don't worry… You're both fine…" I said.

At the moment I was reclined farther back in the bed than I had been earlier. The intensity of the spasms I'd experienced had apparently caused a bit of concern as well, in particular regarding the status of my incisions. That in turn had led to an examination of the wounds just to be sure nothing had torn. Along with that came an unscheduled change of the dressings. This was the first time I had seen the injuries—that I could remember anyway. From the quick glimpse I caught of the jagged rows of staples, it was obvious that I would be sporting some pretty serious scars. Of course, there really wasn't anything new about that, so it was really the least of my concerns.

Now, however, due to all that extra activity, the pain in my gut was even further agitated than before. It was vying hard for my attention, and without a doubt, winning; but I still wasn't ready for the dump of painkiller into my veins just yet. I had a pretty good idea that once I did cave in and press the button, the ensuing nightmare would be taking on a whole new level of intensity. To me, that much was a given.

Unfortunately, that conclusion also left me in a quandary. On the one hand, I wondered if the horror of the darkened dream might bring answers. On the other, I questioned whether or not they might be answers I didn't really want. Still, under the circumstances, I knew it was eventually going to happen whether I liked it or not. I only hoped that I would be prepared for whatever it was I would see.

The stretch of impromptu quiet finally came to a close when Ben elected to offer a personal observation. "Ya'know, if I didn't know better, I woulda thought you were goin' all *Twilight Zone* on us earlier. I mean, that's kinda what it looked like."

I opened my eyes and rolled my head toward him. "Actually, I was, sort of."

"Whaddaya mean?" he asked. "I thought ya' said Miranda had ya' all locked outta that or somethin'?"

"She did," I agreed then tried to shake my head. "But she doesn't anymore."

"That a good thing or a bad thing?"

"I don't know yet, but I'm leaning toward good."

"Okay… So, you seein' anything out there in la-la land now?" he asked.

"No. Not yet but I suspect it's coming soon."

"Okay, so, not tryin' ta' be an ass or anything, but how do ya' really know ya' got your Witch-fu back?"

"Trust me," I sighed. "I know."

"Do you know how it happened?" Constance asked.

"Ben broke a spell," I replied.

My friend shook his head and huffed, "Yeah, right."

I answered the objection. "I'm not kidding."

"Okay, ya' wanna explain how the hell I managed that? You're the Witch, not me."

"Actually, it was both of you," I said. "Constance told me the victim upstairs had my name carved into him."

"Yeah, well that's an understatement. Poor bastard's prob'ly gonna hafta change his name ta' Rowan after this 'cause of all the scars he's gonna have."

"My point exactly."

"I don't follow," Ben pressed. "We already know the bitch is a fuckin' psycho, and she's fixated on you an' Firehair."

"True, but that wasn't just some sociopathic act on Miranda's part," I explained. "Was it just Rowan, or was it my full name?"

He shrugged, "Both, I guess. Some spots it was just Rowan. But wherever it'd fit it was first, middle, and last."

"I figured as much. That means there was a very specific purpose behind her doing that. She was naming him after me. Literally turning him into a living poppet. An effigy of me, actually."

"Okay," Ben grunted. "So what you're sayin' is she made 'erself a real, live Rowan doll ta' torture by proxy."

"Something like that."

"Okay, but I still don't see what that's got ta' do with me 'n Constance breakin' a spell."

"The poppet wasn't just for her to torture, Ben. He was part of a larger piece of SpellCraft."

"Keep goin', I'm listenin'…"

"It's simple really. You told me that he was both deaf and mute, correct?"

"Yeah."

"Well, she picked him specifically because of that. Then once he had been named as me, she also took away his sight and, by cutting off his fingers, his ability to even use sign language. In effect, she did everything necessary to render him unable to communicate, at least in the short run. She isolated him from the outside world in every way possible."

Constance spoke up with a questioning note in her voice. "So if I understand what you are saying, what she did was some type of magick to keep you from communicating with spirits like you normally do?"

"Exactly. It's called sympathetic magick. She made me blind, deaf, and mute as far as ethereal communication was concerned. I have to give her credit, it was an inspired move. Sick and twisted as all hell, but definitely inspired… And in this case, it obviously worked pretty damn well. It probably still would be if he'd never escaped and ended up here."

Ben shook his head. "Okay, that makes sense I guess… Well, ya'know…sorta… I mean at least as far as anything with you ever makes any kinda sense to the rest of us normal people… But I still don't get what Constance and I had ta' do with makin' it go away."

"Sometimes…" I began then paused and qualified my impending statement "Not always, but sometimes…breaking a spell can be as simple as just knowing that it exists and how it was done."

"No shit?"

"Yeah… No shit."

"And that's what happened here?" he asked.

"Yeah. That's what happened."

"But didn't you already know she was doin' this?"

"I knew she was blocking me, but I didn't know it was a spell. As soon as I was clued in as to how she was doing it and put it all together, the wall she'd built began to crumble."

"I hesitate ta' ask…" he began.

I finished the question for him. "Why haven't I been able to do the same thing with her connection to Felicity?"

"Well… Yeah…"

"Believe me, I wish it were that simple. But like I said, it doesn't always work like that."

"Friggin' wunnerful…" he muttered.

"Yeah," I agreed.

"Okay, but just 'cause we helped, that doesn't mean either of us is gonna start goin' all la-la or anything, right?"

"No more than you normally do," I replied.

"Yeah, Row. Funny. Just fuckin' hilarious. You're a real comedian, ain't ya'?"

I felt myself wince, and then I sighed heavily. "I suppose that depends on who you ask."

"Yeah. Well don't quit your day job."

"Which one?" I asked.

"The computer genius gig," he replied. "'Cause in case ya' don't remember, I officially fired ya' from the other one. It was too close this time. My nerves can't take it anymore."

"Bullshit."

"I'm serious, Row."

"Well, I don't know that you have the authority to pull that off," I told him.

"I think my L. T.'ll back me up."

"Yeah, well you can both tell it to the voices in my head. Besides, the Major Case Squad apparently has competition."

"Yeah," he grunted. "I heard the Feebs are tryin' ta' recruit ya'."

"I'm afraid I told him, Rowan," Constance interjected. "Sorry."

"Not necessary. I'm glad you did. I wasn't really planning to keep it a secret."

Ben waited a moment then asked, "So, ya' gonna do it?"

"Right now, I honestly don't know."

"Ya'know I'd hafta start callin' you a Feeb too, right?"

"Why? You haven't called me a Feeb in years," Constance objected.

"Not to your face," Ben replied.

"Oh really?"

"B'sides, that's different. I'm datin' you. I ain't datin' Row."

"And believe me, I'm thankful for that," I grunted. "Well, don't worry. The 'Feeb' thing has already gone into the con column on my list. I don't need anymore nicknames."

"You're starting to sound pretty tired, Rowan," Constance announced.

"Yeah…I am."

She nodded. "And you also sound like you're hurting again."

"It's not really that bad," I breathed through a quick wince.

"Now who's a liar?" Ben chided.

"Guess that'd be me."

"Why don't you just go ahead and hit the morphine," Constance said, telling more than asking.

"So you're pushing narcotics now?" I gibed, although my thin chuckle was cut short by another spate of sharp pains.

"It's there for a reason, Row," she told me.

"Yeah…I know… I think maybe I'm getting close," I admitted.

"Ya' oughta just go ahead, white man," Ben told me. "You layin' there sufferin' for no reason ain't gonna help anything."

"Okay… Okay…" I sighed then lifted my hand into both their lines of sight and made a somewhat exaggerated show of mashing my thumb down on the button. As the pump kicked on with a quick, soft hum I asked, "Happy now?"

"Yeah," he grunted and then took a quick glance at his watch. "Don't worry. You won't miss anything. I've gotta run back upstairs anyway."

"What for?" I asked as the first fingers of dullness started to massage my brain.

"Gotta see if there's an ID on the vic yet. No prints ta' work from, and unfortunately, there hasn't been anyone matchin' his description reported missin'. Hell, hasn't even been anyone who's a deaf-mute reported missin' at all."

"Miranda is using someone else's body," I sighed.

"Yeah, Row, I got that. I ain't spreadin' it around, obviously, but I know the score. We just gotta find who."

"No… Yes… I mean…" I sighed again as the opiate clouded my thoughts and used my exhaustion to nudge me closer to sleep. "I mean…whoever she's using…that person already knew the victim… He was probably a friend or close acquaintance."

"Why do ya' say that?"

I sucked in a deep breath and widened my eyes as I struggled to stay conscious. "Something Miranda said in Texas…" I explained. "She told me she could make the voices stop… That means she already had the spell planned… It wasn't spur of the moment… She knew this victim before I ever came back to Saint Louis…probably longer…"

"Okay…" Ben replied with a nod. His voice seemed hollow and distant as the room began melting around me. "I'll tell my L. T. Saint Flora coppers and MCS are already doin' a door ta' door. Maybe we'll get lucky an' somebody knows 'im."

"Conmmm ban?" I asked.

"What?"

I huffed out an exasperated breath as I tried to make my tongue work in sync with my lips. "Commeen bag?"

“Comin’ back?” he repeated. “Yeah Row, I’ll be back later. Right now, you just rest.”

“It’s okay, Rowan,” Constance told me. “I’m not going anywhere. I’ll be right here.”

“Goond,” I mumbled then tried to add, “Nemmer know…my hab sssome…”

Apparently I didn’t finish the sentence as I heard the echo of Constance’s voice drifting into my ears, “Some what, Rowan?”

However, even if I had managed to make my mouth work, I wouldn’t have been able to answer the question. It was simply too late.

I was already falling toward the muddy, roiling water.

CHAPTER 32

"ROWAN...YOU CAME FOR HER," ARIEL SAYS.

I open my mouth to reply, and the words tumble onto the ground, unspoken and unheard. They shatter, exploding into shimmering gemlike shards, then rain outward only to disappear into the darkness.

"Come with me," she says. "She's been waiting."

We are walking...

The darkness is all around us. I can feel it clinging to me like a shroud. I look down at my own hands but see nothing more than the endless black.

I look over at Ariel and can see her clearly.

I don't even try to ask. It isn't for me to know.

We are walking...

The hollow peal of a telephone ringer worked its way into my ears. It was both infinitely distant and infinitely close by. My brain tried for a moment to make sense of the sound and its proximity to me.

It was completely out of context. But then, so was I.

My brain gave up. It knew I belonged somewhere else right now. I had something important to do, and it didn't involve a telephone.

"She's been waiting for you," Ariel says.

We are standing in front of a large wooden door with intricate carvings.

It is more than just familiar.

It has become a part of me.

The pain that lives beyond its threshold belongs to me.

It calls me.

"It is good that you have come for her," Ariel says. "She's waiting."

"Thank you," I tell her.

The words, like all those before, drip from my mouth in silence. They dribble down my chin then fall, only to land on my chest where they leave bloody stains upon my shirt.

Ariel says, "Go to her, Rowan."

I look up and see the door is now open. I search for Ariel, but she is gone.

I step through the opening and into a new void.

The darkness is replaced by grey.

I'm standing in the center of a small room.

The walls are close.

Too close…

Claustrophobia claws at me.

I have been here before.

I turn in place, searching for her.

In the shadows of the corner an ivory skinned woman waits.

I go to her.

I kneel in front of her.

I reach out and gently touch her.

Slowly, she brings her face up and stares at me.

She smiles and says, "I knew you would come."

"Felicity?" I ask.

Sharp pain arcs through my stomach.

I can no longer breathe.

I look down and see that I am bleeding.

The woman begins to laugh.

She withdraws the knife slowly then plunges it back into my abdomen.

I look at her and the pain rips through me again.

She smiles again and says, "Yes, little man. I knew you would come."

I'm standing in the darkness.

I am alone.

I am standing in the light.

I am no longer alone.

Ariel shakes her head then tells me, "Some people just don't want to stay dead."

The comment confuses me.

I feel something and look down.

She has my hand cupped in hers, my open palm facing upward.

I watch as she slowly drops a necklace into it. I've seen the piece of jewelry many times before.

"Now yours," she tells me.

I feel something in my other hand. I look and see that the mirror image of the necklace dangles there.

I turn to Ariel.

She nods at my palm and repeats, "Now yours, Rowan."

I carefully lower the bauble into my hand to join its mate. As they touch, my skin begins to tingle, then burn.

Ariel closes her hand around mine, folding my fingers over the pair of necklaces.

Harsh pain chews into my flesh.

An unearthly fire sears my palm. I can feel my skin blistering as it fries.

I try to pull away and let go, but Ariel holds my hand in place, squeezing it tightly in both of hers.

I look back to her face.

"For one to live, one must die," she tells me.

Her eyes are imploring.

"Some people need to stay dead, Rowan," she says. "Even if they have to die again."

Dark water rushes up toward me...

The muddy surface roils with tight eddies that appear then disappear.

I see a flash of light on metal...

I hear a woman scream...

I feel pain as she strikes the hard surface of the water...

I feel panic as the swift current pulls her under...

I feel death as the silty river flows into her lungs...

Then, I feel nothing...

I started awake at the end of the nightmare, just as I had each and every time before. This go around, the wobbling peal of an electronic telephone ringer was assaulting my ears. I had a vague recollection of having recently heard the very same sound, but exactly how recent that had been I wasn't at all sure. Where time was concerned, it seemed my perception was more than just a little altered.

The phone started to chirp again, but this time it was cut off at the very beginning of the warble. As the abruptly truncated sound disappeared, it was immediately replaced by a familiar female voice.

"Hello?" Constance said, her tone hushed. A short and seemingly relaxed pause followed her greeting, but only a second later I could literally feel the silence become tense and purposeful. The sensation was unexpected and jarring. My brain was still swimming in the twilight of half-sleep, but the sudden tingle of gooseflesh along my arms forced me to breach the surface. When Constance spoke again, her voice, while still held low, had taken on a vastly different timbre than had underscored it initially.

"When did this happen?" she asked.

I allowed my eyes to open, though they remained half-lidded with drowsiness. I found the room cast in darkness, which was notably different than it had been when I drifted off to sleep whenever ago. The contrast registered; however, it evoked little more from my sluggish synapses than a passing notice. It was light then, it was dark now. Nothing more.

I fought to tread the waters of sleep and hold my head just above unconsciousness. Slowly, my bleary eyes scanned the blue-black shadows of the room. Unlike the preternatural void I had been wandering before, this was purely an earthly absence of light, grounded firmly in reality. My head was rolled to the left, and I could easily make out Constance's shape as she stood next to the bed. A dim glow, probably from the vitals monitors behind me, spilled into the darkness, bringing a surreal illumination to the surrounding space. I took notice that the outline of Constance's body seemed to indicate that she was turned toward the door. Her stance was far from relaxed. But again, it was merely a notice. It meant little in the moment.

I listened as she continued her whispered, businesslike intonation. "He's still sleeping. Yes, so far. So do you have a description? Uh-hmm… Uh-hmm… Okay. Any sign so far? Okay, have you called Parker yet? No problem, I'll do it."

She turned in place, and then there was a dull plastic click. A second later I heard her starting to stab out a number on the telephone keypad. I pushed myself a little farther above the surface of sleep and groped for my voice.

"What's going on?" I managed to croak out in a groggy half-mumble. It seemed like the thing to ask. I saw her outline move again as it twisted toward me.

"I'm sorry, Rowan," she replied softly. Judging from the lull in the other sounds, I assumed she had stopped dialing. She added, "I didn't mean to wake you."

"Didn't," I grumbled, dipping back below the surface briefly and then popping up once again. "Mmmm… Nnnnn… Nightmare did."

"Sorry. Well, this is nothing for you to worry about. It's just a routine status check. Go on back to sleep…" As she finished the instruction, I heard her click the phone receiver then start dialing again.

I tried to believe her, but my skin wouldn't allow it. Now the hair follicles along the nape of my neck danced a painful ballet, insisting that something was wrong. I sucked in a deep breath and slowly let it filter out through my mouth as I focused on remaining awake.

As I continued to lay there, unmoving, I heard Constance speaking again. This time her attention was squarely focused on the answering party at the other end of the line. "Parker? It's Mandalay. What's your status?"

I watched her silhouette as she turned away from me. The petite FBI agent lowered her voice even further as she continued speaking into the telephone. In less than two syllables, her volume dropped from merely hushed to an almost inaudible whisper. The hiss of the one-sided conversation sounded calm but most definitely urgent. However, as was her apparent plan, I could no longer make out exactly what she was saying. After a minute or so of the secretive discourse, she turned back around and settled the handset onto its base.

Between the foreboding of my goosebumps and being conscious of the fact that she had called Agent Parker, I now had a slight churn spinning in the pit of my stomach. I pressed my still sleepy voice into service and asked in a tired drone, "Is something wrong? Is Felicity okay?"

"She's fine, Rowan," Constance whispered. "Like I said, this is just a routine check in. There's nothing for you to worry about. Go back to sleep."

I didn't say another word, but I followed her with my eyes as she left the bedside and stepped over to the window wall. There, using her finger she pulled back the edge of the curtain ever so slightly and then carefully peeked out through the slim gap. A wafer thin shaft of light sliced across her face then splashed its collateral glow over her cheek. It harshly illuminated the severity of her expression and grim set of her jaw. I caught a slight movement in her right shoulder and then noticed a telltale bend to her elbow.

The delineated shadows grew larger, taking over from the light once again as she lowered the curtain carefully back against the frame and turned to her left. She began stepping lightly toward the door, and though I was not fully awake, I was no longer being pulled under by sleep, so I spoke again.

"Are you going to tell me what's really going on?" I asked.

"I already did, Rowan," she replied, voice still hushed. She made a stellar attempt at keeping the concern out of her tone. Unfortunately, for her sake, she failed. "It's nothing."

"Sure," I replied. "Then you started skulking around in the dark with your hand on your gun."

"I'm serious. It's nothing," she repeated. "You're safe. Felicity is safe. Don't worry. Go back to sleep."

"I'm not worried, I just want…"

"Dammit, Rowan," she hissed. "Will you just shut up and let me do my job?"

I immediately fell quiet in the wake of the rebuke. I waited a moment in the pregnant silence and then muttered, "Sorry."

"Me too," she sighed quietly. "But, you just need to let us handle this, okay?"

"You're right," I agreed softly.

"Everything will be fine," she added. "I promise."

"Okay."

There was another thick pause, and then she said, "I guess I don't really need to tell you to stay put, do I?"

"No, I guess not."

She clucked her tongue. "But then again, this is you we're talking about… So as ridiculous as it sounds, I'm telling you to stay put. Understand?"

"Yeah."

"Okay," she replied.

I heard her exhale heavily, almost as if she didn't believe me. Then without another word, she pulled the door open and slipped out, tugging it shut behind her.

I lay there in the darkness, listening to the sound of my heart beating in my chest. Whatever was happening was obviously serious. Whether Constance would admit to it or not, it didn't matter. Her actions definitely weren't in step with a routine status check, and anyone could see that.

My mind raced as I tried to recall what little I had picked up from the one-sided conversation. She had asked when something had happened, and then she had asked if there was a description. From the sound of what followed, I had the impression that the answer to that latter question had been a yes.

I concentrated on the vague pieces of information, trying to fit them together but finding only frustration in the task. My body was still floating in numbed comfort as the unspent remnants of the morphine coursed through my system. I could feel that the drug was starting to overtake me once again. The phantom echo of Constance's voice rang inside my head, *"Go on back to sleep..."*

As my brain slipped back into a sluggish stupor, her suggestion seemed like as good a plan as any. I stopped fighting and let the mantle of slumber surround me. I was just slipping out of consciousness when the phone began to ring.

CHAPTER 33

NOW, I WAS WIDE-AWAKE.

An unearthly chill was chasing itself up and down my spine, and the earlier ballet performed by the hair along my neck had morphed into a full-blown tap dance. The stinging sensation of the gooseflesh pulsed in time with the throb that had set up housekeeping in the back of my skull. And all of this was happening before the first ring had even come to an end.

I waited in the darkness as the telephone blipped out another pair of warbling alerts in languid succession, but still no one came. Of course, with the door closed they probably couldn't hear it. I really didn't know.

I stared at the nightstand where the phone was sitting and tried to judge the distance. In the dark and without my glasses, it wasn't an easy task. Even so, I concluded that it wasn't comfortably within my limited reach, and I'd already been admonished more than once for moving around too much.

As ring four bounced from the walls, I sent my hand searching for the control pendant with the nurse call button. Unfortunately, I found nothing more than a tangle of sheets and blankets. Reaching up next to my head and beneath the corner of the pillow brought the same result. By now, peal number five was demanding attention.

At this point, the ache in my head was bringing with it a sickly familiarity. I knew this wasn't just your average ethereal migraine. It had Miranda's sickly perfume wafting all around it, and that was almost enough to set my gag reflex into motion.

By the sixth ring I was still laying there alone. For all I knew, Constance had declared my room off limits until whatever threat she wasn't willing to admit had finally passed. By the seventh clatter of the electronic bell, it was apparent to me that if the phone was to be answered, I was going to have to do it myself.

I was already on my side, so I stretched out my arm, only to have it meet resistance a full foot away from the handset. I tugged slightly and felt something pulling on the back of my hand. I withdrew my arm and fumbled about then discovered that I had snagged my IV line on the bedside railing at my back.

I rolled slightly and, after a trio of horribly uncoordinated attempts, managed to unhook the loop and free myself. The phone was now well into its tenth ring. Whoever was at the other end definitely wasn't giving up.

Rolling back to my left once again, I pressed myself up against the railing and reached over the top toward the nightstand that held the phone. Once again I came up short; although this time I could almost touch the chirruping device. I sucked in a deep breath and then blew it out as hard as I could, groaning while I stretched. My fingers brushed against the plastic but couldn't wrap themselves around it.

The eleventh ring filled the room.

I allowed myself to fall back to the right and summoned everything my tortured body could give. Rolling as hard as possible to the left, I thrust out my arm and lunged against the railing. My index finger hooked the handset cord, and as I fell back I pulled it with me.

The telephone base clattered over the edge of the nightstand in the middle of the thirteenth ring, unceremoniously bringing it to an end. The device hung there by a thin wire while I maintained a tenuous one-fingered hold on the coiled cord that was attached to the receiver. Pulling my arm back, I managed to fish the handset up over the rail and wrap my hand around it. Breathing heavily from what apparently qualified as extreme physical exertion, I bent my elbow and shoved the handset up against the side of my head.

"Hello?" I said.

Without pause I was greeted with the response, "You sound tired, little man."

The voice that flowed into my ear was one that I had never heard before. However, there was no mistaking who was behind it. If the choice of words wasn't enough evidence, the drawling accent that artificially insinuated itself on top of them was familiar on levels beyond just the audible.

"I *am* tired, Miranda," I replied.

The response that came was unexpected, to say the least.

"As am I, little man," she said.

Her tone lent a bewildering substance to the comment. She literally sounded as if exhaustion was taking a heavy toll. Had it not been for the obvious distinguishing differences in the voice itself, I would have almost believed that I was talking to Annalise instead of Miranda. But, I knew I wasn't. I couldn't identify the body at the other end of the line, but it definitely didn't belong to the malignant soul that was using it at the moment. That simple fact made anything she said to me automatically suspect.

"Are you honestly expecting me to believe that?" I asked.

"It really does not matter what you believe," she told me.

"If that's true, then why are you calling me?"

"To give you one last chance."

"One last chance for what?"

"To be with your wife, of course," she replied.

I felt a wave of anger wash over me at her mention of Felicity. I still had to find a way to undo what she had done to her, so the fact that she was using my wife as a carrot to dangle in front of me was incendiary. But I'd traveled this road with her before, and I knew that was her game. So I took a moment to breathe before offering a measured response.

"What's the catch?" I finally asked.

"We share her," she said.

I stifled a disgusted snort. "You know that isn't going to happen."

She paused and then replied with an oddly dejected sounding tone backing up the words. "I thought that might be your answer."

"I'm surprised you even bothered to ask," I said.

A heavy silence flowed between us. I could hear her breathing on the other end of the line. Now and then I thought I picked up a sound that was akin to distant traffic.

"I don't suppose you want to tell me where you are?" I asked.

"Close," she replied.

"That's a little vague. Would you like to be more specific?"

She ignored the second question and said, "You only have yourself to blame, you know."

"For what, Miranda?"

"All of them," she said.

"All of them?" I repeated.

"Yes, all of them. Everyone who has had to die because you kept her from me," she explained.

"Nice try," I told her. "But a guilt trip isn't going to get you anywhere. I feel enough of it as it is, I'm not taking yours on as well."

"You should feel guilty," she replied. "They are all your responsibility."

"Sorry, Miranda, but their blood is on you, not me."

"Is that what you want me to tell Lisa?" she asked, her voice soft.

The cycling ache that was pressing against the interior of my skull ramped up the scale a bit and then added a sharp stab of intense pain for good measure. The name itself didn't ring a bell, but something about the way she said it told me the situation was heading south in a big way.

I twisted to the right while holding the phone tight against my head and then sent my free hand searching for the call pendant once again.

"Who's Lisa?" I asked.

"The person who used to live in this body," she said.

"And where is she now?" I pressed.

"Where she will be forever, little man," she replied.

"And where is that, Miranda?"

She sighed. "You know. You have been there."

Images of the grey cell from my vision flashed through my mind, and I suddenly felt sick to my stomach.

"Why, Miranda?" I demanded. "Are you planning to keep Lisa's body?"

"No, little man," she replied. "I told you. There is only one that I want, but you will not allow me to have her."

"So then what now?"

"I am too tired. You have won."

"Then you're leaving?"

"Yes."

"Why don't I believe you?"

"You have no reason to," she replied. "I understand that. But it is the truth. I am leaving. Forever."

"But if you leave, shouldn't Lisa come back?"

"Not if she has nothing to which she can return."

Her comments glanced from one another like steel on flint, sparking a recent memory. A searing flash from my tortured visions shot through my brain, and it immediately twisted my stomach into a tight knot.

"Some people need to stay dead, Rowan," Ariel says. "Even if they have to die again."

"What are you going to do?" I demanded, my tone rising in pitch as Ariel's ghostly voice continued to echo in my head.

My hand was still frantically feeling about for the call button but finding nothing more than a twist of sheets and blankets. On a whim I moved it out to the edge of the bed and dragged my fingers along the side until they bumped against the point where the mattress met the railing mount. Digging into the gap, I finally felt a round cord and sought to hook my digits beneath it.

"If you had simply given her to me, little man," Miranda said. "Then this would not be happening."

"What are you going to do?" I demanded once again.

"End this," she replied. "Like I said. I am going away. Forever."

"How, Miranda? Tell me."

"Why do you ask what you already know?"

"Don't do this, Miranda," I told her. "This woman doesn't deserve to die."

"Neither did I," she whispered.

My fingers tunneled beneath the cord, and I slipped them along its length as I pulled. The pendant clattered against the side of the bed but then caught on something as I yanked.

Silence was filling my ear at this point, and a horrible sense of dread was welling in my chest.

"Talk to me, Miranda," I snapped. "You wouldn't have called me if you didn't want to talk this out."

"I overestimated you, little man," she said.

"How?" I pressed, trying to hold her attention. "How did you overestimate me?"

"I thought that you would at least want to see her again."

"You mean Felicity?"

"Of course."

"I do, Miranda. You know that."

"I gave you a chance," she said.

"I wasn't good with the terms of your offer."

"Just remember, you are the one doing this to her."

"Doing what?"

"Once I am gone, what makes you believe you can find her again?"

"I know where to look."

"I have a question, little man…"

"What is that?"

"How long do you think it takes to fall from a ten story building?" As if the words themselves weren't frightening enough, a gut-wrenching melancholy overshadowed the statement.

I was starting to panic. Grasping for something to keep her on the line I said, "Let's discuss this, Miranda. Exactly how would we work out this sharing?"

"It is too late for that," she replied. "If I cannot have her, neither will you."

I was still tugging on the call pendant cord, flipping it with quick jerks in an attempt to shake it loose. Finally, it broke free and I pulled it up. Sliding the sheathed wire through my hand as I released then gripped and then pulled, I dragged the control forward. The moment it was within reach, I jammed my thumb down on the button.

In that moment, Miranda spoke again, offering me a single word, "Goodbye."

I shouted into the mouthpiece, "MIRANDA, NO!"

Barely three horribly prolonged seconds later, I heard a sickening thud and clatter, punctuated by a distant scream, and then nothing.

As the emptiness burned itself into my brain, light filled the room. I could taste salt as hot tears trickled across my face to meet up with the corners of my mouth. I held the now silent handset in a vise-like grip, still pressed firmly against the side of my head. I could feel fingers working against mine in an attempt to pry it loose. My entire body trembled from the mental pain.

And, although through the watery blur I could see the nurse's face, and beyond my sobs I could hear her calling my name, my own voice was nowhere to be found.

CHAPTER 34

"YOU'RE ABSOLUTELY SURE FELICITY IS OKAY?" I ASKED.

This was the second time I had ventured the question in the last five minutes, but at the moment I needed all of the reassurances I could get.

"Yes, Rowan, for the third time, I checked on her myself," Constance told me, an almost impatient tone shrouding her voice. She outlined the answer once again, giving me a demonstrative nod at the end of each sentence. "Agent Parker is still with her. She's safe. Don't worry."

Apparently my personal count was off, but in my mind it didn't matter; I continued to press her on the subject anyway. "But her condition hasn't changed?"

She shook her head. "No. She's still the same as before. No better, but no worse either."

I laid my head back against my pillow and sighed heavily. My throat was raw, and my eyes still burned from the earlier bout of weeping that came along with the almost convulsive hysterics. A quick shot of diazepam directly into a port on my IV had quelled that quickly enough, but it wasn't really doing anything for my foul mood other than to dull it a bit. Between the antibiotics, sedatives, and painkillers being pumped into me at what seemed an almost constant rate, I was beginning to feel like some kind of pharmaceutical dumping ground. But, under the circumstances I didn't really care. In fact, right now I welcomed the numbness.

I brought my forearm up and rested it on my brow to shield my eyes. The severely reclined angle of the bed was allowing the overhead light to shine directly into them, and that wasn't helping with the irritation. However, I just didn't feel much like sitting up at the moment.

"So…" I finally said. "Are you going to fill me in, or are you just going to leave it all up to my imagination?"

"It's not very pretty, Row," Constance replied.

"Trust me, neither is my imagination."

As I was speaking, a quick rap came at the door, and then it opened. Ben followed it in and then turned and levered it shut.

"How we doin' in here?" he asked as he ambled over to the foot of the bed.

Rolling my arm up a bit more so that I could see him better, I grumbled, "Not especially well."

"Yeah," he replied. "Doesn't look much like it." He continued to stand there quietly for a moment and then huffed out a breath as he reached up and massaged his neck. "Well, if you're up to it, here in a little bit they're gonna wanna take your statement about that phone call. Ya'know… While it's still fresh and all."

"I doubt it's going to go stale anytime soon," I replied.

"Yeah…I hear ya'," he said. "But it's procedure."

"Yeah, I know. You can tell them I'm good with that," I agreed as I rolled my arm back down to cover my eyes. My heart definitely wasn't in the task, but I realized the interview had to be done. Much like ripping a bandage off quickly made the removal a little easier to bear, in this case sooner would probably be better than later.

"How is it out there?" Constance asked.

"It's still a fuckin' circus," Ben replied. "Right now we're basically sandwiched in between two crime scenes, two P.D.'s, Major Case, and the Feebs… No offense, of course…"

"Of course."

"And that's not ta' mention the media vultures are all over the parkin' lot too."

"Two crime scenes?" I asked, rolling my arm up once again.

"Yeah," Ben grunted and nodded at me. "The guy upstairs that she turned into a Rowan doll. He's dead."

"He died? I thought he was stable?"

"He was," Ben replied. "And he didn't just die. She got in there and killed 'im."

"How?"

"A clusterfuck across the board, unfortunately," he replied. "She walked right in, told the admissions desk she was his sister and that we had called her. Friggin' media had it all over the tube, so it wasn't really that hard for her ta' find out where he was. So, anyway, whoever was workin' the desk didn't catch the flag, and they sent her right on up to his room even though visitin' hours were over. After that the onus falls on us, I'm afraid."

"How so?"

He gave his head a disgusted shake. "Miscommunication, I guess. I'd reported what you said about 'er knowin' the vic, but apparently it didn't trickle down through the ranks, or it got lost in translation or somethin'. When she said she was family, the security guy on the door let 'er through, no other questions. Ten minutes later she walked out, told the guard she was goin' ta' get somethin' ta' drink, and disappeared. Few minutes after that the nurse went in for her rounds and found the vic dead. He was a coupla' quarts low, and there was friggin' blood all over the floor. It's a goddamn mess."

"That was the phone call you kept pushing me about earlier," Constance added. "We had to assume she was still in the building, which obviously she was. That's why I was 'skulking around,' as you put it. But there was no reason to get you worked up about the situation."

"No, Miranda did that for you."

She blinked and nodded. "True."

I let out a slow breath as I mulled over the explanation and then said, "I guess that was her last shot at trying to use magick to kill me."

"Yeah, could be," Ben agreed. "It's not like she was gonna get at ya' any other way." He paused for a moment, rubbing his neck while staring at some imaginary point in space. Eventually he looked at me and half-shrugged. "Not ta' be morbid and all that, but since ya' brought it up…"

I finished the thought for him. "Why didn't it work? Why am I still alive?"

"Well, yeah," he grunted as he shrugged again. "I mean, not that I ain't happy that you're still with us. But the whole blockin' ya' from the *Twilight Zone* thing seemed ta' work okay. So why not that too?"

"Well, it was a long shot in the first place, and she knew it," I explained. "Magick affecting the ethereal is one thing. Directly affecting the physical is much harder. Besides that, she had already used him as a poppet for a different spell, so she was dealing with conflicting magicks right from the start. But, I guess it was all she had so she went for it."

"So what you're sayin' is it coulda' actually worked?"

"Yeah. It wasn't very likely, but if the conditions were just right, it could have. Especially with me like I am right now."

"That's fucked up, white man."

"Yeah, tell me about it," I mumbled. I took a couple of deep breaths then asked, "What about the second crime scene. I guess that one would be Miranda herself?"

"Yeah," he replied. "Body belongs ta' a Lisa Carlson actually, accordin' to her driver's license. She's the one who came in posin' as the sister, and apparently who you were talkin' to. Found 'er cell phone about fifty feet across the parkin' lot from the impact site, and it actually still kinda works believe it or not. This room was the last number dialed. And…well, I'm sure ya' already know she took a header off the roof of the hospital. Right in front of the main entrance." He grimaced a bit then exhaled heavily before continuing. "Not pretty at all."

"How did she know to call this particular room?" Constance asked.

Ben shrugged. "Dunno. We're lookin' inta' that, especially since ICU rooms don't normally have phones in 'em. But we're thinkin' it was probably the hospital. She was able ta' find out about the vic, so maybe she asked the right person an' got Row's room number and just took a chance.

"Anyhow, once we had an ID, we sent a unit to this Carlson woman's address in Saint Flora… They found…well…I'm not gonna get into it. Let's just say it's more than a little disturbing, and the DNA guys are gonna be busy for a while. Plus, the whole vampire thing suddenly adds up, if ya' get my drift. And from what I hear, there might even be some evidence connectin' the vics from last month. Right now they're waitin' for the county crime scene unit ta' come process the place." Ben paused for a moment then shrugged again. "At any rate, that's pretty much it. Right now, we're still puttin' pieces together, but best guess is that when the hospital got locked down and she couldn't escape, and still couldn't get to you or Firehair, she just took the only way out she could find."

"She said she was tired," I offered.

"What's that?" he asked.

"Miranda. She told me she was tired. That she couldn't keep fighting me."

Ben pursed his lips thoughtfully then gestured as he offered a hypothesis. "So maybe your Witch-fu is better'n you thought it was."

"I dunno. Maybe…" I sighed and pushed my head back into the pillow then spit out a flat, "Dammit."

Despite what I had said to Miranda during that final conversation, I was now taking ownership of the tragedy in full. The fresh guilt was already assuming its place next to my overabundance of other self-condemnations—each of which had been bought and paid for by my curse.

In the back of my mind, I wondered if there was anything I could have done differently that might have affected the outcome. If I hadn't been so fixated on that necklace… If I had just refused to go to Texas in the first place… If I had left it all alone… Then maybe, just maybe, I wouldn't have provoked her into taking action. And then, perhaps four people would still be alive. On top of that, maybe Felicity wouldn't be dwelling in a catatonic stupor either.

As if she were reading my mind, Constance spoke up and said, "You can't take this on yourself, Rowan. It wasn't your fault. She committed these murders, not you."

"Yeah, I've heard that one before," I replied.

"She's right, Row," Ben added. "There's nothing you could've done."

"Rationally, I get that," I said. "But I live in a pretty irrational world, so it doesn't stop me from wondering."

"Yeah, well, trust me. Rational or not, nothing ever does," he grunted. "You ain't the only one with baggage, white man."

A strong knock came at the door, and then it popped open and an unfamiliar face poked through the gap. The countenance belonged to a striking dark-haired woman of conspicuous Asian descent. She looked to be in her late thirties, and from what I could see she appeared to be dressed in regular business casual street clothes as opposed to scrubs like the nurses working the ICU.

"Am I interrupting?" she asked. Her voice held a nondescript but very definite Southern affectation.

I thought I felt a tickle run along the back of my neck, but I wasn't sure. Ever since I'd been injected with the diazepam, I had been a bit dulled to the outside world. I just wished it would work for my headache as well because that was still hammering inside my skull.

"Can I help you?" Ben returned.

"You must be Detective Storm," she said as she stepped farther into the room after pushing the door so that it would swing shut behind her.

I noticed Constance stepping forward and carefully shifting her position so as to place herself in between the woman and me. Apparently even though Miranda was gone, she was operating on automatic.

"Yeah," Ben acknowledged.

Even with Constance between us, I could see that the woman was carrying a folding notepad under her left arm and had what appeared to be a *Glock* riding high in a retention holster on her right hip. A gold shield was clipped to her belt in plain view.

"Wow. The lieutenant told me you were tall. He definitely wasn't kidding," she said and then glanced over at Constance. "So that would make you Special Agent Mandalay."

"Guilty," Constance replied. "And you are?"

"Oh, sorry, I'm Detective Shen. I thought you were expecting me." The woman reached into her back pocket and withdrew a leather case, which she then flipped open with practiced ease and proceeded to display her official ID. "Saint Flora P.D. Lieutenant Sheets with the Major Case Squad commandeered me to come up and take Mister Gant's statement." She glanced past Constance at me and added, "If you're ready that is."

The honey dipped drawl was even more prominent now that she had spoken more than three words in a row. I looked over at Ben and saw that he had an eyebrow cocked upward. He had first hand dealings with Felicity when Miranda had taken over her body, so he knew the uncharacteristic onset of a Southern accent was something that happened to her hosts.

He glanced quickly at me then gave the woman a suspect stare. "Detective Shen… Huh. Ya' mind if I ask…"

"Chinese, but I was born and raised in Mississippi," she replied before he could complete the question. She was already shoving her credentials back into her pocket as she spoke. "You were going to ask about the accent, right?" Her hand now free, she pointed her index finger at her own face and wound it in a trio of quick circles. "It's a little hard to reconcile Southern Belle coming out of this face, I know."

"Sorry," Ben replied. "Wasn't tryin' ta' be a jerk."

Detective Shen gave him a quick shake of her head and a lopsided smile. "Don't worry. I'm used to it. Besides, at least you didn't scalp me first and then ask."

Ben snorted. "Yeah, okay. I guess I deserved that."

"So, I guess we're even," Shen replied, a good-natured air to the comment.

"Yeah, I guess," he said with a nod.

"So, is this a bad time?" she asked.

"Just a sec and I'll let ya' know," Ben told her. He stepped around the end of the bed and crossed behind Constance then snatched the handset from the phone. With a series of deliberate punches from his finger, he dialed a number then held the phone up to his ear. After a short pause he said, "Yeah, L. T., it's Storm. Yeah… Well, he's doin' as good as can be expected I guess. Yeah… So listen, I got a Saint Flora copper up here… Uh-huh… Yeah… That's her… Yeah... Okay, just had ta' check… Yeah… I'll be down in a few… Thanks."

Ben dropped the phone back onto the cradle then looked over at Detective Shen and said, "Okay. All good."

I saw Constance relax her posture, but she remained stationed between Detective Shen and me.

The woman gave Ben a brief look of confusion then said, "Was there a problem?"

"Just never saw ya' before is all," Ben replied. "Had to check your story."

Constance added. "Mister Gant is still technically under federal protection for the time being."

"Sorry," Shen replied. "Like I said, I thought you were expecting me."

"We were. Sorta. Just figured it'd be someone from the MCS."

Shen raised her eyebrows and nodded. "It's a little busy, as I'm sure you know."

"Yeah. I can relate. It's all good," Ben told her. "Just bein' cautious is all."

"That's okay, I understand," she replied. After an uncomfortable pause she directed herself at me. "Umm… So now that that's done, are you ready to give your statement, Mister Gant?"

"Yeah, I can do that," I told her. I still wasn't excited about the prospect of recounting the story yet again, but I also wanted to get it over with.

"Listen, Row," Ben said. "I'll catch up with ya' a little later. L. T. needs me back downstairs."

"No problem," I replied.

"Rowan, do you think you'll be okay with Detective Shen for a minute?" Constance asked.

"I don't see why not," I replied. The tickle was still taunting the back of my neck, but it seemed innocuous. "I mean it's all pretty much over at this point anyway, right?"

"I guess it is," she replied. Seeming far more relaxed than she had been just moments ago, she turned to Ben and said. "I'll walk you out. I could use a bottle of water anyway."

"Yeah," Ben agreed. "I could go for a coffee."

"What about you, Detective Shen," she asked. "Can I bring you anything?"

"No, I'm fine, but thank you."

Constance nodded. "Okay then, I'll be right back."

"Take your time," Shen replied. "Get some air if you want. Mister Gant and I will be awhile, and I'll be happy to stay with him until you get back."

"Thanks," Constance replied. "I know it's just a formality at this point, but remember, nobody comes through that door without a badge or a hospital ID, okay?"

"Got it."

"Good. I shouldn't be long."

Once they'd exited and the door was shut, Detective Shen came over to the side of the bed and looked down at me.

"Rough day, huh?" she asked.

"That's one way to put it," I replied.

"Well, I'll try to make this as painless as possible," she told me.

She turned and wandered over to the window wall and watched Ben and Constance as they disappeared around the corner. Then she purposely drew the curtain shut.

The phantom tickle brushed my neck once again then ran along my spine and spread out to my arms as well. The thud inside my head seemed to grow a little angrier too.

"Why'd you do that?" I asked.

She turned and came back to the bedside then smiled down at me. "I always prefer a little privacy when I do this sort of thing."

CHAPTER 35

"THEN SHE TOLD ME THAT I WAS TO BLAME FOR ALL OF them," I said.

Detective Shen stopped writing for a second and glanced at me. "All of them?"

"Yes," I told her. "All of the victims. She was fixated on my wife for some reason. And, since I was keeping her from getting to Felicity… That's my wife… Anyway, since I was an obstacle to her, she wanted me to know I was to blame for everyone she had killed."

"I see," she replied. "Is that your conclusion, or is it what she actually said?"

"I'm paraphrasing a bit," I admitted.

"We really need to stick to the actual events," she instructed. "Sort of a just-the-facts kind of thing, okay?"

I gave her a slight nod. My head was still pounding, and the tickle along my spine was trying hard to turn into a full-blown tingle. The edge having been chemically honed off my senses wasn't making me happy at the moment. I could tell something wasn't quite right, but I had no idea what it was.

I cast a furtive glance toward the door. Ben and Constance had only been gone for a few minutes, but it was starting to seem like hours. A small knot was working its way into my intestines, and I found myself trying to will Constance to walk back through the door right now.

Apparently, my glance wasn't anywhere near as surreptitious as I wanted to believe. I suppose the fact that it had turned into a somewhat prolonged stare was to blame.

"I'm sorry if I make you uncomfortable for some reason, Mister Gant," Detective Shen told me. "I'm sure Special Agent Mandalay will be back soon enough."

I broke my stare away from the door and looked at her. I swallowed hard then gave my head a shake. "I'm sorry… It's just…"

"I understand," she replied. "Just relax. It's been a rough day for all of us. But you don't have to worry. You're safe now."

"Yeah. I guess so."

"Okay," she nudged. "You were telling me that Lisa Carlson had said you were responsible for 'all of them.'"

"Yeah… Okay… Right… Just the facts," I replied, nodding as I spoke. "So, as I recall she said something like, 'You only have yourself to blame,' then when I asked her for what, she said, 'All of them.' Then I said pretty much the same thing you just did, and she said, 'Everyone who had to die because you kept me from her.'"

I didn't really have any trouble remembering the conversation. It was still painfully clear in my mind. The biggest issue I faced was the on-the-fly sanitizing I had to do. As usual, I just automatically deleted references to ethereal visions and spirit possession wherever necessary. Fortunately, that didn't Swiss cheese my recounting of this particular conversation as bad as it had some of the statements I had given in the past.

"Okay," Shen nodded as she scribbled. "What happened next?"

A sharp lance of pain shot through my head, originating at the base of my skull and ricocheting off the inside of my forehead before clawing its way through the rest of my grey matter. At almost that same instant, a frantic knock sounded at the door. It immediately swung inward without pause, and a nurse barreled through the opening as if on a mission.

Upon hearing the initial sound, Shen had already turned away from me. Apparently, she was taking Mandalay's instructions to heart because a split second after the door began to swing she was in motion. Shifting quickly, she took a pair of steps toward the nurse, effectively blocking any further ingress and placing herself between any potential threat and me.

"Excuse me, officer?" the nurse said, her voice filled with dire urgency.

"Detective," Shen replied.

"Sorry, Detective," the nurse shot back quickly, rushing past the apology and continuing with, "The woman from the FBI. Agent Mann, or something like that. She needs your help out in the lounge area right away."

"Did she say why?" Shen asked.

The nurse shook her head while pointing out the doorway, a wave of what sounded like intense fear rippling through her voice. "No, but there is someone…" she stuttered. "And the tall policeman… He… Please… Something bad is happening out there, and she needs your help!"

"Dammit," Detective Shen muttered then barked. "Let me see your ID."

The nurse looked momentarily both impatient and nonplussed but then fingered a plastic card that was hanging around her neck on the end of an imprinted lanyard and held it up. The detective quickly peered at the hospital credentials then at the nurse's face. Satisfied, she stepped around her while thrusting a finger back toward me and barking the order, "Stay with him. Don't let anyone in."

Shen bolted from the room, and the nurse pushed the door shut behind her. Walking quickly back toward me, she was panting as if the excitement had pushed her beyond her limits. I couldn't blame her. More than enough had happened here today already, so I knew exactly how she felt.

The tickle along my spine had completely bypassed the tingle stage and become a raging fire, spreading outward to consume me. Every hair on my body now stood at attention, and I could feel the gooseflesh literally undulating in tremor-like waves. Whatever was happening out there wasn't good, and even the drugs coursing through my system couldn't keep the cold fear from gripping my chest.

"What's happening?" I asked, with more than just a healthy dose of urgency in my tone. "You said something about Detective Storm. Is he hurt?"

She didn't answer me. Instead, she reached down over the railing and snatched up the call pendant then flipped it off to the side.

"What the hell are you doing?" I asked. It was a stupid question, but it was the first thing that popped out of my mouth. Then, as if arriving late to a party, it dawned on me that I had not seen this nurse before, but her voice sounded oddly familiar. Moreover, it carried with it a more than slight Southern affectation as well.

Still silent, she stamped over to the foot of the bed, released the brake and began pulling. She let out a heavy grunt then yanked hard on the end, shoving her body to the side as she whipped me around. The pulsox sensor snapped off the end of my finger, instantly sending the monitor into a fit. She continued pulling, and a second later I felt a tug then a sharp pain. I grabbed for the IV tubing to keep it from ripping out of the back of my hand, and both the stand and the morphine pump toppled over and clattered across the floor. As we continued to move, the tension increased, and I was forced to pull the IV catheter out before it tore away of its own accord.

She managed to wheel the bed the short distance across the room and bring it lengthwise in front of the door just as someone outside was attempting to push their way in. The wooden slab butted hard against the side of the heavy frame, causing it to shudder slightly, but not budge. I watched her move quickly as she stomped down on the brake to lock the bed into position. Then she stalked around the end and along the side.

Glaring, she covered the few steps toward me, then she laughed. "You are so gullible, little man. Did you honestly believe that I would give up?"

That was when I caught the sharp glint of light from metal. I probably hadn't noticed it before because Detective Shen had positioned herself between us, blocking my view. And after that, everything had happened so fast that it was a wonder I'd noticed anything at all. But now, there it was, a chain around the woman's neck that flowed downward and disappeared behind her scrubs. I didn't have to see the rest of it to know what was dangling on the hidden end.

I could hear shouting beyond the door. Tremors continued to vibrate through the bed frame as something heavy pounded against the opposite side of the barrier. Still nothing budged. I came to realize in that instant that I was on my own.

"You can't make it out of here," I spat. "You have to know that, Miranda."

She lashed out, driving her fist into my jaw. I tried to block her, but my reactions were lagging far behind hers. I tried to roll with it, but her connection was solid and the damage was done. I could feel a sharp sting in the corner of my mouth and taste the blood as it began to flow.

"That does not matter, little man," she snapped. "This is just another body, and you will be dead. Then I will have what is rightfully mine. My only regret is that I do not have enough time to show you what love really is."

"You mean your twisted concept of it?" I asked.

I heard my name being called from the other side of the door, and now a new noise joined the clamor as something struck with a hard ping against the window wall. It didn't take much for me to realize what they were trying to do, but I also had to wonder just how long it would take for them to break through tempered safety glass.

Something told me it would be too long.

Although I was absolutely certain I should be feeling abject fear at my impending fate, I wasn't. Miranda was going to kill me, and I knew it. For a fleeting instant, I thought perhaps I was simply feeling resignation, as a bizarre calm seemed to spread through my body. However, that calm was tainted with a pang of guilt.

I looked into the eyes of the unfortunate woman who was now glaring back at me. The spirit was evil, but the body belonged to someone else, and that rightful owner was in no way responsible for what was now happening. If she killed me, an innocent person would be who ended up standing trial, not the actual killer. If by some miracle they came through that wall in time, an innocent person might lose her life as they did whatever was necessary to save me.

Too many people had died because of me already, and I wasn't willing to allow another sacrifice. My eyes were quickly attracted to her neckline as light glinted from the exposed portion of the chain once again, and in that moment I made a decision.

I imagined there were any number of things in this room she could pick up and use to beat me to death. If she went that route, there was nothing I could do. However, if she came in close enough and if I was correct, there was a way out. It didn't escape my attention that I was dealing with two very big ifs, but I didn't have much choice. If it turned out I was wrong, the outcome would be the same as if I had done nothing at all.

I looked back up at her face and said, "Well then you damn well better kill me now, you fucking bitch."

My intent was to antagonize her. Given past experience, I had no real reason to believe that I could, but I had to take the chance. Fortunately, or so I hoped, the gambit actually worked.

Miranda let out an unearthly scream and lunged forward, clawing as she literally climbed into the bed on top of me. In my weakened state and vulnerable position, I was hard pressed to fight back, so she had every advantage where this close quarters fight was concerned. As she scrambled up on top of me, she purposely tried to bring her knee down on my wounded abdomen, but out of reflex I had pulled my knees upward and thwarted her plan. Still, a searing pain ripped through me, and I howled as she continued her attack. As I buckled under her assault, she rammed her fist into my chest, and I felt the air explode from my lungs.

Half straddling me, she lunged forward again and brought her forearm against my throat, pressing hard. She slipped her free arm in behind my head and bore down in an attempt to lock me solidly into the chokehold.

Somewhere above my head, I heard the hard sound of something slamming into the tempered glass wall as before, but this time a high-pitched ping joined the hollow thud. A second later the heavy noise struck my ears once again and was instantly followed by the bright tinkle of shattering glass as it spilled into the room. The voices on the other side of the wall were much louder now, but even so, everything I heard seemed to be in the form of a ghostly echo.

The lights in the room appeared to be going dark. With the air already forced out of my lungs, I was fading even more quickly than I had imagined I would. I struggled against the weight pressing down on top of me. Miranda had managed to drop a knee across my left forearm to pin it down, but my right remained free.

I tried to swing the arm, but with the limited space I barely thumped it against her ribcage.

"She is mine," Miranda growled directly into my face.

The comment sparked a renewed fury in my gut. Hooking my free arm beneath hers, I thrust it upward, slamming my fist against her chin. A small amount of blood from the back of my hand was trickling down my arm, and it smeared across her face. The force of my strike wasn't enough to do any real damage, but it rattled her enough that she loosened her grip slightly. I gasped in the barest scrap of a breath before she leaned harder into me. But, it was enough to buy me the time I needed. I let my hand drop down to her neck and sent it searching. Groping with my fingers, I found the chain and slipped them beneath it as I began to pull. Miranda reared back with a shriek but continued to choke me. Her motion caused the pendant to pop out from behind the scrubs and into plain view.

With everything I had left, I twisted my hand through the chain and clasped it around the half coin and began to pull. The moment I closed my fist, an unbelievably harsh pain began chewing its way through my flesh. An unearthly fire was searing my palm, and it felt as if my hand was literally blistering, but I held fast.

The wisp of air I had been able to suck in was now beyond depleted. I could feel the brain numbness taking over and see the darkness slipping in to replace the light.

I heard Miranda screaming, "No!"

Then came other voices filling the room, barking out urgent, forceful demands.

The weight suddenly shifted off my chest, and I could feel a sharp tug on my arm, but I refused to release my grip, no matter how badly it hurt. As a hard shudder rattled the bed and a hollow crash sounded in my ears, cool air rushed into my lungs, but I was already slipping under.

When I regained consciousness several minutes later, they had still been unable to pry the necklace from my hand.

Saturday, April 29
12:17 P.M.
University Hospital Northeast
Room 312
Saint Louis, Missouri

CHAPTER 36

"HEY, WHITE MAN," BEN GREETED ME AS HE CAME through the doorway.

"Hey," I returned as I looked toward him then grabbed the remote and muted the fuzzy television set.

Fallout from everything Miranda had done, or in truth, forced others to do, was still dominating the local news and even making a splash on the national scene. Unfortunately, the media was dragging Lisa Carlson through the proverbial mud, and the real story would never be told. In the end, the poor woman had lost more than just her life, and there was nothing I could do to fix it.

"Jeezus, white man," Ben snorted as he drew up next to the bed. "That's what they're feedin' ya'?"

"For now," I replied, pushing aside the tray containing tasteless cream-of-some-unknown-item soup, along with other semi-liquid, semi-solid, mashed and blended foodstuffs. "The pudding actually isn't all that bad. Most days, anyway."

"Yeah, I'll just take your word for it," he grunted. "Want me ta' sneak ya' in a bag of sliders or somethin'?"

I shook my head and pointed toward my stomach. "As good as that sounds, which is odd in itself, I'm not so sure the staples would hold, if you know what I mean."

"Yeah, I hear ya'. They do that to me too. I think it's the onions." My friend sauntered over to a chair beneath the wall-mounted television and parked himself. Nodding toward the nightstand next to me he said, "Nice flowers."

I glanced over at the arrangement. "Yeah. They're from the staff in the ICU… Apparently I'm an unforgettable patient."

"Yeah, no shit. Not every day they gotta bust through a wall." He tapped out a short rhythm on the arm of the chair and waited. After a moment he said, "Stopped in ta' see Firehair on the way here."

"I'm going up to see her after lunch," I said. "They insist I get up and walk, so I told them that's where I want to walk. They've been good about letting me sit with her."

"That's good," he grunted.

"Any word about the nurse? The one who…you know…"

He nodded. “Yeah, but it ain’t all that good. Forensics found her DNA on Lisa Carlson’s body.”

“I’m not surprised. The necklace had to be exchanged for Miranda to switch bodies. They had to come into contact with one another.”

“Yeah, well the question is whether or not they’re gonna try ta’ connect ‘er to the other crimes then charge ‘er with Carlson’s murder. Under the circumstances, it’d probably end up bein’ some sorta manslaughter deal, but she’d prob’ly see time. Especially after what she tried ta’ do ta’ you.”

“They can’t. She couldn’t have killed her. I was talking to Lisa Carlson when she jumped.”

“Row…you and I already talked about this… You know damn well you were talkin’ to that nurse, not Carlson. She pro’bly got all Mirandized and pushed ‘er off or somethin’.”

“I’m sorry, Ben, but I must have been under the influence of morphine or something because I don’t recall that conversation at all,” I replied. “And, I’ve already refused to press charges against her for what happened in that room.”

He cocked his head to the side and stared at me. “You’re tellin’ me you’d lie under oath?”

“I’m telling you I was talking to Lisa Carlson when she jumped.”

“They’re gonna ask ya’ how ya’ know it was Lisa Carlson.”

“Doesn’t matter. But it wasn’t that nurse. That’s all I know.”

Ben shook his head. “Jeez, you really are the Lone Fuckin’ Ranger, ya’ know that? I need ta’ get ya’ a box of silver bullets or somethin’.”

I looked down and stared at the bandages that still encircled my right hand where the necklace had blistered my palm. I had already been warned that there would be a significant scar. But that was something I could live with. An innocent woman losing everything because of me, I couldn’t.

I finally broke my silence and said, “That nurse lost her job, and from what I hear, she’s not coping with the psychological effects very well. She definitely doesn’t need to be charged with a crime she didn’t commit on top of all that. Miranda has already screwed up too many lives as it is.”

“Yeah. Speakin’ of the bitch, Constance talked ta’ Jante this mornin’. Devereaux… Well, Miranda…is un-fuckin-controllable. They got ‘er locked down and pumped full of psych meds, not that they’re doin’ any good. From what they’re sayin’, she’s gone completely off the deep end.”

"I'm still alive and I have both of the necklaces. She's trapped again. Annalise is her only portal into this world at this point. She's angry."

"Yeah, well that's an understatement. Apparently she's bouncin' 'er portal off the walls, the way I hear it."

"I guess I'm not surprised by that."

"I still don't get why she came after ya' when she did. She took a big chance."

"I doubt she'd be interested in answering that question."

"Yeah…I bet you're right," he grunted then asked, "Okay, so what about you?".

"What do you mean, what about me?"

"You copin' okay?"

"Taking it a day at a time," I replied. "How about you?"

"Pretty much the same, but then I was on the outside lookin' in," he said with a nod. "By the way, your dog tore up another one of my towels. I still say the little shit doesn't like me."

"Might be the other way around. Maybe he likes you too much."

He snorted. "Yeah, right. Well, I'm addin' it to your tab."

"I figured you would. How are the cats?"

"Fine," he replied. "I called that buddy of yours…RJ… He's watchin' 'em."

"Good."

As the word faded, a heavy silence rolled in like a swiftly rising tide. I stared at the wall, Ben stared at me, and nothing more was said. Seconds folded into minutes, and eventually my friend cleared his throat.

"Okay, Row," he said. "Are we done with the bullshit small talk?"

"Yeah. I guess we are."

"Okay. So what's up? You're the one who needed ta' talk ta' me right away, remember?"

"Yeah, Ben, I remember." I took in a deep breath and then exhaled heavily. "I know I already owe you more than I'll ever be able to repay, but I need to ask a big favor."

He shook his head and shrugged. "No prob, Kemosabe. Name it."

"I need you to help me kill Miranda."

Friday, May 12
4:32 P.M.
I-10 East
23 Miles Outside New Orleans, Louisiana

CHAPTER 37

"EXIT'S GONNA BE COMIN' UP SOON. LOOKS LIKE WE'RE gonna be about an hour or so early," Ben called over his shoulder.

"Good," I replied.

"I know this is prob'ly a stupid question, but do ya' still wanna go straight there?"

"You're right," I replied. "Stupid question."

"Uh-huh," he grunted. "Just figured I should ask anyway."

We had been on the road since before sunup, and the travel weariness was starting to take hold. My doctor wasn't happy with me making this trip in the first place, but I told him I would take his opinion under advisement, which lasted about ten seconds. I'd been discharged from the hospital for less than a week, and the standing order was for me to take it easy. Even though Ben was doing all the driving, eleven hours in a vehicle was exhausting in its own way. At least we were in his van, so there was plenty of room to stretch out.

I looked over at Felicity. She was belted into the seat next to me, head resting on a pillow as she stared into nothingness. Occasionally she would blink, and earlier when we had stopped for lunch, she had eaten out of reflex and even changed position of her own accord. But that was it. Nothing more. I reached out and took hold of her hand then simply held it in mine.

My wife's parents were as dead set against this trip as my doctor. Shamus more so than Maggie, but neither of them was happy about it. So far, they hadn't given up their attempts to assume legal control of her care, but our attorney had stonewalled them pretty well. Now that I was out of the hospital, they were fighting a losing battle for the most part. And if things worked out as I hoped, an unnecessary one as well.

"How is she doing, Rowan?" Helen Storm asked, turning in the passenger seat to glance back at me.

"The same," I said.

"What about you?" she asked. The tenor of her voice told me she held even more concern for my personal well-being.

"I'm fine, Helen… I'll be okay…"

She twisted a bit more to look at Felicity then smiled and turned back around in her seat.

The hospital had recommended an in-home nursing service. Someone to look after my wife until such time as my strength returned, and then they could train me in the finer points of indigent care. They told me I was in denial when I explained that she wouldn't be in need of it for much longer. Of course, they were always sure to add that if I continued refusing to allow treatment with the anti-psychotic meds, she might never recover at all.

Fortunately, Helen was her doctor of record, and she was no stranger to how things worked in my world. That was why she had come along on this excursion to help with Felicity instead of a stranger who simply wouldn't understand.

A bright chirrup blipped through the interior of the vehicle, low at first then gaining in volume. Ben dug out his cell phone, glanced at it, flipped it open, and then tucked it up against his ear.

"Yeah, what's up?" he said. He paused and listened for a second then spoke again. "We're about twenty minutes out, prob'ly. Depends on traffic. Yeah… Yeah… I'll tell 'im… Yeah, I'll call ya'… Bye."

He closed the device and dropped it back into the console. "That was Constance," he said over his shoulder. "Just checkin' in. Wanted you ta' know the dogs and cats are fine."

"That's great," I replied then looked back over at Felicity.

Glancing out the windows, I could see that on our left, the choppy waters of Lake Pontchartrain were slipping past. On the right was a marshy landscape of the shoreline. I pressed my head back against the seat and closed my eyes. We continued the rest of the trip in silence, save for Ben's occasional grumble about other drivers. I ignored him and simply kept holding Felicity's hand.

Just over two hours later, we were on the deck of a riverboat and pulling away from the dock to head upstream.

WE WATCHED THE NEW ORLEANS SKYLINE SLIDE SLOWLY by as the engines beneath us thrummed and churned the brown waters of the Mississippi, kicking up a foamy wake. Ahead of us, looming in the distance was the Crescent City Connection Bridge, where the Pontchartrain Expressway spanned the muddy river.

"So what now?" Ben asked.

I sighed and looked around. Most of the passengers were inside for the Jazz Dinner Cruise. While there were still a few other tourists on the deck, fortunately we were standing in a pocket of isolation. My guess was that it most likely was a product of the socially repelling effect of a catatonic woman in a wheelchair. I wasn't happy about that societal norm, but for our purposes it was actually useful. We didn't really need an audience for what we were about to do.

Turning back to Ben, I recited a better than one hundred-fifty year old notice from the *New Orleans Bee* that had become etched in my memory over the last two weeks. "Found Drowned. The coroner held an inquest yesterday on the body of a woman named, Miranda Blanque, sister of Delphine Lalaurie, aged forty-three years, who was found floating in the Mississippi opposite the third municipality. It appears that on Sunday night last, she was seen to have jumped into the river. Verdict accordingly."

"Yeah," my friend replied, although I hadn't really answered his question, and his tone more than betrayed that fact.

I wandered closer to the rail and pointed at the shore on the opposite side of the river, which was slowly receding behind us. "Over there is Algiers," I said. "In eighteen fifty-one, that was pretty much directly across from the third municipality, so she likely went into the water somewhere upstream, and her body eventually surfaced around that area."

"But ya' don't know where she went in," Ben replied.

"It doesn't really matter," I said. "This is where she died. This is where she has to die again if Felicity is ever going to be free of her."

I reached into my pocket and withdrew two small glass bottles. Inside each rested one half of the cursed jewelry that had sent us down this path. Each was swimming in salt and could only be seen whenever I slowly twisted the containers and watched for the glint of light from metal.

"How's your arm?" I asked my friend.

"I got ya' covered," he said with a nod.

I carefully uncapped the first vial and poured the necklace and salt into my palm. A tingle began rolling through my body as the metal came into contact with the still healing burn that scarred my flesh. I handed Ben the other vial then nodded toward my outstretched hand. He twisted the cap from the glass container and then hesitantly began to pour it into my palm.

"Go ahead," I urged.

He turned it up, and the second necklace fell on top of the first, riding in a cascade of white crystals.

Now my hand began to prickle as if it had been asleep. The hair on the back of my neck danced, and an explosion of pain arced through my skull.

"NO!" I hear a woman scream.

"Row?" Ben asked. "You goin' *Twilight Zone*?"

"Just a little," I breathed. "But I'm okay… Let's do this."

My friend held out his hand. "This gonna burn me like it did you?"

"It shouldn't," I told him.

"Doesn't matter if it does," he replied. "I just wanna know what ta' expect, so I don't drop 'em and all."

"Thanks, Ben."

"No prob, white man."

I dumped the contents of my own hand into his large palm. He stepped to the railing and then glanced at me. "Just anywhere?"

I nodded. "Yeah, just anywhere."

He drew his arm back and with a heavy grunt he launched the necklaces into the thick air.

I see the roiling waters as they rush toward her.
She's screaming…

A shower of salt sprinkled across us as it was caught by the wind. The necklaces, however, sailed true along their shallow arc before seeming to hover for a brief moment then plummet downward. A good twenty feet out from the stern, a pair of tiny splashes dotted the surface of the foamy wake.

I feel pain as she strikes the hard surface of the water…
I feel panic as the swift current pulls her under…
I feel death as the silty river flows into her lungs…

We stood there in silence, watching the waters continuing to churn. After a languid pause, Ben cleared his throat.

"That it?" he asked

"Yeah," I whispered.

"So what now?"

"We wait," I said.

I slowly turned from the rail and stepped over to where Helen was waiting with Felicity. I looked at my wife's still vacant eyes and then knelt in front of her.

Magick wasn't always instantaneous. It could happen right away, or it could take an entire cycle of the moon. Either way, I would wait for her, and if I was wrong and it didn't work at all, I would find another way to bring her home, even if I had to die to do it.

I watched her face as she blinked and continued to stare into nothingness. With a sigh, I carefully slipped my arms in around her waist and laid my head in her lap.

Tears were beginning to burn my eyes when I felt a hand softly brush against my hair.

Behind me, Ben muttered an exclamation, disbelief rampant in his voice, "Jeezus H. Christ…"

Then a soft, weak, Celtic lilt drifted into my ears. "*Caorthann*… I knew you would come for me… I knew you would…"

Sunday, December 24
4:58 P.M.
Saint Louis, Missouri

CHAPTER 38

"AYE, DO WE REALLY HAVE TO TALK ABOUT THIS RIGHT now?" my wife asked.

I shrugged. "I know, I know… But it's only two weeks away, Felicity."

"So I'll worry about it then," she replied and then thrust a card and ink pen at me. "Here, sign this."

I took the proffered items but simply held them in my hand and gave her a quick nod. "Look, I'm no more excited about it than you are, but you've been subpoenaed to testify at the trial. So have I."

"It doesn't matter, then," she replied. "Annalise isn't Miranda anymore. Miranda is gone. She can't hurt me."

"That's true," I told her. "But Annalise tried to kill you too, so you really need to be prepared for this when you walk into that courtroom."

"I will be."

I sighed. "She's already in Saint Louis, you know. Constance told me that they moved her here the middle of last week."

"Aye, I know, but it's Christmas Eve and I don't want to think about it. We can talk it over this next week," she replied. "Now, sign that card please."

I let out a heavy sigh and then shook my head. "Okay, but next week for sure. So who is this one for?"

"Constance," she replied. "You already signed Ben's."

"Oh yeah, that's right," I said with a nod then laid the card on her desk and scrawled my name beneath hers.

"Just remember," she instructed. "Constance is getting the Irish wool scarf, and Ben the bottle of Black Bush."

"Okay…so, I remember buying the scarf for Constance when we were in Ireland, but didn't we get Ben a piece of dirt?" I replied.

"Not dirt," she told me. "A bit of the auld sod."

"Okay, sod…dirt…whatever."

"I'll forgive you for that since I love you," she gibed. "Anyway, that's in there too. But he needs to learn about good whisky, so I picked up a bottle of *Black Bush*."

"He already knows about good whisky," I told her. "He drinks Scotch."

"Scotch is okay, but Irish whisky is better," she replied.

I tossed the pen on the desk then handed her the card.

She opened it and gave my signature a quick glance. "Your handwriting is as bad as a doctor's," she admonished.

"Yeah, you've told me. So I take it you already wrapped their gifts?"

"Of course. You didn't think I would let *you* do it, did you?"

"I'm not that bad at wrapping stuff."

My wife cocked one of her patented incredulous stares in my direction and muttered, "*Cac capaill*."

"Okay, so they aren't as perfect as you make them," I replied, waving my index finger in the air. "With all the creases, and symmetrical lines, and ribbons and bows and… Well, you know…"

"Aye," she nodded. "The way they're supposed to look then."

"Okay, okay," I laughed, holding up my hands. "I surrender."

"You will as soon as I change into what I'm wearing this evening," she quipped.

"Really?"

"Aye. Actually, it's more a matter of what I'll be wearing under what I'm wearing this evening."

"So I sense an unwrapping theme here," I replied.

"Exactly."

I nodded thoughtfully. "I'm definitely, very, extremely good with that."

"I thought you might be. But you'll have to wait until we get home." Felicity finished stuffing the card into an envelope and laid it aside on her desk then suddenly exclaimed, "*Damnú!*"

"What's wrong?"

"I was supposed to pick up the black and white puddings from the butcher for breakfast tomorrow morning."

I glanced at my watch. "How late were they staying open today?"

"Five," she replied.

"Ouch, too late. I guess we'll have to do without."

She shot me another one of her looks. "Excuse me? I don't think so. You don't muck about with an O'Brien family tradition." She grabbed the phone and stabbed out a number. A moment later she said, "Aye, John? It's Felicity O'Brien. Yes… Yes, I know, I just now remembered. Really? You're a doll. Thank you so much. I'll be there in five minutes then. Bye." She dropped the phone back onto the cradle and smiled. "He's still there closing up. Since we're just around the corner he said he'd wait for me."

"Tell you what," I said, gesturing at her petite figure. "You still have that wrapping to do. I'll run over and pick them up. That way I won't be tempted to peek."

"Aye, good idea," she replied.

I gave her a quick peck on the cheek and started out the door of her basement office.

"Oh, and let the dogs in before you go," she called after me. "And, there's an extra bottle of Bushmill's on the counter in the kitchen. Take that with and give it to John as a thank you."

"Okay, I'll do that," I returned then started up the stairs.

Once I hit the main floor I looked back down the stairs to make sure she wasn't on her way up for any reason and then closed the door. I actually had an ulterior motive for making the run to the butcher shop for her. I needed to call Ben while she wasn't around so that I could check on the status of her gift. It was supposed to have been delivered to his house earlier today, but I'd yet to hear from him, so I was starting to worry just a bit.

I snagged my phone from my belt and flipped it open as I walked through the living room. With a quick stab of my thumb, I hit the speed dial for Ben's number and put the cell up against my ear.

I skirted around the dining room table and into the kitchen as it started to ring. I had made it only a few steps into the room when I noticed that the back door was hanging wide open. I started toward it just as Ben answered his phone.

"Merry freakin' ho, ho, ho, Kemosabe…" My friend's voice flowed into my ear with a jovial laugh.

I never got the chance to respond. A weight suddenly slammed into me from behind, hurling me forward into the island. As I pitched against it, my head bumped directly into a vase Felicity had put there to dry, and it toppled over. Almost in slow motion, the ceramic vessel rolled across the butcher-block island and off the side, hitting the floor with a loud crash.

I pushed back and started to twist, but the weight was on me again, and this time it was literally on my back. An arm hooked around my throat and I was starting to choke. I pushed back again, and as I came upright I began to teeter backwards from the extra bulk. From the corner of my eye, I caught a flash of metal and brought my hand up out of reflex just as the knife was coming down.

I struggled to lunge forward and slammed into the island once again. My cell phone popped from my hand and skittered halfway across the surface, coming to rest well out of my reach against a cookbook at the other end. At the same moment, the weight on my back shifted and let out a bloodcurdling and patently female scream. The arm around my neck loosened just long enough for me to suck in a breath and shout, “BEN!”

The knife came back down, but instead of deflecting it I unintentionally caught it in my grasp. The sharp edge sliced into my scarred palm, and I let out a howl of pain.

Somewhere through all the noise, I heard Ben’s frantic voice screaming from the earpiece of my cell, “…ROWAN? ROWAN?! GODDAMNIT! WHAT THE HELL’S HAPPENIN’ OVER THERE?! JEEZUS H…”

I had no idea how the thin reverberation was even audible to me since at this point the device was lying several feet away. I struggled to push myself up and stumbled backward, slamming first my attacker and then myself into the doorframe, but she didn’t even loosen her grip.

The fresh chokehold from the woman was working. The room was starting to spin as my vision tunneled. My ears were ringing, and I struggled for a breath that simply wasn’t allowed to come. I twisted and then pitched forward, unintentionally ramming my forehead—followed by the rest of my face—into the wall. The squirming weight on my back wasn’t helping my balance, but in the grand scheme of things, that was the least of my worries.

A flash of thought bounced through my head, tweaking what consciousness was left in my brain. It reminded me that this wasn’t exactly how I’d imagined meeting my demise. But then, I’d held fast to an unspoken feeling for quite some time now—a sense that my death would be violent. If this didn’t qualify as such, I’m not entirely certain what would. I’d come close many times. Maybe this was the one.

A blaze of raw pain seared my right palm as I desperately tried to work my fingers in behind the pale forearm that was attempting to crush my windpipe, and it was nearly succeeding by all present indications. However, the bone-baring gash in my hand was rendering my task nearly impossible, as my fingers didn’t seem capable of carrying out the orders my brain was giving them. Unfortunately, my left hand was of no help either because it was otherwise occupied by holding fast to the wrist of my attacker’s other arm. I would have simply let go were it not for the fact that she was still clenching the eight-inch butcher knife tightly in her white-knuckled fist, and this was the only way I could keep it at bay.

The blade already had enough of my blood on it as far as I was concerned.

I abandoned my vain attempt to loosen the constriction clamped around my neck and thrust my hand forward instead. A fresh lance of pain screwed its way through my palm then up my arm as my hand hit with a wet slap against the wall, leaving a bright red smear in its wake. I stumbled out of control as I propelled myself backward, the frenzied weight still clinging to my back by way of my tortured neck.

I had yet to actually see the woman who was now trying to kill me, although I had a better than solid idea who it was. Still, given everything that had led up to this moment and the fact that I had been attacked from behind, there was a sick churn in the pit of my stomach telling me I could be wrong. That maybe, just maybe, I had made a critical error where magick and the dead were concerned. It was that acrid, nauseous feeling that was keeping me from fighting back with the unbridled fervor it seemed it was going to take to save my own life. Until I knew for sure whom I was up against, I couldn't take any chances.

With the lack of oxygen beginning to shut down my brain, the rest of my muscles were beginning to weaken as well. I could feel my right arm buckling against an unnatural strength that was trying to drive the butcher knife downward into my chest, and my legs were quivering as they took on the properties of an elastic band stretched to the breaking point.

Still careening wildly in reverse and unable to see any obstacles in my rearward path, my luck with staying upright finally ran out. In a single misstep, my heel hooked around what felt like the leg of the coffee table, effectively negating what little balance I had left, and the two of us launched into a backward free-fall. A heartbeat later, the dull rush of a crash punctuated by shattering glass ornaments sounded in my ears as we brought the Christmas tree down with us.

The arm was no longer around my neck since the force of the impact had shaken my attacker loose. I gulped hungrily for the air as I tried to roll away, only to entangle myself even farther into the branches of the artificial tree as well as the still winking strands of lights. Twisting back the other direction in a bid for escape, I lost my newly found breath as a knee came down hard on my stomach.

The acid churn in my gut suddenly twisted into a fearful knot as I looked up into an all too familiar face framed in fiery auburn hair, and then I saw a sharp glint from the blade of the upraised butcher knife in her hand.

"You bastard!" she screamed. "You sonofabitch! You killed her! You took her away from me!"

I tried to call my wife's name as I reached for the weapon, but she couldn't hear me. Any faint sound I could muster with my again empty lungs was completely drowned out by the ungodly concussive explosion of a handgun fired a scant few feet away within the tight confines of the room. Hot blood sprayed my face, the knife clattered harmlessly to the floor, and her lifeless form slumped downward across me.

In the muted distance, sirens began to play, drawing closer as each morbidly long second ticked past.

I looked up at Felicity. She was still stiffly holding our semi-automatic pistol stretched out at arm's length in front of herself. There was a glassiness to her eyes as she stared, but I could tell it was merely shock and nothing preternatural. Given what she had just been forced to do, I would have expected no less.

"Are you okay?" I asked, still panting as I regained my breath.

She nodded mechanically.

"Relax and put the gun down, honey," I told her. "The police are going to be here any minute. Just cooperate with them and everything will be fine."

The muffled sounds of racing engines were drawing close, and now emergency lights were flickering through the windows. A siren burped out a half tone as it switched off in front of the house, and I could hear distant, hurried footsteps coming up the driveway.

In that moment, a bell on the toppled-over Christmas tree jingled an abrupt, sad peal…

Tuesday, January 29
9:37 A.M.
FBI Field Office
Saint Louis, Missouri

EPILOGUE

"SO, EVEN AFTER I TOLD DOCTOR JANTE TO TAKE A FLYING leap, you still want me to come work for you? You're kidding, right?" As the question tumbled from my mouth, I was training a bemused stare on the section chief seated behind the desk in front of me. Given the look on his face definitely wasn't one of jest, it didn't take any of my uncanny psychic prowess to tell me his reply was definitely not going to be "*Well damn, you caught me. I'm just kidding.*"

In fact, the truth is I wasn't really expecting an answer at all. The words I had spoken were in and of themselves rhetorical. Verbalizing them was, in effect, merely a way for me to express astonishment at what he'd just said and not really a serious quest for an answer. That much was nothing if not obvious.

Or so I thought.

He leaned forward in his seat, adopted an even more stony expression, and answered me anyway. "I can assure you, Mister Gant, I am… *The bureau*…is entirely serious about this."

Well, at least his answer verified what I already knew, not that it was necessary. Score one for the Witch I guess, even if it was a perceptual gimme.

I shook my head. "Pardon me for saying this, but *the bureau* hasn't exactly earned my trust lately, if you know what I mean."

"I understand. I've read your file."

"Yeah, I can't say as that I'm surprised by that," I grumbled. "I mean after all, who hasn't?"

"This bothers you," he observed with a slight nod.

I didn't hold back on the sarcasm. "Whatever gave you that idea?"

"Mister Gant…"

"Sorry," I said, stopping him with a wave of my hand. I let out a long sigh before going ahead and grimacing slightly at my indiscretion and then added, "I shouldn't have said it like that. It's just that it has become a bit of a sore spot recently. I mean, if you've done all this reading about me then you should know why I'm not a fan. Hell, just last month Annalise Devereaux escaped on the FBI's watch, and you know how that turned out."

"Yes, I do. But you're mistaken. It wasn't our watch."

I shook my head. “Yeah, I’m familiar with the blame game, trust me. But that doesn’t matter. To be honest I think what bothers me most is that I even have a file in the first place.”

His forehead visibly creased for a moment. “With all of the consulting on high profile homicide cases you’ve done, why wouldn’t you? I’m not sure I understand?”

“It’s not *that* exactly. What I mean is…” I started and then allowed my voice to trail off as I shrugged. With another quick shake of my head I told him, ”Don’t worry about it… I really wouldn’t expect you to understand.”

He paused for a moment and then answered with, “I see.”

“No, you probably don’t,” I replied. “But I’m not really up to explaining it right now. It’s a long story with some pretty unpleasant chapters. But, you said you already know that, so who am I to say?”

“All right,” he conceded with a quick nod. “Then maybe we should return to the question at hand. Am I to take your obvious misgivings about the bureau as a no?”

“I don’t know just yet,” I shrugged as I replied, my tone far from certain. “Besides, to be honest I thought I already was working for you. I mean after all, I have a file and everything.”

Obviously, the attack of sarcasm simply wasn’t willing to go quietly.

He made a point of ignoring my underlying flash of attitude this time and simply replied, “In essence, you are. Or, at least, you have been. Simply not in an official capacity.”

I raised my eyebrows. “And that seems to have been working out just fine, don’t you think?”

“So far.” He agreed, giving me a hesitant nod that framed his guarded words with nondescript ambivalence. “But I’m sure Doctor Jante explained our reasoning.”

“Yes, she did.” I nodded my head and huffed out a breath. “But, I still don’t see why you want to fix something that isn’t broken?”

He cocked an eyebrow himself. “I really wouldn’t expect you to understand.”

“Touché,” I answered. “I suppose I’d have a good laugh at the irony there if I wasn’t feeling just a bit cornered at the moment.”

“That certainly isn’t the intention, Mister Gant, and I apologize if I’ve led you to feel that way. Granted, the bureau would like an answer as soon as possible, and we are certainly hoping for a yes, or we wouldn’t have made the offer, obviously. However, please understand there is no pressure either way.”

"Well, you've got an odd way of showing it."

"Again, I apologize if that is how it appears," he told me. "However, if you are interested in entertaining our offer, we don't need to know immediately; in fact, you really should take some time to think about it. Consider all of the ramifications… And, of course, discuss it with your wife."

"My wife… Uh-huh…" I mumbled, my voice trailing off momentarily before erupting into a half-stifled snort. "Yeah, right. So, I don't suppose you'd be willing to loan me some body armor before I do that would you?"

The section chief grinned for the first time since we'd started this discussion then let out a soft chuckle.

I was absolutely positive the FBI had a file on Felicity too. I knew it for a fact because I'd seen it. But, based on his jovial reaction, it was plain to me that while he might have studied mine in depth, he hadn't even opened *hers* just yet.

AUTHOR'S NOTE:

While the city of St. Louis and its various notable landmarks are certainly real, many names have been changed and some minor liberties taken with some of the details in these stories. In an instance or two, they are fabrications, such as the existence of a coffee shop/diner across the street from the Metropolitan Saint Louis Police Headquarters. These anomalies are pieces of fiction within fiction to create an illusion of reality to be experienced and enjoyed—In short, I made them up because it helped me make the story more entertaining, or in some cases, just because I wanted to. After all, this is *my* fictional version of Saint Louis.

And since we are talking about ***fiction***, please note that this book is *not intended* as a primer or guide for WitchCraft, Wicca, or *any* Pagan path. It is important to mention that the vast majority of rituals, spells, and explanations of these religious, spiritual, and "magickal" practices used in these works are, in point of fact, drawn from actual Neo-Paganism – *but they are not tied to any one specific tradition or path.* The mixture of practices engaged in by the characters in these novels is often referred to as "Eclectic Paganism" and "Eclectic WitchCraft," being that they borrow from *many different religious paths and traditions across the full gamut of spirituality* in order to create their own. Therefore, some of the explanations included herein will not work for all Pagan traditions, of which there are countless. This does not make them *wrong*, it simply makes them *different*.

If you are actually seeking in-depth information on the subject of Paganism and WitchCraft, there are numerous **Non**-Fiction, scholarly texts readily available by authors such as Margot Adler, Raymond Buckland, Scott Cunningham, and more.

Also, remember that the "magick," and of course, the psychic abilities depicted here are what some might call "over the top," because it ***doesn't really work like that***, as we all know. But, like I have been saying all along, this is ***fiction***. Relax and enjoy it for what it is…

Finally, if you are saying, "I'll bet he had to write this note because someone took these stories way too seriously," give yourself a cigar.

MORE FROM M. R. SELLARS

ROWAN GANT INVESTIGATIONS SERIES

(In order of release)

HARM NONE
NEVER BURN A WITCH
PERFECT TRUST
THE LAW OF THREE
CRONE'S MOON
LOVE IS THE BOND
ALL ACTS OF PLEASURE
THE END OF DESIRE
BLOOD MOON
MIRANDA

(Available in both print and e-book editions)

SPECIAL AGENT CONSTANCE MANDALAY SERIES

MERRIE AXEMAS: A KILLER HOLIDAY TALE
(e-Novella)

IN THE BLEAK MIDWINTER
(Available in both print and e-book editions)

OTHER

YOU'RE GONNA THINK I'M NUTS…
*(Novelette included in **Courting Morpheus** Horror Anthology)*

LAST CALL
*(Flash-Fiction Short included in **Slices of Flesh** Horror Anthology)*

SPECIAL E-BOOK ONLY OMNIBUS TITLES

GHOUL SQUAD
(Harm None, Never Burn A Witch, and Perfect Trust)

DEATH WEARS HIGH HEELS
(Love Is The Bond, All Acts of Pleasure, and The End Of Desire)

ABOUT THE AUTHOR

A member of the ITW (International Thriller Writers), M. R. Sellars is a relatively unassuming homebody who considers himself just a *"guy with a lot of nightmares and a word processing program."* His first full-length novel, *Harm None*, hit bookstore shelves in 2000 and he hasn't stopped writing since.

Sellars currently resides in the Midwest with his wife, daughter, and a pair of rescued male felines that he describes as, "the competition." At home, when not writing or taking care of the household, he indulges his passions for cooking and chasing his wife around the house. She promises that one day she will allow him to catch her.

M. R. Sellars can be found on the web at:
www.mrsellars.com

And on major social networking venues…

CPSIA information can be obtained
at www.ICGtesting.com
Printed in the USA
LVHW09s0007251018
594757LV00010B/239/P